The Springs

Also by Anne Britting Oleson

The Aventurine Morrow Thrillers:

Aventurine and the Reckoning

— and coming in September, 2023 —

Aventurine and the Bailgate

The Springs

a novel by

ANNE BRITTING OLESON

Encircle Publications
Farmington, Maine, U.S.A.

Encircle editor: Cynthia Brackett-Vincent

Cover design by Deirdre Wait
Cover illustration © Getty Images

Published by:

Encircle Publications, LLC
PO Box 187
Farmington, ME 04938

info@encirclepub.com
http://encirclepub.com

This book is for everyone who grew up in Grover's Crossing.
Pung It!

PART I

ONE.

THE SWEAT BEADED Marty's forehead, and she dabbed at it with the balled handkerchief between her fingers. This despite the desultory breeze puffing off the blueberry barrens beyond the high windows. Early in the season yet, those bushes still bore only the smallest green blur of leaves. Her father had often laughed at the sight of the white clapboard church and its square tower, rising from the blazing surroundings in the fall as though from the flames of hell. *But don't tell your mother I said that,* he'd mutter, leaning in close and winking. Even in his final illness, the muttered words, the wink.

Marty rested her eyes on the casket where her father's wasted body now lay, his narrow face immobile and somehow made plastic by the heavy makeup the funeral home stylist had chosen. He looked, she thought desperately, less like her father and more like a wax effigy, something that might appear in Madame Tussaud's. The thought of her father, then, in a tableau with Abraham Lincoln, or with Clark Gable, or perhaps even with Jack the Ripper: it made her want, suddenly, to giggle hysterically, and she jammed the handkerchief against her lips and pressed her eyes closed before her mother should notice. *Sorry, Dad,* she muttered to herself, and then held the handkerchief harder to her mouth, because, of course, her father would have laughed his great booming laugh, the idea of his appearing at Madame Tussaud's was so hilarious.

Her skin prickled. Her mother was looking at her. Marty knew that even before she opened her eyes. Sylvia was looking at her with the expression that had become so common over the last couple of years. Narrowed eyes, narrowed lips, disapproval in every etched line around her mouth. Quickly, Marty scrubbed at her cheeks, pretending tears that did not fall, then lifted her gaze to the triptych of stained glass over the altar. *Stop it, Dad.* The three windows featured a pale-skinned Jesus in blue robes, flowing brown hair surmounted by a halo of radiant yellow, children gazing up adoringly, fluffy white sheep off to his left and right looking far more intelligent than any sheep Marty had ever come across. At the peak of the tallest window, the dove of peace was performing incredible feats of dive-bombing from the heavens: if Jesus and the kids didn't look out, they'd be pecked to serious injury or death.

Stop it.

Marty hadn't cried at the hospital, holding her father's hand until the lines on the monitors flattened and the alarms had sounded. She wasn't crying now. "I don't want to die, worrying about you crying for me," he'd admonished from his pillows when he still had the strength to speak. "Think about the laughs." There had been a lot of laughs. Most of them muffled quickly into silence, followed by *Don't tell your mother.*

Caro was at the far end of the pew curving to her left. When Marty glanced over, her housemate raised her eyebrows slightly, a signal since elementary school, and so subtle that few would notice. Marty lowered her lids and opened them again slowly, the tiniest expression of exasperation. Caro knew. The open casket, the makeup, the mournful dirges from the funereal section of the hymnal, pages edged in black. All of it her mother's choosing, none of it Marty's. As though her mother were staking claim to her father in death. Caro nodded encouragingly, the slightest dip of the chin, then turned away toward the minister, her face a study in rapture. The sun through the stained glass spattered her in precious jewels, and Marty felt a quick surge of love for her friend of longest standing. Caro knew.

"Martha," her mother hissed into her ear. A hymnal was thrust into her hands.

"Stand if you are able," the minister invited, his hands outstretched.

Everyone rose stiffly to their feet. Except for Alaric Morgan, two rows back at the end, who stayed seated next to his niece Isabella's wheelchair. Marty, looking back over her shoulder, met his eyes, but then he looked away.

Marty had first seen Alaric a couple of weeks after he had returned home to the farm the previous spring: delivering the mail in Painter's Springs meant seeing everyone eventually.

He had been at the end of the long driveway leading up into the farmyard, waiting. For the mail? For her? He stood beside the mailbox—she could see him up ahead as she slapped the door of the Fentons' mailbox closed behind *The New Yorker* and a couple of bills. He had one hand in his pocket, the other shading his eyes as he looked up along the road.

Then, as she pulled up to the last mailbox before the farm driveway, he did—to her—the inexplicable: he turned on his heel and headed up toward the barn.

Alaric had to have seen her. He had to have been waiting for her, or at least for the mail—why else would anyone stand at the foot of his driveway at a bit before ten in the morning like that?

And then, having seen her one driveway away—he had simply walked off.

Strangely, even though she had heard that he'd come home changed, it had hurt. The hurt had surprised her.

Mar and Car, Lar and Lar. It had been the four of them, for years. Marty, Caro, Marty's older brother Larry, Larry's best friend Alaric. The guys had been two years older, always just ahead in school; but as there weren't very many of them from the Springs taking the bus to Danby and the district high school, they rode together, and when the boys got licenses, the girls piled into the sprung and trash-filled back seat of Larry's old Bronco. Marty and Caro were far too young for the teenaged boys to take an interest in, but it was friendship, the kind where the girls felt protected from the kind of meanness commonly directed toward freshmen.

They had been friends. Close friends. Important friends.

Or so Marty had thought.

Then Larry and Alaric, freshly graduated from Danby Regional, had enlisted together. Gone to basic training at the same time. Spent ages in the service together, far apart, until they'd finally been posted to Fort Bragg together. And had eventually wound up deployed together.

Until Larry had come home alone, in a casket, the victim of a roadside IED.

Larry's death, Marty knew, had been what had killed her father.

Of course, there had been the cancer. Of course there had been that. Still, Roger Ahearne had beat it back once, had taken his share of chemo and radiation, and had fought on. He'd been in remission for a couple of years before the monster in his bones had awakened once again, and deep in her secret heart, Marty knew that continuing the fight had just not been anything Roger was up to, with Larry gone. Again with the treatments, but, watching him, she knew his spirit simply was not in it this time.

Try, Dad, she'd urged him, though they both knew it wouldn't happen. Roger didn't have the strength; he didn't have the will. In the beginning, driving him into the cancer center on her days off, Marty had resented it fiercely. *Live for me,* she wanted to shout at him—wanted to shake him, force him to listen to her pleas—but instead she'd merely grip the wheel of the Jeep until her knuckles whitened, steering between the blueberry barrens and the gravel pits and the granite quarries on the slick black road. She'd always been his favorite—had always *thought* she was his favorite, as Larry was so obviously her mother's. In death, however, Larry was claiming him. Marty wanted to shake her brother, too, but the place where he had been in her life was only air.

Only once—Marty swore to herself that it was only once—when she had endured her mother's pulling away in pinched disappointment one too many times—did she wish that her parents would trade places. That her mother would die and her father would live. Only once. She was shocked at her own cruelty, her own callousness. She turned away quickly from her own feelings, just as quickly as Alaric Morgan had turned away from her approaching mail delivery.

John Foreman was speaking words she recognized as a benediction. The interminable service was winding to its inevitable conclusion.

"Go in peace," he said, again holding his hands out, unconsciously mimicking the dove above his head. Then, surprisingly, he added, "Spread the light."

Tell a joke, Marty appended in her own head, watching steadfastly, still not crying, as the funeral director approached the casket where her father lay.

TWO.

CARO SLAPPED THE dashboard of the Vue once she'd turned the key in the ignition, hoping to convince the air conditioning to work at least for a while before she picked up Sophie at Pete and Melissa's. It didn't work. What little breeze had blown in from the barrens through the church windows during the funeral service had since died away, and despite leaving her own car windows lowered, she found the sun had beaten down on the maroon roof, and the inside of the Saturn was baking. She sighed, running her hands over the steering wheel, adjusting her legs, in her skirt, on the hot seat.

Hot seat, she thought. *I see what I did there.*

Caro dreaded going back to Pete's, wished there had been someone else to leave Sophie with during the funeral, but all her fall-backs for a babysitter, including Joanne at the daycare, had been in attendance at the church as well. And Sophie would not have withstood the length of the service without fussing. This had been the better choice in that respect. But all others? Caro sighed again, flicking the blinker to indicate her turn out of the parking lot of the church.

At least Melissa would be working. Caro would only have to deal with one of them.

As she drove up onto the overpass, Caro tried to remember what had sparked her attraction to Pete to begin with. It was so hard to remember—and that was stupid, for it hadn't been all that long ago, that night at Dooley's down by the waterfront in Danby. All right, she could admit it—Pete *was* handsome, in that dark brooding way she had found so appealing from the time she was a kid: back when she had had a fluttery little crush on Mr. Rochester, before trading him in for the equally unattainable Larry Ahearne. Had Pete been a Larry substitute? Larry lite? She had asked herself this so many times since things had begun to go bad between her and Pete. As for Larry: they'd grown up, hadn't they? Larry had gone off to join the army, and she'd felt stupid writing him letters. Like a teenaged girl sending mash notes—she had cringed at the thought. So she hadn't written.

So to Pete Vargas. Good-looking Pete Vargas. He was fun, too, at the beginning, and daring; he laughed a lot, and Caro loved the laughter. When he had touched her, dancing at Dooley's, she had shivered. So she'd let him take her home, and they'd stayed together, more or less, for four years.

When she told him she'd discovered she was pregnant, well into that third year, he'd risen silently from the couch, set his beer can aside, and left the house with a squeal of tires. He had not returned for five days.

Slowly Caroline climbed out of the car, flexing her shoulders, knotted now from sitting so long in the wooden church pew. No, she corrected herself: her shoulders were knotted from tension, the tension she always felt when having to deal with Pete now. More so in the past couple of months, since Melissa had moved into the house with him. Pressing her shoulder blades back and lifting her chin, she looked up at the two dormer windows emerging from the green metal roofing. Frog's eyes, she always thought when she saw them. Even with the new roof and siding, the house seemed strangely reptilian.

A childish shriek from the rear of the house stayed her hand before she could knock. Caro stepped back to the walkway, avoiding the skateboard with the missing chuck lying across the path. The shriek was followed by high giggles—Sophie's giggles. Carefully Caro made her way around the corner past the work truck and to the back. There she found Sophie, in her green bathing suit with the bejeweled sea creatures, running back and forth through the sprinkler. It wasn't the water that elicited the excited laughter, but rather the golden retriever puppy bounding after her, tumbling with her when she stumbled and fell.

"Mama!" she cried. The puppy leaped at her, knocking her down in the wet grass, and her giggles pealed out again. When she stood, there were two muddy streaks of footprints down her legs. She ran through the water again, the puppy following, and scrubbed at her skin with her chubby hands. "Mama! It's my puppy! His name is Karl!"

The pup took this opportunity to charge at Caro, but stopped just in front of her and shook itself off. More laughter from Sophie. When Caro looked up, a stream of sunlight chose that moment to burst through the evergreens at the back of the yard, illuminating Sophie's damp hair, bringing out all the highlights. Caro caught her breath. The puppy turned and ran at the back door, where Pete had just emerged, holding a towel.

"Soph," he called. "Come get dried off now."

The immediate sulk. No one could go from sunshine to cloud as fast as Sophie. She crossed her arms over her chest and stuck out a lip, standing firmly in the spray of the sprinkler.

"I don't want to, Daddy."

"It's time, honey. You need to get dressed and come home with me now." Caro ran a hand over her sweaty forehead.

"And Karl?"

"Not Karl, Sophie. Karl stays with Daddy." Caro hated calling him that.

Karl, not at all helpfully, joined Sophie in the spray, and she dropped to her knees in the grass beside him. She wrapped her arms around his wet fur; though he wriggled, she did not let go. "But Karl is my puppy. Daddy said so." Her voice was rising. A meltdown was on the horizon.

"He is your puppy, sweetie," Pete said. The look he cast toward Caro with his black eyes was unreadable, but Caro felt the familiar tightening in her chest anyway. Some sort of blame. Whatever it was, whatever was happening, it was always, *always,* somehow her fault. "But he lives here."

"Why don't I live here?" Sophie demanded. "Why don't I live with Karl?"

"Then you wouldn't live with me," Caro protested. Falling into the same old tug of war. She never meant to, and she always did. "You wouldn't want to live without me, would you?"

"You live here, too," Sophie ordered. With the impossible logic of a three-nearly-four-year-old.

The bark from Pete wasn't really laughter. At least, it wasn't really pleasant. He moved to the spigot and turned the knob; the spray from the sprinkler subsided and disappeared. Still Sophie held on to Karl, if anything, squeezing him more tightly, despite his wriggling now becoming more frantic. She buried her reddened face in his matted fur.

"Come get dried off," Pete said. "Mama says it's time for you to go with her."

Mama says.

Caro felt her jaw hardening. She turned away from her ex-husband, back toward her daughter.

"Karl needs to get dried off, too," Sophie said. Slowly she straightened, and Karl took this opportunity to leap away, bounding through the grass, which, Caro thought spitefully, needed to be mowed.

Pete held out the towel. Sophie moved toward him, unwillingly, dragging her feet. When she was within arm's reach, he turned her, tossed the towel around her shoulders, and wrapped her up, pulling her close. She giggled.

"Go get Karl a towel," she ordered.

Pete straightened, tucking the towel around Sophie.

"Can you get her clothes?" Caro asked.

He shot her another look, a frown narrowing his dark eyes, before he turned back into the house without answering.

Caro took a deep breath, then bent down. "Come here, Soph. Let me help you."

Sophie was having none of it. Her jaw jutting in a scowl, she turned away just as Pete had done.

The screen door slapped shut again, and Pete dropped a bundle of clothes on the step before capturing the puppy in a second towel. "Come help dry him off," he invited. Sophie's face cleared immediately, and she dropped to her knees, her chubby hands reaching toward the wet fur. Her own towel dropped into the damp grass.

Caro picked up the clothes. Tee shirt, shorts, underpants. "Where are her sandals?"

Pete barely cast her a glance. "Was she even wearing sandals when you left her?"

"Of course she was. The pink ones." Did he think she'd bring her daughter without shoes? Or was this just gaslighting? It wouldn't be the first time.

"Did Mama put your shoes on to come here?" he asked.

"I don't know." Sandals were not, apparently, on Sophie's agenda. She rubbed Karl's wet fur vigorously with both hands.

"The pink ones," Caro repeated. Desperately. "The ones Aunt Marty gave you."

The mention of Marty's name, and the reminder of the gift the sandals had been, sparked something in Sophie. "Aunt Marty gave them to me," she said, straightening. "They have butterflies on them. I put them someplace safe."

Her small feet slapped up the steps, and she wrenched the door with all her might. Then she disappeared inside.

Slowly Pete rose to his feet, Karl in his arms wrapped in the now-muddy towel. He looked after Sophie, then turned to Caro.

"Aunt Marty," he said.

Caro sighed inwardly. *Not again.*

"You two sleeping together now?"

His handsome face was twisted into a leer.

Caro straightened her back, forced herself to lift her chin and look him in the eye. "If we were, Pete, it wouldn't be any of your business."

"My daughter's welfare is my business."

"And that means what? You and Melissa have hardly been keeping to separate bedrooms."

He took a step closer, invading her space, and she could see the faint film of sweat on his upper lip. "Is that jealousy I smell, Caroline?"

"That's bullshit you smell. Don't kid yourself." But she took a step backward, as he knew she would. She always had. He had always liked to make her give up her ground, and she hated herself for doing it.

He held up a hand, and his smile was ugly. "Just keeping an eye on the welfare of my daughter, that's all." Without looking away, he scratched behind Karl's ears, and the puppy wiggled happily, his tongue lolling. *The only one of us who is happy,* Caro thought bitterly.

In fact, when Sophie returned to the yard, with her pink butterfly sandals on the wrong feet and the straps flapping, Caro scooped her up, and her daughter immediately began to scream.

"Karl!" she shouted, fat tears coursing down her red cheeks. She leaned away from Caro, arms outstretched to the puppy. "I want Karl! I want to stay with Karl!"

Caro tightened her arms. "Kiss Karl," she suggested, moving Sophie closer to the dog. "Kiss him and tell him you'll be back in no time."

But Sophie began to kick, shouting every combination of *no.* It was all Caro could do to hold on.

"All righty, then," she said through clenched teeth. "Kiss Daddy. You'll be back to Daddy and Karl next weekend."

Pete leaned forward to kiss the top of Sophie's dark head.

With Sophie's flailing tantrum, it was difficult to get her strapped into the car seat in the back of the Vue. Pete had followed them around the house, Karl still in his arms. Sophie strained to look around Caro to the dog, crying his name, trying to undo the straps. At last, Caro was able to slam the back door.

"Bye, Sophie! Daddy and Karl love you!" Pete called. When Caro brushed past him, sweating, exhausted, and furious, he leaned in and murmured, "Why do you have to be so mean?"

She drove out of the yard a bit faster than she should have. But at least the angry tears didn't leak out until she could no longer see her ex-husband in the rearview mirror.

THREE.

Alaric brought in the mail, delivered today by Marty's sub, and set it on the table. He still wore his suit, and now he reached up and loosened the tie at his neck. He felt as though he were strangling.

"Thanks, love," his mother said over her shoulder, her hands spinning the potato against the peeler, the skin falling away in a long thin strip. She set the potato aside in the deep porcelain sink, reached for another. She had changed out of her dark dress. Alaric was not surprised. There was always work to be done, in the kitchen, in the garden, somewhere. He could not remember a time when his mother was not busy. Always having something in her hand, moving purposely toward some goal only she knew ahead of time. On the farm, the family always saw her results, but rarely noticed her work. "Anything good?"

Almost as an afterthought, she turned to look at him, her smile strained. Alaric shook his head, pushed the small pile toward her. There was something on top from the bank, a thin envelope, not a statement. It was addressed to both his parents, but his mother would, he knew, leave it for his father to open. The potatoes all peeled, she cut them into chunks, rinsed them, and put them on to boil in the pot on the stove. He glanced up at the clock over the sink. Early yet. Not yet four.

"Potato salad," Georgie said, reading his thoughts. He nodded. "Isabella's gone to her room," she continued. For a moment her shoulders slumped. "I just didn't know what to do, you know? I'm sure it wasn't very good for her, going to Roger's funeral." She winced, and then took a deep breath before pulling an onion from the vegetable bin and attacking its yellow skin with her paring knife. "But we couldn't have left her here alone. What if something happened?"

Alaric glanced through the kitchen door to the hall, toward the back bedroom. Bella's room now. The guest bedroom, it had been when he was a child; though why they had needed a guest room when they rarely had guests—and none who stayed overnight—he didn't know. It could have been his parents' bedroom, and then he and his brothers could each have had their own room upstairs. He had rather resented that room, and its lack of use, on the nights he'd lie awake and listen to Brett's snoring.

Brett. He felt a twinge for his dead brother.

And Sarah, of course. His dead sister-in-law.

Alaric let out a long soundless sigh. There was far too much death. He felt that old foreboding wash over him, the sense of being cursed. His entire family was cursed. Perhaps, he thought, and not for the first time, all of Painter's Springs was cursed.

Bella's wheelchair had been under its cover out on the big porch, at the corner beyond the newly-installed ramp. He'd noted it in passing on the way in. His parents, at the behest of the physical therapist, were trying to encourage her to use the crutches more, to practice with the leg braces. To strengthen her legs. His arms always ached, just watching her try. He wished he could give her words of encouragement, though he knew she would not welcome them.

Bella was twelve. Had his parents left him alone on the farm when he was twelve? Of course, he'd never been alone. There had always been Brett, and Richard.

And none of them had been in a wheelchair.

After a few moments, the onion cut up for the salad, his mother turned to him again, her eyes reddened. He held up a hand, smiled at her. The corners of her mouth lifted, but her expression, when she looked into his face, was tired.

Too much death.

Impulsively, he skirted the table to bend and kiss his mother's cheek. For the briefest of moments she clung to him, and then quickly returned to the peelings in the sink.

In the old stable office beyond the barn, which he had slowly remodeled into a kind of efficiency apartment since he'd returned—medical discharge; the term made him grimace—he put the dented kettle on the hotplate and drew the tin of teabags from one cupboard, a mug and teapot from another. The teapot had square corners and scenes from *Hamlet* on it; the mug was plain green and oversized. While he waited for the water to boil, he fixed his tea things, then ran some water into the jug he used to water the petunias in the window boxes on either side of the door. The actions were deliberate, and calming.

Too much death.

Alaric wished, as he rinsed the pot, and then poured the rest of the boiling water over the Earl Gray bag, that he had not gone to the church, the funeral. Yet there was no way he could not have. Roger Ahearne, the father of his longest and best friend: of course he had to go. Alaric had failed the son; he could not fail the father. He owed his attendance to Roger. So he had walked up into the barrens toward the church, preferring not to ride with the family in Georgie's car. He had made it in plenty of time. In the lot, Sylvia Ahearne had stood beside Marty, her dress pressed, her distance complete, as the funeral director had opened the rear door of the hearse. He hung back, not wanting to interrupt, not wanting to be seen. It had been warm, and he had shifted uncomfortably in the suit, yet he had stayed beyond all the cars, watching.

When the family arrived, long after the casket had been carried into the church, he had emerged to push Bella's wheelchair up the ramp, finding a spot for her at the end of one of the side pews. He had been conscious the entire time of her shrinking away from him. Granted, she pulled away from everyone in the family, and had since the accident, but somehow he felt it more pronounced with him. Of course, he couldn't blame her. She resented her new limitations, the body she had found herself in; more than likely, she resented him as well. John Foreman, the minister, had invited the congregation to rise if they were able, and he could feel the impotent fury rolling off his niece: waves and waves of white-hot flames.

Alaric had felt the impotent fury himself, knew it well. When he had cradled Larry's head against his chest and shouted into the radio for aid. Again when he had returned home, with his own invisible wound, unable to face the family, Larry's parents, Larry's sister.

Alaric had so much to say to them. The words simply wouldn't come.

Tea poured, he sat at the scarred gate leg table beneath the window and pulled his book toward him. It fell open at the ace of spades he used as a bookmark. *Crime and Punishment.* He'd started on a regimen upon his return home: visit the library every week on the single afternoon it was open, to check out the classic literature he'd never read. Nothing modern; he didn't want to read about things happening in this world, in this time. He'd already had enough of that. *Moby-Dick. The Hunchback of Notre Dame. Jane Eyre.* All the books he might have read in high school had he paid attention; all the books he might have read in college had he gone. At first he'd forced himself through the pages, but these days he immersed himself, looking carefully at all the flawed characters, at their guilt, their anger, the holes in their own lives that they fell into. Raskolnikov. Ahab. Quasimodo. Rochester. They seemed kindred spirits.

He blew on his tea and sipped it, steeped black and bitter, the way he felt. On the page before him Raskolnikov lifted the hatchet and swung at the pawnbroker. The act on which his life, and his story, turned. At least Raskolnikov had had an opportunity to plan for it.

In the first few weeks after returning home, Alaric drank himself to sleep every night. It wasn't that he needed the liquor, or even that he liked it. He just needed a sleep without dreams. Because all of his dreams were of Larry.

In the dreams, they were singing, just as they had been that morning, riding in the armored vehicle across the night-cold desert—no one in the cab to tell them to stop, as the unit commander was in the truck up ahead of them. The song was "Strange Magic" by ELO, something he'd never forget as long as he lived. He remembered Larry's voice climbing the register as he imitated Jeff Lynne's falsetto; that part was always vivid in the dreams.

Right before the blast.

In his dreams the blast was as much a surprise as it had been that morning. Every time he dreamed it, he suffered the shock and surprise again. He was aware of flying, of shattering glass, of tearing metal. He saw the lightening sky and could do nothing but stare up at it from the sandy ditch in which he lay. Alaric lived through that scene, like watching a clip from an old war movie, over and over again. Sometimes it was in real time: the blast, the flying, the finding himself lying in the sandy roadside ditch, staring up at the fading stars in the early morning sky. Crawling to Larry, holding him in his arms. Sometimes the sequence was slowed down, clicking into place before his eyes, frame by frame. He woke from the dream of it some nights, sweating and shaking, his mouth opening wide for the scream that never came out. From singing to silence, all within the space of a few hours. That was the strange magic. It was as though Larry, in leaving this life, had taken Alaric's voice with him.

There had been the field hospital. The hospital in Baghdad. Germany. Walter Reed. There had been puzzlement from the doctors, the cajoling and then threatening from the command staff, and then the tentative, reluctant diagnosis of PTSD.

FOUR.

Sophie had cried herself to sleep on the short drive back down onto the point. Caro gazed down into her daughter's face, still blotchy from angry tears, as she carried her toward the house. As always, she felt her heart swell, even though right now, the wash of feeling was tinged with relief. How she loved Sophie, more than life itself—but how Sophie could exhaust her. She pressed her lips to the sweaty forehead. In her arms, Sophie stirred but did not wake.

Marty must have seen her pull in, for she was holding the porch door as Caro approached. "You look beat," she said, pitching her voice low. "Do you want me to take her?"

The sympathy in her voice nearly brought Caro back to her tears. She shook her head. "I'm okay. I'll just put her on the couch for now." Biting her lower lip, she brushed past into the living room. There was an afghan on the back of the sofa, and she tucked it around Sophie, adjusted the curtains over the French doors, then turned to find Marty holding out a glass.

Gin and blueberry tonic, with a few frozen berries from last year's crop sunk to the bottom. Caro took a grateful sip. Marty led the way back to the porch.

"I should be taking care of you," Caro protested, but it was a weak protest. She took a seat on the wicker loveseat across from Marty, who had put her bare feet up on the coffee table. The canvases, turned to the wall, ranged behind her. "Today was about you, not about me."

Marty's drink was dark beer in a pint glass. She took a long draw and licked the foam from her upper lip. With her other hand, she smoothed her dark skirt over her knees; she had not yet changed. "It's been a bad day all around," she observed. "Pete being an asshole?"

"Again. Still."

Marty nodded, took another sip. Outside, the shadows were lengthening. From the living room the schoolhouse clock rang once: half-past something. Caro tensed, but heard no stirring from the couch.

"I should wake her up," she fretted. "I don't think she had a nap at Pete's, and if she naps too late, she stays up too late."

"Let her sleep for another fifteen minutes. Give yourself a break." Marty dropped her head against the curved back of the wicker armchair. "We all deserve a break."

Caro found her glass nearly empty. "I could sit here and drink all night until I passed out," she admitted. "Pete makes me feel like that." She rolled her eyes. "He wanted to know if I was sleeping with you yet."

Marty laughed, and quickly covered her mouth. "Again? He's really got some weird hang-up about our sex lives. What did you tell him?"

Caro shrugged. "That it wasn't any of his business. The usual."

"He just can't deal with your moving out of his house and into mine. It can't be that he behaved like an ass and couldn't keep it in his pants. It had to be that I seduced you."

The memory of his dark eyes, the gaze so calculating as he goaded her, niggled at Caro. She shifted uncomfortably on the sofa, the wicker scratching at the back of her legs. Reaching down, she adjusted the cushion. It was worn, and they really needed new ones. "There was something else in it today," she said slowly, frowning, trying to capture the feeling of unease. "Something different."

Her pint glass now empty, Marty set it next to her feet on the table. She tilted her head, narrowed her hazel eyes. That was the thing about Marty, Caro thought: she always took worries seriously, didn't just laugh them off. "Different how?"

Now that she had voiced her suspicion, Caro felt at a loss. "Calculating."

"What do you mean?"

"I don't know what I mean." Caro sighed, rubbed at her tired eyes with the ball of her hand. "I just got a weird feeling from him today."

A dump truck rattled up the road from the turnoff that led to the lighthouse. The load tarp was rolled up; whatever it had been carrying was emptied now. Gravel, probably, to level the road before it was paved later this summer. The truck was speeding, and Marty's expression was of annoyance; she was familiar with every road in the Springs, Caro knew, every speed limit that was never enforced by the police department that didn't exist—and the Sheriff's Department very rarely sent a patrol down to the point. Probably the dump truck driver was in a hurry to get home and start his weekend. She dropped her gaze to her empty glass, wondering whether it was worth it to go get another.

"Like..." Caro's voice trailed off, and she grimaced as she tried to explain the feeling. "Like this time it was a game he was playing—he wasn't serious, but he was trying to score points. Trying to set something up."

"A fight?" It wouldn't be the first time Pete had tried to stage an argument so he could win.

Again Caro shrugged. She too set her glass aside. "He said something weird. Something about looking out for his daughter's welfare."

Marty pursed her lips, wrinkled her nose, as though she were smelling something unsavory. "His daughter's fine. *Your* daughter's fine. Even if you and I had entered into a relationship, Sophie'd be just fine."

"I know. I don't know where he was going with that. I mean, Melissa lives there now, at the house. He gets to be in a relationship, but if I'm in one, it's a problem for Sophie's welfare?"

"He's just being an asshole," Marty reassured her. "Yanking your chain. Like he always does."

Still the worry lay between them, smelling foul. Pete couldn't be trusted; they both agreed on that without saying. Caro met Marty's gaze, her own not quite as steady. She hated dealing with Pete. Hated it. It was exhausting. She despised how he could still make her cry.

The pad of small footsteps. Sophie appeared at the door, dragging the afghan behind her. She wiped at her forehead with the flat of her hand, deranging her dark, sleep-mussed hair further. Glancing from one to the other, she crossed to Caro and clambered up into her lap, all awkward elbows and knees. There she curled up with her head beneath her mother's chin, the howling anger of the afternoon forgotten.

Caro smiled wryly.

"I'll start dinner," Marty said.

Usually Marty enjoyed cooking, but tonight she was too tired to think about it. Chicken on the grill—she hoped the gas would hold out—with roasted asparagus, quick and easy. Teriyaki sauce, she decided, pulling the bottle out of the refrigerator.

She contemplated another bottle of Newcastle Brown, and then decided against it. With the lowering sun, the spring temperature had dropped precipitously: too cold to eat at the picnic table. She brought silver and napkins to the dining room instead.

When Marty finished grilling and called the others, Caro carried Sophie in to sit her in the booster seat to the left of her chair. Marty had left a dishcloth at the side of the butterfly plate, and Caro tucked this around her daughter to tie it loosely at the back of the neck. Marty slid the serving platter onto a trivet and slumped wearily into her seat. She felt suddenly, bone-crushingly, exhausted.

Caro paused in cutting up a chicken thigh for Sophie. She leaned forward, peering into her friend's face. "You look bad."

Marty forced a laugh. "Thanks. You're such a pal."

The chicken cut, Caro turned to the asparagus.

"No," Sophie said. "I want it long."

Throwing up her hands, Caro lay three spears on the butterfly plate. Sophie immediately took one in her fingers and began to chew on the end.

"Really, I mean it." Caro served herself, leaning back again. "I'm sorry I was so wrapped up in my bitching about Pete before. And you just sat there and listened! You made me a drink! I should have been the one—"

Marty shook her head. She took a drink from her glass, water now. "It's all right. It's just been a long day."

"Did something happen after the funeral? In the church hall, after I left?"

Again Marty shook her head. Who could have asked for a better friend? After the committal at Pine Rest, Caro had returned to the church hall, and, cup of coffee in hand, had spoken to Sylvia, then hugged Marty, again. And again. She had stood close for the better part of an hour before leaving to pick up

Sophie. Nothing had happened then, at least nothing untoward. People pressing Marty's hands, speaking remembrances of her father. It had been hot, the air close, the atmosphere absolutely claustrophobic. Marty winced, thinking of it again. The last of the stragglers had wandered away, driven off, no doubt, by the heat; the church ladies had busied themselves washing up in the kitchen. Marty had taken her mother back to the house, where it had all gone to hell. Where it always all went to hell.

"Just the usual," Marty said now.

Caro lifted her dark eyes. "The usual. Sylvia?"

"Mom."

"Of course."

Of course Caro had known Sylvia for nearly all her life—at least, for as long as she and Marty had been in school together, from that first day of kindergarten at the elementary school up on the barrens. "You can't listen to her, Marty," Caro said, her voice low.

Caro always knew.

Marty shrugged helplessly, cutting her chicken with more force than perhaps was necessary. She took a bite before answering. "It's just so hard sometimes. I mean, I've always known that Larry was her favorite." Larry, the boy. Larry, the first-born. "But now—now—" It was hard to go on. She forced the words out, like someone probing a festering wound. "She's so resentful. She wants Larry. She doesn't want me. Dad's death—" she sniffled "—just magnifies that."

"You know that can't be true."

"Of course it's true. That Larry's gone? And I'm alive? She can't bear it." Still, heeding her father's words, Marty didn't cry. Even though, she thought critically, this would be a really good time to do it.

"Don't say that."

"She wishes I'm the one who died, Caro. You know it. I know it." The dinner she'd thrown together now seemed just that: thrown together, tossed onto a plate, totally unappealing. She slid a spear of asparagus across onto Sophie's plate; the little girl looked up at her, eyes wide.

"You're not going to die, Aunt Marty, are you?" Sophie's voice was small, but determined. "I don't want you to. I'm not going to let you."

Sweet Jesus. Marty had only been thinking with half her mind, forgetting that words were food for Sophie's ears, just as asparagus was for her appetite. She summoned her biggest smile. "Oh, no, Butterfly. Not I. You and I still have things to do. Places to go. People to see."

Worry allayed, Sophie picked up the asparagus spear and broke it in half.

"Don't play with your food, Soph," Caro said automatically.

"It doesn't fit in my mouth when it's long," Sophie countered with the contradictory logic of her nearly four years.

Caro picked up her water glass, and then set it back down again without taking a drink. Her eyes remained focused on Marty's face. "Something happened. Tell me."

It was hard to speak the words. When Marty had left Sylvia at the house, had carried the trays of leftover sandwiches into the kitchen. When she had bent to kiss her mother's cheek, and Sylvia had pulled away. Oh, she pretended to be turning to the coffee maker on the counter, but Marty knew. It had been a dance they'd performed between them repeatedly since the news of her brother's death had been delivered by soldiers in dress uniform. Marty knew it. They both knew it.

So Marty only shook her head. "Just the same old thing," she said sadly. "It doesn't matter."

Caro's touch on the back of her hand was brief. "Yes, it does," she said as she stood to collect their plates. "It does. It matters to you, so it matters to me."

After the dishes had been loaded into the machine and the kitchen and dining room lights turned out, Caro made a great show of glancing up at the mantle clock in the living room. She reared back in mock alarm. "Sophie!" she cried. "It's time for dancing!"

With her nightgown on backwards, Sophie careened into the living room. "I hope we didn't miss it, Mama!"

If only she could bottle that energy, Marty thought, sinking onto the couch. And if only the poor child knew. They never missed the dancing. Marty had to stifle a chuckle, as she always had to with every evening's pre-bedtime sideshow. Caro used the remote to click through the screens on the television, until she called up an episode of "Friends." She jumped through the first few seconds until the theme song began. With the first notes from the Rembrandts, both Sophie and Caro threw their hands up and began to whirl like dervishes.

"Dance, Aunt Marty!" Sophie shrieked, staggering into Marty's knees before twirling away again.

"Do it," Caro suggested, not for the first time. Her cheeks were flushed. "It's aerobic! Much better than yoga!"

Marty, as she did every night, left them to it. By the end of the song, both were breathless and laughing. When the umbrellas stopped spinning, and when all the characters had dropped to the couch, Caro grabbed the remote and snapped off the television.

"Kiss your Auntie who is too old to have any fun," she ordered her daughter. "It's time for story and bed."

Sophie did as she was told.

"Some day," Marty murmured to Caro as she passed toward the stairway, "that child will learn to tell time, and you'll be in trouble."

Caro winked and squeezed her shoulder on the way by.

FIVE.

IT WAS SATURDAY and Isabella had overslept. She had been dreaming of her bedroom in the house on Fayette Road, the house where she'd always felt safe, the home where she'd lived with her parents for as long as she could remember. To wake here, in the glaringly white guest room at her grandparents' house—at first she was shaken, and then remembrance came with its flood of sadness, and all she could think of was going back to sleep, trying to find that safe place in the dreamworld, the place that didn't exist any longer.

She hadn't really overslept. In truth, no one had awakened her. Gram always did, during the week, in plenty of time to get dressed, have breakfast, and be driven to this new school Bella hated. On the weekends, it was breakfast and chores, things like feeding the chickens, which Gram encouraged her to do to strengthen her legs. *She needs to be active,* the physical therapist said at each weekly appointment, and which the counselor echoed. *She needs to be occupied. She can do small things to help around the house. She needs to move.*

This morning, the Saturday morning after Mr. Ahearne's funeral, no one had roused her. Bella had slowly become aware of movement in the kitchen, the sound of pans on the stove, of water running, heavy footsteps that could have been Grandad's, that could have been Uncle Richard's. Whistling, quickly muffled—that would be Gram; she was always whistling, which seemed weird to Bella. Guys whistled while they worked, but not here on the farm.

Now there was silence, as though everyone had left the kitchen, gone about their business, and no one had noticed that she was missing. For a moment Isabella lay on her back in the bed, pulling the light comforter up around her chin. As though they had all forgotten her. She turned her head, brushing the tangle of hair out of her eyes, and looked at the closed door, on the hook of which her bathrobe hung. Out of the corner of her eye she could see the yellow glint of the bedside lamp, still lit, off the silver of her crutches and braces.

If they'd left the house, even Gram—she had two choices: stay in bed all day, or attempt to wrestle her legs into the braces herself. She had nearly decided upon a course that would have her lying here under the comforter until someone came looking for her, when her stomach growled. Immediately she became aware of the hollowness: dinner had been—she looked over at the clock radio on the bedside table—sixteen hours ago. She was starving. And no one was coming to help her. No one cared.

The anger was what roused her, made her throw back the covers and sit up. She turned slowly, experimentally, lowering her feet to the floor. Clothes. She needed to dress. The bureau was near the window, but she knew she didn't have the strength in her legs to take the few steps without the braces—and then she'd only have to take the braces off again to get dressed. For a moment, she felt like just throwing herself back down among the pillows and giving up entirely. Then she saw the clean laundry basket, set on the floor just inside the door at some point, by Gram. Scowling in concentration, Bella took one of the crutches from its place leaning against the bedside table, and stretching forward, used the rubber foot to hook the edge of the basket. The first attempt to pull it toward her was a failure: the basket tipped and slid away from the crutch. She let out a long frustrated breath, bit her lip, and leaned forward again.

This time she inched the laundry basket slowly. Bella had to tug a little to get it over the edge of the braided rug, being mindful all the while not to lean too far forward—she didn't want to fall. When at last the basket was at her feet, she anchored the rubber foot of the crutch for balance, then dragged the basket upward one-handed. It tipped. Some clothing tumbled out. A shirt. Some shorts. She ignored them, and pulled the basket the rest of the way up onto the bed. The underwear, she knew, would be at the bottom; smalls, as Gram delicately called them, always were. There was a pair of jeans on top, and a couple more shirts. Dragging her pajamas off, she donned the clean clothes slowly.

Next, the socks and then shoes, which she couldn't reach to tie, and last, the braces. Isabella adjusted the fittings, just as Gram always did. Crutch at each hand, she slipped her upper arms into the silver cuffs, and pulled herself to her feet.

Wobbly, she thought, breathless and defiant, *but upright*.

The door to the hallway was always tricky, though she was getting better: turn the knob, shuffle back, pull the door open. She left it open now, the unmade bed visible to anyone passing by, and slowly made her way along the hall to the kitchen. As she suspected from the lack of noise, it was deserted. There was no sign of Gram; probably she was getting the eggs from the henhouse, or working in the vegetable garden. Bella paused for a moment, straining her ears for the sound of the tractor, but all she heard was a single sharp bark from the dog, somewhere far off. Uncle Richard's hound, following him around the farm; the dog was slavishly attached to him, and for a moment she wished for a pet that would follow *her* around. She made her way to the bathroom.

Back in the kitchen, her glance fell on the table, scrubbed clean, the pewter jug of lilacs on the runner in the center. Tiny purple trumpets of flowers, browning slightly at the edges, lay scattered on the table beneath the blooms. She itched to draw them, but first, breakfast. At her place, a single bowl and spoon, the box of shredded wheat, and the small jug of milk.

Bella inhaled furiously. No one had awakened her, come to help her get up this morning, but it wasn't an oversight. They'd left her breakfast and gone off, just like that. *Get up when you can. Get up* if *you can.* Even her grandmother. Even Gram.

The betrayal turned quickly to resentment, leaving a bitter taste in her mouth. Isabella stumped loudly to the table and fell heavily onto the chair with her back to the door. Hunger overtook everything. She poured out the cereal, sprinkled it liberally with sugar from the green bowl, and then poured the milk over all of it. Fine. She would eat it all, and they could all go to hell.

No one came in as she ate. No one came in as she dragged herself awkwardly to her feet and put her dishes in the sink behind her—the dishwasher was too difficult to manage. She adjusted her arms in the cuffs of the crutches and moved to the door.

Isabella could hear the sound of the tractor in the distance now, but she couldn't see it. Plowing, she figured, though she was a bit hazy about the workings of a farm. That's what they did in the spring, though, right? Probably Uncle Richard would be down there—wherever—and Grandad, and Uncle Alaric, who never said a word, but who worked as hard as any of them.

Where was Gram? Not in the vegetable garden, where nothing

much had sprouted yet, maybe lettuce and spinach, but where the tin pie plates, strung up to mark the borders and to keep the deer at bay with their metallic noise, flashed in the sunlight. Her car was across the yard, parked in front of the garage, so she hadn't gone to town, to the shops, to run errands. But she was nowhere to be seen.

Fine. They wanted to be like that, then it was fine.

Bella negotiated the step to the granite stoop, then from there to the walkway. She'd been working on stairs with Alice, the physical therapist; now she concentrated on her steps, awkward, dragging. And her balance, that was the hard part. Each time she planted a foot, she felt a jar in her hip. She had never thought about how lightly she had stepped, how easy something she hardly ever thought about, like walking, had been before. Now every step took determination. Right now she was angry, resentful. She turned her halting steps toward the path beyond the garden, the one that led into the pines.

Isabella had overheard Gram yesterday afternoon, the strange seemingly one-sided conversations which happened a lot around the house. Gram hadn't thought Mr. Ahearne's funeral a good place to have taken her after school, but couldn't they have left her alone at the farm? Well, she, Bella, was alone now. How quickly things had changed. Well, they could come look for her if they wanted her—and it would take them a while to find her, following the woods path to the one place they'd never think she'd go.

In all the summer visits to the farm, before, Isabella had learned the lay of the land; she knew where everything was, knew where every path led. Still, it took longer than she thought it would, on these damned crutches, to get under the shelter of the trees. Once in their shade, too, she found the footing treacherous—slippery from the browned pine needles. She slowed her pace, feeling the sweat run down the small of her back beneath her shirt. She tried to take deep even breaths, like the PT told her to. This was hard work. She looked over her shoulder, to the sunny yard, the house. She could turn back now, but she hadn't proven her point. No one had seen her leave; no one knew she was gone. She needed them to see what they'd made her do. She took a deep breath, blew her bangs off her damp forehead, and took another step into the woods, and another.

It was hard work. But she was still furious. She pushed on.

By the time the path led her to the rear archway of the cemetery, she was beyond exhausted, and would have liked nothing more than a drink of water. Her arms ached with the effort of propelling her forward; her legs ached from unaccustomed use, and from something else: the brace below her left knee, holding her leg straight as she swung along, had rubbed painfully.

Not much further now. Not much further. Her parents' stone, all gleaming new granite, was two rows over and further into the sea of graves. There were multitudes of Morgans here; probably the first had been buried in this cemetery at around the same time the farmhouse had been built, in the 1850s. The grassy roadways between the sections of the cemetery were rutted from the cars that maneuvered their way along—as they had yesterday, for Mr. Ahearne. Isabella had to be more careful now; there was no point in dragging herself all the way down here, only to fall in the last few feet. She could see the stone. Just a bit further.

Finally, there it was. Carved into the front, which faced the distant road: MORGAN. Carved into the back, her parents' names, her parents' dates. Brett. Sarah. The earth, which had been rounded last summer, was beginning to settle, the grass feeling its way back. It had been nine months. The car accident had been nine months ago. Isabella shook her head to clear her vision, but it didn't help. Perhaps it wasn't her vision that was unclear; perhaps it was her understanding.

Bella rested against the stone, slightly warm from the sun, and felt the tiniest of breezes trace across her skin. She leaned forward to release the lock on her left knee, and, without the support, she overtipped, and fell roughly to the ground.

At first, the pain. Isabella might have cried out with it—she wasn't sure what sounds were punched out of her gut with the impact—but then she pressed her eyes closed, unable to tell where one searing part of her body ended and another began. Hips, legs, torso, arms. She turned her face to the mossy ground at the base of the stone and let the sob well up in her throat.

It had been nine months.

SIX.

Alaric had spent the morning helping his mother in the barn, bringing down things from the loft where they'd been stored, as she directed. Old furniture, some lamps, a box of dented cookware, another of dishes. Some of it had been up there for ages, or at least since he'd gone into the service. He had last climbed the ladder to collect a plate from the dish set for his own kitchen, as well as a single mug, and a bowl; there had been no need for more than one of each, as he hadn't expected—nor wanted—company. He wondered whether Georgie would notice that the box no longer contained a set for eight. If she did, she'd ask, he guessed. Unless she already knew; she always seemed to know, though Georgie always weighed things out in her mind before speaking.

She'd gone back inside now, and, after washing the barn dust from his hands, Alaric tucked a bottle of water into his back pocket and set off on a walk. The sun was climbing up in the sky. It was warm enough on his skin that he chose to take his walk along the roads.

At the end of the long driveway, he turned to the left and headed toward town. Not before checking his watch, though; Marty made the mail run down here early, around nine-thirty, and he didn't want to meet her on the road. Then he shook his head—it was Saturday, and Marty's sub delivered on Saturday. Unless taking a day off yesterday for her father's funeral had rearranged the schedule.

He liked this walk. It was familiar enough that he could shove his hands in his pockets and wander, thinking, looking along the sides of the road for the changes as the days and the seasons wore on. He could watch the buds form, then slowly unfurl into tiny pale flags before holding their leafy faces toward the sun. He could see the maples fur out with their awkward scarlet flowers, then see those flowers fall. He could listen to the susurration of the streams splashing downhill from the multitude of springs in the woods as they joined forces in the deep ditches beside the road, rushing into culverts on one side and out again on the other. He could listen to the birds as they realized it was spring and sang out their raucous mating invitations: *"smale fowles maken melodye,"* as Chaucer—another writer he hadn't read in high school—would say.

The next driveway wasn't far off from his own, and the one after that even closer, the house lots carved out of Morgan acreage ages ago as the working farm had shrunk. After that, the stretch of woods, streams and rivulets pulsing out of it like veins carrying lifeblood. At the big culvert, he stopped to look down over the old post-and-cable guardrail that the Painter's Springs road department hadn't got around to replacing yet. The small black cat was perched down there on the rocks, overlooking the roiling water, as she frequently was. He snapped his fingers, and she looked up, blinking her wide yellow eyes. Slowly she unfolded her paws from beneath her and stood, arching her back and stretching. Then, when he did not call to her, she sat back down, her tail curled around her feet, only the tip twitching. He waved and walked on.

At the place where the roadside curled into the spring, he slowed. Shadowed by the trees despite the morning sun, the ancient copper plaque on the front of the stone trough was greener than he remembered from years past... or maybe he had simply never thought to look in years past. *Oxidation*, he thought, and the word appeared in front of him. *Verdigris.*

The water poured from the pipe that grew out of the hillside, splashing into the trough, then siphoning off again through the groove at the side. The gravel underfoot was soft from the constant dampness, and whispered as he walked over it. Alaric looked down into the water, vaguely green from a century's worth of algae bloom and die-off, and he wondered, not for the first time: why was the plaque dedicated to the memory of Benjamin Painter, and not for Lawrence Ahearne? Where was the monument to Larry?

Bending at the waist, he plunged his hands into the water, which was bone-chilling cold. His fingers ached, and his wrists, and he explored the way the water hurt. The ripples moved over his skin and away from him as the water drained off to the side, but it was spring and there was always more flowing to take its place. It seemed that there was always more, flowing toward him, hurting him, flowing away. The pain the cold water inflicted on his joints melded with the pain he always carried around with him, and Alaric forced himself to remain still, to really *feel* it... until he began to be numbed to it. This morning it seemed to take longer than usual. He welcomed the numbness, though, as an old friend, when it came.

He straightened at last and shook the spring water from his hands before wiping them down the legs of his jeans. That's when his gaze fell upon the stone, tucked against the retaining wall behind the trough. Small, painted a brilliant glittering green. He leaned forward again, reaching out to take the rock between his fingers like a magic talisman. On its front, narrow black lines sketched out a small turtle, its shell divided into tiny sections, its one visible eye a brown dot. A single word was painted along the side in red: *courage.*

For a long time Alaric only stood there, the stone cold and smooth against his skin. He looked down at the word, and then slowly raised his eyes to the trees crowding in behind the retaining wall.

Courage.

He wasn't sure he knew what that was. At least not anymore.

There had been a time.

When he was in high school, when Larry and the girls and he would rattle around the blueberry barrens in that old pea-soup-colored Bronco. They had not been afraid of anything. When he'd crank down the window on the passenger side; when he'd crank up the radio because a really good song had come on. Tom Petty, maybe. "The Apartment Song" was a really good one for belting out into the summer night. Alaric had been a much better singer than Larry, who always took the backup parts, garbling them as he laughed. *Mar and Car.* They'd laugh, too, from the back seat, but they sang on anyway. Van Morrison, "Jackie Wilson Says." Queen, that old standby "We Will Rock You," the four of them pounding their knees, the seats, the roof of the Bronco. *Stomp-stomp-CLAP. Stomp-stomp-CLAP.*

Had that been courage? Or stupidity?

Whatever it was, it had died.

Singing, though. That had been a long time ago.

Alaric slipped the green stone into his hip pocket and walked on.

He didn't know what made him take the left turn onto the Brimfield Road, the way that led to the cemetery. Nearly noon, the sun was higher now, and he was working up a sweat. But he welcomed that, just as he had welcomed the cold from the spring water. *Extremes.* He felt himself bursting in all directions. He liked to know he was capable of feeling them.

The trash barrel just outside the metal archway was full, overflowing with faded plastic flowers collected during the spring cemetery clean-up. Some of them, he had to admit, he'd thrown away himself: he couldn't bear the thought of memorials to the dead being made of plastic. Not when there were real flowers to be had. He had been careful, though, to plant seeds at every stone he'd taken artificial flowers from: marigolds, sunflowers, cosmos. Sometimes a wildflower mix. He thought of something he'd read about English churchyards left to wildflowers, to invite birds and butterflies. That would happen here, if he were the one to say so. But he wasn't. The town crew mowed everything, once a week, like clockwork, to within an inch of its life.

The archway itself needed a good coat of Rustoleum, the white paint stained and chipping. Alaric made a mental note to himself. That was something he could take care of easily enough. Had he realized where his steps would take him this morning, he would have brought the can of WD-40 to give the gate a few squirts, but when he pushed it open, he found it wasn't too creaky. Still, another mental note. He glanced up before passing through. Pine Rest. He frequently wondered who gave cemeteries names. Who had arranged the first burial, thinking, *I'm going to put a cemetery here, and I'm going to name it Pine Rest.* Who did these things?

Alaric dropped the catch on the gate behind him with a thunk. That's when he heard the gasp, as though a sob had been bitten back.

He was not alone in the cemetery. Surprised, Alaric stood motionless, straining his ears to listen. Perhaps he should leave, turn around and walk back the way he had come. No doubt his father and brother would need his help after lunch anyway, if his mother did not. The idea of interrupting someone's grief horrified him, and he felt the pain in his palms again. He had not meant to intrude, and he was sure whoever had come here to commune with the dead would not want the intrusion either.

It could be anyone. It might be Sylvia Ahearne, returning to Roger's graveside the day after his burial. How long had they been married? Thirty years? Thirty-five? She must be having a horrible time of it, planning her husband's funeral so soon after her son's. At the same time he felt the wave of sympathy for her, he felt himself pulling away. Sylvia had hardened after Larry's death, hardened toward him, hardened toward the world in general. Her blonde hair had gone swiftly gray—or she had stopped dying it—and her face had fallen into stern lines. No. If it were Sylvia, he couldn't be anywhere near that grief. He sensed that it would turn to fury, and he couldn't bear the thought of that fury being turned on him.

But. What if it were Marty?

Alaric inhaled slowly, suddenly indecisive.

He thought he ought to try to comfort Marty, if it were she. They had been friends. She was the one person who would know just what Larry's death had meant to him, what Larry's death had done to him. Had he ever stopped to wonder what it had done to her?

Alaric's thoughts screeched to a halt. He could hear the brakes screaming, felt the jolt all the way through his body when he at last came to a complete stop. He put a hand out blindly to catch himself, grabbed the obelisk dedicated to one of the Painters next to the path.

If it were Marty, that was all the more reason why he should flee before she realized who it was that had entered through the gate.

He stood still, holding his breath. Listening. Past the soughing of the pines to the rear of the cemetery. The sob was not repeated. The air around him pulsed with the presence of a person who didn't want to be heard, didn't want to be seen. The two of them balanced each other precariously on the morning air. Slowly Alaric turned his head, his eyes scanning the stones. The person keeping him company in the cemetery would be hiding, so he looked at the edges of each stone carefully, studying its outline for the shadow that would indicate someone bowed behind it. Slowly. His hand still on the cool granite obelisk, he turned. Slowly.

There. A trace of blue. A shoulder? Toward the back, where all the Morgans found themselves when their days were done. Someone sitting with his family.

Released from his stillness, Alaric tucked his hands into his pockets, touching the stone there like a talisman, and moved forward into the grassy lane between the graves. He stepped carefully, making no noise in the new grass, sensing his own breath move in and out without a sound.

He approached from the side, slowly, like one does with a skittish calf, and when he saw her, he relaxed. Not Marty. Isabella. Then he tensed again, but in a different way. His niece sat huddled, her back against the stone that marked her parents' grave. His brother, his sister-in-law. Brett and Sarah. Bella had her eyes squeezed shut, her hands twisted together. If she were praying, he decided, it was probably that she wouldn't be found by the intruder.

Alaric stopped.

She was seated. Her crutches lay on the grass to either side of her, where they appeared to have fallen. Her legs, the braces glinting silver in the sunlight, stuck straight out before her. He couldn't imagine how she had ended up on the ground; he couldn't imagine how she had come to be in the cemetery in the first place. He willed her to open her eyes and look up. When she didn't, he scuffed a boot on the ground.

Her eyes shot open, her chin up. "Oh," she said. Her voice was small, as though she were expecting trouble. A scolding or something. Her cheeks glistened with the tracks of her tears. When she saw who it was, her shoulders slumped again: no scolding from this quarter, anyway.

Alaric held out his hands, palms up. *Only me.* Slowly he stepped toward her, as non-threatening as he could be, the awkward damaged uncle she always shied away from. Isabella watched him, biting her lip. When he was a few feet away, he lowered himself to the ground as well. The stone he leaned his back against belonged to his grandparents, his father's parents, people long gone whom he had loved as a child. Perhaps they could direct him. As far as he could figure, though, the hope was in vain; the stone remained cold through the back of his shirt. The water bottle was uncomfortable in his back pocket, and he took it out, holding it in both hands.

For a few moments the silence was uncomfortable. Alaric lifted his face to the sun, and closed his eyes. He felt her studying him, her gaze like hands running over his face, trying to understand his profile. He was used to uncomfortable silence. People never knew what to say to him, or how to say it. Why bother, since he couldn't answer anyway?

"I came to visit Mom and Dad," Isabella said at last. This time her voice was defiant, daring him to argue. Which of course he wouldn't. He only nodded, keeping his eyes closed. The sun felt good. He hadn't stopped to feel its warmth in a long time.

The stone against which he leaned was also warming at his shoulder blades, reflecting his own body heat back to him. He shifted slightly, feeling the carving through his shirt. *Frederick Morgan,* he knew it read, *and his beloved wife Shirley.* He knew also that if he kept his eyes closed long enough, the lettering would appear before him exactly as if he were facing the stone, reading the names. He wondered whether Isabella were feeling her own parents' names where her narrow back leaned against them. *Brett. Sarah.*

She was still studying him; he still felt her gaze like a touch, timid but curious. He let her continue, keeping his face angled toward the sun. Like a sunflower. He didn't know where that thought came from, but it made him smile a tiny bit.

"Will you tell on me?"

Alaric turned his head toward her, opened his eyes. Hers were green. He hadn't realized that. He shook his head no. The question seemed so sad to him. A twelve-year-old girl—she *was* twelve, wasn't she?—fearing getting into trouble because she missed her parents. Because she had—*how* had she?—managed to drag herself through the pines along the path, to visit their gravestone. He looked past her toward the rear archway and the pines beyond. It was easily half a mile through those trees. She had to be exhausted.

Now Bella was looking furtively at the water bottle. He twisted off the cap and handed it to her. She drank greedily. When at last her thirst was sated, he pointed to the path, then the crutches on the ground, then raised both palms in question.

Isabella shrugged, plucking at the sparse grass. "I was mad." Still was, if the resolute chin and the drawn-back shoulders were any indication. "Everybody went off. They all left me."

Alaric screwed up his face, thinking. His mother had said she needed his help this morning, and he'd gone to the barn with her. He hadn't seen Isabella. He had never thought about why he hadn't. He tilted his head.

"Nobody woke me up for breakfast," she continued impatiently. "I didn't know where anybody was. So I got dressed and came out here."

Half a mile. Alaric shook his head in wonder. He wasn't sure he remembered what it was like to be twelve. Had he been this determined? Stubborn, his mother would have called him; he could hear the word in her voice. He hadn't been this angry at twelve, but then again, he had had both his parents, had the use of both of his legs.

"What?" Isabella demanded. "You said you wouldn't tell. You promised."

Alaric recognized the attempt at manipulation for what it was. He hadn't said anything, to be honest. He hadn't promised anything.

"They don't want to leave me by myself—I heard Gram say it yesterday. I guess they're afraid I'll hurt myself. Fall or something." The jut of that jawline. Alaric had to admire it. Most of the time she looked like his brother Brett, but right now, he was reading Sarah through the angry set of the expression, the black thundercloud of the brow. "And then, after all that, they went off and left me." She rocked forward from her hips, then back, thumping her shoulders into the gravestone at her back so hard Alaric winced. "They left me," she repeated, her voice smaller. To his horror, he realized that she was crying.

Betrayal. By her grandparents, by her parents, by everyone who left her.

Alaric didn't know what to do when people cried. He didn't know what to do when children cried. And now Isabella was crying, and he was being called upon to do something—what? *What?* He looked down into his helpless useless palms. Should he hug her? Is that what you did? But she was glaring at him now, daring him to try to put his arms around her, and he could feel her rejection of such a move even before he made it. If he could bring himself to. He showed her his empty hands, willing her to understand his inability to comfort. It would be presumptuous, too, wouldn't it be? Pretending that an embrace would make everything better, would replace all the things—people—who had failed her by going missing from her life? Still she glared, her eyes a glittering green in her blotchy tear-stained face.

He raised his hands in surrender, dropped them into his lap. And felt, through his jeans, the stone in his pocket.

Carefully he shifted so he could reach in and pull it out. Then he held it out to her, the paint sparkling in his palm. He kept his eyes on hers.

After a few moments, Bella drew in a quavering breath, and dropped her gaze to his outstretched hand and the painted rock, which rested there. A quick look back up to his face, and then she reached out, frowning, and took the stone with shaking fingers. She held it up before her, reading the single word there—he saw her mouth it: *courage.* He had thought, when he'd taken the little stone from the trough at the spring that he had needed courage, that the painted rock was some sort of message. As he watched Isabella examine it, he knew that he had been meant to carry it to her. To give it to her. To remind her that she needed to find her courage.

Slowly now he climbed to his feet, stretching his back and legs. He retrieved the water bottle and returned it to his pocket. Then he picked up the crutches with one hand, and held out the other to his niece.

The tears had subsided. Holding the rock in her cupped

hands, she looked up at him. "I can't," she said, and pressed her lips together.

Alaric waited.

"They were right," she conceded. "I fell."

He nodded once.

"And now something's wrong with the brace." Bella grimaced and indicated the metal cage around her left knee. "I tore my jeans, and Gram's going to be mad—"

Alaric shook his head vigorously. His mother would not be angry about that.

"—And now there's something wrong, and it's hurting my knee."

He lowered himself again. The ground from which the new grass sprung was damp, and he felt the coldness through his jeans. Carefully, gently, he ran his hands over the metal, feeling the shape, the bend where there shouldn't have been one. He frowned. It wouldn't be difficult to fix, if he just had the correct tools. But they were back at the farm. He tapped the brace, then pointed to Bella, then to himself. Her brow lowered. Again he tapped, pointed.

"I don't get it," she said. "I don't understand."

Frustrated, he leaned back on his heels for a moment, then leaned forward to release her shoe.

"Take it off?" she asked.

He nodded, let out a breath.

Bella shook her head, panicked. "Then I'll never be able to get back to the farm."

Alaric nodded, angled away from her, patted his back.

"Carry? Piggy-back?"

Grinning in relief, he turned back to face her.

Isabella didn't look as though the idea gave her confidence. Still, she allowed Alaric to unlock the brace and slip it off, setting it with the crutches. He straightened, and tapped the single word on the rock in her hands. *Courage.* Then he turned and presented his back to her. Waited.

Bella's hands, when she clutched at his shirt, were hesitant at first, and then more sure. Alaric held himself as steady as possible as she used her arms to pull herself to him. He forced himself to hold still when she wrapped her arms around his neck so tightly he thought she'd throttle him. He could help her then, grabbing her under her knees, shifting her legs around his hips. Finally, reaching down to take the crutches and brace in one hand, he tucked his arms under her legs and slowly got to his feet.

"You can't carry me all the way back."

Alaric figured he could, so there was nothing, really, to say to that. He set off toward the gateway at the back of the cemetery, and the pines, and the farm beyond.

He had carried Larry further, but at least, this time, he could help.

SEVEN.

WHEN THEY RETURNED through the trees to the farm, Alaric ducked around the back of the garden and skirted the side of the barn until he came to his door. They saw no one else in the barnyard, and he knew Bella was relieved. Hands full as they were, he had to stoop and twist to turn the knob. At the shift, he felt Isabella's arms tighten around his neck. He was sweating with the exertion of carrying her that half mile; he grimaced at how out of shape he was. Of course, she weighed about the same as his ninety-pound pack, but she was a more awkwardly distributed load. Still, his own breathlessness surprised him.

Inside, he dropped the crutches and the brace to the futon, then turned to lower Isabella to one of the two kitchen chairs. He had one water glass, which he filled at the little sink, and set before her on the table. His one tea mug was upended in the dish strainer, washed out after breakfast; he filled this for himself, and drank it down in a few gulps.

Isabella was looking around the single room with curiosity. Alaric filled his mug again and set it on the table, then pointed to her knee. Now he could see that the leg of her jeans was in fact torn, and there appeared to be a bloodstain.

She prodded the torn place and winced. "It does hurt."

Alaric held his hands out and rolled his wrists up and down. Then he pointed to her leg again. Pointed to his eyes, pointed to her knee.

"You want to look at it?" Bella frowned, but leaned over and rolled the leg of her jeans up, tugging the material to her knee. Alaric knelt to look at the place where the denim had ripped, where the metal of the brace had scraped away at her skin. There was a spot, red and raw, about the size of a quarter. He stood again, held up his hands to indicate she should stay—*where was she going to go?*—and slipped into the tiny bathroom. From the cabinet he drew Band-Aids, and some antibacterial cream; he held a clean washcloth under the faucet until it was soaked and warm.

When he returned and began washing at the spot as gently as he could, Alaric heard her intake of breath. Yeah, it probably stung like hell, he imagined. He glanced up apologetically, and saw her biting her lip. He redoubled his efforts at gentleness. At last, he set the cloth aside and dabbed on some of the cream, covering that, at last, with two of the Band-Aids, just to be sure.

"Thanks." Bella's voice was small, and Alaric looked up in concern, trying to read her for a pain level. But she slewed her eyes away, shyly, he thought. He sat back on his heels, gathering up the supplies and rubbish. Well, of course she would respond with shyness now, having spent the last nine months shrinking away. He recognized her behavior in himself; while she pulled away physically, in ways that were easy to see, he pulled away psychologically. The roots were similar. He tapped her water glass, and smiled, before returning the bandages to the tiny bathroom.

Alaric returned to root in the junk drawer at the end of the counter for a pad of paper and a pen. *I'm going to get my tools*, he wrote. He pointed to the leg brace on the futon.

Bella nodded. "See if they're looking for me," she said.

Alaric nodded in return. She couldn't hide out forever, but he could buy her some time fairly easily. He took up the pencil again. *Can I get you anything before I go? Hungry?*

"Kind of."

He wished he hadn't offered, when he realized he didn't have much in the room. He opened the refrigerator, took out a pint of past-dated milk, smelled it, and made a face. There was a single tomato in the vegetable drawer. He doubted she wanted it. He doubted *he* wanted it.

Bella laughed. "Don't put that milk back in there. Pour it out."

Alaric dumped it down the sink, and threw the carton away. In the overhead cabinets, he found a jar of peanut butter, and a box of saltines, with one unopened sleeve inside. He set those on the table before her apologetically, and got his single knife from the sparsely populated silverware drawer. He ripped off a paper towel—the roll was getting thin; he'd have to do something about that—and handed it to her.

"You don't have much in here, do you?" Bella observed.

Alaric shook his head, picked up the pencil again. *Nobody comes over here.*

Bella cocked her head, eyeing him. "That's sad. Isn't it?"

I like it that way.

She looked abashed. "Do you want me to go?"

The tone of her voice, suddenly forlorn, cut straight through him. He shook his head vigorously. Then he bent to the paper again. *Stay here. Eat crackers. I'll be right back.*

Isabella nodded. She opened her mouth to speak, then closed it again.

He held out his hands, a question.

"Can you get another pair of pants from the laundry basket in my room?"

He figured he could.

It took longer than he expected. The tools were hung over the workbench in the barn; Alaric collected what he needed, and stuck them haphazardly into his pockets. He could hear his brother and his father talking out by the tractor shed, and he moved stealthily, trying not to draw their attention, halting momentarily by the door to place them by the sound of their voices. "Haven't seen her," Richard was saying. "You sure she didn't go to the store with Mum?" His voice was low, and sounded hollow: they had to be inside the shed itself.

His father coughed. "She must have. Bella's not in her room. Your mother must have changed her mind about taking her, and just forgot to tell me."

Sure enough, when Alaric looked over to the garage, he saw that his mother's car was gone. That meant the house was clear. He skirted the vegetable garden, and with a quick glance over his shoulder, let himself in through the kitchen door, feeling distinctly like a housebreaker. Down the hallway, opening the bedroom door: the bed was unmade, the contents of the overturned laundry basket jumbled on the braided rug. There was a pair of jeans on the top of the pile. He took those and headed back to the kitchen. The clock over the sink showed just after noontime; no wonder Isabella was hungry. He grabbed a loaf of bread from the box, then a package of sandwich meat and the jar of mayonnaise from the refrigerator. His mother had been washing the kitchenware they'd brought down from the barn loft; he swiftly snagged another plate, as well as a second knife, fork, and spoon. The yard was still clear when he let himself out of the kitchen door. Arms and pockets fully laden, he dashed across to his own door. Isabella looked up when he entered; she had been doodling on the pad of paper before her. Alaric kicked the door closed behind him and leaned against it dramatically, a man having completed a dangerous mission. He breathed an exaggerated sigh of relief. Isabella laughed, and the sound echoed in the small room. She clapped a hand over her mouth and looked around. He grinned.

"You look like you robbed a bank or something."

Alaric winked at her.

He crossed to the counter, set down the plate, meat, and jar. Then he pulled the silver and the tools from his back pocket. He handed her the jeans.

Bella glanced up at him awkwardly, her cheeks flushing. Easily understood.

I'll wait outside. Shout when you're done.

Georgie's car was still missing. He heard the tractor start up and move off, back toward the fields. Alaric leaned against the wall, squinting against the sun. His father thought Isabella was with his mother; his mother thought Isabella was with his father. That bothered him. *Find out if they're looking for me,* she'd ordered. But they weren't, and he felt a sudden deep sadness for her. And a sharp disappointment in his parents. How could they be so careless with her, he wondered, the one of them who needed so much care? He inhaled deeply. What would have happened had he not stumbled across her in the cemetery? She'd fallen. She'd hurt herself. How long would it have taken for someone to find her?

Alaric quickly fought the anger down. An accident. A mistake. That was all it was. His mother, in going out to the barn, had never thought that Isabella, resentful Isabella, grief-stricken

Isabella, would have done the next best thing to running away from home. Who in their right minds would have expected her to? Who would have thought the girl would have had it in her to navigate all the way to the cemetery on those crutches?

Still Alaric's thoughts careened back to Bella amongst the gravestones. She had fallen. He was holding his breath, because suddenly he felt the loss of balance, the granite stone rushing up toward him. He felt himself twisting his head away, then he felt, through his knees and all the way up his spine, the jolt of hitting the ground, the sharp stab into the skin below his knee. He almost believed that if he looked down, he would find a tear in his own pants, blood on his own shin.

Yet he was still upright, still leaning against the warm wooden wall beside his own door. He hadn't fallen. It was just the vivid imagining. Alaric forced himself to breathe. How frightened she must have been. Yet she had choked back that sob when he'd dropped the latch to the gate; she hadn't wanted to be found crying. He blinked again against the sunlight. He understood that. He understood it very well. And he respected that steel.

Alaric made sandwiches, and they sat across from each other, eating.

"Should have stolen some lettuce while you were at it," Bella said.

He made a face. He pulled the pad of paper closer and wrote *tomato.*

"I don't like tomatoes," she protested.

Alaric picked up the pencil again, but was interrupted by a frantic knocking at the door.

"Are you in there? Alaric?" It was Georgie's voice, rising, frantic. "Alaric?"

He reached the door in two strides and pulled it open. His mother stood there, hand raised to knock again, her face pale.

"Alaric, Isabella's missing. I can't find her anywhere. I thought your father and your brother, when they came in for lunch—"

He stepped back to allow her entry. Her gaze fell on Bella, seated at the table, half a roast beef sandwich in her hand.

"Oh—" His mother's eyes darted from one to the other. "Oh, Bella. I didn't know where you were—"

Alaric tilted his head, swept an arm around. The answer, he indicated, was obvious. Here. Then his mother's glance took in the crutches leaning against the arm of the futon, and the brace, straightened now, surrounded on the floor by a wrench, some pliers, a can of WD-40.

"My brace needed adjusting," Bella said quickly. "Uncle Alaric did it for me."

Alaric could feel the hum of the air, the noise Georgie's confusion made as she looked between the pair of them. He thought about smiling at her, but decided that would push her confusion over the edge.

"Would you like a sandwich?" Isabella asked. "We were just having some lunch."

The smile did not reach Georgie's eyes, but it was, at least, an attempt. "No, Isabella, thank you." She backed toward the door, but paused. "Check with your father, Alaric. I think he has something he needs your help with this afternoon, before the rain."

When Alaric returned to his seat, Bella grinned at him. "I didn't think she would. And I know you only have two plates anyway."

PART II

EIGHT.

After the rain had stopped in the afternoon—too little, too brief—Marty pulled on her jacket and let herself out, pausing only at the table at the end of the porch to select a rock. A shimmery blue one, she decided, painted with a tiny tree. *Hope,* it read in brilliant yellow lettering. She tucked it into her pocket, then slipped her phone into the opposite one, for balance.

The rain and the accompanying wind had brought a change in the weather, from the unseasonable warmth, back to what might be considered normal for late spring. Along the roadside, the new pale leaves on the trees still fluttered fitfully with the memory of breeze. There were puddles at the ends of the driveways she passed, while in the ditch to her left, water ran briskly toward its level. The rush of it was the rhythm to the melody line of birds she could hear but could not identify.

Partway along the road, Marty turned into the woods. There was a path here, had been as long as she could remember, but it was fainter than it had been when she and her brother had used it on a regular basis as kids, cutting off the corner to get to the spring, and then the Morgan farm. On either side, the heads of ferns curled, tight like green violin scrolls. Overhead, the new leaves whispered to one another. The ground was wet, and squelched under her pink wellies. In her pocket, she curled her fingers around the stone, cool and comforting to her touch.

The path emerged at the far end of the stone retaining wall, the blocks of granite dressed and stacked to hold back the hill. She scrambled down to the turnaround before the stone trough, grateful that none of the cars that often stopped here were in the space now. The water in the trough was overflowing, the groove cut for a drain filled and more spilling over the worn side. Even from here she could see that the last painted rock she had left was gone. Someone had found it, had taken it. A message to the universe, Marty thought, smiling gently to herself—a message that had got through to someone. She stepped through the mud gingerly, her boots sticking, to lean forward and tuck the blue stone into the familiar place at the back corner of the trough, next to the retaining wall. Even in the weak late afternoon sunlight it seemed to glitter.

Straightening, she squelched to the far end of the wall, and hoisted herself up. The granite was still damp from the afternoon's fleeting rain, and she'd probably have a wet seat soon enough, but it was nice, to just sit. Her first memory of coming to the spring had been as a child, holding tight to her father's hand. He had cupped his palms beneath the pipe, and had first sipped the water, then splashed it up into his face. Marty still remembered the numbing cold when she had tried to do the same, but she also remembered that more water had ended up running down the front of her shirt than had made it to her lips. She could still hear the sound of her father's laugh, the feel of the bandanna he had pulled from his pocket to wipe her wet face.

Now Marty watched the spring water splash down from the black pipe that brought it from the hill beyond it. The hills on the cape were full of springs, water bursting to the surface and forming rivulets that traveled above ground, carving pathways through grass and fern, through bracken and woods, and even through stone, if given enough time. The rivulets joined together and made streams, which in turn joined and made larger streams. This time of year, after the melting snows and thawing ground, all the water rushed downhill exuberantly, making its way to lower and lower ground, until somewhere at the outer edges of the cape, it flung itself into the Atlantic, its ultimate goal. On its way, some soaked into the ground and was drunk up by the roots of the trees which began as acorns or as the red flowers of maples, and then grew until saplings, and then beyond until their girths couldn't be encircled by both arms.

Marty had meant to walk on, beyond the spring, past the next few houses, and to the cemetery. She had meant to look in on her father's grave, to neaten up the flowers that had been left there on Friday, long before the rain. Instead, now, she listened, lulling herself with the hush of water. There really was no need. He wasn't there, Dad, and he couldn't really care about dying flowers. More than likely, her mother would have been over first thing this morning, before church, and would have taken care of anything that needed her organizing touch.

She ached for her mother, but with a helpless sort of pain, tinged with a bit of resentment. A pair of mourning doves landed in the tiny patch of grass at the edge of the turnaround, unmindful of her presence, and examined the wet ground. She listened for the soft cooing, but the rushing water drowned it out. Mourning doves, she had read, mated for life; her parents had, too. Now her mother had lost her husband of thirty-odd years. It made sense, in a way, that she would lash out, or worse, that she would dismiss Marty's attempts at comfort impatiently. It still hurt, though. It hurt to have the phone call cut off this morning when her mother had said *if you don't have anything else to say, I'm busy right now.* It hurt that her mother did not, perhaps could not, acknowledge Marty's own pain and sadness. They were just two now, where they had once been four; couldn't they lean against one another? She watched the doves peck at some seeds invisible to her, and suddenly she wished to have her painted rock back, so she could throw it at them.

NINE.

MARTY HAD SLAMMED the mailbox shut and was about to pull out onto the road when she heard the snick against the glass, a sound she recognized, having heard it all too often. *Damn it.* She glared at the round chip in her windshield, gift of a flying bit of rock from the dump truck, which had flown past her on the Lighthouse Road. No tarp covering the load, she noted, and wished she'd been able to get the license plate number. She leaned forward to put her finger to the spot, but then drew back, knowing that she'd probably send the crack to spiderweb heaven with the slightest of pressure.

"Marsden," a voice to her right said, and she jumped.

A stranger stood in the yard of the Cash place, a clarinet case in his hand. He wore dark sunglasses, and brushed his graying hair back as he looked down the road and back to her again.

"Pardon?"

"Marsden," he repeated. "That's what it said on the side of the truck. Got your windshield, did he?"

"You didn't get the plate number, did you?" Marty threw the Jeep into park, and grabbed the pen and pad of paper from the console, to write the company name before she forgot. "I'm going to have to call the insurance company to make a claim for this.

I hope they can repair it. I hope they won't have to replace it." That would take far too much time, and she didn't have another vehicle to deliver the mail in.

"You might try the police, too," the stranger suggested. He took a step closer to the car and lifted his glasses. "The way they come flying along this road—we've only been here a few days, and it's been crazy. It's a wonder they haven't killed anybody yet." Now he shook his head. "I didn't get the plate number, though. Sorry. I'm Simon Barnett, by the way."

Marty reached out a hand to take his proffered one. "Marty Ahearne. I'm your friendly neighborhood mail lady. You're living here?"

Simon shrugged. "Renting. For a month or so. My business partner Nate and I."

"Are you having your mail forwarded up here?" Marty racked her brain, trying to remember any temporary forwarding order she had seen, but came up empty.

He nodded. "Submitted the order online, both of us. It'll probably only be bills, so it's hardly worth it." When he laughed, his face was pleasant, the skin around his eyes crinkling. "That and the occasional script."

Marty took the bait. "Script?"

"For the Harbor Repertory, over in Danby. Nate's in planning meetings for next summer. Nathan Waring? He's going to be the new artistic director."

The name probably should have meant something to her, but didn't.

"And you?"

"Just along for the ride." Simon held up the clarinet case. "Providing soundtracks when necessary." He chuckled. "Usually not necessary. But a man's got to do something."

Marty lifted a hand, then shifted the Jeep back into gear.

"The mail lady's got to do something, too. Like deliver the mail." She grinned. "It's nice to meet you. Painter's Springs is a small enough burgh. I'll probably see you around."

"Like tomorrow, when you deliver the mail again."

She was about to ease away from the verge, when another dump truck hurtled past.

"Bastard," Marty hissed.

"Nathan Waring?" Caro exclaimed, poking her head out from the kitchen. The smell of meatloaf, along with the earthy scent of baked potatoes, wafted out with her.

Marty dripped a bit more red craft paint into the small indent of the plastic palette. Biting her lower lip in concentration, Sophie jabbed her brush into the color and attacked the small rock in front of her. When she had covered the top side, she flipped it over to paint the bottom, mindless of the paint that came off on the newspaper covering the table. There was paint now on her fingers, so she wiped them vigorously down the front of her smock.

"That's what he said," Marty told her.

"This one yellow," Sophie said, grabbing another rock. Marty took the paintbrush from her and handed her a clean one.

"At the Harbor Rep. Nathan Waring is going to be the artistic director at the Harbor Rep next summer." The timer went off on the oven, and with a loud sigh, Caro returned to the kitchen. Much banging ensued.

"You all right in there?"

"Yellow paint," Sophie insisted. Marty sorted through the plastic bottles in the little crate, then, finding a sunshiny yellow, opened it to squirt a bit of paint onto the palette.

"That's what you said, and I am in disbelief. *The* Nathan

Waring." The slam of the oven door, a quick cursty. "I'm in such disbelief here that I am setting myself on fire."

"Don't *do* that, Mama," Sophie ordered, as though her mother frequently went up in flames. "I told you before." She brushed yellow paint haphazardly over the rock, eyed it critically, and slapped on some more for good measure. Then she flung down her brush and scrambled from the chair.

"She's fine, Butterfly," Marty said, but Sophie was already marching resolutely to the kitchen to oversee the conflagration. "There's only one Nathan Waring? *The* Nathan Waring?"

Now the clink of silverware on plates. "You want to get the table for me?" Caro called. "Just got to get these beans, and we're ready."

They settled at the table, Sophie holding out her hands to have the paint scrubbed off. Caro left the smock on her, since the tomato sauce atop the meatloaf would be transferring itself shortly to mix with the red paint.

"Nathan Waring has been directing off-Broadway stuff for years," Caro said as she reached across to empty her daughter's baked potato skins. She put some butter on the potato, and into the skins as well, to melt. "What's he doing here?"

"Summer theater, I guess? Next summer? Whatever artistic directors do."

Caro made a face. "Jesus, Martha Ahearne, you're such a Philistine. This is a big deal. This guy is maybe the most famous thing to hit this part of the state in just about forever." She served herself, then cut open her own potato. "What did he look like? Did you see him? Did you get a chance to talk to him?"

Marty shook her head, lifting her water glass. "Only his business partner. Simon something or other. He seemed nice. He was carrying a clarinet."

The sigh was explosive. *"Philistine."*

TEN.

Caro, before turning out the bedside light, did a last scroll through Facebook on her phone. She clicked the "like" button under a picture Marty had posted of a clammer off Wilson's Head, his footprints following him across the low-tide mud. Then she changed her mind and clicked the "love" button. A list of the 100 books the BBC thought everyone should read: she debated, then opted out of checking herself against it. She was far too tired, and just knew she'd fall asleep in the middle of the list, then drop her phone on her face. She scrolled on by.

People You May Know. Caro usually ignored those suggestions, as they tended to be people who had bullied her in high school, with whom she had no inclination to be friends now. The first name, tonight, though, caught her eye. *Melissa Waybridge, one mutual friend.* She closed her eyes, shook her head. There was no way in hell she wanted to be friends with her ex-husband's live-in girlfriend; it was bad enough that she was linked to *him* on Facebook, because she thought she should know what he was doing for Sophie's sake. She didn't need to be friends with the woman he was sleeping with in the last months of their marriage.

Then she realized what she had seen in the picture.

A hand. A ring.

Caro's eyes snapped open, and she peered at the screen. Enlarged it. Yes, that was a ring, with a diamond. She clicked on the picture. It took her through to the truncated page—*to see what Melissa posts, send her a friend request.* No. She could just stare at the picture here, and know what it probably said, what she could read in the full post, if she wanted.

But she did want, in a sick sort of way. Caro quickly typed Pete's name into the search box, and went to his page. Sure enough, he was tagged. Sure enough, she could read the post.

He asked, and I SAID YES!!!!!

Caro sprang out of bed and dashed down to the end of the hall.

The door was closed. She knocked, quietly but urgently, not wanting to wake Sophie. "Marty?" she hissed. "*Marty?*"

There was a grunt, and Caro pushed the door open. The room was dim, though the moonlight filtered in through the two windows, one of which was open. Marty sat up, and pulled her duvet up around her shoulders.

"What is it?" she asked groggily, rubbing her eyes. "Is Sophie all right?"

"I have to show you this." Caro kept her voice low, closing the door behind her before crossing to settle on the end of the bed. She leaned against the footboard and held out the phone.

She could see Marty, in the dimness, trying to climb her way out from sleep.

"This had better not be some TikTok," Marty growled. But she took the phone. Frowning, she looked at the screen, then used a finger to scroll up, scroll down, the frown deepening.

"Not TikTok," Caro said.

Finally Marty looked up. "He's going to marry her, then." She tossed the phone back and readjusted the duvet. "I hope she knows what she's getting into."

"She doesn't, or she wouldn't do it." Caro sighed, took one last look at the ring—he'd never given her an engagement ring—and shut the screen down. "She believes what he says, that everything that ever went wrong came down to me."

"And that you left him for me?"

"And that I left him for you."

Yawning, Marty shoved a couple of her pillows behind her back—she always slept with more pillows than any normal human needed—and leaned against them. "Well, you're in my bed now," she chuckled. She tossed a couple of pillows down to the end, and Caro grabbed one to hold it to her chest.

"You're not my type," Caro said. Even to her own ears, her voice still sounded anxious.

Marty, her friend of longest standing, seemed to recognize that note, too. "What are you afraid of?"

Caro shook her head. The moonlight cast ghostly shadows around the room, and she wished Marty would turn on the bedside light, but she hesitated to say anything. "I don't trust him. I told you before. He's got something going on, some long game that I don't know anything about."

"Aren't you being a bit paranoid?" Marty asked. She yawned again, and ran a hand up into her brown hair, made prematurely gray in the silvery light.

"Paranoid?"

Marty shrugged, her pajama sleeve sliding down off her shoulder. She reached over and pulled it back up. "I mean, how long has he been dating this person? Melissa?"

"Dating? Don't you mean screwing?"

"All right. Screwing. How long has Pete been screwing this person?"

It was Caro's turn to shrug. "I don't know. A year. Two years. Something like that."

"Oh, come on. I think you know exactly how long."

Irrationally stung, Caro didn't answer. Because of course Marty was right, and she knew exactly how long Pete had been screwing Melissa. Almost to the day. When, exhausted after pulling an all-nighter with colicky newborn Sophie, she had sorted a load of laundry and smelled another woman—another other woman—on his clothes. She knew when he had changed his relationship status on Facebook from *it's complicated* to *in a relationship*.

"So tell me exactly what the problem is that you are having with this."

"Problem?"

"You're echoing me, echoing me, echoing me."

Caro threw the pillow at Marty, who ducked. "Stop being such a bitch."

"Does this mean you don't want to sleep with me anymore?"

Caro threw the other pillow at Marty, who snagged it out of the air and threw it back.

"Seriously, though," Marty gasped at last, once they'd both choked off their giggles with hands pressed to their mouths. Waking Sophie at this time of night was simply not done. "Tell me why you're so wound up about this. I know you don't want him back."

Caro made a gagging noise.

"So something else is upsetting you. What is it?"

That, in the end, was the problem. The feeling of dread in her chest was somehow nebulous, and she was unable to identify its source. Caro threw up her hands, and startled herself with the monstrous shadow on the wall. "I don't know. I don't trust him."

"You never have." Marty yawned yet again. The clock on her bedside table ticked over from 11:59 to midnight. "What makes this time so special?"

"He's up to something."

"Proposing to Melissa to get back at you? I don't think I'm following this line of reasoning."

Caro squeezed her face between her palms. Her skin felt hot. "Of course not. But he's got something going on that I can't quite figure out, and I don't like it."

"And Melissa? Is she in on this vague something?"

"I don't know," Caro moaned. Then she sat up, and the shadow moved with her. "Listen, it's really weird talking to you in the dark like this, when I can't see your face. Can you turn on the light?"

"No."

"Bitch."

Another yawn. "Listen, Caro. My oldest, my dearest, my bestest friend. I'm going to sleep, and I want you to go to sleep, too. There's nothing you can do about any of this tonight. In fact, I don't think there's anything you can do until Pete makes the move that brings his nefarious plan out into the open."

"By then it might be too late."

"Caroline. Listen to me. I love you, even though you're not my type and I don't want to sleep with you. But I *do* want to sleep. I'd like to deliver the mail tomorrow without taking out half the mailboxes on the route." She sighed. "You need to go take some melatonin, and then try to sleep yourself. There is absolutely nothing you can do about Pete tonight."

"I could sneak out and burn down his house."

"But you're not going to."

"But I'm not going to."

"Good woman." There was the sound of Mary blowing kisses, and then rearranged her pillows. "Go on, then. I'll see you in the morning."

Reluctantly Caro got to her feet. She had her hand on the latch when Marty called.

"And stay off your goddamn phone."

ELEVEN.

CARO HAD STARTED in on the tapes just as soon as Marty had gone, taking Sophie to Joanne's daycare before going to the post office to case the mail. Headphones and blue glare glasses on, Caro found herself transcribing in her usual frenetic way: type for a full hour, get up and walk a brisk two circuits of the downstairs, get a drink from the kitchen sink. Then she would reset her timer and do it all over again and again until lunch time. Five hours on the clock in the morning. Three in the afternoon. By three o'clock, when it was time to swing up to Joanne's to gather up Sophie—or when Marty brought her back—her neck would be stiff, her back sore, ergonomic chair notwithstanding. Still, it was work, work she could do from home, work for which, for the most part, she could make her own daily schedule.

Caro was surprised, then, around two, when she heard the knock on the porch door: authoritative, just shy of pounding. She struggled to her feet and made it to the porch just as the second, more impatient knock sounded.

"I'm coming," she called. She opened the porch door, but left the screen door latched. It didn't look like the Jehovah's Witnesses, and didn't they always travel in pairs?

"Ms. Pond?" the man on the step asked. He was wearing a black jacket, and a pair of sunglasses, which he did not remove. Definitely not a Witness. "Caroline Pond?"

She looked over his shoulder into the driveway, where a blue sedan idled. Not a delivery. Not a policeman.

"I am," she said, drawing herself up. "Who wants to know?"

"My name is Walter Landon. I'm a process server with Willis and Strout, attorneys at law." He withdrew an envelope and two sheets of paper from the manila folder in his hand, then produced a pen. "If you would just sign here." He held the folder out, indicating a line on one of the loose pages.

"What is this?"

"A notice and acknowledgment form, ma'am, indicating that you've received the complaint."

"Complaint? Complaint about what?" Caro felt her anxiety level climb. "Complaint from whom?"

Walter Landon was apparently used to dealing with babbling people like her: her questions did not stir him, and he still had not removed the sunglasses—she could see two small versions of herself in the dark lenses. "If you'll just sign the form, ma'am, I'll leave this with you and be on my way."

Caro opened the screen door and took the pen. Quickly she scribbled her signature, wobbly and nearly illegible. *Legal complaint.* Tucking the signed copy of the acknowledgment back into its folder, Landon handed her the envelope and the other copy. Then he turned on his heel and headed toward his car.

Slowly Caro opened the envelope, barely registering as Landon backed the sedan out of the driveway and headed up the road toward town. There were several pages. She looked down at the first.

Plaintiff: Peter D. Vargas.

Defendant: Caroline P. Pond a/k/a Caroline P. Vargas.

Panicked, she read through it all, and the shakes began in earnest.

The attack was over in seconds. Still, it felt as though it went on forever, as an earthquake feels like it goes on forever. Once Caro had ceased her shaking, she forced herself again to look at the papers in her sweaty hands. She had never had a process server hand her a court order before—*she* had been the one to file for divorce from Pete. Yet here it was. She realized that her hands were shaking again, the pages rattling. She backed into the dining room and set the pages quickly on the table, then sank into her chair with her hands beneath her legs.

She was the defendant.

That was her name, right there.

Pete was filing for full custody of Sophie.

Caro squeezed her eyes shut for a moment, willing all of this to be a dream—a really bad dream. However, when she opened them again, the summons still lay on the table as though mocking her.

She wanted nothing more than to leap into the Vue and rush to the daycare center, to gather Sophie into her arms. Caro let out a little bark of laughter, bordering on the hysterical. If she did that—interrupted Sophie in whatever activity the child was hurling herself into with all the intensity of her little whirlwind being—Caro knew what reaction she'd get. Even here, stiff and straight and terrified in this dining room chair, she could hear the sharp protests—*not now, Mama!*—and feel the wriggling body as her daughter fought to get away.

Now she, Caro, was going to have to fight to keep Sophie. Caro pressed one hand to her mouth to keep her lips from quivering, and looked yet again at the summons on the table;

she couldn't keep her eyes from it. Full custody. He wanted full custody of Sophie. He would marry his girlfriend, take custody of Caro's daughter—he'd already got the dog, so all he needed was a picket fence.

Caro went to her desk to scramble through the stacks of paper there. She found her phone and dialed his number, then cut the call before the first ring. What could she say to him? What could she say that he wouldn't reply to with a mocking word, a cutting refusal? Nothing. She knew that. He and Melissa had already thought this out, had even got to the point of paying an attorney a retainer.

"I feel like he's teasing me—no, that's not the word. He's taunting me." Caro's voice was bitter. She wanted to tear the court summons into tiny pieces, then feed them to the garbage compactor, then finally give them the ignominious burial they so richly deserved. "Or trying—purposely—to drive me insane."

She was onto the next stage, and it was good that Marty knew enough not to try to stop her, to calm her. Caro slammed from room to room, waving her arms frantically, a caged animal. Caged by these horrific circumstances. Marty was emptying the dishwasher as Caro stomped past to look out the door into the back yard where Sophie had gone in search of her giraffe, then careened back through the dining room into the living room.

"There's no way to go back this time," Caro stormed. "None. He's crossed every line, burned all the bridges. He wants to go for custody of my child, he'll have to fight me first."

Marty had straightened, a plate in each hand, and was watching her. Caro made her hands into tight fists, and wished she were bigger than her burly ex-husband, so she could really fight him, knock him down, punch him.

"Calm down, Mama," Sophie ordered, appearing in the kitchen, dragging her giraffe by one leg.

"You've got to hire a lawyer."

Caro's anxiety had been infectious, however, and now, after Sophie had gone to bed, Marty was sweeping cobwebs. The broom came in handy for a quick angry spot of brushing away where the wall met the ceiling, spiderwebs that appeared in an old house such as this the moment she let her guard down. Marty flicked on the light and attacked them on the porch with vigor. Her anger at Pete, and at the situation he'd put Caro in, had built through dinner as Caro's had ebbed toward despair. She turned her attention to the living room, then the dining room. Before she got to the kitchen ceiling, she locked the dishwasher and hit the buttons to begin the cycle with more force than was actually necessary.

"I don't know any lawyers." Caro's voice took on that helpless note, the one that crept in at last when she was feeling overwhelmed. Marty had to check her impatience. Caro wasn't helpless; she simply needed to be allowed to work through this next stage before she figured out her course of action. Right now she was slumped on the couch, her hands between her knees. Her resemblance to Sophie in this pose was uncanny.

"Call Matt Copeland," Marty urged. Matt had graduated a year ahead of Larry and Alaric, and had slipped easily into his father's and grandfather's shadows at the family law firm in Danby. The firm had handled all of Marty's parents' legal work since the dawn of time, had had drawn up—Marty inhaled deeply, as she did whenever she thought of it—Larry's will. "He can help."

"It's too late."

Time-wise? Situation wise? Marty couldn't help wonder. "Call him tomorrow, then." A particularly offensive cobweb hung in the corner behind the door to the utility closet, and Marty demolished it with a vicious application of the broom. "First thing," she added. "You need to make sure your backside is covered here."

Caro wandered into the kitchen and leaned weakly against the counter. Her T-shirt and shorts—the day had been warm—lent her an even further look of Sophie. Her dark hair was mussed, as though she'd thrown herself together hurriedly that morning before all hell had broken loose. "Why is he even doing this?"

"Because he's a bastard, and because he thinks he can," Marty growled. "Flexing." She abandoned the broom. Why was she even cleaning at this hour? She drew a glass from the cabinet, and after a moment's thought, drew out a second one. Then she splashed together two quick blueberry tonics and pushed one along the counter to Caro. "It's some weird guy thing."

"Like he'd prefer I left him for a lesbian relationship, rather than consider that I'd just—*left him*?" Caro took a drink from her glass, closed her eyes, and took another. "That sort of weird guy thing?"

"That, and that he has to be the manly man for what's-her-face."

"Melissa."

"Melissa."

They took their drinks through to the porch and settled in the wicker chairs, Marty flicking off the light again on the way. The sun was nearly gone, painting the trees across the road a glowing red-brown, which reflected through the windows. These were, Marty saw disgustedly, desperately in need of a wash. She added it to her mental list of things which needed to be done, and would be, eventually.

One of the big Marsden dump trucks rumbled past. Without looking up, Marty gave it the finger.

"Really? This late?" Caro snarled, holding her glass in both hands.

"Gotta go for maximum annoyance. Flexing, see?" Marty drank deeply. She hoped to sleep well tonight. "And the overtime differential is pretty good, don't you know."

Caro slipped into her daughter's room to stand at the foot of the bed. She gripped the footboard tightly, but then her knuckles began to ache with the pressure. *Breathe,* she told herself, loosening her hands, straightening her fingers, willing herself to relax.

A thin sliver of moonlight fell between the curtains and across the low bed. Caro gazed down at Sophie, at the round face flushed in sleep, the parted lips. Clutched to her thin chest was the giraffe she'd had since she was a baby, also apparently tired out from his adventures in the backyard. His spotted fur was rubbed to baldness around his long neck. On the wall above the bed, butterflies danced in the trees Marty had painted there when they'd first come to live at the house.

Pete couldn't take her away. He couldn't. She wouldn't let him. Just the thought of it left her breathless and weak, her heart pounding against her ribcage, her mouth going dry. She wouldn't let him.

TWELVE.

THE SKY WAS a brilliant blue that went on forever, and Alaric felt it in his lungs as he inhaled. At the spring, he leaned forward to look into the stone trough, past his shadow and into the water, which reflected the endless blue sky back up at him. He was surrounded by blue; he was filled with blue. He took another deep blue breath, and felt the blue trickle down into his feet, into his hands. He thrust those hands into the blue water, watching the ripples move outward from them.

On the rear corner of the trough, backed against the granite retaining wall, a sparkly blue stone lay—exactly where he'd found the green one he'd carried to Isabella in the cemetery. He reached a dripping hand to take it up.

It had lain in the sun for a while, and it was warm in his fingers. The entire rock had been painted the same blue as the sky, and on one side, a small tree, with its intricately reaching branches, sported the tiniest, most meticulously drawn pale green leaves. Spring leaves, a spring tree. A single word, picked out in sunshiny yellow, curved along the side of the tree canopy. *Hope.*

Alaric turned the stone over in his fingers, feeling the warmth of it, imagining the season it portrayed burgeoning around him, on his skin, beneath his feet. Still studying the tree and the single yellow word, he sank down on the edge of the trough, feeling the dampness soak into his jeans. It always happened. He'd have a wet butt when he walked on, but somehow that never seemed important.

Usually he felt ambivalent about the way his senses created experiences now. At times it was just too much, a sensory overload he couldn't escape, a constant sort of mild electrocution, synapses firing in every direction. Now he reached for the experience, focusing on the stone, the blue, the tree, the word. *Hope.* He wanted to believe that it was a message from the universe to him: that someone had painted this stone, with this message, leaving it in this place for him to discover. He wanted to believe that it was supposed to be, that there was intent. He needed the universe to give him hope.

At the same time he shied away from this line of thought, because if there was intent in the universe, that meant that Larry had been meant to die in his arms. That was just too cruel a thought to live with. Larry hadn't been meant to die; Larry should have lived. The universe had made a dreadful mistake. He should have been able to save Larry. Somehow. He had failed.

Alaric felt that failure: a spear through his midsection, just below his ribcage. He would be looking at Marty as she drove past, delivering the mail, and he would be impaled by that guilt yet another time. Time after time. He was always surprised when he'd look down at his gut and not find that spear, not find himself bleeding out from the wound.

Tell me, he thought at the stone. He wanted to sink into its sparkling blue as he wanted to sink into the sparkling blue of the sky. He held the stone lightly, free in his fingers, trying to sense where it had been, whose brush had given it this character, whose hands had set it on the back of the trough. *Who are you?*

The little rock was stubborn in its silence. Uncommunicative. That made him irrationally angry. *Hope.* Hope? There wasn't any hope. Hope had died in a ditch on the side of a cratered road. Alaric gripped the stone and swung his arm back, to hurl the damned thing across the road and into the gutter on the far side.

The sound of a woodpecker stopped him.

Slowly he lowered his arm and listened.

The rapidity of the hollow tapping. Somewhere close, the woodpecker was having a go at a dead tree, trying to make itself breakfast of some sort of bugs, or grubs, or something. Pounding away with its jackhammer bill, slapping its brain against the interior of its skull at a rate which should give it a concussion, or perhaps kill it. Carefully Alaric had a look around, trying to follow the noise to its source. It was no use: there were far too many trees—maples, oaks, aspens—their leaves small and green and hopeful. The woodpecker was camouflaged. It kept hammering on, unmindful of his curiosity. Unmindful that it had interrupted his senseless anger at the world, which would not give him answers. He closed his eyes. Woodpeckers, he had read somewhere, had beaks and heads specially designed to absorb the shock waves of their head-banging, and to transfer them to the rest of their bodies. Woodpeckers were uniquely evolved to do what they did. This, now, added to his confusion. It didn't seem quite fair, but he wasn't sure why.

The sun was warm on his face. Alaric listened to the rapping, until suddenly it ceased, the bird having flown off to more exciting breakfast bars at other hollow trees. He was left with the soughing of the wind through the trees, and the rushing of the water from the spring, into and out of the stone trough on which he sat.

He looked down again into his hands. Someone had left this stone here, on which that person had painted the word *hope.*

Someone had left it, hoping it would be found by another lone someone, who needed a little hope. Who needed to be convinced that there *was* hope.

There isn't, he insisted to himself, still angry, but the anger was tinged with disappointment. He looked at the pale green leaves on the tiny painted tree, and then up toward their counterparts in the canopy overhead. Even if the painter didn't know *him,* the painter had left the stone in the hopes that *someone* who needed it would find it.

Alaric sighed and got to his feet. He considered, for a moment, placing the stone back where he had found it, but in the end, he tucked it deep into his pocket. Maybe he could give this one to Isabella, too.

THIRTEEN.

"Well," Sophie said, straightening her back and pulling the comforter up around her chin, "I didn't think I was going to like that genii guy, but then I did." She turned her challenging gaze first on her mother, then on Marty, daring argument. "He was too big and too noisy, but then he was okay and I didn't care anymore."

Caro clicked the red button on the remote, and Aladdin, and Disney+, disappeared. She was still exhausted and anxious, but each time she'd thought Sophie had nodded off during the film, each time she'd made a move to gather her daughter up, Sophie had perked up in her seat on the couch.

"If he came here and gave you three wishes, Mama, what would you pick?" she demanded now.

"Oh, I don't know," Caro responded, hoping Sophie couldn't discern an obvious lie. She stifled a yawn. "I've got you, after all. So I think I've got all I need."

"You don't need Daddy? Or Karl?"

Caro licked her lips and glanced over at Marty, whose lips tightened in sympathy.

"Karl is a wonderful puppy," she said, trying for diversion. "You're lucky to have a dog like him. His fur is so soft. He's so cuddly."

Sophie nodded. Then she drew her brows together. "But you didn't say anything about Daddy," she persisted. She would not be diverted, and Caro wondered why she had even thought it possible.

"Sophie, honey," she said helplessly. "Daddy and I don't belong together. Daddy belongs with Melissa. You like Melissa, don't you?"

Caro heard rather than saw Marty shift in her chair, but refused to look at her. No, she didn't want Sophie to like Melissa—she was jealous of any relationship Sophie might have with Melissa, and more than that, she was fearful of how Sophie would take it should Pete and Melissa break up. Because even engaged couples broke up; even married couples broke up. At the same time, Caro needed Sophie to feel safe and loved, without the jaggedness of her parents' broken relationship causing her distress.

Sophie's shrug was surprisingly sophisticated. "She's okay. But she's not my Mama, and I don't care what Daddy says about that." She hurled herself the length of the couch and burrowed into Caro's side. "You're my Mama, and he's just silly."

Caro wrapped her arms around the small body, feeling Sophie's bony shoulders and ribs. Her eyes shot to meet Marty's. *What the hell?* she mouthed. Marty's eyes were wide, and she shook her head.

FOURTEEN.

MARTY'S MOTHER HAD the phone in hand when she answered the back door. In the other hand she held a scrap of paper. She jerked her head toward the kitchen. "I'm calling Berube's."

Marty closed the door behind her, frowning. "Since when do you keep this door locked during the day? And what about Berube's?" She followed her mother from the mud room to the kitchen, where she set the two bunches of radishes in the sink, half of what the Millers had left in their mailbox. "What's wrong with your car?"

"Full of questions this afternoon, aren't you?" Her mother's voice held the sharp edge of impatience. She was opening and closing the kitchen drawers. "I need a pair of reading glasses for this."

"For what? These radishes are from the Millers' hoophouse, by the way. They gave me way too many."

Sylvia tossed a quick glance over her shoulder. "Thanks, but I don't really like radishes. Your father—" a quick breath "—he was the one who liked those, not me." She turned away, donning a pair of black reading glasses she'd rustled from a drawer, leaving Marty feeling, once again, as though she was in the wrong. As though she should have known that her father liked radishes and her mother did not, and to not know the difference was some kind of betrayal, and the attempt at giving was simply being cruel.

"Fine," she said. "I'll take them back, then. I'll find someone who might like them." *Who might appreciate the offer. Who might appreciate* me. Then, of course, Marty kicked herself. So judgmental, she was. Her mother had suffered a loss. Another loss. Her mother needed to be cut some slack. *But I did, too,* Marty wanted to cry out. She looked at her mother's back, the shoulder blades so sharp beneath her blouse that they might cut. She wondered what it would feel like to put her arms around those shoulders, to lay her head against her mother's. She wondered what her mother's reaction would be. But she knew the answer: she had tried it before.

"You don't need to take on so," her mother said. She did not look up.

Deep breaths. Deep calming breaths.

"What's going on that you need Berube's?" she tried again.

The scrap of paper lay between them on the table, the telephone number etched blackly.

Sylvia picked it up and turned away again, looking down at the phone in her hand. "I want them to come tow that old Bronco away."

Marty gasped sharply. "*No.*"

It was Larry's Bronco. Larry's truck. The truck of their teenaged years. He had restored it, repainted it, repaired the engine. Starting when he was far too young to drive—though they'd both started driving up and down the cape long before they were legal, to which their father had turned a blind eye. How old had Larry been when the rustling hulk had appeared in the yard? Thirteen? Fourteen?

"Mom," she said, and her voice was raw in her throat. "No. You can't be serious."

"Of course I'm serious." Sylvia cast her a glance. "It's been moldering away in that back garage for ages now. It's about time it got junked."

Larry's Bronco.

"No. Mom, please. Don't do that. It's Larry's Bronco. Larry's." It was hard to get the words out. Her throat was closing up. She felt tears burning in her eyes, but she could not let them fall.

"And Lawrence is gone now, isn't he?" Sylvia spat. "And so is your father. It's time for that death trap to go. Berube's can come and get it."

Marty felt the great gob of grief that had been threatening since the funeral growing, pulsing in her gut. She couldn't breathe. She shook her head, staring at her mother's cold face helplessly. "Please," she choked out—or did she? She didn't know whether she'd spoken the word aloud.

It had been difficult enough when Marty's mother had boxed up all of Larry's clothes and donated everything to Goodwill. Marty had pulled into the yard with mail, and had found Sylvia filling the back of her Forester with boxes and a large black plastic trash bag. When she had seen Larry's old Harvard sweatshirt—that big joke he wore everywhere—in one box, she had opened her mouth to protest.

Sylvia had held up a hand. "Don't start, Martha." Setting another box in the rear of the Subaru, she had then turned on her heel and gone back into the house. Marty, for her part, had grabbed the sweatshirt and fled in the Jeep, fuming all the rest of the way around the mail route.

Three days later, her father had appeared at her house. Roger wasn't driving much anymore, weak as he had been from the treatment, but this evening he had climbed slowly out of the F150 and stood leaning against it, his empty pipe clamped between his teeth.

"Jesus, Dad," Marty said when she saw him. "What are you doing? Come inside and sit down. I'll get you a drink." She held the door, watchful as he made his way up the steps. "Does Mom know you're out driving around?"

He patted her arm on the way by, then made his way to the wicker armchair and settled into it, grimacing. She saw the expression, and was sure she winced in sympathy.

"Don't make a fuss, Martha Jane," he said, but almost absently, as though concentrating on other things. Remaining upright, for one.

Marty dodged into the kitchen for a glass of water; returning, she set it on the low table at his side.

"You're a good girl," Roger said, and winked. "You'd be a better one if this were a whisky, but I know you're doing your best."

"Dad—"

He held up a hand and sipped. "There. Better?"

But his face had been gray with the exertion. His face had been gray for weeks now. He wore a Red Sox hat, to hide the hair that had begun to fall out.

"I could have come to you, Dad. You didn't have to drive over here. Whatever it is you need—"

Roger turned his brilliant blue eyes, sunken a bit in his face, on her. "I needed to talk to you away from your mother, Marty."

She slowly sank onto the wicker loveseat across from him. "I'm so angry with her," she whispered at last. She wiped her tight face with both hands.

"Cut her some slack, sweetheart." Roger took another drink from his glass, and set it down on the table. His hand was trembling, she had seen.

"She's getting rid of him," Marty said, and found a lump in her throat. She forced herself to say the name. "Larry. She's throwing him away."

Her father shook his head. "Your mother's in pain, Marty."

"And I'm not?" she shot back. "You're not?"

He shook his head again, still gazing on her with something akin to pity. "Of course we are, darling. But we're not talking about you, or about me. We're talking about your mother."

Abruptly Marty stood and went to the kitchen for her own glass of water. She could feel her anger and resentment churning, tasting sour and hot. She downed one glass of water, standing at the sink and staring out the window without seeing anything. Then she set the glass on the counter, picked it up again, and filled it.

"Marty," her father called from the porch, "come back here and let me say my piece. Then I'll leave you alone to swear all you want."

She wiped a hand across her hot face again. Then she returned to the porch, and her place on the loveseat. She held the glass before her in both hands, like some sort of magic shield.

"I'm listening," she said. Grudgingly.

Her father drew a long breath, closing his eyes for a moment, as though the effort was costing him more than he let on.

"Oh, Martha Jane," he murmured at last, "if you only knew how much I love you."

Marty felt immediately guilty. "I do know, Dad," she said quietly. Sadly.

"And I love your mother. She's trying to order her world. Larry's death—" A deep breath. "Larry's death has rocked her to her core. She doesn't know which way is up. She's trying to retake control of things."

"Getting rid of Larry's stuff is going to do that?"

"It's Larry's *stuff*, Marty. That's just it. And that's all. It's not Larry. And every day she has to live with that stuff is like ripping a scab off her heart."

Marty's eyes were burning. She was that close to crying, with anger, with frustration, with unutterable grief.

"Just let her do what she has to do. It's not the same thing you and I have to do." Roger sighed, and his expression softened as he glanced over at her. "She's not strong like we are. We have to cut her some slack."

Painfully now he got to his feet, pushing hard on the arms of the chair. He'd slipped his empty pipe into the pocket of his shirt, and now he took it out again and gazed into the bowl longingly. "You need to let her grieve in her own way, and just keep loving her."

"But what if she doesn't love me back?"

There. She'd said it. Marty had always felt it, that her mother loved Larry, and she, Marty, was a distant afterthought.

Her father rubbed the bowl of the pipe as though attempting to conjure Aladdin. "She does. She just doesn't know how to express that right now. But you have to love her anyway, Marty. Because we're all that's left. And pretty soon—" he leaned in to kiss her forehead "—you'll be all she has."

Roger clamped the pipe between his teeth and was out the porch door, into his truck, and backing out of the driveway before she could close her mouth and stand.

"Promise me," Marty now pleaded, leaning toward her mother, hands fisted on the kitchen table. She could hear her father's voice, urging her to cut her mother some slack, but the voice was weak and distant. "Mom. Please. Just promise me that you'll give me twenty-four hours."

But Sylvia had turned away, taking up the teakettle and filling it from the kitchen faucet. How hard her back was, still and unyielding, her shoulders straight, her head imperiously high.

"Twenty-four hours," Marty repeated. She heard the wobble in her voice, and cursed her own weakness. *Damn it,* she thought. She hadn't cried at her father's funeral, but now she was close to breaking down over a damned truck.

Larry's truck. *Larry's Bronco.*

Sylvia opened the dishwasher and began to unload it, a clear dismissal.

"Please," Marty pressed, a near whisper.

Marty ran outside, down the track alongside the small field, to the garage at the rear of her parents' property. The door was padlocked, but the key was around the side, beneath the sill, where her father had always left it. The key turned easily in the lock, which, though a bit rusty, was well-oiled. Still.

Marty wondered, looking in at the Bronco backed into the dim garage, whether her father had been haunted. Had Larry's ghost visited him? Was that why her father had walked out of an evening, past the lilac hedge and through the old potato field? Was that why he would pull open the double doors and stand, smoking his pipe? Was he communing with his son's spirit?

She had found him here one time, before he'd relapsed, when she had stopped off after dinner to deliver some cherry tomatoes and a jigsaw puzzle. Her mother, dinner over and dishes taken care of, was crocheting before the television, where over-happy people spun the big wheel and chose letters. "Out back," was all Sylvia said at the interruption.

Marty had followed the sweet familiar scent of tobacco smoke, and then had seen him, at a distance, before the open doors of the back garage. He tilted his gray head to the side as he held the match flame to the bowl of the pipe. Hearing her, he turned, smiling. "Help me close this up," he'd called. As though he hadn't been the one to open the garage, but had just stumbled upon the open doors, accidentally. As though he hadn't been looking at the Bronco. As though he hadn't been thinking about Larry.

So he *had* to have been haunted. Closing the garage doors then on the truck had felt to her like he was closing his grief for Larry away from her. Perhaps it was his way of dealing with Larry's death, if there were truly any way to deal with it at all. And perhaps it was too raw to talk about, to share with her. Or, apparently, with her mother.

Tonight she had expected the garage doors to open with some difficulty, but the hinges still turned easily, as though they had been oiled not so long ago. Obviously that one time she had interrupted Roger had not been the only time he had come here.

Marty stared hard at the Bronco, coated in years of dust. At first her father had parked it here to keep it out of the weather until Larry returned home. Then, when Larry had been killed, it had been easier just to leave the Bronco out here until they could think of something to do with it. Even now Marty recoiled from the idea of selling it or junking it; that would be like selling or junking her brother. It would feel even worse than Sylvia donating his clothes. Especially if there were such a thing as ghosts, for if there were anything Larry would haunt, it would be this truck.

Marty stood still and silent, staring, willing the ghost, if ghosts existed, to make itself known.

In the Springs, kids learned how to drive early, long before the age of legality. So it was no surprise that Larry bought the truck a couple of years before he became a licensed driver. The Bronco had needed body work, and a new engine, and Marty didn't know what else. With help from Alaric and advice from Roger, Larry had worked painstakingly on both. It had taken two years to get the Bronco roadworthy, but he was patient, hurrying home from school and plugging away in the side yard. Larry worked more on the truck than he did on schoolwork, much to Sylvia's chagrin. But Roger didn't mind. *Skills,* Marty could hear him say. *The boy's learning life skills. Marketable skills. Let him be.* Then, of course, he'd hand Larry a couple of twenties for brake shoes, and remind him to *just pass your classes so your mother'll get off my case.* It was their joke. Larry passed without distinction in high school, but he passed. And their father had deflected the chagrin away from him.

"Are you here?" Marty whispered. To her brother, or her father, she wasn't certain. She wanted not to be alone.

An evening breeze stirred the hair against her forehead; the air smelled of salt water, and she half-registered that the tide must be low at the lighthouse point. She reached out a hand and touched the dusty hood of the Bronco, half-expecting it to be warm; but the truck had been out of the sun, and without a driver, for ages. Impulsively, she leaned forward and drew her finger through the dust. *L,* she wrote. *A. R. R. Y.* Then she wiped the dust down the leg of her jeans and waited.

Nothing happened.

Off to her right, the sun was lowering behind the trees, and the air was beginning to cool. Marty shivered a little bit, wishing for the ragged Harvard sweatshirt. Wishing, a bit disappointed, that Larry didn't choose to haunt *her.*

"You bastard," she whispered.

Then she closed the doors on the grill of the Bronco.

FIFTEEN.

WHEN MARTY PULLED the Jeep into the Morgans' long driveway, the lowering sun threw elongated shadows toward her. House, barn, all were blazingly backlit. She pulled around to the side of the farmhouse out of habit—that's what they'd always done; only salesmen and the FedEx guy ever went to the front door. Here, or at any other house in the Springs.

She paused for a moment, uncertain. She hadn't been here in years. Maybe Alaric wouldn't want to hear what she had to say; the past couple of years made that seem more than likely. Never mind, she thought resolutely, squaring her shoulders and unbuckling her seatbelt. She could knock on the kitchen door, and if Alaric refused to see her, she could ask his mother to relay her message.

Once Marty had clambered out of the Jeep, however, she could hear the ringing bounce of the basketball from the far side of the barn. How often had they arrived in the Bronco, she and Larry, to hear that sound? Her brother would bolt immediately, leaping into whatever game was going on, stealing the ball from an unsuspecting Alaric on the way by, gliding in for the layup. Alaric would swear, but never loudly enough for his mother to hear.

Marty caught her breath. Sometimes some things sliced more deeply than others.

Her own shadow trailed behind her. She crossed the farmyard, following the hollow sound of the dribbling. When she turned the corner of the barn, though, she found, not just Alaric, but his niece, Isabella. She was steadying herself with one crutch, while she spun the basketball up onto her fingertips to try a one-handed shot. The arc fell short.

"Damn it," she snarled. She might not look like him, Marty thought, but she sure sounded like him. *Like he used to.*

Alaric retrieved the ball and dribbled back to her. A few feet before the spot where she stood—there was a line dragged in the dirt, the foul line—he held out the ball and raised his other hand, palm up.

"No," Isabella said, her voice still holding a wealth of annoyance. "Foul shot. Regulation. I told you. I'm going to make it. I'm going to."

Alaric handed her the basketball. She took another shot, missed again. Marty saw the smile tug at the corner of Alaric's mouth, before he bit it back to hand Isabella the ball again with a perfectly serious face. She lined up the shot with one hand, her other arm rigid on the crutch. She missed again. And again. Each time Alaric loped after the ball, his work boots clomping in the dirt, his patience beyond measure.

Marty held herself still in the shadow of the wall, barely daring to breathe, lest the sound alert them to her presence. Watching them. Each time Isabella missed, she swore. Each time, Alaric retrieved the ball, hiding his smile.

At last, the inevitable happened: Bella extended her arm, and her fingers, and the ball, spinning through the failing light, hit the rim—and teetered before dropping through the hoop.

Isabella whooped. Alaric threw his arms in the air, then

charged his niece, lifting her and twirling her, crutch and all, around in the twilight.

"Score!" Isabella shouted. She was laughing so hard the tears glittered on her cheeks. Alaric too had his mouth wide open, but no sound came from him. Marty clutched her hands, suddenly made dizzy by their joy, and her own distress at Alaric's silent laughter.

"Marty! I thought that was your car in the yard."

She whirled guiltily to face Georgie Morgan. She was aware of the sudden cessation of the basketball celebration behind her.

"I've just come to talk to Alaric," Marty said. She felt herself flushing, and was grateful for the failing light that made her discomfort less obvious.

Georgie waved a hand toward her son and granddaughter. Alaric had the basketball cradled in one arm; Isabella was adjusting the cuff of her other crutch on her right arm. "I see you found him. Them." There was a slight frown between her brows. She leaned forward, lowering her voice. "They're spending a lot of time together lately. I guess it's probably good for them." The air seemed to echo with words she didn't say. Marty felt her neck prickle. She shifted uncomfortably. "Well, it's good to see you, Marty. I'm sorry about your father—he was a good man." Georgie reached out to pat Marty's shoulder. "But now I've got to get Isabella squared away for the evening. I'll leave you to Alaric."

Marty followed Alaric into what had been the old stable office. She was surprised to find it was no longer the dusty tack room she remembered, albeit vaguely. Alaric had obviously done major work on it. A long narrow room: against the back wall, a closed-up futon, made up neatly under a blue cover. To the right, a table and two chairs under the window. A door beyond the counter was ajar, and she could see the side of a shower stall: a tiny bathroom. Alaric gestured to the chairs, then turned to wash his hands under the faucet as she crossed the room. His back, to her, seemed stiff, tense, as though the unguarded moments under the hoop with Isabella had never happened. At least, she told herself, he hadn't turned away from her when she had asked if she could have a minute. He hadn't looked at her and then walked away.

Another thing that Marty had noticed when Alaric had opened the door for her was the smell. She had expected—what? The sweaty smell of gym socks? The sour smell of unemptied trash cans? Maybe yesterday's fish? Instead she smelled the light spring scent of lilacs, and when Alaric flicked the light switch by the door, she could see why: on the table, a tarnished silver pitcher was full to overflowing with the tumbled purple blooms. Marty halted in her tracks on the way to the offered chair, studying the flowers; they were like a still life, their shadows cast on the whitewashed wall below the window, a single branch on the runner at the base of the pitcher. A feminine touch she hadn't expected. She felt, for a moment, irrationally queasy.

"That's nice," she managed, indicating the flowers.

There were two glasses upended in the strainer next to the little sink.

She was beginning to regret the impulse that had brought her here.

Then Marty shook her head. How stupid could she be? She had to make him this offer, quickly, before her mother made the rash move she'd threatened. And she could hardly call Alaric on the phone to discuss it. Of course she had had to come.

Alaric waved a vague hand in the direction of the farmhouse. "Your mother?"

He shook his head and lowered his hand to just below his shoulder.

"Your niece? Isabella?"

He nodded and smiled. There was a gentleness there. Marty sucked in a breath. Alaric shot her a curious glance, then crossed to the refrigerator. A picture was stuck to the front with a magnet. When she stepped closer to look, she realized that it was a pencil sketch of the lilacs on the table, the still life she had imagined.

Alaric pointed to the house again, held his palm at shoulder height again.

"She did this? Isabella?" Marty leaned in. Just a sketch. The lilacs, the pitcher, even the shade indicating the shadow on the wall behind it. But it implied volume, movement; she almost believed she could smell the flowers. "Isabella did this?" She looked up at him, and then quickly to the picture again. He was too close; she could feel the warmth radiating from him. Hurriedly she moved away.

Alaric nodded proudly. Now he lifted one of the glasses from the strainer and held it out, then pointed to the refrigerator, the faucet.

"No," Marty said. "No, thank you. I can't stay but a minute." She glanced over her shoulder, feeling the urgency, as though Berube's flatbed tow truck was close behind. If she couldn't find help here, then where? If not from Alaric, then from whom? She lowered herself into the chair.

He seemed relieved, and turned to put both glasses away in the overhead cabinet. Over his shoulder she could see two mugs, two plates. Probably if he opened the drawer beside the stove, there'd be two place settings of silverware.

Turning back, Alaric frowned at her slightly, in puzzlement. He pointed to her, to the floor, held up his hands in a question. *You. Here. Why?*

"My mother," Marty said, and stumbled over the words. "She gave me twenty-four hours—"

When she didn't immediately go on, Alaric tipped his head, raised his eyebrows, and made a little circle with his hand. *For?*

"The Bronco," Marty said. She cleared her throat. "Larry's Bronco." She saw Alaric wince and quickly glance away, before forcing himself to look at her again. "She's given me twenty-four hours to get it out of the back garage before she gets it towed off by the junker."

Alaric shook his head, his face full of the same alarm she felt.

"I need your help," she said quickly. His reaction was the one she needed. The one she had been hoping for. "Can you take it? Can you save it?" The tears were building up behind her eyes, the tears she had been forcing back since watching her mother's hand on the telephone, since her father's funeral, and she didn't want Alaric to see her cry. She didn't want anyone to see her cry. She looked around desperately.

He made no move.

"I'm sorry." Marty held up her hands and got to her feet. "I shouldn't have barged in here and dumped this on you. It's just—" she hiccupped, "—you're the only person I could think of. The only one who could help me. The only one who *knows*."

Suddenly there was a folded red bandanna in her hand. Marty stared at it dumbly, before glancing up at him in question. Alaric pointed to the handkerchief, then to her, and made a motion as though wiping his eyes.

"I'm *not* going to cry," she protested, more fiercely than she intended.

Alaric held up his hands. *Sorry.*

Turning away for a moment, he drew a pad and pen from the drawer near the refrigerator. He wrote quickly, then turned the page to her. *Dad's tractor.*

"Be careful, then," Howard called from the back door, his thumbs in his pockets. "Light's going. It'll be dark soon. Don't want to be out when the big bad wolves are on the prowl."

With a startled exclamation, Georgie hustled off toward the henhouse.

Alaric threw a glance at Marty over his shoulder as he strode toward the equipment shed, where the big John Deere was housed for the night. He jabbed a finger once toward her, once toward her Jeep.

"No," she said. "I'm coming with you." She kept her eyes on his straight back, his long legs, and tried to keep up. By the time she reached the shed, he'd already climbed up into the seat of the tractor and turned the key. The engine coughed a few times, then settled into a steady growl. Alaric ducked his head as he drove the tractor out into the yard, headlights cutting the twilight.

He saw her, defiant with hands on hips, and slowed to a stop, pointing again, and more vehemently, toward the Jeep.

"I'm coming with you," she shouted over the river of engine noise.

Alaric frowned, then shrugged, and then, amazingly, smiled. He leaned down and held out a hand. After a moment, Marty grabbed it and hauled herself up onto the side of the tractor, as they had done so many times before, summers, heading out into the fields to hay.

As he followed Marty's directions along the overgrown path to the garage at the rear of the Ahearne property, Alaric tried to keep his eyes on the track carved by the headlights. She was too close; he was uncomfortable, and at the same time, realized he would have been disappointed had she led him to her mother's home in the Jeep. He slowed the tractor as they neared the garage, and she jumped down, a bit awkwardly, to let him wheel around to back toward the double doors. When he killed the engine, he looked furtively at her tense shoulders, the way she held her head stiffly. Her anger was red and burned his hands, and he realized that the anger had built the closer they had come to her mother's. He wondered at whom the anger was directed. He wanted to reach out and massage her neck, to knead the tension out of her shoulders, but instead he climbed down and jammed his hands into his pockets. What if the anger was for him? He'd be angry at him, if he were in her position. The memories, with their noise and fire, threatened on the edge of his mind. They taunted him. He'd failed Larry. He'd failed her. He couldn't help it: he looked down for the spear in his gut.

There was a hasp across the double wooden doors on the old garage. Marty disappeared momentarily around the left side, and returned with a key. The lock snapped open under her hands.

"Help me," she said. She had pocketed the key, and now grabbed one of the doors. Alaric took the other, and together they swung them open, more easily than he had expected. Someone had been keeping the hinges tight and oiled. No sagging, no scraping here.

"My father," Marty said. She shook her head. "Dad used to come out here."

Alaric nodded, and turned his attention to the open mouth of the garage.

And the Bronco. He hadn't seen it in years.

Lar and Lar.

It seemed to Alaric, as he stood beside Marty before the open doors, that all his favorite memories were tied up with this old

Ford Bronco. Looking into the dimness from the fading light of evening, he could only make out the front end: grill, hood, windshield. The dented bumper, which he and Larry had reattached after hitting the deer which had bounded into their path from the granite outcrop up in the barrens. The pea-green paint, streaked and dusty; he knew if he ran his hand over the panel, it would come away black with dirt.

For a long time Alaric didn't move. He stood before the Bronco, Larry's Bronco, his hands still jammed in his pockets, feeling his throat work as he swallowed convulsively. He hadn't seen the truck since the night before they'd both shipped out.

After an age, Alaric warily forced himself to approach the Bronco. He was unsure what he expected; there were far too many memories attached to this truck, trailing along noisily like so many tin cans tied to the back of a honeymoon couple's limo. Voices swirled around him, the howling laughter of his younger self at a terrible pun from Larry; he could hear the thumping bass line from the radio turned up too loudly, while they had sung with abandon. How had they ever survived their high school years with their hearing intact? He could hear, too, the squealing of tires and the spitting of gravel as they took off once again, far too fast, down to the Lighthouse Point Road. He could hear it all, he realized, even with his hands pressed to his ears. How had they got there? He shoved them into his pockets again, quickly. But it was too late, and Marty had noticed.

"Are you okay?" she asked from far away. The back seat? Her nervous voice cut through all the other sounds. "Alaric?" She placed a tentative hand on his arm, and just as quickly dropped it again.

Alaric thought he should wave her concern away, but after

a moment, he only shrugged. *The only one who knows,* she had said back at his room. Oh, he knew, all right, he thought bitterly. He knew far too much, most of which he could never tell her. That was why he'd avoided her all this time; he half-wished he had avoided her this evening.

But that would have meant that Sylvia Ahearne would have called Berube's and had them come to haul the Bronco away. To junk it. Back at his place, he had felt the urgency rolling off Marty like storm waves. He had taken her urgency in as his own. If he had not come with her, the biggest—and the last—part of Larry in existence would have been lost.

Instead of turning away, he held out his fingers and turned his wrist as though twisting a key in the ignition.

Marty unhooked the carabiner from her belt loop and sorted through the keys until she found the one she wanted. She held it up. "Larry left them with me," she said in a small voice. "I've had them with me ever since."

She had kept her promise to Larry.

He had not.

In the waning light, the key seemed to glow and grow larger in her hand, as though imbued with some unimaginable magic. Alaric realized he wasn't breathing, but staring at the key, and beyond it, at Marty, the woman who held it. The dying sun sparked off her brown hair, bringing up the reddish lights, throwing her face into shadow. He wondered what would happen if he dropped to his knees before her now, prostrated himself, begged for forgiveness.

Except, of course, he couldn't speak. Hadn't spoken for years.

He turned away quickly and gestured to the truck.

Marty shook her head. "It won't start," she said. "I tried before I came to get you."

Alaric knew better than to take the key and try himself,

something he was sure his father and his brother would do. He wondered whether Roger Ahearne had run the engine every once in a while, just to get the bugs out; had there been another key? Of course, in the last year of his life, it had probably been too difficult for him to get out here and start the Bronco anyway. Still—and Alaric frowned at this—he could have asked Marty to do it. But apparently hadn't.

He turned his attention back to the tractor. Marty watched as he backed it closer to the garage doors; she lifted her arms and directed him—*closer, a bit more, more, stop there.* Then he jumped down again to unwind the heavy tow chain from the back of the frame. He glanced up at the streaked sky, wishing for more light, and suddenly Marty was on her knees beside him, aiming the flashlight of her cell phone under the chassis of the truck. Once he had the chain sorted, he pointed to her, then to the cab of the Bronco.

He mimed turning a steering wheel.

Marty nodded. "Neutral, right?"

She knew perfectly well to shift into neutral, but Alaric gave her a thumbs up anyway, and waited for her to squeeze into the garage, open the door, and slide into the truck. She closed the door behind her with the familiar thunk that brought the noisy memories rushing back and, this time, he let them swim around him: the music, the radio, the singing. When she waved, he climbed aboard the tractor and inched forward, watching over his shoulder as the chain lifted from the ground and tautened, mouthing the words he couldn't sing. The Bronco slowly emerged from its longtime cocoon.

As they passed the Ahearne house on the way to the road, he thought he saw the white flash of Sylvia's face in the window. He felt her angry grief in the palms of his hands.

Alaric had no idea where to put the Bronco—eventually, it would go into the equipment shed, where it could be worked on under the block, but that meant some rearranging of automotive projects in various states of completion. He'd see what Richard and his father thought in the morning. For now, he stopped before his door in the old stables. Marty braked the truck behind him, and set the brake before climbing out. She stood by while he re-stowed the tow chains. The night was full on now, and the lights on the peaks of the outbuildings cast weird shadows. Her face was in darkness, her white blouse glowing strangely pale blue. Bats fluttered and swooped overhead; she paid them no heed. Alaric restarted the tractor and drove it to the other end of the yard, and the shed.

She was still standing in the same place when he returned, but she had a hand on the hood of the Bronco, as though petting it, as though making sure it knew it was safe. Next to her hand, the name, Larry, was written in the dust, and he knew she had done it. A tiny wind hushed through the yard and lifted her hair away from her brow. Alaric was gripped by a sudden desire to reach out and brush that hair with his fingers; biting his lip, he slipped his hands into his pockets, obviating any gesture such as that. He dropped his gaze to her hand on the hood, white and long-fingered in the strange lighting, and wished she would lay that hand on him: along his face, on his arm as she had done earlier. As he wished this, he felt a tingling on the skin of his forearm, like the falling of a light rain.

"Thank you," she said. He heard her sniffle as she twisted at the key ring in her hands. At last, she held out a key to the Bronco as though holding out Communion.

Alaric took a step nearer and reached out a hand, palm flat below hers, careful not to touch. She dropped the key and their fingers remained a fraction of an inch apart. He did not think he could bear it if their skin touched, and he was grateful for the tiny distance.

They stood silently in the farmyard for a few moments. The tiny breeze had died back as suddenly as it had blown up. In the chicken coop, a confused rooster called for sunup and didn't get it. They were surrounded by the rustlings and scufflings of a farm at night. Alaric glanced over his shoulder at the house, the blue light from the baseball game on television in the living room, the steady glow from the room Bella occupied, in which a light always burned. As he looked, he saw the twitch of her curtain, the hazy moon of her face. He felt only curiosity from her, and he waved.

"I've got to go," Marty said, her voice thick with something he didn't understand. Maybe didn't want to understand. She turned toward her Jeep, where she'd left it near the back stoop. He fell into step beside her, and opened the door for her when they reached it. She slid into the seat and clicked her belt into place. He closed the door and thumped the window frame once before stepping back.

"It's yours now," she said, and started the Jeep. "The Bronco." She turned to look up at him through the open window, and her eyes glittered in the dimness. "Fix it. Drive it."

Alaric nodded.

"I'll bring the title around when I find it."

He nodded again, wanting her to go, wanting her to stay.

She slipped the Jeep into gear, and threw one more glance at the Bronco, monochrome where it stood. "Take care of it."

The last words hit him hard, and he was swirling back to the roadside in Afghanistan, holding Larry in his arms, as she drove away.

SIXTEEN.

O N HER DAY off, Marty usually cleaned house—but, she decided firmly, not today. She looked down at the vacuum she had hauled out of the utility closet, and thought again, *not today, Shark*. Really: she should ditch this one, and buy one of those extraordinarily expensive ones that just woke up in the morning and vacuumed without any human interference. She looked around. They'd sure have a cleaner house.

There had been a time when she'd clean her house and it would stay clean for weeks without anything more than minor maintenance like scrubbing the toilet, and loading and unloading the dishwasher. That had been before the advent of Caro and Sophie. Sophie, the tiny human whirlwind, who dropped things where she stood, who tracked in dirt and grass and pine needles, who left dandelions in strange places, forgetting them as they dried and went to seed inside the house. Marty shoved the vacuum back into its closet and closed the door behind it. Housework had been much easier then and had taken an hour out of her life every week, tops. But what was the trade-off? She sighed, and smiled. She'd never lived with small children, and she'd wondered, when she had impulsively invited Caro to move in after the break-up with Pete, how she would manage it. Strangely, it hadn't been difficult at all, despite the occasional Lego mishap. She liked the way the house sounded, being thoroughly lived in. She hadn't really noticed the echoing nature of living alone until she was no longer living alone.

Again the sigh and smile. What Marty really wanted to do this morning was paint. She hadn't started anything new in months, and it felt uncomfortable. As though there were something inside her, something growing, impatient to get out, making her anxious. The longer she put off picking up the brush, the more it felt as though it didn't really matter, because she wasn't any good anyway, and never would be. If she thought about it, which she tried not to, she realized the contradiction of those two feelings, but they fought it out in the battleground of her head all the same.

This morning, though. Marty had awakened to the songs of the birds, raucous in their morning greetings, rolling over to find it was six-thirty already. She never set her alarm clock on her days off, but always woke around the same time anyway. Not today. She might have heard, through her dozing, the sounds of Caro moving around in the kitchen, making coffee, trying to be quiet, but banging pans anyway. Caro had never been a quiet one.

Caro had had to go into the office this morning for a staff meeting, and had taken Sophie to Joanne's for the day. That left the house empty, and now, giving herself a rousing pep talk and a cup of coffee, Marty opened the porch doors and windows to let the cobwebs—literal and figurative—blow away. She sat at the table.

It was covered with rocks. Some had a base coat—blue, orange, black, red. Some of those had tiny figures painted on them; she was especially fond of tiny animals. Some were ready to be left around town. Some not. It had been something to do over the winter, when she had felt herself draw inward: she had never been a good winter person. She had felt no inspiration then, nothing that told her she needed to paint—*something.* Now she pushed the rocks aside, and reached under the table for her paint box. A mason jar full of brushes sat on the windowsill, and the morning sun struck off the prisms of the glass, casting colors around the porch. A blank canvas waited for her on the easel off to the side. For the longest time, she had thought its whiteness a kind of reproach. This morning, though, the whiteness meant possibility. An invitation. Marty rummaged in the box for a drafting pencil and the sharpener.

Don't think.

She took a deep breath and leaned forward.

Marty lost track of time.

The light on the porch had changed, the prismatic colors cast by the brush jar having crawled down the wall and onto the floor as the sun rose in the sky. The shadows of leaves now played over the table, and her hands when she reached for the sharpener. She sat back and considered the lines of her sketch, feeling vaguely dissatisfied. Something was missing. She frowned, sharpening the pencil; she chewed absently on her lower lip. Even in outline form, there was a force that wasn't coming through, a thing she knew she was supposed to include, but couldn't bring to the surface of her thoughts.

She set the pencil aside, and tucked the sharpener back into the paint box.

Some people could start without the plan the light pencil sketch would present to them. Some people could just squeeze out dollops of oil paint onto their palettes, pick up a brush, and have a go. Some people. Perhaps that was her problem? The reason why her paintings hung about the house, or were leaning, facing the wall over there at the end of the porch. The reason why she had not had a painting hung in a group show over at Nova in Danby, or had not been offered a show herself. Four applications rejected in the past year. Perhaps she wasn't free enough. Perhaps she wasn't confident enough. *If I don't sketch it out, I'll forget.* It was like Caro's constantly making shopping lists, every week when they went to the grocery store, so she wouldn't forget some vital ingredient in the wealth of offerings on the shelves. If Marty didn't sketch the ideas, she was afraid she'd leave something vital out when she began to paint.

Marty rubbed her eyes, and poked herself in the forehead with the drafting pencil.

Exasperated, she threw the pencil onto the table and pushed away from the easel. Standing, she shook out her arms; her shoulders had long ago begun to tighten up with her concentration. She raised her hands, grimacing, then dove forward from her waist: floor, shins, floor, up again, hands to center. The grimace wasn't part of the half-sun salutation. She did a couple more just to loosen up her muscles, trying to relax her face. The clock in the living room rang the hour. With a huge sigh, she went through to the kitchen to draw herself a glass of water. This she downed, and then drew herself another. The base of the faucet was leaking a bit, she saw with half her attention; she'd have to get that fixed. How old was this faucet, anyway? It was the one originally here when she'd purchased the house. She examined the leak curiously, before she realized what she was doing: putting things off. Procrastinating. She took the glass back to the porch and sat, resolute.

There was something missing in the picture, but she had to take the plunge. Marty thrust away her mother's warning voice: *if you're tired, you need to stop before you make a mistake you can't undo.* She wasn't tired. In a way, along with the frustration, she was feeling the edges of exhilaration. She was working. *Arting,* Sophie called it. She was arting.

Marty set the glass aside, and reached for her oil palette. There was nothing to do but forge ahead. If she screwed it up, there were always other days, other canvases. But if she stopped now, who knew when she'd work up the courage to come back?

Greens, she thought, touching each of the paint tubes for luck. Blues. But first: grays. Silvers. Blacks.

By the time Caro returned around noon, the great stone trough had begun to take shape beneath the brushwork. It was rough, Marty knew: but once she had the shape of it, the heft of it, then she could begin to play with shading it. She had been right in her gut earlier; the grays had needed to be tempered with green— there was a mossy feel to the stone, the dampness of a hundred years. She could begin to dapple it, too, with the sunlight filtering through the trees above it. Those trees were suggested roughly by the sketch, as was the stone retaining wall to the rear. She sank back and examined her work critically, making mental notes of what she wanted to do as she built outward across the canvas.

Don't think.

"Whatcha doin'?" Caro skirted her chair to go through the living room to the kitchen. There was a thump of bags on the counter, and the rubber suck of the refrigerator door opening. A cabinet. Glassware on the counter, the hiss of a bottle opening.

"I've already got a drink," Marty called.

"Not of this."

"It's too early."

Caro returned and handed Marty another glass. "Can I see, or would you rather I not look just yet?"

Marty sighed, sipping. Sparkling water, tasting vaguely of blueberry and lemon, her favorite combination. That was what she liked about Caro—well, one of the things anyway. That she understood, without asking, that there were times when Marty held her in-progress work close, not yet being prepared for the judgment of anyone else. She took another sip.

"It's okay," she said, standing. She set the sparkling water next to its plain cousin on the table, and reached her arms high above her head, feeling the knots in her shoulders, her neck. When she stretched up on her toes, her fingertips grazed the ceiling. She sensed Caro move closer.

"The spring," Caro said.

"At least it's recognizable. I don't entirely fail at representational art."

"Of course it's recognizable. It's not like you're an amateur."

"It's not like I'm a professional either." Spreading her feet, Marty turned her left foot forward and bent her knee to slip into a warrior stance. Her hamstrings felt tight. How long had she been sitting? Years.

"Let me buy one of your paintings. Then you'll be a professional."

"Woo. I can fill out a schedule C for the IRS." Marty turned to the other side, bending her right knee, still staring at the start of her work. Too early to tell, really, how it would turn out. She didn't even dare to have a sliver of hope. The nagging feeling had receded, though, the feeling that something was missing. No doubt it would return in the middle of the night. *Don't think.* She found herself being stern again. The thinking was the thing that would paralyze her. If she thought too much, she wouldn't paint enough, because insecurity would strangle art. Arting.

As though reading her mind, Caro stepped closer and put a hand on her shoulder. "I can't tell you how happy I am to see this," she said quietly. "Really."

"The spring? You can just walk down there any old time."

"Stop it. You know what I mean."

"All right. The painting, then?"

"A painting." Just as quickly the hand was gone, as though Caro might worry that she'd trespassed. "Something other than those little rocks. Which I love, because they're so adorable. But—they're placeholders, somehow."

They were. Marty straightened and threw her arms around Caro. "You're the best, you know. And I'll paint you any picture you want, and don't think you have to pay me for it. That's just foolish, because I owe you so much."

"I want to. I want you to be a professional painter." Caro took a deep breath, then pulled back to look into Marty's face. Her dark eyes were earnest. "I want you to be able to go to your mother and tell her you've had a commission."

Her mother. Marty pressed her eyes closed for a moment.

Caro stiffened slightly. "I'm sorry. I'm sorry I said that."

Marty only retrieved her glass and took another long drink. "Don't be sorry. You're right. She still thinks I wasted my time and her money, earning a degree that doesn't support me." She turned back to the painting and let out a sigh.

The light was different, and Marty suddenly felt deflated. She set the now-empty glass aside and began to clear up her materials. The turpentine was under the sink, locked safely away; she'd have to get it out to clean the brushes. She had a flash of memory of a story her father always told, of finding Larry, as a toddler, drinking turp he'd found under the kitchen sink, and of the ensuing rush to the hospital. No need for a repeat with Sophie.

"It's going to take me a while."

"I'm not worried. Just impatient. I can't wait to see this painting once you're satisfied. And I can't wait for you to take up my commission."

"What will that be?" Marty took one last look at the trough on the canvas, with the ghost trees swaying above it, then turned resolutely to take care of her mess. Though of course, she knew the answer, even before she voiced the question.

"Sophie." Caro smiled to herself, downing the last of her sparkling water. "A portrait."

"She'll never sit still."

"You might do it from a picture. I might know just the one."

SEVENTEEN.

THERE WAS NO knock on the door. Just the squeal of the hinges, and a heavy step on the porch.

"Caro?"

In the kitchen, Marty's neck prickled, and she straightened, closing the door of the dishwasher. Pete's voice. Pete, walking into her house like he owned the place, like he had every right. She picked up the broom on her way through the living room to the French doors. She checked the time on the mantle clock, in case she'd lost track: no, the clock read nine twenty-five. She could hear Caro urging Sophie along upstairs, probably into her clothes.

Pete was not alone. Melissa was with him, standing close by, either proprietorially, or for protection. She was looking around with open curiosity, her eyes under their winged liner taking note of the wicker furnishings, the paints on the small table where the dappled morning light played, the paintings leaning back-to against the walls. Marty tightened her grip on the broom handle.

"Ah, there you are, Marty," Pete said without a greeting. "I'm here to pick up Sophie." He took a step forward, a few feet more from the door, and Marty sidestepped, blocking the way into the living room. She didn't want him any further into her house. Hell, she didn't want him—them—in her house at all.

"Pete," she said. She couldn't keep the contempt from her voice.

He smiled, wolfishly. He took a step closer. She held the broomstick across her body.

"She'll be down in a minute, I'm sure," Marty added. She looked pointedly at the clock behind her. "You said you'd be here at ten."

He shrugged, shaking his hair out of his dark eyes. "Thought we'd get a head start."

"We thought we'd get to the beach before the crowd." Melissa laid a hand on Pete's arm, the hand sporting the diamond ring, which winked in the morning light. She too had been encroaching on the porch.

"Caro probably hasn't even fed Sophie breakfast yet," Pete tossed over his shoulder, making a disgusted face. "We'll probably need to stop somewhere on the way and get her something to eat, poor kid." He flicked a challenging glance at Marty, sneering. "Probably these two couldn't get themselves out of *their bed* to take care of her." The sneer said it all.

Marty lifted her chin, wondering if the broomstick would crack if she swung it at him hard enough. This is what Caro had to deal with every single time she left Sophie off and picked her up again over at Pete's house: the overbearing attitude, the cynical assumptions, the attempts to mow her down. No wonder Caro was a quivering wreck on those weekends.

"No, Sophie has had a full breakfast. Waffles and fruit, if you're interested. I'd show you the dirty dishes, but I've already loaded them in the dishwasher."

Too much. She'd said too much. She knew that when Pete turned his wolfish grin back to her. He was trying to goad her, if only for his own sick pleasure. She couldn't let him succeed.

She wasn't Caro. Not for the first time did she wonder why Caro had actually married the guy. Sure, there was something animal about him, but as far as Marty could see, that's all it was: animal.

She plucked the Disney backpack from the wicker chair nearest the door and held it out to Melissa. The backpack Sophie, in her excitement at the prospect of going to Reid State Park, had insisted they get ready the previous evening. Ariel beach towel. Extra clothes. Sunscreen. Cheese crackers. Water bottle with Sebastian the crab crawling on it. Marty had added a container of seedless grapes after breakfast.

"Sophie's been packed for a while," she said pointedly.

There was a stomping on the stairs behind her. "Slow down, sweets," Caro's voice warned.

Pete took another step forward. Marty sidestepped, broom still across her body, and smiled sweetly, as though she wasn't willing to kneecap him, even in front of his child, should he take any more liberties in her house.

"Pete's here," she called over her shoulder.

"Daddy!" One last thump on the bottom stair, and Sophie careened through the door just as Marty lifted the broomstick. Sophie hurled herself at Pete's legs, laughing. She wore a butterfly-covered sundress, ruffled at the shoulders, and a white straw sunhat. "I'm wearing my bathing suit already!" She giggled again, then peered around Pete. "Hi, Melissa! I'm wearing my bathing suit already!"

Marty felt Caro at her shoulder. Stiff, tense, as though expecting the metaphorical punch.

Pete raised his eyes to her. He didn't take long to deliver. His hands rubbing Sophie's shoulders, he said, "You know you're supposed to call her Mom. You know your daddy's going to marry her." His dark eyes never wavered from Caro's face, and he seemed to take a malicious pleasure in his words.

Sophie drew away slightly, her dark brows drawing together, her chin lifting in that stubborn way that said she would be resisting. "She's not my mom. She's Melissa." Sophie twisted slightly under Pete's big hands, and pointed back at Caro. "*That's my mama.*"

Pete's jaw tightened. Melissa looked as though she'd been slapped and might cry.

"We'll talk about this later," he growled. Sophie's mutinous expression did not lighten. "But now we have to hit the road."

Sophie spun to give both Marty and Caro a lightning hug, then skipped to the screen door. "Bye, Mama and Aunt Marty! I'll see you when we get back?"

"Tomorrow," Pete reminded her, casting a venomous look over his shoulder.

"Have fun," Marty called.

"Love you," Caro shouted at the small retreating back.

Pete let the screen door slam with more force than was absolutely necessary. "You know she's not your aunt," they heard him say.

EIGHTEEN.

THE HOUSEWORK DONE—OR as much as either of them cared to do on such a sunny day—Marty and Caro headed into Danby to do the week's shopping. Caro had tucked her meticulous list—made after consulting the interior of the refrigerator, freezer, cabinets, laundry room, and broom closet—into her purse, while Marty did a mental inventory, noting only those things they didn't have for the recipes she'd gleaned from *New York Times Cooking*. She preferred Zen shopping, as Caro called it with a tinge of rancor, wandering up one aisle of the grocery store and down the next, reveling in and not buying most of the products on display.

"How do you even remember?" Caro demanded, as Marty examined the lemons and selected the three that felt best in her hand. She slipped them into her reusable produce bag and pulled the drawstring.

"How do you not?" They moved on to the tomatoes.

In the baking aisle they found Simon Barnett and another man, whom Marty could only suppose to be his business partner, *the* Nathan Waring. They were arguing over flour. The cart between them was mostly loaded with meat and beer and eggs. Stereotypical bachelor establishment fare, she thought, and stifled a laugh. Simon looked up at the snort, and grinned.

"Hey, Marty," he said.

The other man turned, his brown eyes roving from Marty to Caro and back again, as though taking notes. Beside her, Caro had gone rigid. Marty knew without looking that her friend's eyes would be wide: the startled doe look.

"This is my housemate, Nate." Simon fluttered an airy hand. "Nate, this is Marty, our mail lady, and—" he raised his eyebrows in question.

"This is my housemate, Caroline Pond," Marty supplied. She held out her hand, and Nate shook it, but his eyes had returned to Caro. As usually happened, from the time they'd been in high school.

"Caro," her friend corrected, a bit breathlessly. When Nate took her hand, he did not immediately let go. His smile spread over his face slowly. *Calculated*, Marty thought cynically, as though he were casting a role. Then she chastised herself for her cynicism. Maybe it was a role Caro might need to play, after this morning, to keep her mind off Pete and his idiocy.

"We're trying to figure out what to get to make pancakes," Simon continued. He indicated the shelves of flour. "I like pancakes in the morning."

Nate shook his head, still smiling. "I keep telling him bacon is all we need. Pancakes are not for real men." There were, in fact, several packages of thick-cut bacon in their cart.

Marty glanced over Nate's shoulder at Simon and raised her eyebrows. He cocked one of his pale brows in response. "Flour is not the thing," she informed him. She took a few steps back along the aisle and reached for a blue and white box on the top shelf. "Jiffy mix," she said, handing it to him. "Every grandmother's kitchen north of Boston has a box of this." She tapped the back, which was covered in recipes. "You can make nearly anything with it."

"You sound like a commercial spokesperson," Nate said.

Caro giggled. Marty rolled her eyes. Simon winked at her.

"So you both live pretty close to the place we're renting," Nate said. He had, Marty was glad to see, finally let go of Caro's hand.

"Around the corner." Caro still spoke in the slightly breathless voice, as though she couldn't quite believe that she was meeting one of her idols. "Not far."

"Close enough that you could come around for drinks, or dinner, or something."

Behind them a woman cleared her throat gently.

"We're in the way," Simon said, pulling their cart aside. He dropped the box of Jiffy mix on top of a couple of cubes of beer.

"We've got to be moving on anyway," Marty said. Caro's expression melted into disappointment.

"Listen," Nate said. He'd taken Caro's elbow now and drawn her out of traffic. His smile showed off perfect teeth. "We're new in Painter's Springs. We don't know anybody. And I really want to get a feel for the town, for what it's like up here. So seriously— why don't you two stop over for drinks tonight? Or dinner?"

"You'd better get something other than eggs and beer, then," Marty laughed.

"We've got sausages," Simon countered, hands on hips. "And Jiffy mix."

Marty shook her head. "Better you come by our place. We could grill something up. The house with the long enclosed porch, just before you turn onto the Lighthouse Point Road? On the right, white house with green shutters." She glanced down at the time on her Fitbit. "Say around six? Six-thirty?"

The two men glanced at each other. Simon nodded. Nate made a face and tipped his chin. "Sounds good. We'll bring the beer."

Caro's face broke into a wide grin.

"Leave the Jiffy mix at home," Marty said.

Marty blitzed the garlic, rosemary, and shallots in the food processor, then slathered the mixture on the rib eyes and set them aside to marinate. Then she turned her attention to soaking the ears of corn in the sink.

"Should we eat outside?" Caro asked, rooting around in the bottom drawer. She straightened, holding up the red gingham tablecloth and eyeing it critically. "Is this clean?" She smelled it.

"If it's in that drawer, it's clean," Marty said. "Potato salad? With or without eggs?"

"No eggs." Caro made a face. "And no peas, either. They're from New York. They'll think we're weird." She shook out the cloth, wrinkled, but otherwise okay. "What if we cook this all up and they're vegetarians?"

"They had all the meat in the universe in that cart," Marty reminded her, dumping potatoes from the bag into the other sink. "And all the beer." She snorted. "They couldn't have made it more clear that they lived in a man cave than that, I don't think." She got out the peeler and started in on the first potato, humming to herself. Caro banged out of the kitchen door, and Marty watched her cross to the picnic table. At least this little impromptu get-together was keeping Caro's mind off Pete; she fell into such a funk on the weekends Sophie spent away from the house. Suddenly Marty thought of Alaric, and his spartan man cave; she paused, wishing she might invite him, though knowing that he would be too uncomfortable to come. She sighed, returning to the potatoes.

The tablecloth anchored, Caro returned to the kitchen.

"Besides," Marty continued. "*You* never asked them anything. *You* were absolutely dumbstruck. Like you were in the presence of a god."

Caro opened the cupboard to bring out a set of pint glasses, and after a moment's consideration, four highball glasses as well.

"Nathan Waring *is* a god. Just because you're a Philistine and don't know diddly—"

"I know Bo Diddly," Marty shot back automatically.

"Ha. You sound like your dad with that old saw." Caro set a bottle of single malt and one of vodka next to the glasses. She paused, leaning against the counter, her hands clasped before her in adoration. "If you knew what I know, you'd realize that Nathan Waring is just about the most important off-Broadway director around."

"Probably around Painter's Springs, you're right."

"Stop it. Seriously. I mean, it would be absolutely awesome if he's actually going to do some summer theater up here next year. I'd audition."

"You're starstruck."

"I am. And you're probably just jealous."

The potatoes peeled, Marty began cutting them into chunks and plopping them into the saucepan full of water. "Oh, probably. Though I did think the God of Off-Broadway was borderline handsy in the grocery store."

"You *are* jealous!"

"Sure thing." Marty put the pan on the burner. The clock in the living room rang out the hour. "Why don't you get along upstairs, Cinderella, and get those mice to help you change into your ball gown? I'll mind the fort down here."

"What about you?"

Marty looked down at her jeans and flowered blouse, protected by a faded Deering Ice Cream apron. "Yeah, I'm good. I might brush my hair later."

"You're impossible." Caro pounded up the stairs.

NINETEEN.

Their father supervised as Alaric and Richard at last unbolted the mounts, having attached the chains to the engine, and centered the hook of the hoist. They'd brought Howard out a lawn chair—had even wiped the dust off—which he ignored. He was more inclined to hover, more out of curiosity than to do any real work.

"Dad," Richard sighed at last, leaning back on his heels to watch as Alaric tautened the hoist chain as a test. "We do have it under control, you know." He slewed an impatient glance across the engine at Alaric, who lifted an eyebrow slightly.

Howard threw his hands up, but made no move to back out of the equipment shed. "Sure you do. Sure you do."

With the lift motor turned on, none of them heard Isabella's metallic footsteps. It was not until she had paused, a safe distance away outside the doors, that the glint off her crutches caught Alaric's eye. A quick lift of the chin to indicate he had seen her, then he returned his attention to the rising engine. Once it was high enough, out of the engine compartment, he shut down the motor and indicated that Richard should check the locks for safety.

Isabella was frowning intently, the look, Alaric recognized, that she wore when she was trying to puzzle something out, trying to understand. Howard followed his glance.

"Here, Bella," he barked, still leaning against the doorframe. "Your uncles brought you out a chair."

Alaric pointed to it, and then waved a hand. *Move it back out of the way.*

His father looked between them, then shoved away from the doorframe to drag the chair to the side, out of the way of the Bronco's tailgate. Isabella looked warily between the three of them as she settled into the seat, dropping the crutches to the side, and unlocking the knee brace.

Alaric winked.

They turned their attention back to the engine, swaying slightly where it hung from the winch hook. To Alaric, it seemed an old friend, someone he hadn't seen in years. Which, of course, he hadn't, not since he had helped Larry strip it down and rebuild it all those years ago, when they were just kids. More than half a lifetime ago. It looked tired now, grimy with the years' buildup of dust on the block and the coils of wiring. He put a hand to the grimy blue metal cover of the air filter, expecting to feel the cold against his skin, surprised at its warmth. There was something else, too, a quiet steady beating of a heart he both felt and didn't, as though the engine recognized his touch. He snatched his hand away again.

"Dad," Richard called. "Make yourself useful. Get in the cab."

"What do you want now?" Howard growled impatiently.

Alaric opened the door, tapped the steering wheel. He pointed out into the yard.

"I'll do it," Isabella offered.

"No, no, no," her grandfather said. "You stay put, out of the way, girlie." He climbed into the truck and clunked the door closed after himself.

Alaric and Richard leaned into the front end of the Bronco, and it slowly creaked backwards, past Isabella in her chair, and into the shimmering early evening.

"Turn the wheel hard, Dad," Richard shouted. "We'll put her next to the hay wagon for now."

Slowly they maneuvered the truck in a slow curve until they'd backed it to the side of the yard where the wagon and the winnow and a winter plow lined up. Alaric kicked a block behind the driver's side front tire, then brushed his hands down his grease-stained pant legs.

"Hey," said Howard as they returned to the shed. "The hood."

They had removed the hood from its hinges in order to pull the engine. It leaned against the side wall, pea green and grimy. In the dirt was written one word. Larry.

Alaric looked at it for a moment, haunted. Then he turned away to pull the engine stand into place. His jaw felt hard, and he clenched his hands against what he knew he would feel there.

"Larry?" Richard said. "Larry Ahearne? Who'd write his name there?"

Alaric turned away, and met Bella's eyes. She opened her mouth to say something, but just as quickly closed it again. She frowned. When she looked at the name in the dirt, her frown deepened, and her eyes narrowed, as though measuring a danger.

TWENTY.

Marty leaned forward to gather up the plates, and Simon quickly moved to help, balancing the serving platter and bowls in his arms. Nate made a half-hearted move to rise, but Marty waved him back down. "Stay here. We've got this covered."

Simon stood with his crooked half-smile. "Caro, stay here and keep an eye on him, will you? Keep him out of trouble."

Caro looked up. "He gets into trouble?"

Nate lifted his beer bottle and tipped the remains into his mouth. "Always. Would you like to join me, my pretty?"

Marty rolled her eyes. She held the door for Simon, then let it swing closed behind them. He set down his load on the counter, and flipped the faucet to begin rinsing. Marty got out the foil to cover the rest of the potato salad, before putting it away in the refrigerator. When she turned, Simon had the dishwasher open. "Clean or dirty?" he asked.

"Those are dirty." She looked out the window beyond him, and saw Nate with his hand on Caro's wrist, leaning over her palm like a fortune-teller.

Simon laughed at her expression. He waved a long-fingered hand. "Don't mind him. He's just playing. He does that all the time."

Marty offered the bottle of sparkling water, and Simon held out his empty glass. She poured some for him, some for herself. He leaned against the counter, the overhead light picking out the silver in his blond hair. He was smiling.

"You've been friends a long time," she observed.

"A long time. And I'm grateful. Nate always hires me when I'm in need of something to lift my spirits."

It was an opening, and Marty was obviously meant to take it. "Lift your spirits?"

Simon shrugged. "Bad break-up. I thought James was the one. He obviously wasn't. Nate thought I might want to get out of town, come up here on this research jaunt."

"I'm sorry."

Simon's lips turned down at the corners. "Don't be. As Nate says, I always choose the wrong ones, and I'm lucky to have him to whisk me away to nurse my wounds." He turned to look out the window with her. "Don't worry about Nate. He's larger than life, but basically harmless. Just watch out, though—he's the sort that rummages through your refrigerator and your medicine cabinet, to understand your motivation."

"I hope he's harmless. Caro deserves some fun. She's just had a bad break-up herself."

"The ex-husband she mentioned?"

"Pete. That's the one. He's got their daughter this weekend."

They cleaned up the kitchen. Simon was surprisingly easy to work with, or around. As Marty wiped down the counter with the sponge, he drew the pack of cards from the windowsill. He picked up his drink, tucked the bottle of sparkling water under his arm, and grabbed the bag of corn chips. "Listen," he said on the way out the door, "don't feel like you have to stick to water on my account. Just because I've got to be the DD and all."

"You're a good man," Marty laughed. She picked up her own

blueberry and lemon. "I'll just keep you company, shall I? No worries."

They lit the citronella torches, which cast flickering shadows over their hands as they played for corn chips.

"They say that everyone who looks into their family history will find a secret sooner or later," Simon mused, shuffling the deck for the next hand. "Me, for example. I'm my family's deep dark secret."

Marty shook her head. "Not us. Not the Ahearnes."

She watched as Nate set his empty bottle on the grill shelf, with the row of others he and Caro had demolished. Dead soldiers, he had called them, and both Marty and Caro had winced, though only Simon had seemed to notice. Nate drew another bottle from the cooler at their feet.

"No secrets," she added. "Just seething resentment."

Simon laughed.

"I'm serious," she protested. "The Ahearnes. Your typical two-child family: father, mother, brother, sister. For a while there, we even had a dog."

Simon slapped his hand to his forehead in mock horror, then gathered the shuffled cards into his hand to deal. "Not a typical two-child family! Those are the worst kind. And a *dog*, even."

Marty couldn't help but laugh herself. "It was a beagle. It was named Dewey."

"I loved that dog," Caro chimed in. She reached out as Simon dealt her a card. "He had the absolute best beagle ears."

"And your family?" Nate leaned back in his chair. His face was in shadow.

Caro shrugged and lifted her bottle of Guinness. "I lived with my grandmother, growing up. I spent more time at Marty's house than at my own. I was the adopted third child in that typical two-child family."

Marty looked down at the cards in her hand, frowning. Two queens—hearts and diamonds—ten of hearts, four of clubs, five of clubs. She bit her lip, grateful for the flickering torch light that made her non-poker face impossible for anyone else to read. She was no good at this, had never been any good at this, even years ago when Larry had tried to teach her, when the four of them would play down on the beach for change they'd scrounged from the floor of the Bronco. She glanced up to see Simon looking over his cards at her, his brow lifted sardonically. He made a face. She plucked out the four and five and lay them down on the table, choosing to live dangerously.

"Two," she said.

Simon dealt her the cards. He took one, Caro one, Nate one.

She tried to keep her face still, lifting the corner of one card. King of hearts. Then the other. Jack of hearts.

Caro tossed two corn chips onto the picnic table between them.

Marty, playing it close, met the two corn chips and raised them two more.

"As for me," Nate said, swirling his beer in the bottle, then taking a drink, no doubt for effect, "I had a typical Midwestern upbringing. My parents were named Norma and Randall. I was their only—and therefore their favorite—child." He took another sip, and set the bottle down. He held his cards fanned in his hand, but was not looking at them. He appeared to be waiting.

"Norma?" Caro wrinkled her nose in distaste.

Marty leaned back from the table, eyeing the pile of corn chips on the gingham between them. The kitty.

"What's wrong with the name Norma?" Nate demanded, though with surprisingly little heat. Despite the number of bottles lined up on the grill shelf, he didn't appear to be feeling any effects; he still hadn't looked at his hand again since he'd taken the one card. She narrowed her eyes against the feeling, again, that he was examining them and taking mental notes. For material. It made her uncomfortable.

Simon was watching her with some interest. When he laid out his hand at the call, he held four aces. He smiled and raked in the corn chips.

"What's this?" Nathan said.

At first Marty couldn't place his voice, wafting to them from inside the house.

The moon was rising, as was the breeze. One of the citronella torches had gone out. The house flung its moon shadow over them at the picnic table. Simon gathered the cards, turned the top of the corn chip bag over on itself.

"What's what?" Caro called over her shoulder. Her voice sounded wobbly; she had probably drunk just a bit too much, though her pace had not kept up with Nate's.

Then Marty knew, and her stomach dropped. Nathan had gone inside to use the toilet, but now his voice was muted, faraway—or as far away as the porch could take him. She started from her seat. Simon reached for her, missed, and stood to follow her hurried steps into the kitchen.

"Nate, what the hell are you doing?" he shouted.

Nate, on the porch, held a small study in his hand, a three-quarter view of Sophie.

"Put that down," Marty hissed. She felt hot with protective anger. What the hell? Who would come to your house for dinner, and then go through your things? *Rummaging in your refrigerator and your medicine cabinet.*

Simon brushed past her and took the little painting from Nate's hands. He turned to Marty. "Where do you want this?"

Caro had followed them in. "Oh, Nate, no," she said. "Marty doesn't like people looking at her paintings before she's ready."

Nathan was all innocence. "Why not? They're interesting." He turned to the painting on the easel, the stone trough of Painter's Spring, still unfinished, though the lower left corner swelled with grays and greens. "This one's kind of cool. It's that spring up the road, isn't it?" He lifted a hand.

"Don't touch that," Marty gasped. "It's not dry."

"And not finished, either," Nate said, rather unnecessarily. "You've got some work to do, I guess."

Simon set the little painting of Sophie on the table and took Nate's arm; Nate promptly shrugged off his grip.

"I want to look at the rest of these," he protested, sweeping a hand grandly toward the canvases leaning against the wall.

"And I don't think Marty wants you to." Simon's voice was wry, and tired, as though he had been through this—or something similar—before. "Come on, chappie. I think it's time for you and me to ride out into the sunset." He grimaced apologetically at Marty, and began herding Nate toward the door. "The card game's over, and you've got a meeting in the morning. Come on, Nate."

Surprisingly, Nathan allowed himself to be pushed along gently to the porch door. He was searching his pockets. "Where are my keys?"

"In my hand," Simon said. "I'm driving."

"Are you in any shape to drive?"

"Better than you."

Taking a deep calming breath, Marty followed them to the door, and held it while Simon urged Nate down the three steps to the driveway. "Thanks for coming," she said, though right now, as enjoyable as the evening might have been to a point, she was happy to see them go. Happy to see Nate go.

"Thanks for having us." Simon slammed the car door once his housemate was inside. He took a step back toward her and lowered his voice, casting a hurried glance over his shoulder. "Sorry about Nate. Sorry about his going through your paintings."

"She doesn't like people to look at them when they're not finished," Caro repeated. She leaned against the doorjamb. When she raised a hand in farewell to Nathan, Marty could just make out his raised white palm in response: waving like the Pope.

"I don't," Marty said, her voice still hard. She felt Nate's hands, pawing through her unfinished work, like a kind of violation.

"She really doesn't," Caro reiterated. Her voice was unsteady.

"I'm sorry," Simon said again. He took one more step back to the porch, and lowered his voice a tiny bit more, so that Marty had to lean forward to hear him. "Do you have any that are finished? I'd really like to look at some, if you do. Sometime. When you're ready to show them to anyone."

"I don't—I just don't know," Marty faltered.

"It's just that I really liked the two I saw, unfinished or not." Simon saw her flinch in the porch light, and shrugged. "I don't know if you're represented or anything. It's just that I know some people over in Danby. I mean, some people who might be interested."

"I don't know," Marty repeated. She wrapped an arm around her midsection, a defensive move.

Simon smiled his otherworldly smile up at her. "Think about it, okay?" He crossed to the car, climbed in, and with a wave of his hand, drove off.

"Think about it, okay?"

Caro's voice mimicked Simon's.

"You've had too much to drink," Marty said wryly.

Caro laughed. "Probably." She slipped out into the back yard to extinguish the torches, then returned. "We should clean up the back tomorrow. I don't think I have the energy right now."

Marty shook her head. "You go on up to bed. I'll take care of it."

"You sure?"

"Sure, I'm sure."

Marty listened to Caro's footsteps, unusually awkward on the stairs; listened to her go along the hallway to her bedroom, then out again to cross to the bathroom. Marty went to the kitchen to turn on the back floodlight. In truth, there wasn't much mess. Their cooler—she could leave that there and return it to the house on the Lighthouse Point Road tomorrow. The empties—she found the green bag for returnables, and let herself out into the backyard, where, she noticed, the crickets had gone raucous. Beyond the circle of the light, fireflies sparked gently, then faded; not as many, she realized sadly, as when she was a child. She checked the citronella torches to make sure they were extinguished; she was enough of a fireman's daughter to always double-check. Then she gathered the bottles, the glass clinking in the bag. She collected the bag of corn chips, tucked the deck of cards into her back pocket.

It had been an unsettling evening. She liked Simon, found him compatible, friendly. As for Nathan Waring: she didn't like him at all. *Give him a chance,* Simon had pleaded. From the sounds of it, Nate had been a good friend to Simon for years, just as Caro had been to her. There was something about him, though, that just grated, a bow dragged along out-of-tune strings. Something false, as though his overstepping boundaries was intentional, carefully designed to elicit a response. *Motivations.* Everything he did was designed to uncover motivations.

Marty turned out the spot, and, when her eyes had adjusted, she looked up at the stars, scattered across the sky, forming spring constellations that she'd learned in junior high science and then promptly forgotten. Except, as always, for the Big Dipper. She looked for, and found, the squared bowl, the curve of the handle. She found the North Star and stared up at it, imagining the sky spinning around it, imagining her life spinning around it. What exactly was her North Star? What was she spinning around?

The questions gave her a headache, and she wondered whether the answer would have come more easily had she not stuck to the sparkling water. Drunken people had all the answers. Then she caught herself for the judgmental bitch she was being, and half-laughed in the darkness. The night was getting cool, the dew settling, and she shivered. She picked up the bag of bottles and closed the door, locking it after her. Then she snapped off the kitchen lights.

TWENTY-ONE.

Marty had her eyes closed, and was slumped in her chair, feeling drained. She felt the hands on her shoulders, small and sure, and slowly relaxed into the gentle kneading.

"You've been going at it for hours," Caro said. "I'm so glad."

As if on cue, the mantle clock rang. And rang and rang. Twelve times. Four hours. Marty had been painting for four hours. Except when she'd been staring out the window, trying not to think.

"I haven't seen you so wrapped up in something for such a long time."

Marty's stomach growled.

Caro laughed. After a moment, Marty joined in, but for her, it was more the relief of the tension that had wound her while she painted. Good tension. She welcomed it. She twisted in her chair to look up at Caro.

"It's time for breakfast, I think."

"More like lunch."

Slowly Marty stood, stretching her spine, dropping her shoulders, raising her cramped and paint-stained hands over her head. She went up on her toes to touch the ceiling. The day had warmed up considerably while she had been working, but as with everything else, she hadn't noticed. Now she realized she was sweating. "Let's compromise and call it brunch. It is Sunday, after all." She took a final look at the wet paint, then turned to Caro, who looked a bit pale. "Have you eaten?"

Caro shook her head squeamishly. "No. I didn't feel all that hot this morning." Her hair was damp and disheveled, as though she'd merely run her hands through it upon getting out of the shower. "Still don't feel all that hot."

Marty made a move to pat her on the shoulder, then stopped; the paint on her hands was still tacky. "We're getting old, you and I." She smiled ruefully. "Remember when we were able to stay up all night drinking?"

Caro sighed. "You weren't drinking."

"I'm too old. I know my limits." Marty picked at a bit of gray paint on her thumbnail. "Besides. I had to keep the designated driver company. It would have been just too cruel for all of us to get tiddly while poor Simon sat and watched."

"Tiddly." Caro winced.

"Is there any coffee?"

This time Caro chuckled before wincing. "I gave you some a while ago." She pointed to the flowered mug on the table next to the jar holding the dirty brushes. "It's probably stone cold by now."

Marty picked it up and sipped. It *was* cold, and disgusting. She set the cup down again hurriedly. The coffee had a slight oily film over the top, which reflected prismatic color. Nice in paint, not nice in coffee.

"I know you don't like people looking at your work before you're satisfied," Caro said. She retrieved the flowered cup and went to the kitchen. Marty could hear the offending liquid gurgling down the drain. When she returned, Caro had an entirely new coffee mug, which steamed gently. Marty took it and sipped gratefully.

"You lit into Nate about it hard enough last night," Marty said, casting a sideways glance. "Pretty sharp about it, you were. Might have spelled the end of a beautiful relationship." She took another drink. "Kind of wasn't expecting that."

Caro flushed. She had her own mug, the one with the kittens playing guitars. "You think I'd sell you out for some guy?"

Marty lifted an eyebrow. "Not just *some guy*. *The* Nathan Waring, the off-Broadway director. And where he's concerned, I believe you think I'm—and I quote—a Philistine."

"But you're my *favorite* Philistine," Caro protested. She chuckled, then pressed her eyes closed, a hand to her forehead. "Holy Mary."

Marty joined in the chuckle, but not the wince. She turned back to the partially-finished painting, sipping hot coffee and considering critically. She'd made a pretty good start on the trees on the left-hand side, with the play of dark green and light. This, she hoped, would suggest the movement—the constant movement—of the leaves, the sunlight playing through them.

"You've got that look on your face again," Caro said, her voice softening. "I'm so glad. It seems like it's been such a long time." A pause. "And I'm not looking at the painting. I swear. I've been turning my head when I walk to the door, every day since you started. I swear."

Marty came back up slowly from her contemplation of the colors, a diver returning to the surface. She half-smiled. "You. That's okay. *You* can look." Once she'd said it, she realized that the words were true: after all this time living together, after all these years of friendship, she didn't mind Caro's eye, even on unfinished pieces. Caro knew. Knew when to comment, knew when to remain silent.

Still, her confidence faltered as Caro stepped closer to the easel. Marty abandoned the porch for the kitchen, where she drew a couple of slices of bread from the box and dropped them into the toaster.

"Do you need a refill?" she called back over her shoulder. She lifted the coffee pot, eyeing the remains. Not very much at all. She wondered how many pots Caro had gone through since dragging her hangover out of bed.

"No, thanks. I'm swimming."

"Tylenol?"

"Now that's an offer I can't refuse."

When the toast popped, Marty buttered it, shook a fair amount of everything bagel seasoning onto it, and returned to the porch. She handed the now-seated Caro the bottle of pain reliever. "I didn't know how many you wanted—two, or ten, or the whole bottle."

Caro shook out a couple of pills and downed them with her last gulp of coffee. "I like this," she said, her eyes still on the painting. "So far."

Marty snorted. "To paraphrase someone who thinks he's a critic, I guess I need to finish it."

"I guess you do."

Caro's expression shifted to indecision, as she glanced between the painting and Marty.

"Just say it," Marty nudged.

Caro took a deep breath: what she always did when she was certain she was going to offend, but needed to do it anyway. "What Simon said last night." Her words were hesitant. "About thinking about letting him talk to somebody."

When Marty snorted again, it was a defensive response. "Like the man can do what I haven't been able to do on my own."

"That man is Simon Burnett. Have you Googled him? He's not just some guy off the point."

"Not that there's anything wrong with that."

"Oh, come on. You know it really *is* about who you know. And who do we know? But now we've met somebody who might know somebody, if you get my drift. And if his connections can get you into a gallery—a group show or something—even if it's right here on the midcoast…"

Marty drank down her coffee. Caro was usually the anxious one, but this conversation was planting a knot in her stomach, a knot that was growing larger. Her palms, too, were damp; she set the cup down and wiped her hands on her coverall. "I'm thinking about it, Caroline," she said at last. "I fell asleep last night thinking about it. I woke up this morning thinking about it."

"Think harder." Relentless, Caro stood up, and set her empty coffee cup aside. "Listen, Marty." She took Marty's arms in a tight grip and shook her gently. "I know you don't paint for the fame and fortune—"

"Good thing. I've made precious little from it so far."

"Shut up and listen to me, will you? I'm trying to be sincere here, and this headache is making it harder. I know you're not in it for the money, but if there's a chance—the tiniest chance— don't you *dare* turn up your nose at it." She took a deep breath, and shook Marty again. "Talk to Simon about it. Let him look at some of your finished pieces."

The toast was gone, and Marty had no idea when she had eaten it. She took both coffee cups back to the kitchen and put them in the sink. She couldn't remember whether she'd ever pressed *start* on the load in the dishwasher last night.

"Marty." Caro's tone was ominous. Marty smiled to herself. "You're practicing avoidance. Cut it out."

"Okay." Marty squared her shoulders and returned to where Caro stood, arms crossed belligerently. She smiled to herself again. *My favorite Philistine.* "Okay. On one condition."

"Which is?"

"You help me go through these—" she waved a hand toward the canvases leaning against the wall "—and choose some to show Simon."

Caro's pointed face broke into a radiant smile, and she threw her arms around Marty's neck. Then she backed off, holding her head. "Oh. Ow. I shouldn't have done that."

There were more than Caro had expected, but Marty knew how many canvases there were. She knew what each one would show even before she turned them around for Caro's perusal.

Caro had seated herself again in the chair beside the easel. She held up an admonishing hand. "Don't tell me anything. No commentary. Let me just look."

Marty pressed her lips together determinedly. She turned over the nearest, a study she'd done of the front corner of the house, with the peonies in riotous bloom. There was a second next to it, with the petals scattered on the grass beneath the drooping head of the flowers.

"I didn't know about the first one," Caro said, frowning. She had her palms pressed together between her knees as she leaned forward. "But I like them together. Like a diptych. It's the passage of time." She indicated an empty spot near the French doors. "Put those there, and show me some more. I need to think about those."

One by one, Marty flipped the canvases at Caro's direction. As she did, she became less and less aware of Caro, and more aware of her own reactions: a vague dissatisfaction with most of the paintings, sometimes a strong dislike, and even less frequently, a sense of surprise, tinged with real pleasure. *I made this.* For her part, Caro directed a surprisingly few to her *no* pile.

"I love your work, Martha Ahearne," she breathed, leaning forward. "And I don't think I am biased. Not very." There was only one small canvas left, and when Marty made no move toward it, Caro pointed. "What's that one?"

Of course Marty knew, and it was the knowledge that caused her to hesitate. She bit her lip, and then slowly bent to it. Her hands curled around the mounted canvas protectively, and she looked down into it without speaking.

Larry stared up at her with his wide-open gaze, his blue eyes startling under his mop of dark hair. He leaned against the hood of a truck—the Bronco, though the paint thinned out at the edges, leaving the ghosts of the pencil sketch to each side. A kind of periscope view, Marty thought—small, looking through the wrong end. Though all ends were wrong, weren't they? She had managed to suggest the freckles, which had lightly dusted his tanned cheeks, but no matter how she had tried, she hadn't quite managed to get the sardonic curve of his mouth right. He had an arm slung over the side mirror, and his look challenged the viewer. No, it was Larry, but not quite Larry. Nothing, she thought sadly, would ever quite be Larry. She had begun the painting for her father, but then—he had died, too.

She felt rather than saw Caro draw close, to peer over her shoulder. She heard Caro's indrawn breath, and then felt the grip of Caro's fingers around her wrist.

"Oh, my God, Marty," she murmured. "Oh, my God."

"I never finished it," Marty said, indicating the circular fade. "I couldn't bring myself to go back to it."

"Oh, it's perfect the way it is," Caro whispered. Her voice— was it shaking? "Look at him."

When Marty exhaled, she felt as unsteady as Caro sounded. "Maybe. I mean—I could show him. I could show this. But—I could never sell it."

Caro leaned her head into Marty's shoulder. "No. Of course you could never sell this painting."

TWENTY-TWO.

O N MONDAY MORNING, Caro found herself anxiously following Matt Copeland's secretary down a hallway and into an office on the left. The building was a low yellow house overlooking the inlet in Danby; she saw two doors opposite each other at the end of the corridor that were undoubtedly Matt Copeland's father's and grandfather's corner offices. Probably with much better views than this one, she noted, the single window of which, over the lawyer's shoulder, had a brilliant view of the former chicken rendering plant. Matt stood as she entered, proffering a hand.

"Miss Pond," he said, his grip warm and assured. "Caroline."

The secretary closed the door quietly behind her. Caro slipped into the chair facing the desk, the blotter of which was clear of papers, though there were long folders in both the in and out boxes at the corner, and a screensaver on the computer just behind him showed three grinning boys with fishing poles, the middle boy missing a front tooth.

"Caro," she corrected, folding her hands in her lap.

"Of course. And I'm Matt, just like in high school." He opened a desk drawer and withdrew a legal pad and a shiny silver pen. Caro vaguely remembered him; he had graduated, as Mary had pointed out, the year before Larry and Alaric, three years ahead of her and Marty. Matt Copeland still looked incredibly young, with close-cut blond hair, and wide eyes that gave him a look of constant surprise. She rather thought that must play in his favor when he went up against adversaries in a courtroom; they had to be always underestimating him.

"You've come about a custody matter," he prodded.

Caro took a deep breath. From the manila envelope she'd brought, she withdrew the paperwork the process server had delivered the previous week, and passed it across the desk. "My ex-husband, Peter Vargas, has decided to sue for full custody of my daughter, Sophie." She swallowed hard. "Sophie is almost four years old."

Matt took the proffered pages and scanned them slowly. There were v-shaped lines between his pale brows as he jotted notes on his pad, then read some more. He flipped a page. Caro held her breath, and clenched her hands tightly together until her knuckles ached. Finally he set the papers aside. Caro wished she could read the black hatch marks he had made on the legal pad, but his handwriting was impossible, and probably would have been no better had it been right-side-up. He drew a sharp line beneath his notes.

"If you wish to retain me on this matter, I'll need to have my secretary make a copy of these." Matt's voice rose at the end of his words, turning them into a question.

"Please." Caro's voice broke. "Please. I'm desperate."

He nodded, then picked up the phone. "Sierra, could you run some copies for me?" He lifted his wide eyes, his expression sympathetic. "And could you bring some coffee?"

The secretary reappeared almost immediately, her footsteps muffled on the carpet; she set a tray on the desk between them, took the legal papers, and disappeared again.

He noticed Caro's surprised glance at the coffee tray, and chuckled. "That's my grandfather's rule here at the office. A secretary has to be discreet, have knowledge of Office Suite, and be willing to bring coffee." He poured out, then moved the creamer and sugar bowl closer to her. "Anyone objecting to that need not apply."

Caro opened her mouth and then shut it again.

Matt chuckled again. "Oh, no, not sexist at all—our previous office manager, Paul, made the best coffee, before he left us for law school." He leaned forward. "Paul used a French press. Sierra makes great coffee, don't get me wrong, but for her, it's not an art." The preliminaries over, he leaned back in his chair, which creaked. Behind him, a seagull landed on the outside window sill, and opened and shut its yellow beak. "Tell me about you and Peter Vargas, and your daughter. Sophie Vargas?" He glanced down at his legal pad again, the v-shaped frown reappearing.

Caro set aside her coffee cup, which rattled on its saucer, and began. "When we divorced last year, we agreed upon joint custody." It had seemed the path of least resistance then, and she had felt too bruised and exhausted to put up any extra fight.

"How is your time split with Sophie?" The silver pen was poised.

"Sophie is with me during the week—I work from home as a medical transcriptionist, so some days Sophie goes to a daycare home up the road. Pete and I alternate weekends."

"Not a fifty-fifty split, then?"

Caro inhaled. "No."

"Has it ever been? Since the divorce?"

"No."

The pen scratched its way across the yellow page. Matt drew another line, then flipped over to the next page. Outside the window, the seagull continued its complaints, muted by the glass. Caro stared at it, mesmerized.

"And money. What about child support?"

Caro remembered that she had shoved her copy of the original divorce decree into the manila envelope as well. She fumbled for it now, pushed it across the desk. "I'm sorry. I should have given you this with the others." She caught a breath. "I'm just not very good at this stuff."

Matt smiled gently. "Not many are. I wasn't when it was my turn. Don't panic." His voice was reassuring, and Caro tried hard to relax, even though she could feel the tell-tale sweat along her hairline. He took up the stapled decree and shuffled through it. After a moment, he looked up. "This reads that, according to wage information submitted, you make more than Mr. Vargas does?"

Caro felt her jaw harden. "I am a transcriptionist for Harbor Area Medical. Pete works for an HVAC friend of his, and gets most of his pay under the table. He also drives a company truck."

Matt's eyebrows climbed higher. "You have proof of this?"

She flushed. "What proof is there? But I agreed not to say anything about it if Pete would ask the judge to forgive child support payments."

"Because you would have had to pay him, in a joint custody agreement."

"Because on paper, the numbers would mean I would have to pay him."

"And the judge—" he glanced down "—Judge Russell, went along with Mr. Vargas's request."

"Yes." In truth, Caro's memories of standing before the judge in district court were a bit hazy. All she had wanted at the time was *out*. She could remember feeling panicky, being willing to agree to nearly anything. She could even remember how the wooden rail felt beneath her hands. But what anyone had actually said? In what order they had said it? No. She had just wanted out of the marriage. The biggest mistake of her life.

"So let me get clear on this, okay? Bear with me." Matt scribbled again on his pad. This time he bit his lower lip. "No money has ever changed hands, between you and Mr. Vargas, for the support of your daughter Sophie."

Caro nodded. "That's right. She's covered on my health insurance plan from Harbor Area. I pay for the days she goes to daycare."

"She's with you twelve days out of every fourteen."

"Yes."

"And has been for—" he flipped the pages again "—the last sixteen months."

"Yes."

The door opened behind them, and Sierra returned with the original summons and the copy in a legal folder. Matt handed her the divorce agreement, and she whispered out again, with the barest hint of a smile as she passed.

A second seagull attempted a landing on the outside sill, but the first lifted off just enough to flap its wings vigorously, to drive it off. Then the first seagull settled back into its accustomed position.

His note-taking finished for the moment, Matt Copeland sat back in his black leather desk chair and swiveled gently back and forth. "And now Peter Vargas is suing for full custody." He spoke more to himself than to her, but Caro nodded anyway. "Have you given him any reason to argue that you're not a fit parent?"

Caro gasped.

Matt held up a hand. "I'm sorry, but I have to ask the questions. You know they'll be asked in court. Are there drugs in the home? Excess drinking? Is the home unsafe for a child?"

"None of those things. We share a house with an old friend from school, and both of us love Sophie very much. She's very well cared for."

Again, the hand, to fend off her rush of defensive words. "I'm sorry. You just need to be ready for this line of questioning in court. You know I'm going to be asking those questions of Mr. Vargas." He paused. "Can you think of any reason why Mr. Vargas might think he has a chance of succeeding with this suit?"

Caro lifted her hands helplessly. "I can't. I don't know why he would do this. But Marty—"

"And Marty is?"

"My housemate. Martha Ahearne. You might remember her from school, too."

He nodded, wrote. "Yes. I remember her. It was a pity about her brother."

"Yes."

"So continue? You were going to say something about Marty?"

Caro returned her gaze to the seagull. He was watching her with one red-rimmed eye. She looked away. "Marty says he's flexing. He's asked his girlfriend to marry him. He might be trying to establish a sort of nuclear family this way, or as Marty suggests, he's trying to show off his power to her."

"And to you."

"And to me." Caro raised her eyes gratefully. Matt Copeland seemed to get it, to understand the ugly undercurrents of her situation, and she felt a wash of gratitude.

"So you feel that he might be using your daughter as a pawn in some way, rather than looking out for her welfare."

Caro nodded again. "He was very angry that I wanted a divorce. My friend Marty had recently bought a house, and had invited us to be housemates, to split costs. Pete has always insisted that I left him because Marty and I are in a relationship."

The lawyer's face remained impassive. "And are you?"

"No. Marty's been my best friend since elementary school. It's just the kind of person she is, to offer us a place when we need it, while I'm saving for a house of our own."

Yet again Matt held up the hand. "Don't get defensive. Just remember that, if this is the kind of thing he's going to say in court, we have to be prepared to answer. He might be trying to make an argument that your relationship situation is unstable, that you move from one relationship to another that quickly, which might be detrimental to your daughter's well-being."

Caro tilted her head, frowning. "That's just projection. After all, Pete's the one who has a new fiancée, a year after the divorce. Melissa lives with him in our old house, and I think it's their plan to get married that has him going after custody." She spread her hands. "I haven't even gone on a date since I moved out." Dinner with the neighbors—that didn't count, did it? She flushed.

If Matt noticed, he made no sign. He nodded. "We can make that point. We can posit that you've spent your time focusing on the needs of your child."

"I have." Caro thought of Sophie's face, flushed in sleep, her hand fisted under her chin, the butterflies that Marty had painted fluttering on the wall over her dreams. She smiled gently to herself. When she looked up again, Matt Copeland was watching her, his gaze calculating.

"You are going to have to prepare yourself," he warned. He jotted down a few more things. "Custody battles are notoriously ugly. Whatever the motive, people who sue for custody generally do not shy away from positing the most negative things about the other parent in court."

"Pete already says ugly things," she sighed. She looked again to the seagull, who was still watching her suspiciously. "He said them all through our marriage—during which he was unfaithful several times—and he's simply ramped that up now."

"So I'm giving you homework, and my email address." Matt

took a business card from a small silver stand at the side of his desk, and circled something with his silver pen. He slid the card across to her. "In the next few days, I want you to think about all the sorts of things Mr. Vargas might try to argue in court, and all the ways we might counter those things. Additionally—" and he cleared his throat "—I'm going to ask you to write down all the things you might tell a judge that would sway his decision as to Mr. Vargas's fitness as a parent." Caro's jaw dropped, but the lawyer continued. "You've already given me some things we might shape to our advantage: the fact that your daughter already spends twelve days of fourteen with you. The fact that Mr. Vargas has been generating income and not declaring it on his taxes, and has thus avoided paying child support when you so clearly provide the majority of support to your daughter. We can use his relationship status if he chooses to bring up yours. But I need you to write down and email me anything else we can use. *Anything.*"

"I didn't know it was going to be this hard." Caro's voice sounded small to her own ears. Intimidated.

For the first time, Matt Copeland's eyes narrowed, and Caro realized that he knew exactly how to play his own appearance for maximum effect. "I think it might be in your best interests to file a countersuit, for full custody, yourself."

"But—Sophie—"

His tone softened. "Full custody, though with visitation at your discretion. None of the actual time with him has to change, if you don't want it to. And just remember that this agreement can always be modified by the court—if, for example, your daughter wants to live with Mr. Vargas when she's older." If he saw her wince, he again chose not to react. Instead, he leaned forward and clasped his hands on the blotter before him. "Think of this, Caro, as a game of chess. Mr. Vargas has made his opening move. We make a countermove. Eventually, we might come to some sort of compromise with the aid of the judge." He stood up, and held out a hand. Slowly Caro got to her feet and took it. Matt's grip was warm. He smiled reassuringly. "But one thing's certain. We don't go down without fighting. Okay?"

"Okay."

He walked her to the door and opened it. "Sierra will talk to you about the retainer." He smiled again. "I'll prepare our filing in the countersuit."

Caro reached for her checkbook.

TWENTY-THREE.

"I HAD TO give Matt Copeland a retainer before I left," Car said, slumping onto the sofa, glass of water in hand. In her other palm she held a pair of Tylenol caplets, which she tossed into her mouth before drinking. "A thousand dollars. When it dips below five hundred, I've got to give him some more."

Marty was also drinking water, and had also availed herself of the Tylenol, which they kept on the windowsill over the sink for just such occasions. She glanced over at her friend in concern.

"I don't know where I'm going to get any more money, Marty," Caro said, her voice low.

"We'll figure something out."

"I know it's part of his plan," Caro continued after a moment. She picked up the television remote, turned it over a time or two in her hand, then set it on the end table. She leaned her head back and stared at the ceiling. "Pete's. He's going to drag this out until I'm all out of money, and he'll win by attrition." She set her water glass down next to the remote, and squeezed her eyes shut. Were there tears? Marty couldn't be sure, but now might be a good time for them. "And then he'll take Sophie away from me. He'll take her away."

"No, he won't."

"Matt said we won't go down without a fight." Caro's fists clenched now, as though she were preparing to get into this melee, physically.

"And he's right." Marty drained her glass and set it on the floor beside her chair. She lifted her eyes to the ceiling, and to Sophie, in the room above them. So far so good, no sound of tiny footsteps crossing the floor to the stairs, to demand they come up to bed, as Sophie did some nights. That made her think of the latches, and she quickly got up to slip them at the tops of the front and rear door frames. Then she returned to her chair.

"But I don't know how I'm going to pay for this." Caro's voice was climbing now. Her expression was panicked, a small animal in a cage.

"I told you." Quickly Marty crossed to sit next to her on the couch. She put her hand on Caro's fist; the skin beneath hers was hot. And those were, in fact, tears tracking along the sides of Caro's face. "Oh, honey. We will figure something out. I have some money set by. My share of Larry's life insurance policy. I can help."

Caro turned a white face to her. "Oh, Marty. I can't let you do that."

Marty shrugged. "It's not a matter of you letting me do anything. I do what I want. And I want to help keep Sophie safe and happy. I love her, too. I don't think Pete's having full custody is the best move for her." She squeezed Caro's hand. "And I know Larry would want this money to go toward this."

Caro turned her hand over beneath Marty's and twined their fingers together. "I'll pay you back. I swear I'll pay you back."

"We'll worry about that another time." Marty held up their hands. "Right now, we do what we have to do. As Matt Copeland says, we won't go down without a fight."

Caro sniffled. With her free hand, Marty reached for a tissue from the box on the side table, and held it out. Caro took it, stared at it dumbly for a moment, then blew her nose.

A shriek came from upstairs.

They both bounded up the staircase, Caro in the lead.

The shriek had subsided into heartrending sobs. "Mama!" Sophie cried out.

Caro shoved open the door, which she always left slightly ajar anyway. Marty flicked the light switch, to reveal Sophie sitting up in her bed, the covers tangled about her. She clutched the giraffe to her chest. Her mouth was open, her face flushed and blotchy from crying. Caro sank to the bed and took the little girl in her arms, dark head pressed to dark head.

"Mama!" Sophie cried again, clutching at Caro.

"I'm here, baby," Caro said, stroking Sophie's small back. "I'm right here." She kissed her head. "Aunt Marty's here, too. We've got you."

But Sophie would not immediately be comforted. Her cries again became unintelligible sobs, and she pressed her face into her mother's shoulder. The bedsprings creaked as Marty lowered herself to her other side, reaching a hand to her shoulder.

"It's just a dream, Butterfly," Marty murmured.

"Scared," Sophie sobbed.

"Of what?" Caro asked softly. "Nothing's here. You're safe. I'll keep you safe."

"But you weren't!" The fear had suddenly changed to anger, and Sophie shoved her mother away with small fists. Then she pounded at Caro's chest, shaking her head until her hair swung about, and the tears scattered. "You weren't there! I was scared and you weren't there!"

"Hush, Butterfly," Marty soothed. "Look. Mama's here now. It's all right."

"It's not, it's not, it's not!"

Caro tried to gather the little girl into her arms again, but still Sophie fought her.

"It was just a dream," Caro repeated. She met Marty's eyes over Sophie's head. "Tell me about it? Maybe I can fix it. Maybe Aunt Marty and I can fix it."

Just as suddenly, the fury disappeared, and Sophie drew her knees up, wrapping her thin arms around them. She hiccuped, her face streaked with tears. "No." The single word was clear. She dragged the back of a hand across her wet cheeks.

"We can fix it," Caro said again. "Tell us about it."

"No. I can't. I can't ever tell."

Caro's expression grew more perplexed. She wrapped her arms around Sophie again, trapping the little fists between them, and after a few moments, Sophie's resistance wound down. Still she repeated, "I can't ever tell. I can't."

"All right, then," Caro whispered into her daughter's hair. "You don't ever have to tell. Maybe another time. But it's all right now. I'm here. You're safe. I'll keep you safe." She kissed Sophie again. "Do you want a drink of water?"

In the paradoxical way of small children, Sophie clung to Caro. "Don't go," she said, her voice tiny. "Stay here."

"I'll get it," Marty said. She touched the little girl's head softly, then touched Caro's as well. "Mama can stay with you."

There was no cup in the upstairs bathroom, so Marty went down to the kitchen to run the water. When she returned to Sophie's bedroom with the sippy cup, she found both of them curled up together, and somehow, miraculously, Sophie had dropped off to sleep again. Marty set the cup on the nightstand, pushing a book out of the way, then kissed them both, pulled the blanket up over them, and shut off the light.

"I love you, Aunt Marty," Caro whispered in the darkness.

"I know," Marty said, pulling the door closed.

TWENTY-FOUR.

ON TUESDAY EVENING, Simon agreed to come over and have a look.

"Don't bring Nathan," Marty warned on the phone. "This is going to be hard enough with just you."

Simon laughed. "Don't worry. He's off at a meeting anyway. Something about the summer theater programming, and contracts."

He pulled into the yard promptly at seven. Marty, her palms sweating, opened the porch door for him. "You drove."

Simon's smile was surprised. "I *do* drive. You've seen me do it."

"But you could have walked. It's only a mile or so."

He looked appalled. "Me? Walk? I'm a city boy. If the subway doesn't run, I'll drive myself, thank you very much."

"Subway. In the Springs. Huh," she scoffed. Simon followed her through to the kitchen, where she offered him a drink. "Seltzer? Lemonade? Something harder?"

"Lemonade's fine." He leaned forward to look out the window over the sink, into the back yard where Caro had put both her lawn chair and Sophie's tiny one in the wading pool. Caro sat in hers, but Sophie ran around the pool in a circle, twirling the giraffe over her head and laughing uproariously. *I'll try to wear her out,* Caro had said.

Marty poured two over ice, and handed him one. The dishwasher gurgled away between cycles. He brushed his silvering blond hair out of his eyes and drank gratefully. "Thanks. This hits the spot. It was a warm one today."

The ancient circular thermometer outside the window still hovered around 75°.

"Not going to be good sleeping." Marty leaned against the counter with him. "It's getting to be time to put the air conditioner in upstairs. It gets pretty unbearable in this old house."

They fell silent for a moment, the ice clinking in their glasses as they drank.

"You're nervous," Simon said at last. She offered more lemonade, and he held out his glass.

"Yes." Marty poured more into her own glass, and resolutely put the pitcher away in the refrigerator. She turned to face him. "I'd be better off if I were out there with Sophie, and had Caro in here acting as my agent. She's a lot better at talking about my painting than I am."

Simon shrugged. "She's a lot further removed from it, as well." He set the glass down and crossed his arms. "Listen. I really liked what I saw the other night. And while I can't promise anything, I've been hanging out with the guy from Nova over in Danby, while Nate does his thing. Nova's putting on a group show in a couple of weeks, and I know he's pretty full, but I thought maybe I could convince him to include something of yours."

Nova. There was a painting in the living room, over the fireplace, that Marty had bought at Nova, spending far too much money for: a simple imagining of the Rockland Breakwater against a background of blue sky and blue water. It was impossible to tell where the horizon lay, save for the thin line of stone, and the exclamation point of the lighthouse. She remembered the first time she'd walked past the painting, displayed alone in the bow window of the gallery. She'd been immediately struck, but had to convince herself to pay over more money than she could justify, having just bought the house. *Nova*. She bit her lip, looking up, half-expecting Simon to be pulling her leg. His eyes were steady, though, his expression sincere.

"Nova," she said. "Pat Wakefield?"

"You know him?"

Marty flushed. "Met him, yes. Got him to look at my work? No."

Again Simon shrugged. "Like I said, I can't promise anything. But could I just look? Maybe there's something I could take a picture of, maybe a couple, and show them to Pat next time I see him this week."

It sounded as though Simon saw Pat Wakefield frequently. Marty shot him a look from under her brows, but his expression was giving nothing away. She filed the impression away for further consideration later. As though it were any of her business.

"I suppose I could text the pictures, but I always think the personal touch is best, don't you?" Simon retrieved his glass and indicated the way back to the porch. "Shall we have a look?"

Marty's lemonade was gone, so she set her glass carefully in the wet ring Simon's had made on the counter, and led the way.

In the end, Simon took pictures of six paintings from the ones Caro had set into her *yes* pile: Sophie and her pail, the seagulls tracking on the beach, her father Roger tying his boots, the fallen tree, the potato peeling, and Larry leaning against the Bronco. He had Marty set them on the spare easel, and turn on the overhead light, the one she never used.

"I'll let you know what Pat says," were his parting words, as she held the porch door for him. He slipped out into the early evening, and smiled up at her. "No promises. But—" and his smile widened "—if he doesn't take at least one, he's an idiot."

TWENTY-FIVE.

THE NIGHTMARES CONTINUED intermittently, and each time, Sophie steadfastly refused to tell either Caro or Marty about the thing that frightened her so. At bath time, Marty discovered Caro surreptitiously examined her daughter for bruises, her expression clearly one of fear and fury: nothing. Caro found an old nightlight in the kitchen junk drawer, but even that reassuring glow did nothing to lessen Sophie's fright at her dreams.

"Have you asked Pete whether she had the nightmares at his house last weekend?" Marty asked on Wednesday morning. She yawned, feeling the effects of interrupted sleep, and decided that taking another travel mug of coffee on the mail route might not be a bad idea. Neither rain nor hail nor snow, sure, but if she fell asleep and drove the Jeep off the road and into the blueberry barrens, nobody would be getting the mail. She pulled another mug down from the cupboard and filled it, added a dollop of creamer, and snapped the lid into place.

Caro's eyes were sunken, the dark circles pronounced. She looked up, and then away quickly. "I haven't."

"Maybe you should?" The keys were on the hook beside the back door, and Marty gathered them up. "If we could figure it out, we might be able to do something about it."

Caro pressed the balls of her hands into her eyes. "I know. I should. I *have* to. But I feel like I already know what kind of an answer I'll get from him."

Marty squeezed her shoulder on the way out the door. "I know. He's such an asshole." She sighed. "But I just think the timing's odd. That right after Sophie comes home from her weekend with him, she starts up with these nightmares. I can't help thinking that something happened when she was with them."

"I know." When Caro lifted her head, her eyes were blazing. "And if I find out he's hurt her, I swear to God I'll kill him."

"I'll help," Marty said. She paused. "But Pete's never hurt her before, has he?"

Caro bit her lip and shook her head.

"Could it have been Melissa, do you think?"

The blaze grew in Caro's eyes. "I'll call him this morning. I'll find out. I'll kill the both of them, I swear it."

Marty squeezed Caro's shoulder again. "Call me as soon as you talk to him. And hold off killing them until I get home."

The screen door swung shut behind her.

Caro fed and dressed Sophie, then delivered her to Joanne's before settling down to work—a bit late, but it couldn't be helped. She'd just make up the time on the other end. When she took her break a couple of hours in, she dialed Pete's cell phone. It went to voicemail almost immediately.

"Call me," she said, knowing he wouldn't. He usually didn't. He usually claimed that he never got the message.

At lunch, she fixed a salad and called again. Voicemail again.

"Please. It's about Sophie."

Knowing again that he probably wouldn't call back.

So she was surprised when the phone rang, just after four. She picked it up, looked at the number on the screen, and quickly punched the green icon.

"What is it?" he demanded without preamble. "Is something wrong with Soph?"

Caro felt her hackles rise. He could wait all day to call, and then come off all concerned?

"Yes, Pete, there is," she said, fighting to keep her voice steady.

"Is she sick? Did she hurt herself? What the hell happened?" His voice was accusing, as always. *Why weren't you watching her? Why didn't you take better care of her?* He was no doubt taking copious notes even now to use against her in court. "Where is she, Caroline?"

"She's at daycare right now." Caro found herself looking at the monitor, just to be sure of the time.

"What's happened, Caro?"

She took a deep breath. "Pete, since she came home from the weekend with you, she's been having nightmares. Sometimes several times a night."

There was a pause. Then, "Nightmares? Kids have them all the time."

"Not like this." She had to remain calm. She was not exaggerating, not making a big deal out of nothing. "Pete, she wakes up terrified. Screaming. Sobbing."

"Sophie's an imaginative kid. Give her a nightlight. She'll be fine."

Caro could feel the tension headache starting, creeping up her neck and into the base of her skull. This always happened. Pete was always able to make this happen. "No. I gave her a nightlight. I already tried that." She took another deep breath. The headache was beginning to pound. "Don't dismiss this, Pete. Sophie is terrified of something, and I think it might have to do with something that happened when she was with you this weekend. I need you to think about what it might have been. Even something relatively small."

"You think I did something?" The sudden force of his reply took her by surprise, like a blow to the side of the head. She held the phone away from her ear. "You think I'd do something to Sophie? What kind of an animal do you think I am? What kind of a flaming bitch are you to even suggest I'd do something to her?"

"That's not what I said—"

"Oh, but that's what you meant, isn't it?" There was a long pause, during which she could hear her ex-husband breathing heavily in his anger. Caro realized that her palms were sweaty, and gripped the phone more tightly. "This has something to do with the custody case, doesn't it? You want to make out that I'm some sort of abuser? Is that it?"

"That's not what's going on here, Pete," Caro protested.

"No? Sure as hell sounds like it to me," he shouted down the line.

"This isn't about you. It's about Sophie. She's all I care about here. She's frightened of something, so frightened that it's giving her nightmares. I just want to figure out what it is—"

"Then why don't you ask her? Instead of calling me at work to accuse me of abusing her."

"I never accused you of abusing her. You're twisting my words. I'm trying to find out what happened so I can fix it for her, okay?" Caro squeezed her eyes shut, pressing her fingertips to her temple. She felt the tears welling up. Tears of anger and frustration. She knew this pattern so well. "I asked her. Marty asked her. Sophie won't tell us what's wrong."

"Did you ever stop to think that she won't tell you because there's nothing wrong? She's a kid. She's having nightmares. She'll grow out of them." A deep breath, and the roar continued.

"And you keep your bitch lover out of my kid's business. I swear I'll be so glad to get her out of that house."

"Don't dismiss this, Pete—"

"Oh, I'm not. I'm calling my lawyer right now to let him know what you're trying to do. It won't work, Caro."

"Please—don't do this. Does Melissa have any idea—"

"And don't you be dragging Melissa into this, either. You flaming bitch."

The phone went dead.

Caro dropped her head onto her arms and sobbed. It always happened like this. She had known it would.

Caro scrubbed her face and put on her sunglasses before heading out to pick up Sophie. She felt weak and bedraggled, and stopped for just a moment to call the Chinese place up off the highway. A pu-pu platter for two, with an extra side of fried wontons—not the healthiest of dinners, she supposed, but it would obviate the problem of cooking something up. She felt the hysterical laughter bubbling up: could Pete use this against her in court, that she fed Sophie Chinese take-out? She was so tired, from her fractured sleep; they were all so tired. She felt like hell; Sophie had been fussy in the morning, and Marty, if she didn't get some sleep soon, was going to throw them all out on their ears.

Well, no, she wasn't. Marty wouldn't do that.

Sophie was amongst the last of the children to be picked up; she still appeared to be fussy, whining as she haphazardly threw blocks into a box.

"Gently, Sophie," Joanne said, pushing her frizzy blonde hair up off her forehead.

"I don't want to pick up," Sophie said. "I want to play more."

"Look, here's your mother now," Joanne countered brightly. "Finish that up, and get the picture you painted, so you can bring it home and hang it up."

Joanne obviously didn't realize that space on the refrigerator was at a premium, with all the paintings held to it with magnets. Caro forced a smile through her now-splitting headache, and slid her sunglasses up atop her head.

"You still look like hell," Joanne observed. "I thought you looked beat this morning, but if anything, you look worse now."

"Thanks." It was a good thing they'd known each other for years.

Joanne cast one more glance over at Sophie, who was nearly finished with her chore. Then she drew Caro aside. "Listen, is there something going on with her? With Sophie?"

Caro's guard came up quickly. "What do you mean?"

Another glance at Sophie, then Joanne lowered her voice. "Soph woke up crying from nap time. She just would not be consoled. Jill finally wrapped her in a blanket and read to her in the rocking chair."

Caro sighed, wiping her face with a hand. "And I'm betting she wouldn't tell you what was wrong, either."

Joanne shook her head.

Now Caro rubbed her eyes, which did nothing to help her aching head. "She's been having nightmares since the weekend. I don't know what's happening. I can't get her to tell me what's in her dreams that scares her so."

Joanne made a face, her thick brows drawing together. "Night terrors, do you suppose?"

Caro shrugged her shoulders helplessly. "I don't know. I have zero experience with those. And I didn't know you could get them during an afternoon nap." She glanced back at Sophie, who had gone to the bench along the wall to retrieve her painting.

"Should I call her doctor, do you think? I'd do anything to find the thing that will help her."

"And help you, I'm sure." Joanne patted her shoulder. "I don't know. It's probably a good idea." She bent down as Sophie approached. "Have you got your backpack?"

"Oh!" Sophie thrust the painting into Caro's hands and dashed off in the direction of the cubbies.

"If she does say anything to you about what's bothering her—what's in her nightmares—anything, would you let me know?"

"Of course," Joanne said, brushing her hair back once again. She leaned down and kissed Sophie on the crown of her head. "You know I will."

Marty was already home. She took one look at Caro's drawn face and pulled down the highball glasses. She splashed a healthy couple of fingers of scotch into each and handed one to Caro.

"Hang your backpack up," Caro called after Sophie, who had tossed it onto one of the porch chairs.

"Did you call him?" Marty led the way out through the kitchen door to the picnic table. She settled onto the far side and leaned back, looking up at the swaying branches of the oak at the side of the yard. "Pete?"

Caro set the tumbler down and straddled the other bench. "Yeah. Sorry I didn't call you."

The door slapped, and Sophie tripped down the steps, clutching her stuffed giraffe. She danced her way to the swing set, where she climbed up the slide, and sent the giraffe down. He stuck halfway.

"It was that bad, then?"

Caro shook her head. Maybe the headache was abating. "What is it they say? The definition of stupidity is doing the same thing over and over and expecting a different result?"

"That bad."

"He started yelling at me about how I was baselessly accusing him of abusing Sophie in order to sway the judge in the custody case."

"Holy God."

"Yeah. Then he said if Sophie wouldn't tell us about the nightmares, then there were no nightmares."

Marty watched as Caro lifted the glass and downed it. And immediately began coughing.

"Easy, there, killer," she said.

Sophie slid down the slide, a tried and true way of forcing a stuck giraffe down. Then she picked it up and clambered up the ladder again, determinedly. Much as though she had not had her sleep interrupted by those nightmares for the past several days.

Caro wiped her mouth with the back of her hand. They both glanced across at Sophie, giving the giraffe a stern talking to before sending him—halfway—down the slide a second time. She frowned at him.

Caro leaned forward and lowered her voice. "When I picked Sophie up at Joanne's just now, Joanne said she'd awakened herself during nap time with crying, and wouldn't say what scared her." The scotch obviously had not helped; Caro looked decidedly worse.

Marty reached across the table to touch the back of Caro's hand. Sophie, down again from the slide, twirled past with the recalcitrant giraffe, stopping only briefly to hug first her mother, then Marty. She tossed the giraffe into the air, then darted off after it, singing, something that might have been from *Cinderella*.

"So what do we do?" Marty asked quietly.

Caro turned her dark tired eyes to her. "I guess I call her doctor in the morning. Joanne thought maybe night terrors?

We just need to find out what's bothering her and put an end to it. I can't help thinking, still, that Pete knows and isn't saying anything."

"Deflection?"

Caro shrugged hopelessly. "All I know is that lack of sleep is killing us all." Sophie tossed the giraffe up and caught him this time; if he didn't care for the slide, this probably wasn't making him happy, either. Now she was singing "Let It Go." "Well, maybe not Sophie. But she's made of sterner stuff, I guess, than either you or I." Slowly she stood. "You want some Chinese food?"

Sophie heard that, anyway. Back atop the slide, she shouted, "Shiny food!"

"Silly human!" Marty called to her.

Sophie struck a pose. "I know, I know." She held out a small hand, as though pushing the objection away. "Don't talk baby talk and all that." Her tone was bored. She looked nearly four going on forty.

"I'll get it," Marty offered.

"No, you stay here. I've got to move, or I'll collapse into a puddle of hysterical inertia where I sit." Caro collected her glass, made a face into its empty depths, and headed toward the door.

"Hysterical inertia?" Marty laughed after her.

"Shut up. You know what I mean." Then she turned back, lowered her voice once again. "Oh, and Pete did say that he couldn't wait to get Sophie out of our nest of lesbian vipers."

Marty bared her teeth.

TWENTY-SIX.

In late afternoon, Marty slipped one of the rocks into her pocket and headed out for a walk. Caro was plugging away at her transcription in the little room at the back, and, her brushes and workspace cleared away, Marty could not settle. It was the painting, she knew. She was finally working on something, after all this time, and she felt it inside her rib cage, growing, expanding. It pressed on her lungs and made it hard to breathe. Right now, she knew that she had to let her tank refill—that she had emptied herself of ideas in her morning painting and had to wait for more to come to the surface. She had no doubt the ideas were there, just as an iceberg was there, most of it hidden beneath the water. But she also knew that she had to work those ideas slowly, allowing them to float to the surface in their own time. Forcing things would only lead to disaster—a seriously half-assed job. She jammed her hands into her pockets and set off at a brisk pace. At the end of the driveway, she turned left.

Friday afternoon, and there was no traffic on the road. Marty could feel her heart pounding in her chest and slowed to a more leisurely pace. She found herself eyeing mailboxes critically, noting which ones had not yet been righted fully after being abused by snowplows during the past winter, and which were too tall or too short according to post office regulations. After all these years—of pulling in, flipping open the doors, dropping in handfuls of envelopes and magazines and flyers, then slamming the doors shut again—she could feel the motion required for each action in her right hand and arm. *Even on my day off I'm working.* She shook her head.

Marty turned left again, and the spring was just up ahead, the tar cracking and falling away at the side of the road, and the pull-in rutted. Better to feel the paintbrush in her hand, the tiny movements that left a dab of color here, an outline there. Because delivering the mail might pay her a salary, but she wasn't a mail lady. She was a painter.

She was a painter.

Marty found herself smiling, a distilled kind of happiness. A painter, but not a Painter.

At the edge of the turn-out, she paused, studying the stone trough, the stone wall, the swaying trees above all. With her painter's eye. She took a step to her right, and another, and then squinted, trying to line the reality up against the image she had constructed on the canvas from her memory. It was no use; she never really painted the reality, but tried to capture a feeling. Was that what was missing, when she approached this canvas? The feeling was elusive.

A car passed, and Marty realized that she was nearly standing in the road, nearly oblivious. She was a painter, apparently, and not a pedestrian; but if she managed to get herself run over, she'd be neither. Carefully she made her way across the rutted dirt to the trough, examining the plaque as she did so. Did this belong in her painting, she wondered? The painting might not be fact, but it was truth, so maybe there did need to be a plaque on her trough—though perhaps it didn't need to have the literal inscription. She narrowed her eyes, thinking, and reached into her pocket with muscle memory, to take out the painted rock and place it on the far corner of the trough. Then she plunged her hands into the cold water, holding them there as long as she could bear it.

Finally she clambered up to her usual seat on the retaining wall. Was her painting of this spring, and this trough, dedicated to the memory of some long dead Painter? Or was her painting dedicated to memory? But even that thought made her impatient; and she realized it was because of the thing she was missing.

Don't think.

Marty closed her eyes, wiping her damp hands along the legs of her jeans. Above her the boughs had begun sighing in earnest, as they measured the wind. She held a hand before her, without opening her eyes, and felt for the direction. Not from the ocean, the provenance of most of the breezes in the Springs, but from the west, beyond the barrens. That usually meant rain. Marty had been so intent upon her work this morning that she had not thought about the weather; it would be just her luck to have walked out into a burgeoning rainstorm without noticing. Not brilliant, she chided herself. She opened her eyes and looked up into the trees, where the leaves tossed restlessly and whispered among themselves. She could see a sliver of sky over the road, and it looked gray and uneasy. Yeah, she'd probably done it now. With her face upturned, she felt the first raindrop just below her eye.

Too late. She could get up now and run for it—and she couldn't remember the last time she had run, in all seriousness—but there was no way she'd make it back to the house in time. She shrugged to herself. Fine. She'd just sit for a while and let it come to her. Maybe she was supposed to be feeling the rain. Maybe that was what was supposed to refill her proverbial tank.

Marty turned her gaze to the trough, where the pipe brought the water in at one end, and the groove in the stone let it out at the other, to run off along the base of the wall until it joined the stream from the woods, through the culvert that led it under the road, and downhill on the far side. Right now, the water was running off fiercely, but she knew from experience that, as the spring and summer wore on, the rush would diminish, to a flow, to a trickle, to nothing in the heat of August. That's when the fire danger would be at its worst, for if the springs couldn't bubble up from underground, then the ground was as dry as bone, as dry as death.

But the rain now had begun to pock the surface of the water in the full trough, and Marty watched it, fascinated. The raindrops fell in, the water sprung up. She wished she could slow the action and reaction down, to witness it in slow motion. In stop motion. The great sadness of it was that water in motion was nearly impossible to depict—the spirit of the water could never be captured. She sighed, lifted her face again, to feel the raindrops on her skin. They were no longer scattered, no longer gentle. When she listened, she heard their hush through the leaves overhead; when she watched, she could see them running along the veins of the oak leaves, to drip from the ends of the pointed lobes. There were birds, but their songs were now counterpoint against the sound of the rain. She wished for a way to capture that layering of sound visually, but it was an idle wish. There were limits. For her, there were more limits than for many. She held out her hands before her, paint beneath her nails, and let the drops pelt her palms.

She was going to be soaked.

She didn't really care.

For the first time in a long time, she was nearly satisfied with her day's efforts.

I am a painter, she whispered to herself. *I am a painter.*

She was not alone.

Marty's neck prickled, and at first she thought it just the rain, running down inside her collar. She cupped her palms, watching the rain pool in them, and then slowly turned her head.

Alaric. Of course. Marty didn't know why she wasn't more surprised. Who else would be hanging out at a roadside spring, letting the rain soak them, when they could be inside where it was safe and dry and warm? She had not seen him since she'd returned to the farm to give him the title to the Bronco.

He nodded, just once, a greeting. He remained under the canopy of the trees, at the lip of the hillside. His eyes were shadowed; she could not see his expression.

"Hello," she said, her voice rising above the rain. She held out a hand, sweeping over the stone trough, the stone wall. "Join me."

Alaric did, slowly. All of his movements, she was beginning to realize, were slow, economical. No energy wasted. Yet there was energy there—he pulsed with it—coiled inside him, as though he were constantly holding himself in check. Conserving that energy to withstand the next big blow.

Marty sucked in a breath.

When he stepped from beneath the trees, he held his face up and let the rain fall on it. There was a frown between his eyes, as though he were trying to work something out. A puzzle. He had his hands in his jacket pockets; he always had his hands in his jacket pockets, when they weren't busy among the bits and pieces of some task. Or trying to speak.

Now, having reached the end of the trough, he held up a hand, still looking to the sky. When his eyes dropped to Marty's face, he held out both hands. *Why?*

She laughed. "It's just rain. I'm not the Wicked Witch of the West. I won't melt."

He raised his eyebrows and nodded.

"I've been thinking." Marty surprised herself with the admission, though she stopped herself before she babbled on about *what* she'd been thinking.

Alaric touched his forehead, then his chest, and then nodded. "You, too?"

He nodded again.

Marty looked up past the leaves, toward the sky. The rain was steady now, having settled in for the long haul. Her father's words sprang to mind: *I can hear the grass growing.* A joke, but with a hard edge—the grass grew, and that meant more work with the mower. She dropped her gaze to Alaric, whose hands were back in his pockets.

"This is good for the hay," she said. "It'll be tall."

Alaric made a face, held a hand up at his waist. Tucked it back in his pocket.

Marty considered him from beneath her rain-beaded lashes. How changed he was. When they had been kids in high school— and that seemed centuries ago now—he hadn't exactly been gregarious, but neither had he been the shy, retiring type. He'd talked; but more than that, he sang. Exuberantly. She had a flash of memory, of spinning down this road at the end of day in the Bronco, with Larry and Alaric singing "Twilight Time" by the Moody Blues, taking turns at the high part, which neither of them could do well.

"Come sit," she invited again, indicating the length of the retaining wall. Plenty of room for both of them, and possibly twenty other people.

Alaric hesitated.

"We're soaked. A few more minutes won't matter."

Alaric moved stiffly to the wall, and sat a couple of feet away. Where Marty had had to hoist herself up, because of her height, Alaric had only to settle back. Sometimes she forgot how tall he really was. Lanky.

For a time there was silence. This was suddenly interrupted by an argument of crows, in the pines across the road. Several, from the sound of it. Marty turned her head toward the noise, wondering what they were arguing about. Several tones, several voices. Maybe they weren't arguing at all—crows were familial—but warning each other of some intruder, driving the intruder off: fox, deer.

Alaric, too, was looking into the pines. He held up three fingers, then a fourth. When he noticed her watching him count, he shrugged. Then he pointed to her, drew a smile on his own mouth.

"I'm smiling?"

He nodded, held his palms up in his *why* gesture.

Marty looked up into the rain again, and found it strangely conducive to the disjointed mood she felt welling inside her. "Thinking. Remembering."

Alaric made the gesture she'd seen before: pointing to his forehead, then his chest.

"You do that, too."

He nodded.

"I was thinking about us. About the Bronco. You and Larry singing." The words were out, then she realized what she had said. What a stupid thing to say to a man who could no longer sing. To a man who could no longer speak. She clapped a hand to her mouth. "Oh, Alaric. I'm sorry. Sorry. I shouldn't have said that."

He only shrugged. He swung both arms around, indicating the surroundings, then he pointed to his toes. When she looked puzzled, he repeated the gestures, but with a deepening frown. Marty felt worse, for not understanding, and bit her lip.

"Everything?"

Alaric swept a hand from shoulder to knee.

"Body? Every*body?*" It was like charades. Marty had never been any good at charades. She wished he could write out what he was trying to convey, but the pouring rain obviated any use of paper and pencil.

He stood, took a few steps on his toes, sat back down again.

"Everybody tiptoes," she said.

Now Alaric leaned back, grabbed a stick from the tall grass behind the wall, then bent to write in the mud at their feet.

Larry.

He drew a circle around the name.

After a moment, he hurled the stick across the rain-slicked road.

Everybody tiptoes around Larry.

Marty slumped. It was true. Nobody ever talked about her brother. Certainly not her mother, with her frenzied clearing out of any trace of him from the house where they'd grown up. Even Caro avoided the subject, glancing sideways uncomfortably sometimes when Larry's name came up in conversation.

"I miss him," Marty whispered now. Her voice was nearly drowned out by the rain.

For a long time she kept her gaze on the road, where a torrent of dirty rainwater ran alongside the cracked tar, before washing into the stream that ran through the culvert to the other side. When she finally turned back to Alaric, she found he was watching her, his body still as a statue. She met his eyes; he nodded and tapped his chest. *Me, too.*

She could only nod.

Me, too.

When she let herself into the house, she immediately began peeling off her soaked clothes: jacket, her lilac Chuck Taylors—Marty tried to ignore the mud on them—her shirt as she ascended the stairs two at a time. In the bathroom, she stripped off her underwear and ran a bath, throwing in some rose-scented bubble bath she found on the shelf. Hot as she could bear it: no point in catching pneumonia, or pleurisy, or whatever those Victorian ladies would catch if so much as a raindrop fell on them.

Marty slid beneath the bubbles and closed her eyes. She hadn't run a bath for herself for ages, and had forgotten just how comforting the embrace of the warm water was. The scent of roses was strong, maybe too strong; well, she had poured in a dollop, and then, vaguely dissatisfied, had poured in more. People would be able to smell her coming, anyway. She smiled to herself, feeling her muscles relax, feeling the warmth replace the cold at her core. She took a deep breath. *Deep cleansing breath*, the yoga lady instructed from inside her head.

"What the hell were you even doing?" This was definitely not in the calming tones of the yoga lady.

For a fleeting moment Marty had wished she had locked herself in. She'd seen Caro's Vue still in the driveway, although, when she'd checked her Fitbit, she had seen that it was nearly time for her to sign off work to pick up Sophie at the daycare. In fact, Caro, when she swung the door open now, was wearing her jacket, obviously on the way out. She'd just taken a weird detour up the stairs, apparently.

"Walking." Marty sunk lower in the hot water, the bubbles crackling in her ears. She had not taken a bubble bath in years, but somehow, that had just seemed the logical antidote to her wetness.

"It's raining, you idiot."

"I noticed. It started when I was about a mile out, and I knew I was going to be soaked by the time I got home, so I didn't bother to hurry."

Caro shook her head. "What if it had started to thunder and lightning?"

"It would have been very, very frightening."

"You're hopeless."

Despite herself, Marty giggled, and then, taking another deep breath, began to sing about killing a man. She lifted a hand from beneath the bubbles, and conducted Caro's entrance.

The mood was infectious. After a moment's resistance, Caro joined in. Her voice was uncertain at first, but as the words, and the tune, spooled out, it grew in strength. They sang the verse all the way through, then launched into the next, before Marty collapsed in a paroxysm of laughter. She gulped a mouthful of water, spat it out, and snorted. Caro laughed, too, though at the singing, or at the coughing, it was unclear.

"Oh, God," Marty gasped. "The bubble bath tastes gross. Not like roses at all."

Caro shook her head. She still laughed, doubled over, leaning against the doorframe for support. "You're such a freaking idiot," she gasped. Then, "I haven't sang like that since Alaric, and Larry—in high school—"

Her voice broke off, her expression stricken. There was surprise, and grief—and guilt?—in her face.

"Oh, Marty," she whispered.

Marty thought of her own hand, clapping over her lips, when she'd said nearly the same thing to Alaric. In her mind's eye, she saw the circle in the mud, with Larry's name incised in the middle of it. *Everybody tiptoes around Larry.*

"Say his name, Caroline," she said, sitting up in the bath, wrapping her arms around her knees beneath the shelter of the thick bubbles. Water sloshed onto the floor. "Say it."

Caro's dark eyes grew round.

"Larry. *Larry.* My brother Larry."

Each time she repeated the name, it felt to Marty as though she were conjuring, speaking the words to a spell. Not calling him back; it was far too late for that. Invoking his spirit. Perhaps invoking some healing energy. Did it hurt to speak of him? For Marty, this instant, it wasn't so much a pain as a hollowness, a Larry-shaped space where he had once been, which was now empty.

"Say his name," she repeated, glaring up into her friend's pale face. "Larry."

Caro's mouth worked, as though she were trying to form words which would not come. At last, a whisper: "Larry."

"He's dead," Marty said. "He's not gone. I need people to talk about him, not erase him. I still love him."

Caro's eyes were still wide as she looked into Marty's face, her cheeks still blanched. "Oh, Marty," she said, her whisper nearly inaudible. "Oh, I still love him, too."

They stared at each other for a few moments more before Caro drew herself up and tugged at her jacket.

"I've got to go get Sophie," she said, as though she'd just remembered.

As Caro pounded down the steps, Marty sank back again into the bath, trying to regain some semblance of balance.

"Larry," she repeated. Loudly.

She would not tiptoe around her brother any longer.

TWENTY-SEVEN

DR. GRIFFITHS SLIPPED her stethoscope over her head and handed it to Sophie, perched on the exam table and swinging her sandaled feet so that her heels thumped lightly against the side. She held her giraffe against her narrow chest.

"You'll need to check the giraffe's heart," she told Sophie. "And her lungs."

"It's a *he*. His name is Gerald." Nevertheless, Sophie stuck the ends of the stethoscope into her ears, and pressed the silver disk against a spot somewhere between where the giraffe's neck ended and his legs began. She frowned.

The doctor stood near, but did not hover. That was one of the things Caro liked about her.

"All systems go," said Dr. Griffiths, raising her eyes from the computer cart to meet Caro's. "Everything, physically, looks fine."

There had been no signs of abuse, and about that Caro was relieved, but not surprised. Physicality was not Pete's *modus operandi*, for the most part.

She nodded. "But the nightmares?"

Sophie had left off pressing the stethoscope into various parts of the giraffe's body, and was looking furtively from one to the other of them. The frown had deepened. She plucked the instrument from one ear, the better to hear.

"We do have options, if Sophie won't talk about them to you, or to me." Dr. Griffiths turned her even gaze to Sophie. "Will you tell *me* about them?"

Seeming to shrink into herself, Sophie took the other earpiece out, and formally handed the stethoscope back to the doctor: exam finished. Game over. "No."

The doctor draped the stethoscope around her neck once more, and put her hands into the pockets of her lab coat. She nodded. "Why do you need to keep it a secret?"

Caro's head shot up. The one question she had not thought to phrase in just that way.

Sophie turned her face slightly toward her mother, as though gauging her expression. Only slightly. Her lips pressed together stubbornly.

"I'm good at secrets. Would you like to whisper it in my ear?" Dr. Griffiths kept her voice calm, almost impersonal, as though, should Sophie again say no, they would simply go onto another topic of conversation. Caro admired that, wondering how on earth one learned to keep anxiety from leaking into every word, every gesture. She found herself wanting, irrationally, to tell the non-judgmental Dr. Griffiths all her secrets.

Now the doctor was leaning forward, and with another quick glance to her mother, Sophie put both hands on the doctor's shoulders and pressed her face into the graying hair. She whispered something.

"Okay," the doctor murmured, without straightening. "Why not?"

Sophie muttered something else, then pulled away quickly.

Dr. Griffiths stood up, and tucked her hair behind her ear again. "That makes perfect sense to me." She nodded, her eyes on Sophie's face. "If you were told not to, I can see why you wouldn't want to."

Sophie nodded, too. "Can I get down now?" She set the giraffe gently on the exam table behind her. When Caro reached for her, she shook her head sharply. "I can do it by myself, Mama."

When she had hopped down and retrieved Gerald, Dr. Griffiths lowered herself to one knee. "But you know, Sophie—and I can't tell you this strongly enough—that if somebody ever hurts you, or scares you, and makes you promise not to tell anyone: that's a promise you don't ever have to keep. Do you understand? If someone hurts you, ever, you can tell your mother, or you can tell me, or you can tell you Aunt Marty. You won't be in trouble."

Sophie's blue gaze roved over Dr. Griffiths' face for a moment. There was another sideways peek at Caro, and then, lower lip between her teeth, Sophie nodded.

"Someone told her not to?" Marty asked when she got home. "What the hell does that mean?"

Caro tilted her head and narrowed her eyes. "We both know exactly what that means," she said tightly. She looked out the window over the sink to where Sophie sat on the swing, rocking gently back and forth, digging her toes into the grass beneath. She was watching as the water ran from the hose into the little wading pool, but strangely, not playing with it. Not once in the past ten minutes had Caro had to tell her to put the hose down and let the pool fill.

"Pete?"

"Of course. Pete."

"But no signs of abuse?"

"Dr. Griffiths says no, not of physical abuse."

Marty let out an enormous sigh of relief. "I'm sorry. But I was so worried, Caro. So worried about that." She took a long breath. "But that leaves her with those nightmares, still, the ones Pete denies and at the same time, probably tells her not to talk to us about. Should you let Matt Copeland know about this?" Her tone made it obvious what her opinion was on the matter.

"I'll add it to the list," Caro said grimly.

TWENTY-EIGHT.

"Do you ever…"

Alaric looked up as Isabella's voice trailed off. She had become much better about talking to him, and had taken to visiting with him before dinner—tonight, after dinner, since truck parts were on order and they couldn't work. Still, there were times when she was still reticent, times like when conversation at the dinner table—Alaric still ate inside with the others, mostly as a favor to his mother—veered dangerously close to the topic of Bella's parents. She still held Brett and Sarah close, as though unwilling to share them, or what remained of them, with anyone else. Alaric supposed he could understand that; what remained of Larry was *his* and he felt no desire to share with his family either.

His thoughts slipped sideways to Larry's sister, Marty. He hadn't brought Larry back to her and that weighed heavily on him. He pushed Marty away from his mind and turned back to his niece. He held up a hand, flat-palmed. *What?* Then he spun the hand in the air. *Go on.*

Bella chewed on her lip, her head leaning against her left hand. In the light from the window over the table, he could see the ghostly white scar along her hairline, something she usually

184

combed her hair over in an attempt to hide it. In her right hand, she played with a pencil. He looked down at the napkin and saw the beginnings of a cow. Quickly he stood, rustled in a drawer, and returned with a blank sheet of paper, which he placed beside the napkin. For a moment she frowned at it, then at him; then a smile broke out.

"Thank you," she said. Her voice was small, as though thanking him for something other than the paper. He almost knew what it was.

Alaric twisted his hand in the air again, and raised his eyebrows.

"It's hard to go on," she said, frowning. She pushed her oak-colored hair away from her cheek.

For a moment his heart raced. He'd said that before, to the counselor at the hospital. Written it. To the counselors at all the hospitals. Before they'd offered him drugs and discharged him to go home. *It's hard to go on.* He looked at Isabella sharply.

"I mean, I don't know how to ask you things. What if I upset you? What if I make you mad?"

Alaric let out a long relieved breath. *Not that, anyway.* He tipped his chin, held out his hands, and then shook his head.

"But what if I do?" Bella's question, he realized, was dead earnest.

He touched his forehead, shrugged.

Bella frowned at him. "I don't know what you're saying." She shoved the paper he'd given her across the table, and handed him the pencil. "You need to write it."

I won't get mad. Don't worry.

She sighed. "I have to worry, don't you see? Because you're my only—friend." She turned her head quickly, looking out the window into the farmyard as if something interesting had suddenly begun to happen out there.

School?

Bella shook her head. "I'm too weird. I've got these crutches and stuff. I'm an—orphan. Whose parents—" she hiccupped, "—died tragically."

She was the new kid in school, too, which, he had to think, didn't make anything easier. If he remembered correctly, the cool kids were stand-offish with new kids until they proved their worth at something: soccer, or troll-catching. Until new kids did something acceptance-worthy, they hovered on the edges of school society. School, he thought violently, was cruel to kids. He was so grateful to have had Larry, from the time they were first put on the kindergarten bus. From then until he held Larry, bleeding out his life-blood, in his arms.

He grabbed up the pencil and wrote so hard he scratched a hole in the paper. *I'm not going anywhere.*

"Promise?"

He forced a smile and held out his hand, pinky crooked.

Bella looked puzzled.

He pointed at her hand, and at his little finger. After a moment, she hooked hers through his.

Ask me, he wrote.

"He was your best friend," Bella said slowly.

He nodded.

"Does it hurt a lot?" She was careful not to look at him. He was grateful. Alaric, too, turned to look out at the fading light; the farmyard, enclosed by outbuildings as it was, drew evening on more quickly than the fields that surrounded them. The pines to the north didn't help.

Every day.

Bella squeezed her face between her hands. Alaric looked

down at his own hands, imagining groping his way along this conversation, as she was doing. Sometimes he forgot how young she was.

"Mostly I hate people who still have parents. It's not fair. I hate them."

Alaric nodded.

She looked up and away. "Do you hate people who still have their friends?"

The question was a sucker punch. Alaric felt his head snap back, a blow to the chin. Stupid. He should have been on the lookout for that question. He should have expected it, should have raised his defenses, his hands and arms strong from all the push-ups he did upon getting up in the morning.

He squeezed the pencil between his fingers, feeling it strain, knowing it would break if he squeezed just a bit more—a bit more—

I hate myself.

Suddenly *everything* was jangling all around him. The noise of the refrigerator. The sound of Richard on the tractor out of sight somewhere. He thought he could hear the low-pitched hum of his father's television inside the house, where the Red Sox game was on. Even Bella's breathing—even his own breathing— was too much to listen to. He put his hands to his head and squeezed, trying to keep the overload out. Above it all, he could hear explosions, gunfire, and a voice—his own voice, which he almost didn't recognize—screaming for a medic.

Had he ever said this to any of the counselors at the hospital, at any of the four hospitals? *Said.* The word was laughable. Had he written this to them, this bald, unforgiving statement? *I hate myself.*

The loathing that dropped over him was a heavy blanket, suffocating, dark. He tried to fight his way out of its confines, but it grew more and more constricting, and he thought he might as well surrender to it. He had never used these words. And here he was, committing them to paper—committing to them—for a preteen girl. He was surprised, and shocked, and ashamed.

"Alaric," she was calling, from far away. "Uncle Alaric?"

He couldn't answer her.

"Alaric? Oh, God, I shouldn't have asked anything. I shouldn't have." There was a grip on his arm, which didn't seem to be his arm. "Oh, God, oh, God." A metallic noise, and the table beneath his elbows wobbled. "Oh, *fuck*." Then he felt the embrace, her thin arms around his shoulders, her unsteady weight against his side. Her face was pressed into his hair, and after a moment, the blanket lifted and he felt the dampness of her tears. "Come back," she whispered. "I'm sorry. Come back."

How could she be speaking his own words to him?

Come back. I'm sorry. Come back.

PART III

TWENTY-NINE.

WHEN HE HAD himself under control again, Alaric put his arm around Isabella to steady her. He could feel her shaking against him with the effort of standing without her crutches, which, he saw, were still leaning against the other side of the table.

He tipped her face up with a trembling finger and looked at her. So like Brett, but with a hint of Sarah around the eyes, and the cheekbones. Her face was tear-streaked. He pointed to her chair. She shook her head. "In a minute," she said. She was examining him as well, her eyes glittering with the tears. "I need—I need to make sure you don't go away like that again."

Alaric shook his head, touched his chest with his fingertips. *Sorry.*

It must have taken her a monumental effort to pull herself up and around the table. Alaric was aghast. It must have taken her a monumental effort to drag herself around to comfort him, and yet she had made the effort. He touched his lips, one of the few real signs he knew. *Thank you.* He hoped she understood. Slowly he got to his feet and maneuvered her into his chair. Then, not knowing what else to do, he went to open the freezer door. Ice cube trays, nothing else.

"What?" she demanded. Her voice was still shaky.

Alaric returned to the table and took the opposite chair. He picked up the pencil. "*I thought there was ice cream.*"

Bella laughed, wiping at her face with the back of her hand. "Scary thing equals ice cream. You're like my dad." She hiccuped over the word, but the faint smile remained.

We could go get some.

"At Burke's?"

Alaric nodded. *I'll drive.*

The bad joke was worth it just to hear the unsteady laugh again. "You'd better. I don't have a license. Not to mention these." She rapped a knuckle against the brace on her left leg.

He flapped a hand dismissively. He still felt wrong, but the sounds had faded, back to something at least partway normal. Or what he remembered normal to be, back before everything had gone to hell.

But he did hear the footsteps on gravel, and looked out the window to see his mother making her way across the yard.

"Oh, geez," Bella moaned. "Don't tell her I swore, Uncle Alaric. Don't tell her I swore *that word.*"

It took a moment for Alaric to remember which word, but then he forced a grin, and crossed his heart.

Georgie had paused at the screen door, peered around at the dimness inside, and then knocked.

"Do you have Isabella with you, Alaric?"

"I'm right here, Gram," Isabella answered.

Georgie opened the door. "It's getting to be time to get ready for bed. Nearly eight, and you should have a wash. Only a couple of school days left."

Bella looked pleadingly at Alaric, who had stood upon his mother's entrance. She tapped the piece of paper, touching the words *ice cream.*

He lifted his hands and nodded.

"We were just thinking about running to Burke's for ice cream," Bella said. "It's so hot."

Indeed, Georgie pushed her hair away from her damp forehead.

"We could bring some back for you," Bella wheedled.

Georgie looked from one to the other, and shook her head, a half-smile playing about her mouth. "Go on, the pair of you."

Alaric handed Bella her crutches. She slipped her arms into the cuffs, and pulled herself to her feet. They followed Georgie out into the yard, where the bats were already swooping overhead.

"Do you want to take my car?" Georgie asked.

Alaric pointed to the battered farm truck, and smiled his thanks.

"Don't be late." She stood watching them make their slow way along the side of the yard to the garage, where the vehicles lined up before the closed doors. "And I want a hot fudge sundae!"

Alaric helped Bella from the truck, and they got in line.

With Burke's newly opened for the season, and with the heat of the evening, a fair number of people had the same idea: the line in the brightly-lit lot was long, and slow-moving. Alaric nodded to a few people; one old couple smiled at Isabella before turning away with their cones, shaking their heads. Bella felt distinctly out of place; she hadn't thought this through. She hadn't been to Burke's in a long time—the last time was with her parents. She winced at the thought, looking at the kids running around, shouting, as though it wasn't so hot. She tried not to hate them. But it was hard, so hard. A boy who might have been a couple of years younger than she got a bit mouthy with his mother, and it was all she could do not to slap the chocolate-dipped cone out of his hands with her crutch. Alaric touched her arm, then wagged a finger at her.

"Can't do anything when you're around," she complained in mock annoyance.

Alaric rolled his eyes.

Bella looked desperately back toward the truck, but she had to order. Alaric drove, and she ordered. It was only fair. Of course, he paid, too. They inched forward in the line. She was aware of the eyes upon her, and she bit her lip.

Alaric touched her arm again. When she looked up at him, he pointed to his eyes with two fingers, then waved a hand in a small circle.

"It's like being in a sideshow, isn't it?" she asked in a low voice. He shrugged, smiled, and then, leaning close, he shielded his hand from the surrounding people, and lifted his middle finger.

Bella laughed. Alaric smiled innocently.

At the window, she ordered a small strawberry on a plain cone for herself, and a medium maple walnut on a sugar cone for Alaric. Then, remembering, she ordered a small hot fudge sundae for Gram. "Don't know why," she said, as they stepped aside from the window to wait, Alaric having paid and dropped his change into the tip cup. "It's all going to be melted by the time we get back anyway."

Alaric shrugged, lifted his closed hand to indicate pouring.

"I know. Soup. But she said."

A sudden quick shout from one of the tables under the awning at the side of the building. "Alaric! Hey!"

They both turned, to find Marty Ahearne waving to them. She sat across from the lady she shared the house with, and a little girl. Isabella couldn't remember their names. Alaric smiled warily and lifted a hand, and Bella felt the slightest twinge of jealousy. The table was otherwise unoccupied.

"Come sit with us when you get your ice cream," Marty called.

After a moment, Alaric nodded. This was not what she had planned. Bella turned resolutely to read the placards taped to the insides of the windows. Onion rings. Root beer floats. Fried pickles. Banana splits. When the girl called their order, she stepped forward, then stopped: of course she couldn't carry the damned thing and maneuver the crutches at the same time. Alaric took both cones, and the sundae in the to-go cup, then jerked his head toward the picnic table. Bella narrowed her eyes; she didn't want to. Alaric jerked his head again, and narrowed his eyes right back. Then he turned on his heel, leaving her to stump along after him or not, as she saw fit. But Bella wanted that ice cream—she could feel the sweat trickling along her backbone under her shirt—and she had no choice.

He sat next to the housemate, who was rather pretty, and the little girl, who looked just like her. This left Bella the seat next to Marty, who, she guessed, was pretty enough, but brown-haired where the other was dark. Bella glared at Alaric balefully as she lowered herself gingerly, then she took the cone without saying thank you.

"Hi, Isabella," Marty said. "It's a hot one. We had to come out for ice cream, too."

She was holding a half-finished cone that looked like chocolate chip; the ice cream was melting down over the edges of the sugar cone, and into the napkin and her fingers. Bella felt a niggling little satisfaction at that. She licked around the base of her cone quickly, to ensure she didn't lose any of her strawberry ice cream.

Marty waved at the others. "Do you know Caro? And this is her daughter, Sophie."

"I'm Sophie," announced the little dark-haired girl. She had ice cream on her face, but she wiped at it, somewhat ineffectually, with one of the thin napkins. "That's my mother." She waved her spoon—her cone was upside down in a dish—at Caro. "It's hot."

Bella nodded, aloofly, going at the other side of her cone.

"Glad to meet you, Isabella," Caro said. She had a low voice. Bella examined her from under her lashes. "Sometimes at our house we just have to have ice cream for supper. Cooking supper is too much. Thinking about what to have for supper is too much."

Now Isabella wondered which one she should hate: the one who came to the farm, or the one Alaric sat next to? Which one Alaric might be giving his attention to. Marty, next to her, the mail lady—she was the sister of his friend. Bella watched her out of the corner of her eye, thinking about Uncle Alaric's best friend, the one who died. Her brother, the one who died. Across from her, Caro seemed engrossed in the mess her daughter was making, barely sparing any attention for Alaric. He didn't seem to mind.

Bella's thoughts were flying every which way. She ate her ice cream slowly, her eyes still narrowed. A puff of hot wind, smelling of French fries, lifted her hair from her forehead, and the trickling down her spine continued. Alaric had had something happen, back there in his room, a big reaction, a *bad* reaction; it had something to do with talking about his friend. His friend, Larry. She thought of her feeling of helplessness, calling to him, trying to bring him back. And she'd done it. But here was the sister, cheerfully licking away at an ice cream cone, as though her brother's death didn't matter, as though Alaric's reaction didn't matter. So she hadn't seen it, but surely she should sense something? Bella wanted to lash out somehow. But when she looked across the table, there sat Uncle Alaric, also licking away at his maple walnut cone as though something earth-shattering hadn't just happened an hour ago. Every once in a while, his eyes would flicker toward

Marty and away again. He didn't think she noticed, but Bella did. She resented it.

Bella didn't speak. Of course Alaric didn't. But Marty didn't, either, and didn't seem to be worried about the lack of conversation. Bella resented that, too.

Abruptly Sophie announced that she was done. Her ice cream had melted sufficiently to float the colored sprinkles; the cone had a few bites taken from it, and had been unceremoniously thrust back into the mess, where it listed slightly. Caro pulled a wipe from her purse and tried to clean up Sophie's face, but the girl wriggled away from her mother and got to her feet. She dodged around the end of the table and scrambled up next to Bella.

"You have crutches," she announced, as though that were news.

Her forthrightness took Bella by surprise. People—like the elderly couple in the line—usually looked at the braces and the crutches, and then let their gazes skim away quickly.

"Sophie!" Caro gasped.

Beside her, Bella realized that Marty had gone still and watchful. Even Alaric seemed to be waiting on her reaction.

"Yes," she said. Her voice wavered, and she tried again, more forcefully. "Yes, I do."

"Why? Did you break your legs?"

"Sophie," Caro said again, her voice sounding strangled. "That's rude. Leave Isabella alone."

"It's all right." It wasn't, really, but she would not let these strangers see that. She licked the melting ice cream back quickly, and then turned to Sophie. "My legs were broken, and they still don't work right."

"And these help?" Sophie lifted one of the crutches in both her hands. She frowned at the cuff, and the handle.

"Until I get stronger, yes." It was hard to say the words, but Bella pushed them out into the hot and suddenly still air.

Sophie looked up, her blue eyes curious. "And do you go to the doctor? And is your doctor nice? My doctor is nice." She stood up next to the bench now and slipped her arm through the cuff. The crutch stuck out in front of her, blocking the way past the picnic table.

Nice? Bella hadn't thought about Dr. Mack that way; mostly she just resented having to go to him, having to be the sort of person who kept having to go to an orthopedist. "I suppose he is," she said. "Here, pull that crutch in before you trip somebody and their ice cream."

Surprisingly, Sophie did as she was told. She set the crutch back where she had found it, leaning against the edge of the table. She giggled. "They would fall down, and their ice cream cone would go splat! Maybe into their face."

"And that would be mean, since it's so hot," Isabella pointed out.

Sophie nodded. "They could always go home and play in their swimming pool," she considered. "I have a swimming pool. It's blue." She skittered a glance sideways. "I don't like it much."

"I wish I had a swimming pool."

"You can come over to my house and play in mine." Sophie smiled a sticky smile up at her. "Can't she, Mama?"

"Any time she wants," Caro said.

But now, his ice cream cone finished, Alaric tapped gently on the table between them. He pointed to the take-out bowl, where the sundae melted away, becoming less and less defined under its domed cover.

"Not now, though," Isabella said. "We've got to take that home to my grandmother. It's going to be a drink before we get there."

Sophie's face fell, and for a moment she looked rebellious,

before her expression subsided into disappointment. "I wish I had a grandmother," she said, ducking her chin.

You can come over and play with mine, Bella almost said, but she caught herself.

Alaric tapped the table again, and held out a hand for the remains of her cone. The ice cream was nearly gone, so Bella finished it quickly, and ate the cone. She handed Alaric the crumpled and damp napkin, and he made a face at her.

Before she could begin the laborious process of drawing herself to her feet, Sophie wrapped her arms about Bella's middle. "I'm glad you're named Isabella," she said, her voice muffled. "It sounds like you're a queen of something."

THIRTY.

Caro knew she'd promised Marty that she'd stop Facebook stalking Pete and Melissa. Still, after she'd tucked Sophie in, read four different Eric Carle books to her, and turned on the nightlight and the fan, she sank back on the couch and opened the app on her phone. She glanced upwards in apprehension: she might have ten minutes before the nightmares began; she might have three hours. If she had been a more sensible woman, she would be getting into bed immediately. Dropping off to sleep immediately.

Out on the porch, Marty had been struck by an idea, and now was leaning forward, limning something in gray-green. Caro could just make out her profile, her brown hair curling along her cheek. To cover herself, Caro switched on the TV, clicking through menus until she found "The Great British Baking Show." Paul and Mary, she knew, would provide good cover.

Pete first. She flicked through his profile. He never posted anything except the occasional picture of an HVAC installation. More often, other people (read: Melissa) posted photos and tagged him in them. She scrolled, squinting. *Got engaged.* She snorted, but then covered that with a little cough, in case Marty looked up. There they were—the pictures she knew would be there from the weekend. Caro traveled backwards through time. Not many from Sunday—the backyard of Pete's house, the puppy Karl, who appeared to be growing into some kind of small bear. Not many of Sophie, and none close up, none facing the camera. Caro felt a weird nagging, and scrolled back further, looking for Melissa's inevitable picture dump from the beach.

Finally. *With Pete Vargas at Reid State Park.* Caro forced herself to calm her breathing, and looked up quickly at the television, where Mel and Sue were frolicking briskly through the grounds of a country estate. *I'm not trolling,* she thought in Marty's direction, *I'm investigating.*

The park sign, from inside the car. The sign indicating the different beaches and parking areas. The parking lot with what Caro always thought of as the new bath house, though it had been there for years: it still struck Caro as wrong, used to the old one as she was. So Pete and Melissa had chosen to take Sophie to the lagoon side of the park—she breathed a sigh of relief—which was a good choice for a nearly-four-year-old.

She glanced up furtively, but Marty was still intent upon her painting. She was coating her small brush from her palette, then leaning forward over her canvas. The table was scattered with tubes and jars, the rocks pushed over to the side. Those rocks, Caro had often thought, were Marty's equivalent of Caro's online solitaire game: Marty drained her brain of ideas painting her real pictures, and then paused, painted a rock or two, and then continued with her real work. Her important work.

Caro returned her attention to her phone screen.

More pictures. Sand dunes. Rose bushes not yet in bloom. Sophie on the walkway between the dune fences, her sunhat hiding her face.

That wasn't the lagoon.

Stupid, stupid people.

Pictures of Pete, up to his knees in the surf. Sophie running from the waves. A selfie of Melissa in bikini and big sunglasses, on a blanket. Another with lots of cleavage and pursed lips. And another one. Caroline grimaced.

"What are you doing?" Marty drawled, as though she knew perfectly well what Caro was doing.

"Nothing," Caro sang back innocently. "It's just that this foolish person has chosen to use a *bain Marie*. No matter how many times I've watched this, I can't help asking how idiotic a person can be."

"Sometimes a *bain Marie* is a good choice. Don't knock it." Marty turned back to her painting, dabbed her brush, no longer interested in this conversation.

Caro turned up the sound on the television a click. Bakers were panicking slightly. She sympathized. She dropped her eyes once again to the pictures. How many selfies had Melissa taken? Had she even gone into the water?

More. Pete and Sophie advancing up the beach, away from the surf, hand in hand, she dwarfed by him. Caro scrolled past that one quickly, the resentment making her feel a bit squeamish. Sophie draped in her Disney princess towel, eating a tortilla chip with great intent. A seagull also eating a tortilla chip.

It all looked so nice on Mile Beach, the sky beautiful and blue, the surf pounding, the sun sparkling off the sand. A perfect day at the beach, Caro thought bitterly, with a happy little wannabe family. And look! More selfies: Melissa and Pete and an impatient Sophie, refusing to look at the camera—she'd probably been told to smile for *Mom*. Melissa and Pete by themselves, both wearing sunglasses now. Melissa and Pete kissing—Caro's stomach turned slightly. Several more of Melissa and Pete in various states of affection.

But where had Sophie gone? Probably sulking behind them

on the blanket, in the way she had when events weren't moving in the direction she had mapped out in her stubborn little brain. Caro scanned the next few pictures of Melissa and Pete enjoying themselves and each other for the benefit of social media and posterity.

Then Caro saw the sunhat. Beyond Melissa's tanned left shoulder, further down the beach, chasing a seagull, dangerously close to the surf. Pete and Melissa were laughing, and the ocean was reaching out, in its treachery, for Sophie.

This time Caro couldn't keep the mewling cry from escaping. "What?"

"Marty, come look." She leapt up from the sofa, holding the phone out. Marty, hearing her distress, dropped the paintbrush and rushed in through the French doors. "You have to look at this."

Marty took the phone, and immediately frowned. She looked up into Caro's face, and then down again. "Pete and Melissa?" Her lips turned in distaste. "Haven't I told you to pay no attention to them online?"

"I had to. I had to see if there was anything in their pictures from the weekend that would help us figure out what's going on with Sophie." Caro felt the tears start. "Oh, Marty. She said she didn't like her pool anymore. She wouldn't play in it, even when I sat in it. Oh, Marty."

Now Marty peered down more closely at the photo. Caro reached over and scrolled back a couple, to where Sophie appeared in the selfie, looking a hundred kinds of displeased, then slowly forward, one at a time, as Sophie disappeared, and then after a few, reappeared, making her way down the beach, away from the oblivious Melissa and Pete.

There was one more, the last one. A picture of Pete and Melissa, again kissing, while behind them a large wave had knocked Sophie down. A small arm was the only part of her to be seen in the roiling water, and the sunhat had been flung up the beach.

"Oh, my God," Caro whispered. "Oh, God." Just looking at the picture terrified her, but she could not look away. She was sweating, and could feel the shakes coming.

"The bastard," Marty said. She half-turned to look up the stairs, her expression dark as a thundercloud. "That God-damned bastard."

Get screenshots, Marty had instructed, her voice icy. *Matt Copeland will want them.*

Ever practical, Marty was, and Caro was grateful. With a purpose, her shaking had nearly subsided, and she had held back her tears, though she suspected she'd be having a good cry before she fell asleep. If she could ever fall asleep. *Sophie had come this close.* How could Caro sleep knowing that her daughter had nearly drowned? That she had come so close to being swept out into the ocean, her little lungs filling, her cries unheeded? There had been no other pictures after the terrifying one where the tiny Icarus had plunged into the ocean with no one the wiser. No doubt that was when Pete and Melissa had realized that Sophie had disappeared. Caro had seated herself at the desk and had painstakingly screen shot every one of the photos, and then, thinking carefully, had downloaded each into a file, which she named *Pete Vargas—Reid State Park* with Saturday's date. Melissa must not have realized that the near-tragedy was playing out in miniature behind her left shoulder, otherwise she never would have posted those last couple of pictures. Caro was working on composing a cover email to Matt when the cry she had been dreading came from upstairs.

Pushing open the bedroom door and turning on the light, she saw the glitter of the wide terrified eyes, and threw herself onto the narrow bed to gather Sophie into her arms.

"I needed you, Mama," Sophie sobbed into her shoulder, and Caro's heart tightened in her chest.

"I know," she whispered back, her voice thick. "I know, and I'm sorry. I should have been there. I should have come to the beach with you. I should never have let you go with Daddy and Melissa."

Sophie stiffened and drew away.

"I'm not supposed to talk about that," she said, dragging an arm across her eyes, and sniffling. "I'm not supposed to tell you."

"You didn't tell me," Caro said carefully, reaching for a tissue from the bedside table. "I figured it out by myself."

In the glare of the overhead light, Sophie's small face was all planes and angles, lower half shadowed. She looked, Caro thought with that catch in her chest, other-worldly. A fae child. Which she could have been, *could have been*, had she not been pulled from the unforgiving waves. What had Pete been thinking, taking a small child to the surf, rather than keeping her safe in the shallow lagoon? What had Pete been thinking, turning his back on this tiny, stubborn little person? *What had Pete been thinking?*

The tears she had held back broke through her flimsy resolve, and Caro felt them running, hot, down her cheeks.

"I'm sorry, my sweetheart. I'm sorry for not being there when you needed me," she whispered, and held out her arms again. After a moment's pause, Sophie slid into her embrace once more.

"I kept yelling for you, and I kept getting water in my mouth, and it tasted awful, and then, when the man got me out, I threw up all over him." Sophie hiccuped, her tiny body convulsing once, twice. "But I'm not supposed to say."

Caro shook her head. *I'll kill him,* she thought. Still, she kept her voice low, reassuring. "It's all right. I figured it out by myself, so it's not a secret anymore. You don't have to worry about that."

She became aware, slowly, of the figure in the doorway: Marty, in her robe, standing silent, listening.

"Daddy said," Sophie protested after a moment. Then, "Melissa was just crying."

Didn't keep her from updating her social media. A catty thought, but then, Caro decided, Melissa deserved it. She'd like to shake Melissa, too.

"It's all right." Caro ran a soothing hand up and down Sophie's back, feeling each vertebra, the sharp wings of her shoulder blades. She paused for a moment, Sophie's words crowding her mind. A lifeguard? "And I'm sure the man wasn't worried about your throwing up. He's probably had people do it before. Do you know who he was?"

Sophie shrugged, and hiccuped again. "I don't know. There were two men. One had a surf board. They were nice. But then we left. And Daddy yelled a lot, and Melissa cried. I didn't cry." She reached up to wipe Caro's face almost reproachfully. She seemed quite proud of her stoicism; and that, Caro was sure, was why she had been crying in her sleep all this time since.

Caro pressed her lips to her daughter's hair, and breathed deeply. Sophie's clean soap scent filled her nose, and she felt more hot tears tracing their way along her face. "Is this what you've been dreaming about, then? Is this what's been scaring you at night?"

After a moment, she felt the tiniest of nods against her shoulder.

"Can I talk about it now? Really?" Sophie sniffled. "I don't want Daddy to get mad. I don't like it when he yells."

I don't, either. "Does he yell a lot?"

"Only sometimes. And I don't like it. Most of the time he's good, but not at the beach."

A point in Pete's favor, Caro thought wryly. *Most of the time he's good.* I'll kill him, she thought again. I'll kill them both.

In court.

"Daddy says that I'm not going to live here anymore, that I'm going to go live in his house with him and Melissa. He says I'm supposed to call Melissa 'Mommy,' but I just think that's dumb." Sophie wriggled in Caro's arms, and Caro loosened her grip, but did not let go. "I'm supposed to live here. You're my Mama, and Melissa's not my mommy, and this is my house, even though my puppy doesn't live here."

That damned dog.

Caro nodded against Sophie's head.

"And I just wanted to look at the waves, and there was a seagull, and it had an orange eye. Daddy and Melissa were just taking pictures of themselves, so they didn't need me, see? I didn't know the waves were going to knock me down. I didn't know I wasn't going to be able to get out until the man came."

Suddenly there were tears, oceans and oceans of tears. Sophie clung to Caro, but somehow there was something new and different about this outbreak, as though a dam had been breached. Caro turned slowly and lay down, pulling Sophie to the pillow beside her, cradling her against her chest, and letting her cry it out. If she allowed herself to drain her own tears, who was she to tell Sophie not to cry?

Caro heard the floor creak, and then the lights went out, leaving only the glow of the nightlight in the corner. Marty pulled the door closed behind her.

THIRTY-ONE.

Caro's next appointment with Matt Copeland fell on her day off, and Marty took a chance on someone being home at the Morgan farm in the afternoon, after the school bus angled past toward the Lighthouse Point Road.

Sophie, unstrapped from the car seat and set on her feet in the wide barnyard, looked around slyly. "Is there a horse?" she demanded, hands on hips. "There's supposed to be a horse."

Marty closed the rear door of the Jeep. "I never told you there was a horse. I said nothing about a horse."

Sophie cast her a withering glance. "You said 'farm.'" She drew the words out with infinite patience. "And farms have horses, Aunt Marty."

Georgie Morgan had opened the kitchen door. Her smiling face held a hint of curiosity.

"Hi," Marty called, urging the suddenly shy Sophie forward. "It's probably imposing, and I know Isabella probably has homework, but I wondered if she might have a minute or two to show Sophie some of your animals."

Marty could see Isabella over Georgie's shoulder, at the kitchen table. She was studiously reading a thick book, pretending not to have looked up, expressions fighting their way across her face, when Marty had appeared. The curiosity, the slight tinge of jealousy, the curiosity again when she heard her own name. Slowly she lifted her chin again.

"Sophie?"

"Is this where you live, Isabella?" Sophie asked, pushing past Marty's legs, shyness gone as quickly as it had come. She looked up at Georgie. "And is this your grandmother?"

Georgie chuckled and opened the door wider. Sophie brushed past her and climbed up on the chair next to Bella at the long table.

"Sorry," Marty said, her voice lowered. "But Sophie really took to Isabella when they met the other night at Burke's."

Georgie clucked, a grandmotherly sound. "No need to apologize, dear. Come on in." She waved Marty to the table with the others. "Make yourself at home. You've been here plenty of times before."

"But I haven't," Sophie announced.

"No, dear, you haven't," Georgie said. "You're right, though—I'm Isabella's grandmother. You're Sophie? She's having a bit of a snack now, after school. Cookies and lemonade. Do you like cookies and lemonade?"

"I do," Sophie said. She swung herself up onto her knees to lean forward for a look at Isabella's book. She frowned. "But I don't go to big school yet. So I don't have books like that." She sounded concerned, as though the lack of big books would negate any claim to cookies and lemonade.

"Sit in your chair properly," Marty admonished, "and mind your manners. You're a visitor, remember."

She heard Isabella sniff. Again she wondered why the girl didn't like her; she'd felt the waves of animosity at the ice cream place, and the tide had apparently not turned yet. She turned to Isabella and smiled determinedly.

As Georgie set another couple of glasses on the table and filled them with lemonade, the ice clinking, she smiled at Marty. "It's all right, dear. You know how many young people have sat at this table before." She replaced the pitcher on the refrigerator shelf, then brought down the cookie tin from the cabinet over the stove, to replenish the supply on the plate. "Molasses cookies," she told Sophie, who looked at them suspiciously before helping herself to one. "Do you like molasses cookies?"

"I don't know." Sophie nibbled cautiously at the edge. She frowned, considering, then took a bigger bite. "Mm. I think I do." She looked up with her frank blue eyes. "Did you make them? Grandmothers make cookies, don't they?"

"That they do," Georgie said, laughing delightedly.

"I just had to check. See, I don't have a grandmother, so I don't know."

Georgie looked up quickly to Marty, who could only shake her head.

"What's this book about?" Sophie, still nibbling at the cookie, now turned her attention to Isabella. "Does it have pictures, or is it a chapter book?"

Sliding her glass out of the way, Isabella turned the book so Sophie could look at it. "It's history. What happened to people before we were born. There are some pictures, but most of them aren't nice. Wars and stuff."

"No animals? Marty said you had animals here." Sophie took a long drink from her glass, holding it in both hands.

"We've got real ones," Georgie said. "Would you like me to show you them?"

"No," Sophie said. Marty cleared her throat and mock-glared, and Sophie quickly amended, "No, thank you." She smiled at Isabella. "I want Isabella to show me. She's my friend."

For a moment, Georgie looked like she thought this might not be the best idea.

"She's got crutches, because her legs don't work right yet," Sophie continued blithely. "But we can go slow."

Marty closed her eyes.

Before Georgie could voice the objection she seemed to want to, Bella pushed away from the table. "Let's go, then." She bent down to adjust her braces, then donned her crutches and hoisted herself up. "Are you ready?"

"Can I take a cookie?"

Bella shrugged. "Just eat it up before the chickens see it. Otherwise they'll mug you for it."

They made their way, a slow procession, out of the kitchen and into the farmyard.

"I'd hold your hand, but your hands are busy." Sophie skipped a few steps ahead of Isabella, then back again.

"They rather are."

Trailing behind them at a careful pace, Marty could hear the ironic note in Isabella's voice, though of course Sophie missed it. She pressed her lips together to keep from chuckling. Beside her, the slight worry lines had returned to pucker Georgie's forehead.

They passed the garden, newly fenced in to keep out deer and other assorted beasts intent on vegetable feasts, and then the small barn. Beyond that was the coop. The chickens were not penned in the daylight, but milled around in the sparse grass, talking amiably to themselves. Quickly Sophie shoved the last bit of molasses cookie into her mouth and wiped her hands along her sundress. With the advent of strangers, the hens protested to one another, and skittered about. Bella paused, leaning forward on her crutches, and cooed at them.

"Are you talking chicken talk?" Sophie demanded.

Isabella laughed. The sound seemed to surprise her grandmother. Her footsteps, beside Marty, faltered before picking up again.

"Chicken talk," Isabella giggled. "I like that, Sophie. Yeah, I guess I'm talking chicken talk." She cooed again; the chickens seemed to be calming after their initial agitation. Two edged closer to Isabella, pecking at pebbles at her feet. They answered her genially.

"Do you know what they're saying?"

Isabella shook her head. "I haven't got a clue. But they like it when I make the noises. Why don't you try it?"

Sophie frowned fiercely in concentration, and made an attempt to imitate Isabella. The two chickens fluttered backwards, their claws scrabbling, then settled again, pecking at the ground. Sophie cooed again. They came closer.

"I'm doing it, Isabella!" she whispered. "Did you hear me do it?"

"I heard you, Soph."

The excitement was too much. Sophie hopped up and down, an eruption of glee. The chickens scattered. For a moment she looked as though she might cry, but then Isabella laughed. Sophie looked up at her uncertainly, and then laughed, too.

"What's all this noise?"

Marty turned, and it was Richard, wiping his hands on a red rag. His face was sunburned, his faded T-shirt sweat-stained. His smile was broad.

"All done for the afternoon, dear?" his mother called.

From inside the big barn came Alaric and his father. "A couple more things to take care of before dinner," Howard Morgan said. "New fence posts wait for no man." He was wearing a worn pair of overalls, and Marty could almost hear Sophie's pronouncement: *farmers wear overalls, don't they?* Alaric shoved his hands in his pockets and held back a little. Marty lifted a hand in greeting, and he nodded, once.

"We're just showing Marty and Sophie some of the animals, Grandad," Georgie said. "Sophie seems quite taken with the chickens."

"Isabella showed me how to talk chicken talk!" Sophie announced.

"You should take her back of the big barn to look at the spring calves," Howard suggested. He smiled fondly at his granddaughter, and then tweaked her nose. Then he leaned over and tweaked Sophie's nose into the bargain. "Did you make Bella laugh?" he demanded. He winked at Marty. "Our Bella doesn't laugh. She's as serious as they come."

"Howard," Georgie said warningly.

Sophie put her hands on her hips defiantly. "Isabella does too laugh. We were laughing at the chickens. I don't think they liked it."

Howard grinned under his bushy gray mustache. "I think you're right. Chickens are even more serious than Bella." With a hand to his back, he straightened. "Any more of that lemonade, Gram? Or did these hoodlums drink it all up? I've got a bit of a thirst on."

"But—"

"I'll take Sophie to see the calves," Isabella said. She lifted her chin toward the house. "It's okay, Gram. I can manage."

Georgie didn't look convinced. But her husband took her elbow and guided her back toward the kitchen door. "Don't fuss, Gram. You're as bad as the chickens."

"I think I could use some of that lemonade," Richard said. He shrugged, tucked the red rag into his back pocket. "Nice to see you, Marty." He followed his parents across the yard.

That left Alaric. "You coming with us?" Isabella asked. Her voice was rougher than it might have been. Marty caught the glance Isabella threw between Alaric and her, and suddenly knew the source of the slight animosity.

Alaric had tilted his head to the side, his gaze on his niece steady. After a second, she flushed, and then he nodded.

Sophie was quite taken with the baby cows, too. Most were in pasture, Isabella explained patiently to her, except for these two, and their mothers. Sophie squealed and tried to shove torn grass through the fencing. After a moment or two, the curiosity got the better of them, and the four cows came to investigate. The first touch of the calf's mouth on her hand sent her giggling. "Cow lips! I felt cow lips on my fingers!"

Isabella laughed. When Marty looked over at Alaric, she saw the smile—so infrequent, she realized, which made it all the more sweet—break out over his face as he watched his niece. She wondered how much Isabella had laughed over the past year, and figured it probably wasn't much. Then she thought of all the times Alaric had seen her, on her mail rounds, in the church, wherever, and had turned away; he probably hadn't been smiling all that much, either. Well, neither had she, she supposed, except for when she witnessed Sophie's antics. Bringing Sophie here had been the right thing to do, she decided, despite Isabella's suspicious dislike.

In her pocket her phone chirped.

Isabella glanced up sharply. "Is that a bird?"

"No, silly," laughed Sophie. "It's my mama. She's calling Aunt Marty on the phone." She leaned closer, conspiratorially, and lowered her voice. "My mama is the only person who calls Aunt Marty on the phone."

For some reason, Marty felt herself flush at the words. She forced a laugh. "It's true. If anyone else calls, I don't answer it."

"Well, she can answer it now," Isabella said. She flashed a glance in Marty's direction. "Go on ahead. We're not stopping you."

That earned her the tilted head and stare from her uncle again, and Isabella fell silent. Then Alaric pointed at Marty and clapped a quick hand to his ear.

"Probably I'd better," Marty said apologetically. "I am traipsing about the countryside with Caro's daughter, after all. Do you mind?"

Alaric shook his head.

Sophie gathered more grass to shove through the fence. Marty stepped away from the sound of her delighted squealing.

"It's about time," Caro said on the line.

"We're at the Morgans' farm. How'd it go?"

"The Morgans', eh?" Her tone was calculating.

Marty shook her head, drawing in an impatient breath. "Your daughter is feeding the calves grass, more or less." More shrieking laughter from over her shoulder.

"That's what they all say."

"So how did it go?"

"I'll tell you about it when you get home. Nothing bad. Stuff to think about. More homework from Mr. Copeland before the preliminary hearing. I just wanted to let you know I was here, and ask you what you wanted me to start for dinner."

"Something cool. We'll be home soon." She punched the red button and slipped the phone back into her pocket. When she turned back, only Alaric looked her way. He held up both his hands, flat-palmed, to the sides. *Everything okay?*

Marty nodded, surprised at her ability to figure out Alaric's meaning. Then she scolded herself: he was one of her oldest friends. Then she thought: but much changed. *Much* changed. Because everything was changed.

"It's all right. Caro just wanted to let us know she was home and starting supper."

Sophie's head jerked up, and her lower lip began that familiar stubborn jut. "But I don't want to go home. Isabella and I are having fun."

Isabella's expression was inscrutable.

Only Alaric was now looking down at Sophie's set jaw, the determined lip. He frowned, glanced over at Marty, then down to Sophie again.

Sophie, hands on hips, glared at the adults in turn. "I don't want to go," she repeated.

Alaric squatted down until his face was even with hers. He pointed to her, to Isabella, at the ground. Then he rolled his hand.

"You don't talk," Sophie said, sidetracked. Again Marty held her breath at Sophie's forthrightness. How she spread out in the open all the things that adults seemed to want to—need to—gloss over.

Alaric shook his head, holding Sophie's gaze.

"So I don't know what you mean."

Alaric repeated the gestures, then looked to Isabella.

"Uncle Alaric means you can come here to visit me again," Bella translated. "Any time you want to."

Sophie nodded. "Maybe tomorrow. Maybe every day. And when it's hot, you can come to my house to get in my pool."

Isabella smiled, only a little bit strained. "That would be nice."

Sophie had refused to go to bed, even after the dancing—*there's so much more I have to tell you, Mama*—and then had fallen asleep on the couch in what, ironically, looked like child's pose. The giraffe was crushed beneath her. Caro, still looking exhausted and shaken after the past week of broken sleep, carried her daughter upstairs, while Marty cleaned up the kitchen. She felt bone-tired herself, but it was beyond the tired of exercise; or instead of the tired of exercise, she thought wryly, as she'd done pretty much nothing since the hurried yoga of the morning before painting. *Hurried yoga.* She laughed quietly at herself, at the contradiction. She turned off the kitchen and went through to the porch, to sink into her chair between the table and the easel.

Marty was a slow worker, and she knew it. Today had been the first extended work on the painting of the spring since the weekend, and something about that twisted her insides. The ideas, roiling around, trying to find a means of escape. Of expression. She could flick on the overhead light out here, open the paint box and get out the palette; she could do that now. The face of her Fitbit told her it was eight-thirty, but she could tell, more or less, from the slant of early June evening light outside the windows. It was too late, she was too tired. The thought of prepping her palette seemed like more work than she could bring herself to attempt.

"So," Caro said. She leaned against the doorframe, the living room light behind her making her into a formless silhouette. She probably did that intentionally. Marty had not heard her pad down the stairs from Sophie's room.

Marty leaned her head on her fist. "So?"

"The Morgans. You went to the Morgans' farm."

"I told you we did. More to the point, *Sophie* told you we did. Repeatedly."

"And I've got you to thank, now that she's going to pester me until the end of time to get her a cow."

"Don't forget chickens."

"Oh, I won't. She won't let me forget chickens." Caro shifted slightly against the doorframe, arms crossed. "So."

"You keep saying that. Learn some new words."

Caro sighed dramatically. "Because inquiring minds want to know."

Marty knew what she was driving at, but knew also that it felt as though Caro was poking a rough finger at something tender. It was easier to play dumb. "What do they want to know?"

"What's going on with you…" A long emphatic pause. "And Alaric."

Marty turned in her chair, nearly upsetting the jar of brushes, which she righted just in time. "What?"

"So there *is* something. I knew it." There was wonder, and not a small note of satisfaction, in Caro's voice.

"No."

"You've been over there a lot lately."

"Don't be ridiculous. Not a lot. You know Isabella invited Sophie to come to the farm sometime. We had some spare time this afternoon, and so Isabella was showing Soph some of the animals."

"That's *this* time." Caro now abandoned the doorframe, and sank into the wicker chair, which embraced her in a white glow. "And Isabella, according to Sophie, also showed her some lemonade, some cookies, her grandmother." Caro was ticking her fingers. "Chickens, cows, her grandfather, her uncles."

"Uncles," Marty echoed. "Both of them. Both Richard and Alaric were there." She sounded defensive to her own ears.

"And one of them went to the calf pen with you, Sophie told me." Caro was still probing, and Marty was certain her eyebrows would be raised as she persisted in the interrogation. "She said it was the one who doesn't talk. So. Alaric."

Marty sighed, a long-suffering sound. "So. Alaric."

"The one you gave Larry's Bronco to."

This time Marty threw up her hands. "I had to. You know that. Mom was going to junk it. I couldn't let her do that. Alaric was the person who could understand that."

This time it was Caro's turn to inhale loudly. "*I* could understand that," she reminded Marty. "I was there, too, with you guys, way back then. Don't forget that. I know what that Bronco means. To us. What it meant to Larry."

"But do either of us know what to *do* with it? What to do about it?" Marty's voice was rising in frustration, and she thought to control it. "If I'd brought it home here, it would sit out there in that driveway until it rusted away to nothing, and that would be the same as if I'd let Mom have it towed away." She pressed her hands to her face. "It had to go to Alaric. Surely you can see that."

Caro held up a hand. "All right. I'll grant you that much, that Alaric would know how to care for that truck. And we wouldn't."

"So there's no big deal there, either. Nothing." Marty slowly deflated. Argument over.

"Except for the times you've gone over there in the evening."

"Once. I went once. Delivered the title. That was all. Alaric was out in the hayfields with his father. I left the title with Georgie. I never saw Alaric."

"Oh, but you wanted to, didn't you?" Caro wagged a finger knowingly.

"Just stop it, okay? Even if there were something between me and Alaric, Isabella would never allow it. She doesn't like me. She's really protective of her uncle."

"Her Uncle *Alaric*."

"Yes. Her Uncle Alaric," Marty agreed, peeved. "So if I'm after somebody over there, it would have to be Richard, and Richard is definitely not my type. Or maybe I'd be after Howard, but he's married, and far too old for me, and therefore also not my type."

"All righty, Player Queen," Caro laughed in the darkness.

"Player Queen?"

"You're protesting too much."

Marty looked for something to throw. She settled on a roll of paper towels.

It wasn't true, Marty argued, later in the darkness of her own midnight room. She lay on her back, hands at her sides, staring up at the invisible ceiling, listening only to the hum of the oscillating fan, which wasn't doing much to move the stifling air. There was nothing going on between her and Alaric. He was a friend, from childhood, whom she thought she had lost, when he had returned so different, so wounded, so *changed*. She had thought, naively, that he might share her pain upon his return, that they might grieve for Larry together. But she had not reckoned on the differences in their griefs—the differences that made him avoid her. Until now. Until the Bronco.

Outside her window, there was a sudden crack of thunder, which made her heart stop for a moment. When she had steadied her breathing, she tried to place the sound. Somewhere to the southwest, she decided, inland from Danby, towards Augusta. As she strained her ears, she could hear the wind growing outside, sighing in an accompaniment to the fan. More rolls of thunder, on and on, like the sound of a bowling ball meandering slowly up an alley. The wind was picking up. Marty lifted a hand to wipe the sweat from her forehead. It was impossible to sleep on nights like this—and hard to imagine nights like this so early in the season; this did not bode well for the months ahead. At least the rain would come soon. As she listened, she knew the storm would not pass them by this time.

Faintly, she heard the squeak of the hinges she and Caro never bothered to oil: the door to Sophie's room. The hush of the fan drowned out footsteps, but she heard the little voice, barely intelligible. *Mama? It's thundering.*

At least there was no screaming. This was not a nightmare, just a normal thing that woke Sophie from her sleep.

Hot as it was, she knew Caro would welcome Sophie into her bed, to cuddle and whisper gently until the storm passed or they both fell asleep. Sophie had never liked thunderstorms, though she had grown to the point where she often slept through them. Not tonight, though. It was too hot to sleep through Rip van Winkle bowling. Caro was good at comfort, Marty thought, and smiled to herself. Even if she was a pain in the butt in all manner of other ways. Marty sighed, replaying their conversation on the darkened porch, where Caro's carefully chosen words prodded. Marty and Alaric. Right. There was nothing there, except friendship of long standing.

The rain began now, and as Marty listened, it quickly grew more intense. She could hear it falling in torrents from the roof. A flash of lightning turned everything in her bedroom black and white, the familiar becoming strange. Marty counted to herself until the thunder cracked again. Only a few miles away now, coming along the highway to Painter's Springs and Lighthouse Point. She had a sudden memory of the beagle, Dewey, that Larry had had when they were kids; the dog was terrified of thunderstorms and would hide under the nearest bed, quivering. More than once she had passed Larry's bedroom to see his long legs protruding from beneath the dust ruffle, and to hear his murmuring comfort to the whimpering beagle.

Oh, how she missed Larry. He had been such a jerk of a brother at times, but overall, a kind person. A fun person.

Another brilliant flash of lightning, another crack of thunder.

She heard Sophie's surprised shriek, and what might have been a comforting murmur from Caro, though it was hard to be sure. The fan slowed and spun to a halt: the power had gone. Somewhere between the highway and the point, a tree had probably come down on an electric line. Marty took a deep breath. The rain, she hoped fervently, would wash the air and cool it down. Otherwise, sleep would truly be impossible now. She rolled over to look at her alarm clock, but, electric, the normally red face was black. She fumbled for her phone, charging—or not—on the bedside table, and flipped through the apps to set the alarm clock. Rain, snow, sleet, hail, downed electric wires—all that stuff: there would still be mail to deliver in the morning.

Marty paused before setting the cell phone aside.

Think of something to win her over, had been Caro's parting suggestion before they'd climbed up to bed, breezing over all Marty's objections. *What does Isabella like?*

Biting her lip, Marty opened the Amazon app. It was slow loading, without electricity and the modem; she was on data, but when eventually the page opened, she typed in *oil pastels*.

THIRTY-TWO.

FRIDAY NIGHT, WHILE they were grilling hamburgers in the back, the phone rang in Marty's pocket.

"It's not me." Caroline held up her hands. "I'm right here."

"And I'm right here," Sophie sang out. She selected another crayon from her box and began to apply a sunshiny yellow to the coat of a lion in the coloring book.

The number had a New York area code.

"Marty? Simon here."

She met Caro's eyes, mouthed his name. "How are you?"

"Not too bad at all." Simon laughed. "Pretty spectacular, actually."

"Are you drunk?"

"Never. But I need to ask if you're free tomorrow afternoon, say about four?"

There was conversation in the background, the clink of glassware.

"I am," she said cautiously. "Why?"

"Pat wants to meet you."

"Pat?" The realization sunk in. "Pat *Wakefield*?"

"That would be the one. Here? At Nova?"

Dumbfounded, she held out the spatula to Caro.

"Are you there? Have you swooned?"

"Shut up. You're serious. Tomorrow, at four, at Nova. You're serious."

"I'm serious." There was a moment of muffled conversation. "And bring two of your pictures." More conversation on his end. "The one of the woman peeling potatoes, and the one of the guy leaning against the truck."

"I've swooned." Indeed, Marty's legs gave way, and she sank onto the picnic table bench.

"I would have expected no less. See you there, then?"

"Yes," she breathed. "Oh, my God, Simon. Yes." Then, "Oh, my God, I think I love you."

He laughed and rang off. Marty dropped her head between her knees.

"Who's Simon?" Sophie demanded, knocking on the back of Marty's head, like knocking on a door.

"Marty," Caro whispered. "Martha Jane. What did he say? *What did he say?*"

"Tomorrow. At four. At the Nova Gallery. I'm to bring two pictures with me." She lifted her head. Caro still stood, holding the big grill spatula like a sword. "Pat Wakefield wants to look at two of my paintings."

Caro screamed and threw the spatula. Then she grabbed Marty's hands and pulled her to her feet, whirling her in a frenzied laughing dance.

"Martha Jane!" Sophie cried, and laughed, leaping down to dance around them. "Martha Jane! Martha Jane!"

Saturday morning, Marty found herself unable to summon calm as she did her yoga warm-up. She could not regulate her breathing, couldn't stay with her breath. She couldn't keep her navel back toward her spine. Her arms were tingling in that way that indicated expectation. Sun salutations were just not cutting it.

She gave up and sat down at her easel. The small study of Sophie lay on the table. She moved it gently to the windowsill, where she could see it out of the corner of her eye as she selected her brushes, ran her hands over the tubes of paints in her kit. On the easel, the unfinished painting of the spring and the trough. Today, more greens. The trees were loosely sketched in on the canvas: trunks, branches, leaves. Only suggestions, though, for the more she thought about it, the more she knew that the main feeling of this painting had to come through movement, through light.

Think about it. It was—might be—happening.

Don't think.

"Stay with your breath," she urged herself, stretching her arms up and over her head. The clock in the living room rang; it was still early. Neither Caro nor Sophie were up. She had slept surprisingly well, but she had awakened early and leapt from the blankets with the feeling of expectation she'd missed until lately. She was alive, she was awake, there was paint, she was creating. She looked over again at the painting of Sophie. She was arting. And someone important wanted to look at her efforts.

I am a painter.

Frowning in concentration, she looked out the window at the trees across the road, doing their own version of morning yoga in the smallest of breezes. All the shades of green. But somehow, too sunlit for what she had in mind. She picked up the tube of veridian and hefted it, then set it aside, knowing it to be too vital for her vision. Cadmium. She squeezed a bit out onto the palette, then ran her hand over the tubes until she found the dioxazine purple, and the white. She hummed to herself as she mixed her colors: the green and the purple, the green, the purple, and the white. Then she leaned forward and set her brush to her canvas.

Marty did not look up when the cup of coffee appeared at her elbow. She didn't have the head space to be grateful, nor to think about the catlike quiet of Caro's movement around the kitchen and living room. Her concentration was narrow and pointed, considering every slight line of color, every mix, every gradation. So delicate, so excruciating. After every few strokes, she would lift her head to look out at the ever-moving leaves; she wanted their motion, but not their colors, so she had to force herself to superimpose the memory of the trees beyond the retaining wall over these.

Don't think.

Marty wasn't thinking. She was seeing. It was exhilarating. And hard.

Promptly at four, Marty stood outside the door of Nova and took a deep breath. She had scrubbed the paint off her nails—all except this purple limning her cuticle, she noticed, chagrined—and donned a smart belted summer dress at Caro's insistence. She'd even borrowed Caro's big square sunglasses; more arty, Caro had judged, looking at her in the mirror.

She had the two paintings wrapped in brown paper, and she juggled them as she opened the heavy door to the shopfront. Inside it was cool and dim, track lighting pinpointing several paintings and two alabaster sculptures in the vein of O'Keeffe. Lilies, poppies, all so close up that they might have been anything. She paused, setting the paintings down to slip the sunglasses atop her head and look around.

"Hello?"

"Marty! Is that you?"

Simon appeared from a door hidden behind a wall jutting from the side of the room. Following more sedately behind, the man she knew as Pat Wakefield sailed across the gallery space to take her hand.

"Martha, I take it," he said. "Simon has been raving about you."

Simon looked a little breathless, his face slightly red.

"Let me take these from you. Out to the office, shall we?"

She followed Pat Wakefield through the cool white room. When she passed one of the sculptures, she saw that it wasn't of flowers, as the paintings were, but was of two smooth and stylized human forms, entwined in a dance, or an embrace. She resisted the urge to run her palms over the alabaster surface, just to feel the cool smoothness.

The room he led her into ran the width of the building, and, with the way Danby was built into a hill down to the harbor, was higher above street level than the front; the wide windows overlooked the one-way cobbled street, and the coffee house with the umbrellas on its deck across the way.

"Espresso?" Simon asked. "Capp?"

There was a machine on a granite counter to the left. Deep armchairs took center stage. The desk and other paraphernalia, Marty realized, were off in the corner, as though business was a necessity, and Pat Wakefield could pretend it wasn't.

Marty took the chair Pat indicated. It was extraordinarily comfortable, as was the air conditioning in here as well.

"May I?" He indicated the two paintings.

"Of course." Marty only released her tightly clasped hands to take the cappuccino Simon handed her. He put a small cup of espresso on the low table to the left of Pat, without asking his preference, Marty noticed. He slipped into the armchair between them.

Slowly Pat slipped his long fingers under the tape and pulled it away. He slipped the first painting out and set it on the long shining table between them. It was the one of the lined hands, peeling potatoes in a deep porcelain sink, done in browns, whites and blacks.

"This is what attracted me," Pat said, pointing to the brushwork on the sink. Shadows. The shadows of the hands. The pile of discarded and curling skins. He looked up, his elbows on the knees of his creased slacks, the casual look that probably cost an arm and a leg. He had a single small gold earring in his left ear. "I liked what I saw in the picture Simon brought me, but I thought I'd like to see the actual piece. Details."

"Of course." Marty sipped the cappuccino. It was monstrously hot.

"Let's look at the other, shall we?"

Marty's mouth went dry as he unwrapped the painting of Larry, to set it on the glass table next to the other. She glanced up to see Simon's eyes on her, and his expression was sympathetic.

"I don't usually like portraiture," Pat said. "But this, the way the paint thins out at the edges—like the edges of perception. There's more going on here, but we, the audience, can't know. This boy, too, the way he challenges the viewer. It's striking."

Simon nodded. "There's something out of reach going on between the artist and the subject."

Pat cast him a glance, with a sardonic twist of the lips.

Simon put up his hands. "I'm just saying. What do I know? I'm just a lowly clarinet player."

At last, after an hour's conversation and a second cup of cappuccino, Pat leaned back. "Here's the deal, Miss Ahearne—"

"Marty, please."

"Of course. As Simon might have mentioned to you, I have a group show to mount in a couple of weeks. One of my artists has withdrawn one of the paintings I wanted to hang—sold it right out from under us, which is seriously bad form." His expression was so stony that Marty decided she wouldn't want to cross him. "However, that leaves me with a space I could fill with one of these, if you'd accept gallery representation for it. The other I'd like to keep back, for just in case." He shrugged, smiled. The smile transformed his face. "If those terms are agreeable, I could draw up a standard gallery contract and have you look it over in a couple of days."

Marty could only nod.

Simon beamed as though he were a proud parent.

Caro, predictably, threw her arms around Marty's neck with a screech. Sophie repeated her manic dance, singing *Martha Jane Martha Jane Martha Jane*.

Then realization set in, and Caro drew back. "But—what if someone buys the painting of Larry? We agreed we had to keep that."

Marty shrugged, though the idea tugged at her gut. "That might not even be the one he hangs," she said. "Pat said he didn't care for portraiture. And besides: he's going to hang one of my paintings—that's no guarantee he's going to sell it."

"But what if he does?"

"I'll paint another one."

Truthfully, though, she didn't know if she had another painting of Larry in her.

THIRTY-THREE.

ISABELLA, THEN, WAS not happy the first evening Marty appeared, parking the Jeep near the house and climbing out. From the corner of her eye, Bella noted the way Marty rubbed her hands down her jeans, then straightened her back, as though uncomfortable, as though trying to find courage. Instinctively, Bella touched the stone in her pocket, the one Alaric had given her in the cemetery: courage, indeed. Then, the strange confusion of feeling welled up in her, and she turned her head away. In her lap, she had a block of drawing paper and a pencil, with which she was trying to sketch the action in the machine shed. It was frustrating and hard—she had never been really good with faces, and the engine on the stand was a mystery to her. How did one draw something without knowing anything about what it was, or what it did? And her uncles—they just kept moving: heads, shoulders, arms, feet. She'd get one body part down, and then the next one wouldn't be anywhere close to where it should be. Bella bit her lower lip and tried to be small and inconspicuous in her chair. Maybe Marty would ask a question, get what she needed, and go away.

Bella listened intently, though. She was glad she'd managed to come out earlier and wipe that name off the hood, still leaning against the side wall. With any luck, each of her uncles would think the other had done it.

"Marty!" Uncle Richard's voice, booming and always unnecessarily loud. Alaric had straightened, wiping his hands on a red cloth, and had taken a few steps back into the shadows of the shed: a good sign. "What can we do for you?"

Marty shrugged, tucking her curling hair behind her ear. "Just came to see what progress you're making. Just curious."

"Come look, then," Richard laughed, in the challenging way he had when he was sure you wouldn't understand. Isabella hated that. She hated being condescended to. Richard was her least favorite of her two uncles. Alaric never condescended.

Bella watched from beneath her lowered lashes as Marty approached the engine, her thumbs tucked in the belt loops of her jeans, as though recognizing the invitation to an old west gunfight. Marty winked at Bella on the way by, but then adopted an expression, when she glanced up at Richard, as though she didn't quite take him seriously. Despite herself, Bella inwardly cheered her on. Marty stepped closer, peered at the engine on the stand.

"Pulled the carburetor, I see," she said.

Richard's expression faltered slightly.

Alaric took a silent step closer. Even from her chair, Bella could see his lips twitch.

"Needs to be cleaned," Richard said stiffly.

"I wouldn't doubt it." Marty smiled up at him beatifically, her thumbs still in her belt loops. "My brother was a stickler for maintenance, of course. But I don't know when he last worked on that. The truck's been in storage for awhile."

Richard pulled a rag from his back pocket and started in on his greasy hands. "If you'll excuse me," he said, "I've got to—" He nodded his head toward the house. He didn't even acknowledge Bella when he sailed past the lawn chair.

"The float bowl in that's always interesting," Marty called after him.

When he'd gone into the house with a bang of the screen door, Alaric rolled his eyes. Bella giggled despite herself.

"Pardon me, Alaric," Marty said dryly, "but your brother's a pompous ass."

Alaric rolled his eyes again, then pointed to Bella.

Marty grimaced. "Sorry, Isabella. I've got a garbage mouth. Pretend I never said that."

Bella pressed her lips together. Too late she remembered that she was supposed to be suspicious of Marty and her visit. She cast a glance toward the hood, feeling mildly guilty, where the dirt was smeared from her wiping away the name. It really was too late, because Alaric was dragging the other lawn chair out, to set it near her own. He indicated that Marty should have a seat, and after a moment, she acquiesced. When she settled into the chair, Marty smiled at Bella. *Damn it.*

Alaric went back to probing the valve lifters after casting them a half smile. Pointedly, Bella returned to her sketch pad. For a time she felt Marty's attention shift between the two of them; she would have turned away, but even with the leg braces unlocked, it was awkward.

"Do you take lessons?" Marty asked at last.

Not the question Bella had expected. Adults of her acquaintance usually asked things like *what are you drawing?* And *can I see?* Then they offered critiques as though they knew what she was trying to do and thought they could do better; or they dismissed her efforts with a vague smile and a *that's nice.* Sometimes *that's nice for a girl like you.* The kind of remark that made a person need to smack something: like having leg braces meant you were incapable of *anything*. Then there was Gram, who frowned as though trying to understand, but never said anything.

"I used to," Bella said shortly.

Before. But she wasn't going to say that word.

At the sound of their voices—stilted nature of the conversation notwithstanding–Alaric glanced over and smiled. Maybe nodded. Isabella glared at him, then dropped her eyes to her sketch. Peevishly, she flipped over the page she'd been working on and started a new sheet. This time without him in it.

Richard returned, and cast them a rather uncomfortable smile on the way by. He said something under his breath to Alaric, then with a final glance at the pair of them, he turned his back.

Pompous ass.

Bella liked the sound of that. She tucked the phrase away for later use. Probably not in front of Gram, though. She smirked. Marty was watching. She quickly wiped her expression clear.

"Will you again?" Marty asked. "The lessons? Will you take them again?"

"Maybe." Bella kept her tone carefully non-committal. It suddenly occurred to her that she wanted to take more lessons, wanted to take them *now*. But she wouldn't let Marty know that.

"Are you thinking about working in art when you're out of school?" Marty persisted.

Again, the phrasing surprised her. Not *do you want to be an artist when you grow up?* Bella frowned and shrugged, but she couldn't help thinking about the question. Getting out of school seemed a long way away. She bit her lip and sketched a long narrow line.

"What did you want to do when you grew up?" Bella asked, more to head off any more questions than for a real answer. She tilted her head to the side as she watched Alaric and Richard at work, disentangling some connections, then pulling out a roundish black bit as though delivering a calf. "Did you always want to work for the post office?"

Bella kept her voice innocent, as though there were people in the world—and maybe there were, in Marty's world, but she couldn't imagine why—whose aspirations were to go to work every day for forty years, sorting and delivering bills and flyers so they ended up on Gram's table. Marty looked at first as though she might laugh, but the laugh died, and she suddenly looked as though she wanted to cry instead.

"I wanted to be a painter when I grew up," she said. There was a tinge of sadness in the words, and Bella looked quickly over and away again.

"Did *you* take lessons?"

Marty shook her head. "My parents couldn't afford them. My dad got me supplies—paints and brushes and things—for Christmas and my birthday. And I tried on my own. But I just could never get it right." She took a deep breath. "So I studied in college. It was—magic."

Bella wondered what *it* Marty couldn't get right. She dropped her gaze to her own sketch pad, frowning. She didn't like the way this conversation was going.

"Then I got a job that could pay the mortgage." Marty made a face.

"Do you get your paints out still?" Despite herself, Bella found the answer to this question suddenly seemed of major importance. Like something that mattered.

"I didn't, for a long time." A deep breath. "But I do now."

Not painting. That seemed like some sort of crime. Bella grabbed at the thought hurriedly, trying to use it to bolster the dislike she wanted to feel. Who would want to give this up? Who would let the world take it away?

Then Bella thought of the long stretch of time, *after*—when she hadn't drawn. When she couldn't bring herself to. When it seemed so selfishly wrong to have this thing that she enjoyed, still. Her breath hitched in her throat.

"I'm painting again now. I tried so hard—when my brother died—and my dad got sick. I don't know: I just didn't have the courage. But—" Another deep breath. "I suddenly realized that I couldn't *not*."

Bella measured her breathing. She looked at her uncle turning a piece of the engine in his hands, rubbing it with one of the red cloths that were everywhere in the equipment shed. She wanted to look at Marty, to study her expression, but she didn't want Marty to know she was doing it.

"I'm glad you're here," Mrs. Morgan said. She'd brought a couple of glasses of lemonade for Marty and Isabella. When Marty took the sweating glass with thanks, Georgie noticed the quick glance into the machine shed. "Oh, they don't need anything. Those men have an entire refrigerator in there, hadn't you noticed?"

Marty hadn't, but as if on cue, Richard went to the back of the shed, to return with two bottles, one beer, one water. He handed the water to Alaric. They snapped the caps off, took long drinks, and then, intent on the work, set the bottles aside on the tool bench. Alaric indicated something Marty could not see, and Richard handed him a tool she did not recognize. They both bent back over the engine on the repair stand. Tom Petty sang about being on the Old King's Road.

Georgie leaned in toward Marty. "When you're set, call me, and I'll come for Isabella," she said, her voice low.

Marty nodded, and Georgie set off, back toward the house.

"She doesn't have to whisper," Isabella complained once she

had gone. She rolled her eyes in the semi-darkness. "I know she's going to want to wash me and put pajamas on me and send me to bed by nine o'clock."

Marty cocked her head.

A quick sketch of something Marty couldn't quite see. "She pretends nine o'clock is my bedtime," Isabella said. "But it's really hers."

The aggrieved tone had Marty biting her lip to keep from laughing. Sometimes, she thought, Isabella said things that made her seem older than her years; then suddenly, the twelve-year-old came roaring out again.

"When is your bedtime, then?" Marty asked.

"Nine."

This time Marty could not contain the chuckle; then she noticed the pained expression on Isabella's face, as though the girl had suddenly remembered something. "I'm sorry," she gulped quickly. "What is it?"

"That's what time it—*was*," Isabella said. "With—my Mom and Dad." She turned her face away and was staring up at the evening sky, blinking. A star twinkled on the horizon.

This was the first time this evening Isabella had mentioned her parents to Marty, who now held her breath. It was a crack in the ice. She wasn't sure what to do about it, so she waited. When nothing else was forthcoming, she lifted her sweaty glass to her lips. The lemonade was sour enough to make her pucker slightly. When she looked over again, Isabella, too, was drinking.

"You must miss them so," Marty said. She thought of her own father, the pipe clamped between his teeth long after he was allowed to smoke it; she thought of the feeling of safety she had had, as a child, when he lifted her in his arms and called her *Martha Jane*. She was overwhelmed by a sudden feeling of longing, of knowing that one person in all the world who loved her unconditionally was gone. An emptiness opened up inside her like a sinkhole, and she gasped. Then she took another quick drink of lemonade to cover the feeling.

"I don't want to talk about them," Isabella said shortly.

In the face of her own grief, the thing Marty thought might bring them to some common ground, it was like a slap.

THIRTY-FOUR.

Though Caro didn't recognize the number on the screen of her cell phone, it did have a New York area code. Well, she knew two people now with 917 numbers, so she thought she'd take a chance on it not being a telemarketer.

"Caro, hi."

Definitely not a telemarketer.

"Nate. How are you?" She immediately felt foolish: did she sound like a groupie? And then: did she sound like someone who got piss-eyed last time she met him?

He laughed. "Listen, I thought you might do me a favor?"

Caroline Pond, being asked for a favor by *the* Nathan Waring. She pushed her desk chair away from her keyboard and leaned back. Then sat up again, suddenly wary. "That depends entirely on what kind of favor."

Again he laughed. He had to be aware how attractive that laugh was. "Now you're sounding as suspicious as your friend Marty."

Caro opened her mouth to retort, but he cut her off.

"Nothing nefarious, I promise. It's like this. I really need to get a feel for this place, so I can program for the Rep next summer. What people like, what they don't like. What kind of a place it is, if you know what I mean."

She almost felt disappointed. "Surely some of the people at the Rep could show you around. Take you to visit the mucky-mucks and all that."

"Been there, done that," Nate dismissed that suggestion airily. "Met the mayor of Danby, the head of the Chamber of Commerce, the guy who runs the art gallery, a whole bunch of others." He cleared his throat. "I thought you might be able to show me some of the less-than-official things about the area. Where real people go, what real people do for fun. That sort of thing."

"You want me to show you the town, as they say."

"As they say."

Caro drew in a breath. "Is this a date?"

Nate laughed. "You want a date? I'll buy you a drink."

Now she felt herself flush again. She really did sound all gushy, like a groupie. "I'll buy my own, thanks."

"Ooh, prickly."

Caro glared at her shadowy reflection in the computer monitor. "When do you want to do this, then?"

He still sounded as though her reactions were giving him endless amusement. "When's good for you?"

Now she frowned, thinking. "I'll have to check with Marty, see if she can watch Sophie. Can I get back to you?"

"Soon? Thanks."

She was left staring at the cell phone in her hand.

THIRTY-FIVE.

Tonight when Marty settled into the chair beside Isabella in the yard outside the shed, she could feel the girl's eyes on the reusable grocery bag. Isabella said nothing, after the curt nod. Marty took a deep breath. She hadn't really expected anything. Yet.

"I've brought dessert," she said, leaning forward to make a big deal out of rummaging in the Hannaford's bag.

Isabella still didn't evince any interest. She was watching her uncles tear apart something unmentionable on the engine. Richard would murmur, Alaric gesture, Richard murmur again, all against a soundtrack of ELO. There was no sign of Howard this evening. "Alaric," Isabella shouted over the music, "Marty's brought you dessert."

He glanced over, made a face, held up his grease-blackened hands.

"Actually," Marty corrected, "I brought some for you, too. And for me. Richard, if he wants some."

She saw Isabella's eyes dart sideways, then back again. *Gotcha.* Now she pulled out a whoopie pie and offered it. "Try this, would you? It's a new recipe."

For a moment Marty thought Isabella would refuse, but

then she took the pie gingerly. Like a bomb.

"Am I the guinea pig, then?"

"Oh, I am, too," Marty said cheerily. She pulled another from the bag for herself, and peeled at the waxed paper wrapping. "This recipe uses butter cream for the frosting, and I'd always used the marshmallow filling."

Isabella looked suspicious as she bit into the whoopie pie, leaving small even tooth marks in the chocolate cake. Apparently finding that she wasn't being poisoned, she took another, larger bite. Marty followed suit.

"The problem with these, no matter what filling you use, is that you always need a drink with them." Now Marty withdrew a bottle of root beer and twisted off the cap. "Want one?"

Isabella nodded. Marty handed her a bottle, and drew out a second for herself. They ate and drank in silence—companionable only in that Isabella seemed to forget to be sullen and wary. Every once in a while, Alaric would glance over from the shed, his expression curious.

I'm going to win her over, Marty thought stubbornly. The thought made her smile inwardly. She had no idea why it was so important, but it was. She took another swig from the root beer bottle.

Isabella had taken the last few bites of her whoopie pie, and licked the sticky cake from her fingers, before Marty was even half-done. She folded up the waxed paper carefully, and tucked it into her front pocket.

"Oh!" Marty exclaimed after a moment, as though she had just remembered. "I've got something else in here for you that I thought you might want to try out." She set her bottle on the ground by the leg of the chair, and then bent to the bag again. This time she drew out the long narrow box of pastels, and the fresh block of heavy drawing paper.

Isabella had attempted to go back to rigid aloofness; but Marty could feel her attention being inexorably drawn to the art materials. *Gotcha,* she thought again.

"I hope you don't mind," Marty said carefully, "but I saw the picture—the one you'd sketched of the lilacs on your uncle's table?—and after we talked the other night, I thought maybe you'd be interested in trying these out. Or maybe you already have some?"

She didn't think so; wouldn't Isabella have been using them if she did?

After a long moment, Isabella too set her root beer aside to take the pad and box into her hands. She set them on her lap and slowly opened the box: two rows of stubby pastel crayons lay in front of her, graduating through the colors and the shades of the spectrum. Marty watched out of the corner of her eye, but clenched her fingers together before her, hoping. Isabella reached out a hesitant finger and touched first one color, then another.

Richard circled around to the back of the shed, on a quest for some tool not available inside, but when Alaric made a move to join them outside, Marty held up a hand slightly to forestall him. He raised his eyebrows, and she gently shook her head, then lowered the hand to her knee. *Wait.*

Still Isabella had to remain cool; that much was obvious—she couldn't go from territorial and suspicious to won over just like that. "I think I could do a couple of things with these," she allowed slowly. She glanced over to see how Marty was taking her reaction.

I have many, many years more of playing it cool than you do, little sister, Marty thought sardonically. When she looked up, Alaric winked at her, and she felt her cheeks warm. She looked away quickly, grateful for the failing evening light.

"Let me hold the box for you," Marty offered.

The crayon Isabella chose when she opened the pad was an off-white, but she quickly changed her mind and chose a slightly darker tan. Her first lines were slow, somewhat hesitant, as she tried to get a feel for how the pastels left their marks. Marty leaned back and looked up at the sky, where the stars were beginning to peek out. She felt rather than saw Isabella choose another color. She did not look to see what Isabella was drawing.

It was Richard, returning with a socket set, who came over and whistled before Isabella had a chance to hide her work.

"That's good, Bella," he said. He peered closer. Isabella shrank in her chair, embarrassed. "That's really good." Before either of them could say anything, he turned and beckoned to Alaric. "Come and see this, Lar."

"It's not ready," Isabella protested, her voice unnaturally high. "It's not done."

She sounded desperate, as though she wanted to hide. Or to run away, which was impossible.

Alaric came slowly from the shed, wiping his hands on a rag; he was frowning, but not, Marty realized, at Isabella, but at his brother. He put a hand on Richard's upper arm, ostensibly to get around him, but the move effectively brought him between Richard and Isabella. He leaned forward, and the expression on Isabella's face when she met his gaze was almost heartbreaking.

"I don't want you to look at it," she said in a small voice.

Alaric backed up, held up his hands. *Okay.*

"Why not?" demanded Richard. "Geez, Bella, I didn't know you could draw. That was Alaric! It was really good! Why don't you show him?"

Alaric glanced Marty's way and rolled his eyes, then turned to his brother and touched his shoulder again, a slight push this time. He jerked his head toward the engine. When Richard was slow to move, he jerked his head again. Impatiently. There was a frown between his eyes. They moved off.

Marty realized she'd been holding her breath.

"I won't look," she said quietly. "I understand."

Isabella only shook her head. "It doesn't matter. It wasn't any good anyway." With a swift angry motion, she tore the page from the pad and crumpled it into a tight ball. She dropped it into the chair beside her. "The light's gone, anyway."

And in fact, the night had fallen in the sudden way it had, as though soft black cotton batting surrounded them. The lights on the peaks of the outbuildings had begun to come on. There was a creak from the kitchen door, and Georgie approached, her footsteps crunching on the grave.

"Time to head in, Isabella," she called. "Say goodnight to your uncles, and to Marty." The question from all the other nights had gone from her voice; after the past couple of visits, Marty had become a fixture in the evening yard.

Marty closed the box of pastels, and waited while Bella tightened her leg braces and struggled to her feet. She slipped the box and pad back into the grocery bag and handed it to Georgie. "These are Isabella's. A gift."

"Thank you, dear," Georgie said. She put a hand on her granddaughter's shoulder and led her toward the house.

Marty waited until the door shut again behind them before picking up the root beer bottles. She emptied them out in the grass at the side of the shed, then set them inside the barrel full of returnables. Only then did she retrieve the crumpled ball of paper. Making certain no one was looking—no one peering out from the downstairs bedroom window—she picked it open gingerly, furtively.

The light from the shed fell across her lap and the crumpled page. She could make out the curve of jawline, the fall of dark hair over the forehead, the glint in the eyes. Only the shoulders were suggested, without detail.

It was recognizably Alaric. And as Richard had so clumsily announced, it was good. In just a few strokes with only a handful of colors, Isabella had captured the wry expression of her uncle.

THIRTY-SIX.

BELLA THUNKED IN through the open door—he had heard, on the edge of his thoughts, her measured metallic progress across the yard, but had made no real note of it, so hard was he concentrating on the pen in his hand.

"Whatcha writing?" she demanded. She shed one of the crutches, and with her free hand she opened the drawer at the end of the counter, from which she extracted the pad and the box of pastels. Then she settled into the chair across from him.

Alaric covered up the name he'd written so painstakingly, fighting back all his misgivings, but not before her quick glance had fallen on it.

"Marty," she said aloud. He prepared himself for the barrage of questions he knew would be forthcoming. Still, that was far better than the days when she had avoided him.

Alaric sighed. He turned the paper face down. Pointedly.

"Are you embarrassed?" Bella had opened the box of pastels and now selected a pale blue stick. The ends of many, he noticed, were already worn slightly.

He tilted his head and looked at her, unblinkingly.

"She's kind of pretty," she allowed, almost unwillingly.

Probing, he knew. It wasn't a question; she didn't look up

for an answer. She examined the blue, and then set it aside for a darker shade. She could be as pointed as he: she steadfastly studied the pastels, her pad, the pastels again. Never up. Never at him. The pastels and pad Marty had given her, which had apparently won her grudging forbearance, and for which he found himself grateful.

Alaric waited.

"You were friends in school, right? Because she's the sister of—" she glanced up sideways, hesitant to finish the sentence. He knew she had wiped the name from the hood of the Bronco. Now she licked her lips. "Larry." A near whisper.

Larry.

Everyone tiptoed around Larry.

Alaric took a deep breath and let it out slowly, for once willing the synesthesia. The name felt different today: softer. He looked down at his palms.

"I know you miss him. He was your best friend. We—talked about this."

Now she was watching, from the corner of her eye. Gauging his reaction. Alaric nodded.

"Does she miss him, too?"

He felt the lump forming in his throat. A potato, all knobs and lumps, unable to be swallowed down. He nodded again.

"Does she cry?" This time the rest of the question remained unspoken. But Alaric knew what Bella was asking. After that night at this table, he knew she meant *does she cry like you do?*

He thought for a moment. He thought of Marty's hard face at her father's funeral. He thought of her stiffness and her anger when she had come to plead with him to save the Bronco, when she had spoken of her mother's desire to junk the truck. Not one tear, he realized, and he found himself turning that idea over and over in his hands, feeling its weight, its texture. It had sharp edges. He shook his head, frowning.

"She's like you, then."

He looked at her, held his hand out, palm up. *Huh?*

"She's so sad she can't cry," Bella said slowly, as though thinking it through. "And you're so sad you can't talk."

For a while they were silent. Well, she was, anyway, seemingly waiting for him to react, waiting to see whether she might have crossed an invisible boundary. Again. She was glaring down at her blank page as though waiting for it to tell her what to draw with the blue pastel she clutched so tightly between her fingers that he thought she might snap it in two.

Bella's words were like little probes beneath his skin, itching, bordering on painful. They were the words of someone who had thought carefully about his sadness. More carefully, perhaps, than all the doctors at Walter Reed, or at Togus. And yet—it was an observation from his niece, not a judgment. That seemed strange. Everyone judged. No one said *this is why you're sad* and left it at that. Everyone told you to get over it after all this time.

Her observation extended to Marty, too, a person she had known for a relatively short while. Alaric knew instinctively, though, that she was right. Marty's sadness, like his, was coiled down so deep inside that it blocked something vital. He glanced across the table at Bella where she still glared at the paper. He wondered what the sadness kept her from; but maybe, because her injury and its resulting limitations were so physical, her psyche felt no need to take anything else away.

He needed a drink. He got up to draw them tumblers of water.

"Do you want to ask her out on a date?" Bella asked after a while, her voice surprisingly bland. "She *is* kind of pretty, after all."

Alaric frowned at her, drawing his brows down as far as he could get them to go. These questions, which he had expected as soon as she'd spotted Marty's name on the pad, made him uncomfortable. He really didn't want to talk about Marty anymore. He wanted to think about her, and about Larry, the haunting around which their lives turned.

Now Bella began, finally, to sketch with the pastel, swooping strokes of cobalt along the bottom third of the page. She seemed to have come to some decision, or perhaps the paper had told her what it wanted her to create. "You could go to the movies," she suggested. "Girls like movies."

Alaric shook his head.

"She must like you." Bella switched out the cobalt for a deep gray, to highlight the edges of some of her bold blue strokes. "She gave you that truck."

Alaric remembered again Marty's straight back, her determined shoulders, all of which had been contradicted by her shaking voice. But no, Marty had not cried. Not a single tear.

She was too sad.

Suddenly Alaric flipped the pad over and slapped the top sheet back against her prying eyes. He scribbled quickly on the new page, then spun the paper quickly so she could read it.

What would you do if she said yes?

Now Isabella had gone back to the original light blue. She highlighted the swoops and curls on her page, and he saw now that she was working on the ocean. There was no shore. Only waves. Big waves, overpowering waves. No safety.

"I would be jealous," she said after a moment. "Not much. A little bit. Because I guess I do like her. Some." Bella held up the pastel for a moment, her freckled face creased in a frown. A pastel from the box Marty had brought to her. "But I like you more. I didn't think I would, because I used to think—" she cast a quick look from beneath her long lashes; more testing of the waters as it were—"that you were *weird*. You know. Before I knew you."

Fine one to talk. He drew a big smiley face next to the words.

She punched him in the arm. The pastel went flying.

"Now look what you made me do," she said.

Alaric stood to retrieve the pale blue pastel crayon, where it had rolled under the futon at the far side of the narrow room. First, though, he pointed to the pad, and to her, and slapped a hand down on it.

Bella rolled her eyes. "Of course not."

He didn't quite trust her. He kept an eye on her as he retrieved the pastel.

"Just write her the letter," she said. "I'll get over it. I mean, you two have a lot in common. Carburetors and stuff. Ask her out." She made an innocent face. "To a monster truck show."

Alaric shook his head. Then he smiled, somewhat ruefully. Funny how his best friend, suddenly, the person who knew him best, was a twelve-year-old girl. He took a sip from his water glass, watching as she feathered the edges between the pale blue, the cobalt, and the gray with the edge of her finger.

THIRTY-SEVEN.

TWILIGHT, IN THE Morgans' farmyard. The day's heat had not abated. Marty wiped the sweat beading her hairline at the back of her neck. Tom Petty was making some hard promises from inside the equipment shed, where Alaric and Richard bent and moved around the engine on the heavy duty repair stand, as though dancing. Richard wore a bandanna, rolled and tied around his head, to keep the sweat at bay. Only a couple of things left to do, Richard had said; Alaric had rolled his eyes.

"Bats," Isabella murmured from the chair next to hers. She pointed up to the barn's peak, where the tiny creatures flitted, black shadows against the blaze of the spotlight.

Overhead, clouds rippled across the sky, dark against the fading light. The air was still, and humid, but it hadn't rained for days. Marty hoped it would rain overnight, not the least to lower the fire danger, but it didn't seem likely. Tease and back off—that had been the way of it for most of this spring. It would be summer in another week. The spring at the trough would die back to a trickle. She hadn't finished the painting yet, though it was working; there was still something missing.

"You like bats?" Marty asked idly. She shifted in her plastic lawn chair. Both had been set outside the shed for them again;

they'd been expected. As though their arrival after dinner to watch Alaric and Richard work at rebuilding the Bronco's engine had become a habit.

"You don't?" Isabella had her block of paper; Marty held the box of pastels open on her lap, within easy reach. Isabella doodled little bats, flying, hanging upside down, close-ups of their tiny rodent faces.

Marty shrugged. "It's not dislike," she mused, glancing up toward the spotlight again. "It's wariness, I guess you could call it. Startle reflex. They move so quickly. They zip by so closely."

Isabella didn't look up from her sketching. Her bats all had an endearing quality to them. "But they don't get caught in people's hair. That's a myth. They've got that echolocation that keeps them far enough away not to do that." She turned the page, started in with her drawing again. "Alaric told me that."

Marty could imagine Alaric and his *telling*. The combination of gesture, and scribbling quick words on the edges of Isabella's drawing paper. A little spurt of envy caught her by surprise— that Isabella and Alaric understood each other so well.

"I don't worry about that," Marty said. "It's the sound that startles me. The *whirring*. It's the way I'm not afraid of snakes— but the suddenness of them always makes me jump."

"I guess I can see that," Bella allowed after a moment. She looked up and smiled. The unexpectedness of it took Marty's breath away.

Alaric had been working on the engine for some time now, every evening after supper, after the work of the farm day had passed; the meaty work was nearly done. Sometimes there was little to do, as he waited on the delivery of a part. Sometimes Richard came out to help; sometimes their father appeared, if it was an off-day for the Red Sox, joining them in a chair, but more frequently leaning against the doorjamb, the better to critique his sons' work.

"I didn't think the poor thing was that bad off," Marty had said, one of the first evenings she had stopped by to see how it was going.

Just want to do it right, Alaric had written in the small notebook he now kept in his shirt pocket. He didn't add *for Larry*, but the way he looked up at her with that distant gaze made the unspoken words obvious.

One of the evenings, Marty had stopped at her mother's to drop off some eggs on the way to the farm, and to report the progress of the Bronco restoration.

"You two left the back garage doors open," Sylvia had complained.

Stung, Marty had apologized and left.

Tonight, Alaric didn't even make a sound when he hurt himself; the only way they knew was because he jerked back away from the engine and the stand, gripping one hand with the other, his lips pulled back over his teeth in a grimace. He doubled over.

"Shit," Richard exclaimed sharply, jumping back. "What is it, bro?" He dropped his wrench on the dirt floor and twisted around the stand. "Let me see it."

When Alaric straightened, he glanced out at Isabella, and turned quickly away. But not before Marty saw the blood running over his wrist and along his arm.

"Shit," Richard said again. He pulled another bandanna from his rear pocket and grabbed his brother's arm.

Marty felt Isabella, beside her, go very still. She'd seen the blood, too. The pad slid to the dirt, and she began to tremble. Marty set the box of pastels aside hurriedly, and turned to her. *Alaric's blood.* "Bella?" she said. Isabella's wide eyes were fixed on her uncle. On the blood she had seen on his fingers, running into his palm, and down his wrist. "Isabella? What is it?"

The shaking grew more violent. Marty placed a hesitant hand on Isabella's shoulder, and then, feeling no resistance, leaned to gather her awkwardly into her arms. Isabella buried her face in Marty's shoulder, gulping desperately, a drowning person gulping for air.

"Alaric?" Marty shouted, panicked.

He turned back now, his hand bound up in his brother's handkerchief, his eyes darting between her and Isabella. Quickly he brushed past Richard and rushed to them, dropping to one knee in front of the chairs. He lifted a questioning hand.

"I don't know," Marty cried, attempting to bring her voice under control. She rubbed Isabella's narrow back slowly, trying to calm the shaking, which had now escalated to sobs. "She saw the—she saw your hand, Alaric, and this happened."

Alaric closed his eyes and dipped his chin, then put a hand on his niece's head. When he opened his mouth, Marty thought—*this is it.* But nothing came out. There were still no words. The anguish in his expression was nearly palpable.

Marty couldn't bear to look. She bent her head to Isabella's. "It's all right," she whispered. "It's all right, Isabella. He's right here. Alaric's right here. He's fine."

Still Isabella pressed her face into Marty's shoulder. She could feel the tears dampening her shirt.

"Jesus, Alaric," Richard said, crossing to them. "You need a Band-Aid or something. Let's go in the house."

Alaric looked torn. He glanced from Richard to Isabella.

"There was blood," Isabella said, without lifting her face. Her voice was thick and the words difficult to make out. "I saw the blood. I saw it."

"He's fine," Marty murmured again against the blonde hair.

"Where is he?" Isabella's voice was rising. "Where is he? He was bleeding. I saw it."

It came to Marty at last. Of course. She put a finger beneath Isabella's chin. "Look up, Bella," she ordered. "Look at him. He's right here."

Slowly Bella turned her face, and when she saw her uncle kneeling before her, she released Marty and threw her thin arms around Alaric instead. "Don't go," she sobbed into his neck. "Don't go."

Don't go and never come back.

"You can't bandage that up by yourself," Marty said, her voice still unsteady.

Satisfied at last that Alaric was not going to die from his injury as her parents had done, Bella had scrubbed at her face with the sleeve of her shirt and had allowed herself to be carried into the house by Richard. Not before, however, she threw her arms around Alaric one last time; Marty watched as Alaric, still with the pinched expression, kissed his niece on both cheeks and atop her head. He stood in the darkening farmyard, where the shadows were elongated by the spotlight at the peak of the barn roof, until the kitchen door had banged shut in its frame behind them. He had raised a hand in farewell.

He shrugged now, not meeting Marty's eyes. That stung. It felt like a step backward.

She reached for his hand, where the bandanna was still tied. Then she thought better of it.

"At least let me do that much," she pleaded.

When he made no move, she turned on her heel and walked off toward the stable office. After a moment, she heard his footsteps following. She pulled open the screen door and slapped at the light switch on the wall. The narrow room blazed into light. Leaving him there, she crossed into the tiny bathroom—little more than a closet fitted with a shower, sink, and toilet—and found a washcloth in a basket on the top of the tank. Inside the medicine cabinet, she found some antibiotic ointment and a box of bandages in varying sizes, so she grabbed those as well.

Alaric stood just inside the door, where she had left him.

"Well, sit down," Marty ordered roughly. "Let's do this."

She tossed the ointment and bandages onto the table. Alaric moved awkwardly, as though he'd forgotten how to do it, and stumbled more than sat in one of the dining chairs. His face still held a ghost of the anguish Marty had read there out in the yard. It was still hard to look at. Instead, she turned away and filled the sink, then soaked and wrung out the washcloth.

"Can you undo that?" she asked, turning back to indicate the bandanna tied around his left hand. She waited while he worked the knot—fortunately not a very tight one—with the fingers of his right hand. The bandanna, red deepened by blood, fell away to the floor.

When Marty first began to dab at the mess on his two fingers, she half-expected him to pull away. Hell, she had expected him to send her away when she had offered to bandage the cuts, which was why she'd turned and let herself in before he could. Now she wiped at the blood gingerly, trying to see how deep the cuts were. He held perfectly still, his eyes closed, as though willing himself elsewhere.

"How on earth did you do this, anyway?" she demanded. Not expecting an answer, and if he wanted to write one out right now, he probably couldn't anyway. "We were talking about bats, Bella and I, and then suddenly there was blood."

She could see the cuts now, and though they still oozed a bit of blood, they weren't too deep. Marty probed a bit along the edges with her fingers, and Alaric winced. "Sorry," she said quickly. "I don't think you need stitches, anyway. They don't look that bad." She turned back to the sink and rinsed the washcloth out; the water swirled pinkish red. Wringing the cloth out again, she took his hand and dabbed a bit more. Then she reached for the yellow and blue tube of antibiotic cream. "I think that's as clean as I can make it," she said, and squirted some of the cream onto each of the cuts. "I'm going to have to touch them again, so hang on." With a gentle finger, she spread the pasty stuff around until his skin shimmered with it. Finally, with one hand, she opened the box of bandages and shook them out onto the table. There were two fairly large ones. She ripped them open and lay them, one after another, on his fingers.

He still had his eyes closed.

"You're going to need to get some more big Band-Aids, I guess," she said, leaning back to examine her handiwork. It was then she realized how black with grease his hands were. "Holy cow." She slid the remainder of the bandages back in their box and tucked the lid closed. "Be careful washing your hands. You'd probably better check in with the doctor in the morning, anyway. If your tetanus shot isn't up to date, that stuff will probably kill you."

Marty realized that she was babbling. She had been for a while. Talking herself through the first aid. Alaric had not responded, not even with a gesture, a shrug. She bit her lip, gathering up the bandages and cream and returning them to the medicine cabinet. She couldn't see where he put his dirty laundry—there had to be a basket or something, for him to take his laundry to the house, but a quick glance around didn't locate it. She settled for rinsing the washcloth out yet again, and, after wringing it out the best she could, she draped it over the side of the sink while the water swirled away down the drain.

"Are you going to be okay?" she asked at last.

When he made no indication, she yanked open the end drawer, and pulled out the pad of paper and pen to slam them down on the table.

"Jesus, Alaric! Will you just talk to me?"

For a long moment he looked at her out of his steel gray eyes, and she was surprised by her gut reaction. Then he picked up the pen and wrote quickly.

She was back in the accident.

"Isabella?"

He nodded. Another word. *Scared.* He crossed it out impatiently. *Terrified.*

Marty licked her lips. She pulled out the chair opposite him and lowered herself into it. "I felt that," she said at last. "Her terror. At the sight of—your—blood." She looked up at him, intent. "Does that happen often?" Again she felt the spindly arms around her, holding on for dear life. The narrow back shaking under her hand as she tried to rub some comfort into it.

Alaric shook his head, and shrugged. *Never seen it.*

Marty slumped back against the wall. "Does she see somebody? A counselor or someone?"

This time he nodded. *Appointments.*

Abruptly he got to his feet and opened the cupboard. He took out the two glasses there, and filled them from the sink. His own he drained immediately, then refilled it before bringing them both to the table. He slid one across to her. Marty stared at it for a moment before lifting it to her lips; what she really wanted right now was a stiff drink: a double shot of single malt. If that didn't help, a second one. The gray was leaving Alaric's face; she wondered how he didn't want a drink, as she did. But she didn't ask.

Blood.

"How long—" Marty took a sip, set the glass back down in its damp circle on the tabletop. "How long was she in the car after the accident?"

This time when Alaric winced, the pain was emotional, not physical, she realized. When his answer was slow in coming, Marty was certain she had said the wrong thing, and wished she could take it back. How easy it was to forget that Alaric was not the same person he had been when they were teenagers together, when she could ask anything, say anything. How easy to forget that he was not the same person who had enlisted and gone away at the same time as her brother. Who had not come back.

Larry.

Marty glanced up now, uneasily. She knew they had been assigned to the same duty station after a couple of years apart; she wasn't sure how that had come to pass, but she could still remember that phone call, Larry laughing, Alaric's boisterous shouting in the background. What had happened on that patrol, on that morning, she didn't know. How had Alaric found out? Had he seen? Had he been close enough? Larry's death had taken his voice, but she still had no real idea of the circumstance.

He met her eyes, and looked away again. She felt herself flush.

Again he drew the pad of paper close and wrote. Then he pushed it toward her with a single grease-stained finger.

Don't know. Long time.

He grimaced, grabbed the pad as though afraid he'd lose his nerve.

They were already dead

Long pause. She could hear his breathing. She could hear the clock above the sink, ticking away the seconds. She could feel her own heart pounding, trapped inside her rib cage.

When they cut her out of the car.

When they had parted, Marty found herself sitting in the Jeep, staring at the downstairs bedroom window, where a dim light burned. Nightlight? It wouldn't be surprising if Isabella needed to sleep with a light on. Twelve-year-old girls are not meant to be present at the deaths of their parents. Twelve-year-old girls' parents are not, for the most part, meant to die. Again Marty felt the spasms in her arms as Isabella shook. She touched the shoulder of her shirt where the girl's tears had soaked through. *Poor kid,* she thought, and realized just how futile and trite and meaningless that thought was. She pressed the clutch, turned the key, and headed toward home, where, she determined, she would not sleep herself before she looked in on Sophie, and kissed the little girl's flushed cheek where she lay on her pillow.

THIRTY-EIGHT.

"**D**OWN HERE," CARO directed, indicating the path that cut through the rugosas at the end of the parking lot with the flashlight on her phone. The rose bushes had grown up since she'd come here last, and now the path was barely visible. She shook her head at the laziness of today's high schoolers, and regretted it when the dizziness washed over her; giving Nate the real-people tour of the waterfront bars might have been a mistake. "Pull your sleeves down, or you're going to be sorry." The sun was sinking, the shadows reaching out to her right and the bay.

Caro hadn't clambered down this path in a long time—how many years? With Sophie, she stayed further back, at the park's sandy beach; with Pete, she had never come down at all. Even now, as she listened to Nate scramble and curse behind her, she felt guilty, as though giving up state secrets. He was an outsider, after all. This path, and the rocky cove beyond—both of which left the confines of the park and crossed into private ownership—were the secret places from the days of the four of them: Car and Mar, Lar and Lar. But he'd prised the information out of her over a drink at Libra. He'd wanted, he'd told her, to see the Painter's Springs insiders knew. He'd said it with a smirk she didn't quite like, but made an effort to ignore.

When was the last time she'd been down to the Bird with the others? That was a stupid question, and she chided herself for even thinking it. She knew exactly when: the night before the guys had shipped out. They'd stayed out way too late, had drank way too much, albeit illicitly. It hadn't made seeing Larry and Alaric off in Bangor any easier the next day.

As she and Nate followed the overgrown path toward the rocky beach, Caro noted the mist midway out on the bay, obscuring the Blue Hill peninsula across the way. Rolling in or rolling out? She breathed deeply of the salt water scent.

"Is that fog?" Nate asked breathlessly. He put a hand on her hip, to steady himself, and she stepped away.

"Sea mist."

"Same difference."

Not really, but he wouldn't understand the difference if she explained, so she didn't bother. Caro didn't turn at the sound of his sudden thrashing in the brambles behind her; she didn't look back when he swore again. She'd warned him about the roses, hadn't she? Now she jumped down the last few feet and waited.

"I'm going to break my legs," Nate protested. After a moment, he, too, leapt down, landing heavily beside her.

"You're kind of spleeny, aren't you?" Caro asked. She didn't wait for an answer, but turned to head along the beach, skirting the large rocks glaciers had tossed haphazardly about. Ahead of her loomed the Bird, the rock taller than she was, that sat at the tide line a couple hundred yards from where the path debouched. She steadfastly refused to look back, but she heard Nate following, his steps cautious on the stony beach. On the far side of the Bird was the old fire pit, a ring of stones around a depression filled with scraps of charred driftwood. She flopped down beside it. From this side it was easy to see the grooves that made the monolith look like nothing more than a fisted hand with a middle finger erect. The guys had called it the Bird, and the name had stuck.

For a moment Nate stood awkwardly, and when she did not instruct him, he settled near—but not too near. He clasped his arms around his knees and gazed out at the mist on the water. "Is the tide coming in or going out?"

"Going out," she said. The sound of the water washing in and out filled her with a strange melancholy. She didn't like it.

It had been a mistake to bring him down here. Caro thought back to their last fire here, the four of them singing to the songs on Larry's CD player until the batteries had worn down. She closed her eyes and listened to the hushing of the waves against the stones. She should have come down here by herself before she brought someone else. There were too many ghosts: ghosts of their pasts, because not a one of them was the same person they had been, and Larry was dead.

"What?" Nate asked.

Caro had not realized she'd made a sound. She shook her head.

"It's going to get cold when that mist comes ashore."

"It's not coming ashore."

"How do you know?"

Caro opened her eyes again to look out on the retreating water. "I've lived here all my life," she reminded him. "I know how this works."

A trio of seagulls landed at the waterline, their shadows elongated, and they picked their way gingerly through the seaweed-covered rocks. She watched them idly, wondering if they were friends of Matt Copeland's seagull. Three of them. There were three of *them*, now: she, Marty, and Alaric. Would Alaric come down here? Had he already? He had returned from that last deployment so different from when he had left. He *looked* different to her, though maybe not to Marty. To Caro he looked at the same time both harder, and more frail.

"You're thinking some deep thoughts," Nate said. She glanced over, and saw him brush some windswept hair off his brow.

"You look like you're posing for *Gentlemen's Quarterly,*" she shot back.

"Implying I'm shallow?" He smiled at her, but his blue gaze seemed calculating.

"Not everything is about you," Caro said. And sighed. This was too hard. She thought she'd wanted some casual flirtation. Why not? *Have a little fun,* Marty had urged, packing up Sophie to take her to visit the farm. "Listen. I think probably coming down here was a mistake. We should head back."

"We just got down here. And that was hard work for a city boy like me." When she didn't respond, Nate kept on. "What's wrong with this place?" He waved a hand around. "It's probably frequented, maybe by a younger generation of you and your friends. I mean, this is where the high school kids come, isn't it?"

Caro shrugged, uncomfortable. It might be a blessing if some high school kids showed up now. "It used to be. When my friends were back in high school, you're right. It might be still. I don't really know."

Nate kicked at the stone circle, dislodging one.

Caro leaned forward slowly and replaced the stone.

"Somebody's obviously been making fires here since you came down as a teenager."

"Obviously." So maybe the high school kids weren't such slackers after all.

One of the seagulls lifted off, nearly backwards, and the other two, not to be outdone, joined it on an updraft. They climbed upward into the remains of the sun, circled over the Bird, and flew back toward the point and the sandy beach in the park on the other side.

Nate's sigh was long and pronounced. "Look. I don't get why you're being so prickly. I'm just trying to get a feel for my neighbors, for the place I'm spending my summer. Make some friends, maybe, for next summer. We can go back up if you like. It's not a big deal. But I was hoping you could talk to me a bit more about Painter's Springs. About what it's like here."

Caro sighed as well, her hands sifting the small round stones that made up this curve of cove. Stones that had been washed out and back, grated against one another, for ages upon ages of tides. It was a metaphor, really. Because isn't that what they did here, in the Springs? Grated along against each other for all of their lives. She looked down at her hands, at the stones. These were probably much the same rounded rocks she had sat on with Marty, and Larry, and Alaric. A lifetime ago.

"We used to come down here, even before high school," Caro found herself saying, rattling the rounded stones through her fingers, "to hunt for buried treasure. Marty and me. We were just kids. We'd ride our bikes, hide them in the bushes just beyond the lighthouse."

Nate leaned forward, his arms again across his knees, his eyes on the receding tide. They were in shadow now, only the tideline painted by the sun behind them. He pretended not to notice the catch in Caro's voice, her one small sniffle, and for that she was grateful. "How old were you?"

"I don't know." Caro shrugged. "Eight? Nine? We dug all over this beach and never found a thing. Except a rusty jackknife. Once we found that. And buried it again, in case other pirates came and tried to steal our treasure. I later found out that it was Marty's brother Larry's knife, but when I tried to dig it up again, for him, I couldn't remember where we'd buried the damned thing."

Which was only partially a lie. Years later she had found it, under a chunk of white quartz up under the edge of the bluff, when she'd left them all at the fire and gone off to pee in the darkness. She'd never told anyone, not even Marty, but had slipped it into her pocket. Later, back home, she'd put it in the bottom drawer of the jewelry box her grandmother had given her, the one that played "The Shadow of Your Smile." Every once in a while she'd take it out—still—and turn it over in her hands. The much-traveled, much storied jackknife. If they'd originally found it when they were nine, that meant Larry had lost it when he was around eleven.

She hiccuped a little. Caro remembered his face, then, Larry at eleven, the freckles, the nose that turned up at the end, like Marty's did, like their mother's did. She remembered how he and Alaric would hide in the bushes and throw chokecherries at them as they rode their bikes past, the berries leaving little red spots like blood stains on their shirts. How the boys would run off into the trees, down one of the many paths that crisscrossed the woods on the point. She'd hated them both then, as had Marty, in the way all little girls hated their older brothers and their friends.

"Now you're just looking sad." Nate's voice had softened, and she felt her face grow warm. "I'm sorry. Maybe we *should* go back up. You're right—this was probably a bad idea." But he didn't sound as though he wanted to.

Caro shrugged. "I haven't been down here in a long time. I hadn't realized it was so full of ghosts."

"Every place is full of ghosts," Nate said, his voice low.

Caro wondered if he was right. She wondered what would happen if she retraced her steps with Pete? Was the waterfront bar where they'd met—the one she'd carefully avoided this afternoon and evening with Nate—haunted? The idea of visiting that place, and possibly finding out, had made her skin crawl; so probably it was. Full of absolutely evil spirits. Pete and his dark eyes, for which she'd fallen. Or rebounded.

She drew in a sharp breath. The thought made her nauseated. Disgusted with herself.

"Oh, dear. Now you're angry about something." Nate's laugh had a steely edge. He shifted his seat slightly. "I'm sorry, Caroline. You have such an expressive face. Every thought runs across it waving great big flags."

"I don't know what you're talking about." Still, she looked away hurriedly, toward the retreating waterline, now fully in shade. The shadow of the bluff had long since crawled over and away from them. The sea mist had gone, and across the bay, the peninsula shimmered like a mirage. She did not want him reading any more of her thoughts and feelings on her face. Night was drawing on while they sat there, talking. Arguing. She risked a glance in his direction; soon it would be impossible to see his face. Not that she would be able to read anything in *his* expression. He was more guarded, and she didn't know what expressions meant anyway. That had always been part of her problem.

"We should make a fire," he suggested now. "I'm getting cold."

"The mist is gone," she pointed out. "And you just said we ought to leave."

"I'm a changeable sort. You'll just have to forgive me." Nate clambered to his feet. "But you don't forgive easily, do you, Caroline?" He wandered back up toward the bluff, gathering dried seaweed, and a handful of bleached twigs lying well above the flood tide mark. Then he carried his armload back and dumped it unceremoniously into the stone fire circle.

"Not like that." Caro frowned. "Get those out of there." When he wandered off in search of more, she let out a breath. "I'm finding it difficult to forgive you for this mess." She crawled forward to scrape the twigs to the side, then pulled the half-burned piece of driftwood out of the depression. Carefully she relaid the fire, thinking of all the times they'd done it together, the four of them. *The official Boy Scout way*: the way Larry and Alaric had learned as kids at Camp Roosevelt. A teepee of twigs, stuffed full of tinder, surrounded by a log cabin of larger pieces of driftwood. "Give me a match."

Nate handed her a lighter, then leaned back on his heels, arms across his chest, implying total disbelief at her ability to make a fire. Caro spun the flint wheel a few times until the flame burst out, then reached in to touch it to the tinder. In a moment there were tiny wisps of smoke curling up into the air, and the fire caught and grew, up through the teepee. Larry would be proud. She tossed the lighter back to Nate.

"City boy," she scoffed.

"Any other talents I should know about?" Nate asked. "Swimming?" He gestured toward the water. "Ever give a thought to skinny dipping?"

"No."

"Too cold?"

"Except in the height of summer, which this is not," she pointed out.

"Maybe you're too scared."

"Of what?"

"Of getting naked with me."

Caro turned to look him up and down in the flickering light of the little fire. "You *are* crude, aren't you? And absolutely full of yourself, I might add."

Nate shrugged cheerfully. "Who else am I supposed to be full of?"

The fire crackled beside her, and the smell of smoke mixed

with the salt scent of the ocean. The only thing missing was something to roast over it—sausages, marshmallows. Hell, even a couple of cans of beer to drink beside it, leaning against the Bird, would suffice. Or not: the couple of drinks she'd already had weren't sitting well. Still, in all the days of the four of them, Larry had always kept supplies in the Bronco. Blankets, beer, whatever might be called for.

Caro threw out her hands. "So. This is local color. This is, maybe, where kids hang out in the Springs."

"Pretty much the same as anyplace." His frown was lit from below. He looked around, as though he were trying to memorize the things he saw, the sounds of the tide and the gulls screeching overhead, the crackling of the fire, and the smoke twirling lazily toward the sky, where a single star showed.

"Something tells me that that wasn't the real reason why you wanted me to bring you down here." Caro narrowed her eyes, though not really against the smoke. Funny how you could get used to anything like campfire smoke quickly, again. It was like riding the proverbial bike.

"Something like—my suggestion about getting naked?" Nate's eyes glinted. "You're astute." He dropped to his knees, and pushed a piece of driftwood into the fire, crushing the remains of the log cabin, and nearly killing the flame. Swearing, Caro leaned forward and pulled the piece off to the side in the pit.

"You're not, at least when it comes to building fires." She sat back again. "Have you ever built one before in your life? Ever?"

"Well, no."

Caro shook her head. "I didn't think so. You really have no clue."

Now he laughed, that full round laugh she had found so attractive on the night of the cookout. Here it was so loud that it startled the gulls in the dark, who squawked angrily.

"I have a clue about some things," he protested.

"Like what?"

"Theater," he shot back. "Directing. Remember? I'm pretty good at that. Pretty famous for that."

"That." Caro waved a hand dismissively.

"And I'm pretty good at this." Suddenly the distance between them had disappeared, and his hand was at the nape of her neck, his mouth on hers.

He *was* pretty good at that, Caro thought, caught off guard. She let him kiss her, a long languorous sort of kiss. She was so busy thinking about it that she totally forgot to respond in kind.

"What's the matter?" he asked against her lips.

"You'd better try that again. I wasn't ready."

This time she tried to empty her mind, tried only to feel what you were supposed to feel when an attractive man kissed you. For half a moment she forgot herself in the sensation of being desired—it had been a long time, hadn't it?—and let herself be washed along to the hush of the tide, the crackle of the fire, the romance of it.

Then her mind played that old trick. She was on the beach, kissing the man she had wanted for so long, knowing that it could only lead one place, knowing that it was the one thing she wanted—*the one thing.* Caro pressed herself forward, feeling the blood rush in her head, and she whispered his name.

Nate jerked back.

"Who the hell's Larry?" he demanded.

Caro opened her eyes. It wasn't Larry. Because it could never be Larry, never again.

"Not you," she cried out, surprised at her own vehemence. She scrambled away from Nate, kicking one of the fire pit stones out of place, scraping her hands on the rocky beach. Then she fled back toward the bluff and the path up to the park.

When she got back to the house, only the light over the sink was on; the Jeep wasn't in the driveway. *Thank God.* Marty and Sophie weren't home from the farm yet.

Caro hurled herself up the stairs, stripping off her clothes as she went. In the bathroom she dialed up the shower as hot as she dared, then crawled under it with the soap, scrubbing at her skin. Being there—on the beach—with Nate: how close she had come to lifting off that scab of forgetting. She had almost allowed herself to imagine that things were not so irrevocably changed. She had almost convinced herself that Nate was someone else.

That Nate was Larry.

It was like reliving the shock of learning of his death, four years ago. When she saw how broken Marty and her parents were at the news, and having to hide just how broken she was. She had started then, hiding those feelings, and had just kept on. Because it wasn't her place to love Larry. It had been her place to love her husband. Pete.

Caro turned her face into the hot water and cried then, the tears mingling with the shower. Hiding how she felt then. Hiding how she still felt.

Marty would be home soon from the farm, with Sophie. Hurriedly Caro turned off the water and toweled herself off. Then she threw on her nightshirt and crawled into bed.

A while later, she heard Marty moving around downstairs. She burrowed deeper into the covers, her back to the door. When the slight tap finally came, she mumbled indistinctly.

The door cracked open.

"Hey," Marty said, her voice low. "Sophie fell asleep on the way home. I've put her in her bed."

"Thanks," Caro mumbled. She did not turn over. She hoped Sophie's nightmares, for the most part alleviated, didn't choose tonight to manifest themselves.

A moment's pause.

"Are you okay?" Marty sounded concerned, and Caro couldn't bear it. She felt a tear slide out of her eye and across the bridge of her nose.

"I don't feel very well." Another tear.

"Can I get you anything?"

"I'll be all right," Caro said. "Just need some sleep."

"Okay." Marty didn't sound convinced. "You know where to find me if you need me."

When the door closed, Caro allowed the rest of the tears, but kept her face pressed to the pillow to muffle any sobs.

THIRTY-NINE.

Caro had found him alone on the beach, staring into the fire on the far side of the Bird. She had parked her car on the park access road, just before the closed gate, just behind the Bronco where it had been pulled off into the bushes—the place they'd always left it, back when they were in high school. Even in the dark she had known the way, hadn't bothered with the tiny light from her phone. The waning moon had been enough.

He had to have heard her coming, but he didn't turn, didn't look up.

Caro lowered herself to sit next to him on the tattered plaid blanket, the same one that had always been in the back of the truck. He leaned forward and eased another piece of driftwood into the fire pit. Sparks snapped and twirled up into the dark sky. She could hear the wash of the tide; the past-full moon sparked off the crests of the waves.

"Hi," she said at last.

He turned then, his face shadowed and carved by the flickering light.

"Are you alone?" he asked after a few moments.

Caro nodded.

"Why?"

There were too many ways to answer that question, too many things she could have said. Caro felt the rush of confusion, the heat in her skin that might have been from the fire. Through it all, she felt the single white spear of knowing, running through her, toward him.

Slowly she got to her feet and walked away from the fire, toward the moon, toward the ocean. On the way she kicked off her shoes, pulled her shirt over her head, dropped her shorts, and stripped off her underwear. The water was freezing, but she waded out along the lighted path of moonlight until the waves slapped at her thighs, and then she dove in. Just before she sank beneath the water, she thought she heard him call her name.

Caro swam out a bit further, then dove again and resurfaced. Back on the beach, he was standing, outlined by the flames, a black still form against the blaze. She dove one more time, then turned back. Emerging from the ocean, she felt the cold of the night air and the water running down her back, her breasts, her legs, but her skin was still warm. She walked slowly toward him, her eyes steady on his shadowed face. He did not move. He might not have been breathing. When she reached him at last, she cupped his face in her hands wordlessly, then pressed her mouth to his. For a moment he was still, almost resistant. But then he ran one hand into her wet hair, the other along her hip.

"Why?" he asked again, against her mouth.

Instead of answering, she broke away to settle back on the blanket. She held out her arms. Another, briefest, hesitation— before he pulled off his own sweatshirt and slid into her embrace.

When they were spent, he buried his face in her neck. Her skin was slick with sweat, but somehow she thought the dampness at her collarbone might be his tears. She shuddered, and his grip on her tightened. She felt like crying herself, as though she had been turned inside out so that every nerve ending in her body was open to the air. She kept her own arms around him, loath to let him go, though she knew she would have to. Had he known then? Had he? Instead, she took deep breaths, staring up into the night sky. The moon had risen further; the fire was dying back. The sound of the incoming tide was louder and closer.

"Why?" he asked a third time.

"Because," she whispered, "this is what I wanted." She could still feel him at those exposed nerve endings, everywhere he had touched, everywhere he had kissed. "This is what I've always wanted."

Caro knew then that it was true. That all those nights in high school, riding around in the Bronco, the four of them—she had been wishing that it had only been the two of them. That the nights by this very fire pit had been this night, this one, with his weight on her, his hands on her.

"I have to go tomorrow," he said, the words muffled.

Caro turned her head to press her lips to his hair. "I know. That's why I came to find you." *That's why I made love to you. That's why I'm holding on to you like it's the end of the world.*

When she shivered, he shifted to the side and pulled the blanket awkwardly around her. He sat up to throw the last piece of driftwood into the fire, then lay back down again in her arms, wiping his face with the back of a hand.

"Stay awhile longer," he whispered.

She kissed his hair once more, and turned back to the sky again, caressing his muscled back. She said nothing.

Later, when he'd fallen asleep, she found her clothes—her shirt was soaked, so she put his on. She covered him as best she could with the blanket, then headed silently back to the path, toward home, where—maybe—Pete had returned.

FORTY.

"**I** HAVE TO tell you this," Caro said.

Sophie played in the blue wading pool—which, at her direction, held only a couple of inches of water—leaping and shrieking all the while. Caro sat sideways on the chaise longue, her arms wrapped around herself protectively. She wore her oversized pair of Jackie O sunglasses, as though hiding, or hungover. Was she rocking back and forth? Marty did a double-take. Was that a tumbler of scotch at four in the afternoon?

"Something's the matter," Marty said quickly. She dragged a lawn chair closer and sat on the edge. "What is it? Is it Pete?"

Caro had sounded like hell last night, and had called in to work this morning. She never called in to work.

"No." Caro had turned her head away, looking beyond the pool, beyond her daughter, toward the old overgrown farm pond outside the safety fence.

Marty felt the air go out of her. Relief. Not another communique from Pete or his lawyer, then. Things were tense enough with the preliminary hearing looming on the very near horizon. "What is it?"

Caro licked her lips, picked up the glass, and put it down again without drinking. "I have to tell you this," she repeated, a skipping vinyl record. "And it's bad."

The slight panic raised its head again. If not Pete, then what? Illness? Injury? Marty looked at the splashing Sophie, but there was no clue there. "You're scaring me. You'd better tell me."

This time when Caro lifted the glass, she drained half of it. "I'm afraid you're going to be angry. I'm afraid you're going to hate me."

"I'm going to strangle you if you don't stop this and tell me what's going on." The words were meant to be a joke, but Marty's tone was sharper than she meant it to be. "Tell me."

She realized then that Caro's face—what she could see of it behind the dark glasses—was pale, and pinched. Guilty?

"What have you done?"

Caro took a long breath. "Do you remember, back when I told you, the first time—when I was married to Pete—and I discovered he was sleeping with the bartender from the Outer Banks?"

"Sleeping. Euphemism of the first water." Marty almost spat. "Screwing her in the alley behind the storage shed, as I recall. Yeah. I remember that." She hadn't wanted to say *I told you so,* because you don't say that to your oldest and dearest friend, who is married to a person you don't trust. Oh, she could have. Instead she'd had to console Caro in her angry heartbreak. How she had hoped that would have been the end—that Caro would have shown Pete the door, and good riddance to him. "It didn't take him much longer to turn around and do it again, did it?" Marty cast a quick look at Sophie, now running in circles around the perimeter of the pool, flapping her arms, the water wings she insisted on wearing catching the sun. "How long after Sophie was born did you catch him again?"

"*Before* Sophie was born," Caro corrected. She swallowed. The scotch tumbler was empty now. She pushed the white sunglasses back up her nose.

"Wait—"

"Yes."

"There was another time before Melissa? Another *other* woman?"

Caro nodded.

Marty slid back in her lawn chair. She realized her mouth was hanging open. The sun was in her eyes; she shifted her chair. "You never told me about this."

"No." Again Caro swallowed, and grimaced, as though there was a bad taste in her mouth. Maybe there was. "I'm telling you now, though."

Loud giggling as Sophie leapt once more into the wading pool, and then began kicking the water up around her. Suddenly her feet slipped from beneath her and she landed on her bottom. For a moment it looked as though her face would crumple, but then she began slapping at the water with her hands. More squeals.

"But—why?" Marty frowned, looking down at the empty glass, which now lay on its side in the grass. Which needed mowing, she thought distractedly. Caro had needed to pour herself a stiff drink to tell her this story. "Why now?" *Why not then?* Marty had thought there were two times, two infidelities—but there were three? Why had the third one—second, really—been kept a secret, when she and Caro never kept secrets from each other?

For a long time Caro remained silent. Her throat was working as she tried not to cry. Marty waited. Her neck prickled. She didn't know what was coming, but she already didn't like it.

"Marty. I did a thing." Suddenly Caro's words broke through, water through a breached dam. "I was so angry when I found out—I found her underwear in the pocket of his jeans when I was doing the laundry, if you can believe that. Then I found a diaphragm in the glove compartment of his car when I went to put away his new insurance card—he always forgot to take that out to the car. But—a diaphragm! They'd probably been screwing right there, on the seat I was sitting on."

"But you never told me." Marty wiped a hand across her brow. "Why not? Did you think I'd get on your case to leave him? Because probably you're right, I would have."

Caro shook her head. "It's worse than that, Marty. And you're going to hate me for it."

It would have been easy at this point to say she'd never hate Caro, that they had been friends for far too long; but there was something in Caro's trepidation that stopped Marty from throwing out the casual reassurance. It would have smacked of platitude.

"I guess you'd just better tell me, then," Marty said. She almost wished for a shot of single malt herself. "Just say whatever it is, and we'll sort it out afterwards."

"I found out about this one about four years ago. The very end of summer. September." Caro waited, and when Marty didn't seem to be following her lead, she continued. "It was—it was right about the last time—"

Now Marty frowned, remembering the time. Lots of things had happened then. She had just bought the house. It was the last time Larry had been home on leave, before he was sent back to Afghanistan, the September before Sophie was born—Larry had never got to meet Sophie, which Marty thought sad: her brother loved kids, would love this kid. Marty watched Sophie splashing in the pool for a moment; the little girl had begun to sing, some made-up song about a chicken and a cow. Then Marty looked across at Caro, who turned away. Something was niggling. Something she had missed. "I'm not understanding. Tell me what you mean."

"Larry was here," Caro confirmed. "I was so angry. I went to him—"

"To tell him about it?" A vague relief. Larry had been good to talk things through with. But he would have told Caro to leave Pete, as well. Of this Marty was certain.

"To seduce him."

This time Marty did go inside for a glass, and, after slugging back a shot of the whisky, she brought the bottle back outside.

"I don't know if I want to hear this," Marty said. She set the bottle down in the grass, but not before making sure it was corked tightly—reflex. One couldn't spill expensive scotch, no matter how upset.

She had always thought Larry and Caro would have made a cute couple, when they were in high school; but Larry always dated girls from his class. Caro was part of the four, but apparently not dating material. Even so, Larry's girlfriends had tended to be short-term, apparently not liking the thought of being a fifth wheel with them, or not liking the idea of being in competition for his time. They'd appear, they'd drift away, and then the four of them would climb into the Bronco and drive off to the beach.

"I know you liked him when we were in school," she said slowly.

Caro laughed bitterly. "I had a mammoth crush on him in school. You knew that. If he'd ever thought of me as more than a friend, or as more than just *your* friend, I would have died and gone to heaven. If he'd wanted to seduce me when I was sixteen, I would have stripped naked in the school parking lot."

A wave of longing and loss washed over Marty then, thinking about her brother, how perfect and how idiotic he had been—they all had been—back when they were kids. She pressed the ball of her hand into her brow, wanting those days back, wanting Larry back. Wanting everything that had been lost back.

"Again, why are you telling me this now?"

For a long time Caro said nothing. She leaned forward to collect her glass and the bottle of scotch. Marty watched her splash a couple fingers into the tumbler, and then a couple of fingers more. Without even recorking the bottle, Caro tipped back her glass.

"Because four months after that, Larry was dead. Because five months after *that,* Sophie was born."

Bored at last with the pool, Sophie ran toward them, but slowed, her eyes daring between the two. When neither spoke, she sidled up to her mother. "Where's my towel, Mama?"

Caro's hands were full. Without thinking, Marty picked up the towel and held it out.

"No," Sophie said, tipping her chin stubbornly. "Mama can do it."

With that round face, with the blazing blue eyes and the freckled cheeks staring up at her, Marty wondered why she had never seen it before. That stubborn jut of lip was every bit of Larry's expression.

FORTY-ONE.

MARTY TOOK THE bottle and her glass and clambered into the Jeep. She stuck them in the cup holders—it was highly unlikely that any sheriff's deputies would be patrolling in the Springs, or at least not this far off the highway, and if she just drove straight and steady, no one would know anyway.

Larry's child.

Her brother's child.

Her best friend, for nearly her entire life, who had kept this secret from her.

Marty felt dizzy. Sophie, their beloved Sophie, was her niece. Was her blood.

The shock was wearing off, and the fury was welling up, as Marty had known it would. How could Caro have kept this from her? This most important piece of information? She had had to leave; she had known that as soon as she had felt the confusion growing, knowing what was waiting on the other side. Otherwise, she would have said something that she'd never be able to take back, something that she'd regret when it drove a wedge between them.

Caro had driven that wedge already.

At the road, Marty hesitated. Turn left, and she could be at the Morgan farm in minutes, though no one would be working on the Bronco tonight. Even so, it seemed a safe choice, a busy place, a bastion of everyday. Then she laughed bitterly to herself. The family with the son who could not speak, with the granddaughter who could not walk. They didn't need her tearing in and dropping this on them.

Well, it wouldn't be on *them*. It would be on Alaric, the one who knew Larry the best.

The one who knew Larry the best.

Had Alaric known what had happened between Caro and Larry?

She spun the wheel to the right, heading down the Lighthouse Point Road, past Simon's and Nate's house, and toward the state park. One of the blasted dump trucks was bearing down on her, and she pulled the Jeep as far to the right as she could get, and then, fearing dumping the car off the shoulder at the last moment, she threw up an angry middle finger.

"Bastard!" she shouted out the open window after the truck.

Alaric might have known that Caro and Larry had been lovers. Had had a one-night stand. That Caro had cheated on her husband with Larry. Marty tried on different variations on the theme, trying to decide which she liked best, when she liked none of them. She sighed, slotting the Jeep into the pull-off they'd always used when the gates to the park were closed. They weren't now, but—and she checked the time on her Fitbit as she climbed out of the Jeep—they would be soon. Sundown, whenever that was today. Best not to be caught, unable to get out—or best not to be towed. She grabbed her jacket, and folded it over the bottle of scotch. The glass she opted simply to leave behind as she locked the door.

It was unlikely, though, that Alaric knew about Sophie. Because if he did, then that would mean that Larry had known about Sophie, and Marty was fairly certain her brother would have told her. Fairly certain. Not positive, though, because what brother ever confides in his sister about his sexual conquests? She had never told him about hers; he had never mentioned his. But a pregnancy—a baby—that was something different. No, probably Alaric had no knowledge about Sophie. Besides— there probably had been no time for him to learn about it.

And, she told herself bitterly, a baby? She would have thought her oldest friend would have confided in her about that.

There were only two cars in the lot below the lighthouse. When she shaded her eyes with her hand, Marty could see a couple of people up at the top of the long stairs leading to the summit of the hill and the keeper's house. She looked the other way, but could only see a man walking a dog on the beach itself, and two kids throwing mud at each other. She trudged steadily to the far end of the lot and slipped around the split rail fence marking the end of access. Well, public access. The path to the rocky cove on the other side of the bluff was overgrown, but she could have found it with her eyes closed.

Once she'd made that final leap from the path to the beach, she turned left and headed for the Bird. The sounds of the two kids on the park beach had faded and were replaced by the hush of the waves; the tide had turned and was on its way out. She was almost to the giant stone before she realized that Alaric was there ahead of her. She didn't really want to see him now, didn't want to talk to him. He was too prescient by far: he'd sense something was wrong. But at her shuffling footsteps, he turned, and it was too late to go back.

"I brought the scotch," she said, drawing the Macallan from under her jacket and holding it up.

Alaric had taken one look at her face, then tapped his chest, his temple, and held out his hands. She'd been around him long enough now to be able to translate. *What's the matter?*

Marty shook her head. "I don't want to talk about it right now. I have to think." She had come down to the Bird to be alone, to be able to wade her way through the confusion about what she'd learned. To figure out what to do. So angry, though. She'd try to think, and the fury would wash in again. *So angry.* What a mess. The whole thing was a mess.

She uncorked the whisky and tipped the bottle back. It burned in her mouth. It burned down her throat. It burned in her stomach. She welcomed it; it was something else to think about aside from the anger. Alaric was watching her, his face still. She thrust the bottle into his hand and stumbled across the stones to the waterline. There she picked up a big rock with both hands and hurled it over the breaking waves. It fell into the water with a satisfying hollow sound, the splash eaten up by the tide. She picked up another and threw that as well.

The rocks were really too heavy for her to be throwing, and it wasn't long before she felt the strain across her shoulders and into the muscles of her upper arms. Probably she'd have to have rotator cuff surgery, and her career in the major leagues would be over. Still she threw the rocks, moving down the beach to select more and more. She was aware of Alaric, back up at the fire pit, watching her, but he made no move to join her. Well, he'd come down here, probably to exercise his own demons, after all. He had to do it in his own way. For all she knew, her presence down here was as surprising and perhaps as vaguely unwelcome as his had been for her. She bent down to grab another stone, wet and gray and streaked with lighter bits of quartz, and spun to throw it as far as she could. Another deep splash. Short of breath now, she leaned forward, hands on her knees.

Throwing stones. Not at things. Marty congratulated herself on her forbearance. *Congratulations, me!* Throwing stones, instead of the furious words, which even now welled up, in the way conversations long past and too late welled up.

Caro, why?

Larry, why?

And what did this mean about Sophie? Sophie, her brother's child. Her niece.

Roger had never known. Roger had died without knowing that he had a grandchild. An unbearable grief washed over her, for Roger, for Larry who probably never knew he had a daughter, for Sophie who would never know her father.

This time, when she bent down, she chose a stone she could lift with one hand, and threw that as far out into the tide as she could manage, opening her mouth to let out a roar. Then she threw another, and lifted her head to scream into the evening light. And then another.

The shadows were crawling to meet the tide when she at last returned to Alaric and the fire pit. He had collected driftwood and tinder, and now he paused in creating the standard Boy Scout pyramid inside a log cabin, to hand her her jacket. It was cooling off. She shrugged herself into it.

Alaric drew out the pad and pen from his breast pocket. *Better?* He held the page out.

"No." Her throat hurt from the shouting. Marty threw herself down and scrabbled for the bottle. Alaric had pushed the cork top back in, but now she popped it once again to swig from the neck. "Not even close." She wiped her mouth with the back of her hand. "There aren't enough rocks on this damned beach to make everything better."

Bad, then.

Marty took another drink.

He tore off the page and tucked it beneath the pyramid of sticks. Replacing his pad and pen, he drew forth a battered book of matches, struck one, and touched the flame to the paper.

"Alaric," she said, "I don't understand people."

He pursed his lips and nodded. He studied the flames as they licked the tinder, caught the twigs. The fire grew, climbing up through his careful construction. Satisfied at last that it was going, and that the log cabin would soon be alight, he sat back and crossed his arms over his knees.

Marty held the bottle out.

Alaric shook his head.

"Friends don't let friends drink alone," she admonished.

He took the bottle from her and took a sip. Then he grimaced, and turned the bottle around to inspect the label.

"Don't be making that face, Morgan," Marty growled. "That's the expensive stuff. No cheap drunk, me."

The shadows were upon them now. Marty shivered. Out on the water, light still sparkled, and the peninsula across the bay was bathed in a golden light. When she looked at her Fitbit, she saw it was nearly seven-thirty. Where had the hours gone? She felt like there was an enormous blank from the moment Caro had spoken the words, "*…four months later, Larry was dead; five months after that, Sophie was born…*" until now.

The sun would be down soon; the gate to the park would be closed and locked, though that didn't matter, since she'd left the Jeep in the layby. Where had Alaric left his farm truck?

"Where did you park?" she asked. "There weren't any other vehicles in the layby."

He shrugged. Then he patted his legs.

"You walked."

Alaric nodded. Again he shrugged, then pointed to his head and held his hands out.

"You had to think."

Another nod.

Marty took the bottle back and had another gulp. Her head was spinning. She really wasn't good at this. When she held it out again, Alaric put a hand up.

"You don't drink anymore," Marty said. It wasn't a question, but she wondered why she had not noticed.

He pressed his lips together, made a face. Then he took out the pad and pen again, wrote, and turned it to her. *Drank to get drunk.*

Now it was Marty's turn to nod. "Since you—got back?"

He wrote again. *Used to. Every night.*

"Larry?" Her voice was small. She had a sense she might be probing a wound, but the whisky was in her blood now, and she felt a little out of control. A lot out of control. Besides—she didn't want to be one of the people who tiptoed in circles around Larry.

The eyes he turned on her had darkened.

I didn't want to feel, he wrote.

"I know," Marty said. "I understand that. So well."

Alaric did not look as though he believed her. But he wrote nothing else. A piece of driftwood fell and the pyramid collapsed with a crash and a blaze of sparks that whirled upward. Off on the horizon the first stars had begun to appear. Alaric leaned forward and lay another piece of driftwood across the flames.

The whisky had lost its appeal. Marty corked the bottle again and leaned it against a rock; it wouldn't do to change her mind later and find that all the scotch had drained out onto the beach. Especially after she had made a big deal about it being the expensive stuff. Of course, she hadn't bought it; she hadn't opened it. Caro had been the one drinking the whisky when she'd returned home from the post office. Marty let out a small laugh: she'd stolen her housemate's expensive bottle of scotch.

Maybe she should let the last of it pour onto the beach, a kind of sacrificial libation or something. Or petty revenge.

Marty leaned back against the Bird, feeling the cold of the enormous stone through her jacket and shirt. Again she shivered, and felt small and discouraged, the way she always did when the anger abated. Alaric tilted his chin, raised his palms. *What?*

"Sometimes," she said slowly, "I feel so stupid. Like I should have known some things, but wasn't paying enough attention. Like I saw everything and didn't understand any of it. And that frightens me, that I should be that stupid. It frightens me."

Alaric picked up a long stick and gave the fire a poke. More sparks leapt up, the flames growing taller, and then subsiding slightly. In the deepening darkness, his already thin face looked thinner, lit from below by the orange glow: angular, as though he were a thousand years old. His eyes were hooded; he poked the fire again, but absently.

Marty sighed. She closed her eyes and thought of Caro's stricken face. *You're going to hate me.* "I just can't talk to you right now," she'd told Caro, and, taking up the bottle, had walked determinedly away. She knew she didn't hate her best friend, her friend of longest standing. But *why* hadn't Caro told her? Why? And even stranger, why had she suddenly decided, more than four years after it happened, to tell Marty about it today? Today. Not even a couple of weeks ago, when Pete's custody battle had first begun. What had happened today to make *this* the day the story of Caro and Larry's one-night stand had to come out?

Again she sighed. Her chest felt tight. "Larry and my father and my mother, Caro, and you, and me—everything. I don't understand any of it, and it frightens me."

When she skewed a glance in his direction, she found Alaric still preoccupied with the fire. Or with something else. Sometimes, when he wanted her to, he could make her understand him, could help her read his thoughts. And at other times, like right now, right this minute, he was closed off tightly. Sealed. She found herself staring, wondering about the nature of PTSD. *I didn't want to feel,* he had written.

Still, he had stopped drinking. Had he given up trying to hold off the feelings? Had they grown less sharp over time? Had he simply realized that drinking against the feelings didn't make them go away, but rather gave them time to strengthen and come roaring back once sobriety had returned? Or maybe he had tired of waking sick and hungover every morning. Just as she knew she was going to wake up headachy, come the ringing of the alarm clock tomorrow at six. Marty regretted that scotch now. She regretted how it felt on her empty stomach, which had not seen food since her sandwich at lunch time.

"What scares you?" Marty asked, her voice low. She had heard about—and had read about—people suffering from PTSD being triggered by loud noises: fireworks exploding, balloons popping, cars backfiring. What triggered Alaric? She hadn't seen a bad reaction from him—not like the reaction Isabella had had to his blood when he'd cut his hand working on the engine. Still, she'd seen other things: the inability to deal with people, the turning away when they came too close. Or rather—when she had come too close.

For a long time, Alaric looked away, past the fire, over the stones toward the incoming tide. His throat was working. Marty looked down at his hands, she saw that he was kneading his fingers together. She had again, she thought despairingly, overstepped the invisible boundary, and she cursed herself.

"Look, I'm sorry." Marty touched his wrist, then pulled her fingers away quickly. "Don't answer that. I'm sorry I asked."

But Alaric shook his head, and held up a hand before reaching for the pad and pen, which lay on the beach between them. He scribbled something quickly, then shoved the pad at her, as though he could change his mind at any second.

Dark. Sleep.

Marty swallowed. She held herself still. Something told her he didn't admit this often. If he ever did. She wondered if it had come up with the doctors at the VA hospital. Or whether he'd let them know at Walter Reed.

"Do you—have bad dreams?" She was almost whispering now, her voice only slightly higher than the incoming tide. Treading very carefully, softly on his exposed nerves.

He thought for a moment, then wrote again. *Not dreams. Feelings.*

A gull flew overhead, a gray blur, then dove to join a flock at the tideline, flapping its wings and forcing the others to move back. The dying fire snapped, and Alaric tossed a couple of sticks onto it. The air between them seemed taut, and Marty felt that every word she spoke tested that tautness.

"What kinds of feelings?" This question toyed with boundaries even more than her first, but, pad of paper in her fingers, she looked down at those three words and felt he wanted her to ask further. She hoped to God she wasn't wrong.

He took the paper back. *I can hold them in my hands,* he wrote.

Marty drew her brows together, trying to make sense of the words.

I don't understand either.

Then suddenly he was on his feet, walking away from her, studying the stony beach. Marty gasped and threw up a hand, then drew it back, pressing her fingers to her lips. She felt cold without him beside her. Bereft.

When he reached down quickly to grab something, he reminded her forcibly of one of the gulls, swooping in on prey. Then he returned, dropping to his knees in the sand before her.

When he opened his hand, she saw the piece of brown glass, the edges still sharp, not worn down. Not the kind of sea glass Sophie would spend hours searching for, but something newly broken and ugly. Dangerous. There were traces of blood in his palm where the edges had cut his skin.

Marty drew back slightly. "I don't understand." Her voice rose in frustration. "What do you mean? What is this?"

With his free hand, he wrote *grief.*

There was something ugly and horrifying in the word, and in the piece of broken glass in his hand. Something Marty simply couldn't comprehend. She struggled to her feet and ran, toward the crowd of gulls. Screeching, they flew up into a spiral around her. There was sand down here, wet and cold underfoot.

Alaric could hold feelings in his hands. Feelings were hard and sharp like glass.

No, *grief* was hard and sharp like glass.

Marty's thoughts shied away from the idea that presented itself, and then turned back, tentatively.

Emotions, to Alaric, had shape. Had texture. Had temperature. Had dimension.

When she returned, he had set the pad on the beach where she'd been sitting, and was again staring out at the retreating waves.

He died in my arms. I couldn't save him.

Marty got back to the house, and went straight through to the kitchen to put the half-empty bottle of scotch in the cabinet over the sink. Then she crossed to the living room, where Caro huddled, wrapped in a blanket on the couch. The television was on, but turned down low; Caro didn't appear to be watching it. Sophie was nowhere to be seen—but it was nearly eleven.

"I thought you'd never come home," Caro said. Her face was blotchy, her eyes red. She groped around for the remote, then snapped the television off. "Are you okay?" Then, "Are you still mad at me?"

Marty drew in a deep breath.

"The first thing you need to do," she said, the words scratching out of her sore throat, "is to have the court order a blood test."

"But—"

"If Pete discovers that Sophie is not his daughter, he's going to drop the fight for custody."

Without waiting for a reply, she turned and climbed the stairs to her bedroom. Every bone in her body ached.

FORTY-TWO.

THE RAIN WHICH had surprised her on the mail route had beaten down the seven sisters roses, the burgeoning flowers pressed into the grass by their own weight. Marty sat in the driveway in the Jeep, looking at them, discouraged. It had been a hard day, with her thoughts all tangled. She was still angry. Furious, when she thought about the years of having a granddaughter that her father had missed. Furious, when she thought about Caro keeping this biggest of secrets from her. Furious, when she thought of Larry at all. And grief-stricken—she looked at her palms—when she thought of Alaric's words: *I couldn't save him.*

Finally she climbed out and went to the shed—at one point there had been a rickety garage at the end of the driveway, but she had had it pulled down when she first moved in, and now occasionally thought about having a new one built—and found the secateurs in her gardening bucket. Then, thinking of thorns, she turned back and dug out some gloves. At last, she set about clipping the roses that could be saved. Sadly, there were not many. The petals were scattered and glimmering on the wet grass like teardrops.

Without thinking, she peeled off the gloves and threw them

on the kitchen counter to rinse out the blue glass vase; when she picked up the first bloom to arrange it, a thorn tore at the skin on her hand. *Damn it,* she hissed, looking at the dotted line of blood that appeared.

Blood in her palm.

Marty stared at it.

Grief, Alaric had written to her. So fiercely that his pen had torn through the paper. He had ripped the page, with its bald word, from the notebook, had crumpled it and hurled it into the fire pit on the beach.

His fierceness had frightened her. Grief felt like blood in the palm of his hand. He held grief there. And somehow, he wasn't able to set it down. He carried it. A physical sensation.

Marty flipped the faucet handle up, and thrust her palm under the water. The blood swirled pinkly along her fingers and disappeared down the drain. She pulled her hand out of the torrent, and the blood beaded up again in her palm.

It hurt.

This was the part, she knew, where she should cry. Marty felt lost, thinking of her brother, her father. Her—niece. She felt guilty, because the tears wouldn't come. She felt unnatural: an unnatural sister and daughter. No wonder her mother had no patience with her—she didn't behave like a grieving person should.

But the thought of her mother twisted her lips, and she stuck her hand under the faucet again. The water was slightly warm, the single handle midway between hot and cold. She wished for a moment for the bracing, painful water of the spring. The water from the faucet washed the blood away, and was clear.

"What are you doing?"

Caro had returned, Sophie tagging along and singing the Baby Shark song. Marty had not heard the door. Caro came to the sink and looked down at Marty's hand. She stood slightly, warily, away. Knocked from her reverie—it was hard to maintain focus with "Baby Shark" in the background—Marty slapped the faucet handle back down, then reached for a dish towel.

"Scratched myself," she said shortly, wrapping her hand so Caro wouldn't see the blood; it seemed, somehow, something she couldn't share.

Caro set her purse aside, and reached for another rose. With her thumbnail, she scraped a thorn away from the stem, and plopped the flower haphazardly into the blue vase. The others followed, and the silence pulsed. She saw Marty's critical glance at the finished product, and shrugged. She carried the vase into the dining room and set it on the table runner. "Not pretty, but done. Do you need a Band-Aid?" It was not the question—they both knew—that she wanted to ask.

When Marty pulled the towel away, it was stained, and the blood dotted up again.

"I'll get you a Band-Aid," Sophie announced. "I know where they are." She disappeared into the downstairs bathroom. There was the sound of the toilet cover being closed with a thunk. After a moment she reappeared shaking the blue and white box. "You need to put these on the shopping list, you guys. We're going to run out." She frowned up at them, and then squatted to shake the bandages out on the kitchen floor, sorting through them with a finger. "How big is the blood? As big as your hand?"

"Sophie—" Caro's voice trailed off.

"A square one," Marty suggested, disparate thoughts swirling. She couldn't get away from the blood in Alaric's palm, and looked down again into her own hand. *Grief.* She locked her gaze on the swinging dark hair, the determined expression, and felt something big pushing its way through the sorrow and fury.

She let Sophie work on her hand, the little girl frowning in deep concentration as she peeled the covering from the bandage. Now that she knew, she wondered how she could ever not have seen it: the expressions, the tilt of the head, the narrowing of the eyes. Deep blue eyes. The mannerisms of her brother, which she thought so ingrained in memory, had been in front of her all this time, in miniature, in Sophie. Marty barely registered Caro, gathering up the remainder of the Band-Aids and shuffling them back into their box. She still couldn't quite stomach this secret being withheld from her. She wondered how one bandaged that? And how did one bandage the grief Alaric carried in his hands? How could any of that ever heal?

Then Marty knew. She had to gather up Sophie and place her in Alaric's arms, so he would know what she knew. Perhaps his grief might then be assuaged.

"Marty?" Caro called, from far away. "Are you okay? Are you in shock?"

Marty glanced up, meeting Caro's eyes for the first time since she'd learned. "Yeah. Yeah, I think I am."

FORTY-THREE.

"Look, Martha," her mother said, adjusting the straw hat on her head and drawing the gardening gloves back onto her hands. Marty had interrupted her in the planting of hostas in the front garden. "I really don't have time this morning—"

"Mom, you never have time for me."

Not *this. Me.* How many times Marty had thought the words, but had never spoken them aloud. Everything was so close to the surface today, every nerve raw. Her thoughts jangled, all those sweet bells out of tune. So many things she needed to tell Sylvia, first and foremost about Sophie. Sylvia's granddaughter. She hadn't expected it to be easy, but neither had she expected to be brushed aside so quickly after her arrival this Sunday afternoon.

The words appeared to have surprised Sylvia as well, for her mother drew back, her lips pursed. "Don't interrupt, Martha. It's rude."

Out of the corner of her eye, Marty thought she saw the Bronco go by the end of the driveway. She allowed herself to be distracted, but only for a moment, before turning back to her mother.

"Don't talk to me as though I'm a child, Mom. And don't treat me—just because I'm not Larry—as though I don't matter."

Wow. She had never said anything vaguely like that. For a heartbeat she felt a twinge of shame; her father would not want her to speak to her mother this way. But it suddenly occurred to her that he had never protected her from this treatment, had never stepped in when her mother was at her most dismissive and unkind. It was always comfort after the fact. Reasoning with her after the fact. *You just have to understand. She's in pain.*

"Martha—"

Having started, Marty couldn't have stopped if she'd tried. If she'd wanted to. Over her mother's shoulder, she saw the Bronco go by in the other direction, and in a weird way, it gave her strength. "I know you miss Larry, Mom. I know you do. And I do, too. But I'm here. I'd like to share this with you. I'd like to make it easier for you, and maybe you could make it easier for me, too."

And I need to tell you something important. About Larry. About your grandchild.

That part, though, she had to hold back until she was certain of the reception, until she was certain that it was safe.

"I'm fine, Martha. You don't need to worry about me." Sylvia bent to the porch step to collect one of the pots from the garden center. She had already dug and primed the hole along the foundation border where it would go.

"Did you ever stop to think you should worry about me?"

There it was, out in the open. The hurt since childhood, when she had realized that, to her mother, she was the fifth wheel in their family of four. That she would have to fight for her mother's attention and regard, and more often than not, she would lose that fight. Sylvia had never had enough bandwidth for two children. It had always seemed as though Marty was an inconvenience.

But if Marty thought she was going to break through

somehow with that demand, and to reach her mother, she was wrong. Sylvia straightened now, a hosta pot in each hand. "You don't need me to worry about you, Martha. You've always gone your own way, without regard to my wishes or my feelings." She turned away, taking the few steps to the border, where a trowel was jammed into the ground, and where a half-full bag of mulch stood at the ready. A clear dismissal.

Marty stumbled back, stung. "That's not true."

Sylvia bent forward and set the plant pots down.

Marty stepped around in front of her, so close that when her mother straightened back up, they were eye to eye. "You know that's not true, Mom."

"Explain to me how it isn't," Sylvia challenged. Her eyes narrowed, emphasizing the crows' feet around them.

"I haven't got a clue what you mean," Marty protested, defensive in her anger. "I've done everything I could to make you proud of me—all the honors at school and in college. I've tried to help you here with the house, with Dad. I've never asked you for anything. I've always had a job—"

"Little Miss Self-Sufficient," Sylvia sneered.

Marty threw up her hands. "I don't know how to please you, Mom. If I hadn't done those things, you would have been all over me for not doing those things. I can't win with you. I've never been able to win with you."

"You've got a degree in art, and you have a job delivering the mail?"

"I'm making money, so I can do my art. There's no money in art." This would be the time to tell Sylvia about the Nova Gallery, but Marty held that little success close, to protect it from Sylvia's denigration.

"You might have chosen a degree that would be worth something, then."

It was like arguing with a wall, a brick wall higher than she could climb or even see over. But Marty knew, now, that Alaric had her back; she could hear the familiar pitch of the Bronco's engine as he passed the driveway once again. "You might have noticed that I've always loved painting. If you had ever really been interested in me." She sighed deeply. "You could have supported me. You could support me now."

Sylvia crossed her arms, her feet apart, unmovable. "Support you. When you bought that house, with all the work it needed—"

"Which I had done, which I paid for—"

"And then you invited that Pond girl to come live with you— honestly, I've never known what you could see in her to be friends with her—"

"Caro and I have always been friends. She was—" Marty caught her breath: *not yet.* "She was Larry's friend, too."

"Don't kid yourself. Larry wouldn't have given that one the time of day if she hadn't been your friend."

Marty felt her eyes widen. *Oh, really?*

"She's always been a hanger-on, that one, and I could never understand how you could be so easily taken advantage of."

Marty flushed, and opened her mouth to retort.

"And then that husband of hers threw her out—"

"That's not what happened—"

"And suddenly she turns up on your doorstep, freeloading again, and this time with that brat in tow—"

That brat is your granddaughter. Marty clenched her fists at her sides, clenched her eyes tightly shut. *Your granddaughter. Larry's child.* She didn't know how much longer she could hold it together. Sylvia's voice was climbing the register, and Marty knew hers would, too. She wanted to shout at her mother; she wanted to shake her mother. She felt her fingernails digging into her palms.

"And now you're running around with that Morgan boy, the one who should have died in Larry's place. The one who feels so guilty about that that he's become a mute!"

"Mom—"

"He's damaged, Martha. And it's all mental and emotional, isn't it? No good reason for him not to be able to talk, except there's something wrong with him psychologically."

Wow. Everyone important to her, run down and abused by her own mother. Except Isabella, Marty realized, but there was still time, wasn't there? And still, apparently, enough vitriol running through her mother's veins to escape into the world, in an attempt to poison everything.

"That's not fair, Mom. Alaric is grieving Larry. They were best friends forever."

"I'm grieving Lawrence, too, Martha," Sylvia reminded her, like there was a need. "But I'm still able to speak."

Marty lifted her chin and stared her mother right in the eye. "After listening to this garbage, I can only say I wish you weren't."

Sylvia tore off a glove to slap Marty's face.

Marty's head snapped back, and she put her palm to her skin. She stared for a long moment at her mother, feeling something in her tear; but when she heard the Bronco coming nearer yet again, she spun on her heel and ran toward the road. She threw a hand up, and there was a squeal of brakes, a spray of gravel. As she reached the end of the driveway, Alaric leaned over and threw open the passenger side door. Marty hurled herself inside.

He held up a hand. *Where?*

"Anywhere. Just go!"

She slammed the door. Alaric threw the Bronco into gear and spun the wheels, throwing up more gravel, and they were off.

FORTY-FOUR.

IN THE END, Marty wouldn't let him turn down the Lighthouse Point Road, and when they passed her house, Caro's Vue was in the driveway.

"Your place," she ordered.

Alaric glanced at her once, and spun the wheel. When they reached the farm, he pulled into the yard and slid to a stop before the stable office. He pointed to the back of the house, then jerked his head toward his door. *Hurry.*

Marty dodged around the hood of the Bronco and followed him inside. He locked the door behind them, and she jerked the blinds closed over the windows. When she turned back to him in the darkness, he held out his arms, and she slid into them.

It was their first kiss. Tentative at first, an exploration. Yet to Marty, her mouth against his felt like a kind of homecoming: she had finally reached the place where she truly belonged. She slid her hands along Alaric's back, feeling his shoulder blades, his backbone. Somehow she knew the shape of him, the curves, the movement. She wondered if he felt the same as he ran his hands over her shoulders, up her neck, to cup her chin between them.

Alaric was the first to pull back. Marty looked up into his

face, where his eyes glittered. He tipped his head, then turned his chin toward the futon, a question.

"Yes," Marty whispered. "Yes."

Alaric sank onto the coverlet, then pulled her down beside him. She was having trouble controlling her breathing, but then he leaned forward to kiss her again, and breathing didn't really seem to matter all that much anymore—she forgot to worry about it, or about anything else.

Marty woke to the sound of the door handle turning back and forth. She pressed her face into Alaric's shoulder, pulling the coverlet closer.

He placed his finger against her lips. When she looked at him, he simply smiled and shook his head gently.

"Alaric?" Of course it was Isabella, who probably had never found that door locked to her. The girl's voice was filled with puzzlement. "Are you in there? Alaric?"

When Marty opened her mouth, Alaric leaned forward and covered it with his own. Then he drew back and shook his head again.

The door knob rattled one more time, and then they could hear Isabella's metallic steps moving away. There was a call from the direction of the house, the words indistinguishable. "I don't know," they could hear Isabella answer. "The door's locked." Her steps retreated until they could hear her no more.

Alaric raised his eyebrows and made a rueful face.

"I know." Marty tucked her head under his chin. His skin against hers was warm; he smelled of lime and cloves. A surprisingly old-fashioned smell. "That's why I didn't want to go back to my house. My bedroom door doesn't lock."

She felt his chest shake with silent laughter. Turning, she

kissed his collarbone.

When Alaric drew away and climbed up from the futon, Marty missed his warmth immediately. She sat up and pulled the coverlet more closely around her, watching the way his muscles moved under his skin. He crossed the length of the room to open the cupboard and take out two of the three glasses she knew were there now. He flipped the tap and filled the tumblers, then shut off the water again to return. When he caught her looking him over, he grinned before handing her a glass. He slid in beside her, bent to kiss her breast, then drank.

The water was just what she needed. She emptied the entire glass. "Isabella's going to be so angry when she realizes you were here the entire time."

Alaric nodded and shrugged. *Can't be helped.*

"She's going to be more angry when she realizes that you were here with me."

Alaric repeated the gesture. *Can't be helped, either.* He took the empty glass from her and set it on the side table, pushing aside a copy of *The Canterbury Tales* to make room. His shirt lay on the floor; he nearly tipped out of bed reaching for it. He fumbled for the pad and pen he kept in the breast pocket.

She likes you.

Marty laughed quietly. "She's used to me, you mean. And that took a while, didn't it?"

Not as long as it took her to get used to me. Alaric made a face.

"And now she loves you."

I love her.

A simple statement, bald and unadorned. Marty looked down at the pad and smiled at the sweetness of it. With a hesitant hand she reached out and touched the three words. After a moment, Alaric put his hand over hers.

"How will you tell her?"

Alaric looked at her quizzically. Then he scribbled quickly. *Tell her what?*

Marty slumped back.

"How will you tell her that I'm not going anywhere?" She licked her lip. Might as well go in whole hog, as it were. "How will you tell her you're stuck with me now?"

Alaric blinked. He deliberately set the pad aside on the table. Then he turned back to her, and kissed her hard. Marty wrapped her arms around him, and pulled him closer, until she felt his weight upon her.

FORTY-FIVE.

"So what did you want to see me about?" Caro asked, when Sierra had left the coffee tray and retreated with the softest click of the door. Caro held her hands in her lap. The seagull—the same one?—perched on the windowsill and glared at her with its beady eye.

Matt Copeland brushed back his blond hair, then poured out the coffee. Again he pushed the sugar bowl and creamer closer to her. "I'm sorry to bring you in here like this, but I didn't feel comfortable giving you this information over the phone." He drew the long legal-sized folder to him and opened it.

"It's the paternity test results, then, isn't it?" Caro couldn't meet his eyes.

"It is." Withdrawing a sheet of paper, Matt slid it across the desk to Caro. She could feel him watching her as she drew the page closer with a single wary finger. At the top of the page, a table of several columns screamed at her for attention: a column full of abbreviations and numbers she had no idea about, then columns labeled "mother," "child," and "alleged father." Pairs of numbers cascaded down the columns. She shook her head in confusion. "I don't understand what this means. All these numbers?" For the first time she looked at Matt. "How do I read this?"

"The important information is in the line below the table," he said. He pointed, his arm stretching across the desk. "Here."

Combined Paternity Index: 0

Probability of Paternity: 0

Caro stared at the two lines. There it was. Pete was not Sophie's father. Caro, in her heart, had never really thought he was. She had always known that Larry was.

"It's as you thought, then," Matt said.

She nodded. She felt the tears well up, felt them drop onto her hands, once again folded in her lap. "Yes."

"I take it you have a pretty good idea who Sophie's father is."

She nodded again. A tissue appeared, and she took it gratefully, pressing it into her eyes. "Yes. I know."

"Do we need to ask him for a sample? Get a court order?"

"No." Caro's voice was muffled. "No. He's dead." The tears kept coming.

For a long time, Matt said nothing, simply let her cry. When at last she was finished, she mopped up as best she could; he'd placed the box of tissues on the desk before her.

"Mr. Vargas's lawyer should have the results shortly, if he doesn't already,"" Matt said. He helped himself to his own cup of coffee, with plenty of milk. "I will communicate with them, to see whether they're interested in pursuing these proceedings."

Caro lifted her head quickly.

Matt held out his hands. "Mr. Vargas might choose to. And he is within his rights, as his name is listed as the father on Sophie's birth certificate."

Caro blew her nose, and nodded.

"I think the chances are probably slim," he continued. "He'd most likely only do that to be vindictive. Is he? Vindictive?"

"He can be," Caro said, biting her lip.

"But again, this would have to be vindictive in the long term.

And should he decide to continue with this custody suit, we could press, using the evidence we have, for an increase in child maintenance he'd be responsible for."

"But I don't want his money," Caro protested. She reached for another tissue.

"You don't have to want it," Matt said easily. "You just want to use it as leverage. As a weapon. If he feels threatened by that, he might retreat from a custody position."

"Oh." Caro felt winded, and really quite small. She didn't need a mirror to know that her eyeliner was probably smeared all over her face, and that her lipstick had long since washed away. "Oh, okay."

Matt's smile was kind. He stood and came around the desk, offering his trash can for her used tissues. "It's going to be all right, you know," he said. "We can make this work. You'll be fine. Sophie will be fine."

"That's all I care about." She stood, and saw, one last time, the single red-rimmed eye of the seagull on the window ledge.

Matt saw her glance. "You like that guy? I'm thinking about getting him an office. His name's Malcolm."

Caro giggled, and threw her crumpled tissues away.

FORTY-SIX.

"I WANT TO ask you a favor," Marty said, settling into the kitchen chair opposite Isabella, who was determinedly sketching a barbed-wire fence with a silvery gray pastel.

Isabella looked up quickly, blushed, and dropped her eyes again. She had been uncomfortable around Marty from the time she had seen her emerge from Alaric's room the other evening.

Alaric was filling the kettle, to water the geraniums in the window boxes. Pretending not to be paying attention. Marty could feel him—his presence, his movements—even though he did not come close to her.

"What is it?" Isabella asked. She had traded the gray for an umber, and was now drawing a chicken beside one of the fence poles. "I'm not much good at favors, if you haven't guessed. There's not much I can do." But her voice was without rancor.

"I have a painting in a show at Nova Gallery over in Danby. I'd like you to come to the opening." Marty paused, waiting for Isabella to meet her eyes. "As my guest."

Bella slowly set the pastel into the box again, and did not immediately choose another. "I don't—I don't know—"

"I've invited Alaric, too. I'm really hoping you'll say yes." Marty held her breath.

On the other side of the glass, Alaric was focused on deadheading the flowers. He moved to the other window box, out of their sight.

"An art gallery," Isabella breathed. If she had reservations before, they were wiped away. "A real art gallery."

"Yes." Marty couldn't help grinning. "I'm going to be in a real art gallery, and it would mean a lot to me to have you two at the opening."

"A real art gallery," Isabella repeated. Her gaze, when she looked at Marty now, was filled with a certain respect. "I think I'd like to come."

Joanne was keeping Sophie for the evening, so when Alaric and Isabella arrived in the Bronco, Marty and Caro hitched up their skirts and climbed into the back seat.

"Alaric wants you to know that he cleaned it out specially for you guys," Bella said. Alaric grinned.

Indeed, the inside of the truck smelled like pine air freshener. There were no crumpled McDonald's bags or Dunkin' cups on the floor, and there were no balled-up shirts or dirty socks on the back seat.

"This experience is surreal," Caro murmured. She looked pinched and uncertain.

"Who are you?" Marty demanded. "And what have you done to my brother's truck?"

Alaric, who had been about to adjust the driver's seat, pulled it back again so he could lean in and kiss Marty.

"Gross," said Isabella.

Alaric slammed the door and turned the key. There were seatbelts with shoulder harnesses in the back, which there had never been before. When Marty glanced up into the rear view mirror, Alaric rolled his eyes toward Isabella. Of course. Marty clicked herself in, and after a moment, Caro did as well. Alaric had retrofitted the belts for Bella—with the braces, she'd be riding around in the front seat for a while, but that didn't mean the belts wouldn't make her feel safer. Of course. Marty smiled.

"Can you turn up the radio?" Marty laughed, as they came to the highway.

He'd updated the radio; it was now a bluetooth model. Alaric handed Isabella his phone. She frowned, hitting a few buttons, and then there was Tom Petty.

"He said you'd want this playlist," Isabella said over her shoulder.

Alaric met her eyes for a moment in the rearview, and nodded.

"Free Fallin'." Marty sang. She elbowed Caro once, twice. Then Caro sang, too. Hesitantly at first, but then her voice grew stronger. Marty reached for her hand, and Caro, after a surprised moment, twined her fingers through Marty's and held on tight.

"Looks like I'm going to have to learn the words," Isabella said glumly.

"Going back tomorrow," Simon said, kissing Marty on both cheeks, "but I had to stay long enough for my protegée's opening." He shook Alaric's hand, then Isabella's. He kissed Caro, too, and Marty heard the whisper. "Nate's already gone."

There was a flash of glances between them that Marty filed away.

Pat Wakefield sailed up to greet them, then whirled Marty away to meet some people. She cast a helpless look back at the rest, only to find Alaric, Isabella, and Caro voguing. After a moment, Simon, too, adopted a pose. Isabella broke down first, pointing and laughing. Simon signaled to a waiter. They were fine; they'd be taken care of.

Other painters in the show. A critic from the Portland paper. *And this is Martha Ahearne.* More painters. An artists' representative. *She has two paintings in the show.* Marty found herself passed hand-to-hand. The crowd grew. *One's already been purchased.* She snatched a glass of champagne from a passing tray, and then sneezed when she tried to drink it. Just as well. She pretended she was someone famous, who moved in these circles, and held up the champagne flute languorously as she spoke to more strangers than she had in a year.

Suddenly she was in the rear gallery, where someone from some paper somewhere—she hadn't caught the name—was taking her picture in front of the painting of Larry.

It was then she turned and saw the little colored circle affixed to the side of the frame.

FORTY-SEVEN.

Hɪɢʜ Sᴛʀᴇᴇᴛ ᴡᴀs nearly empty when they left the gallery just before ten, save for the patrons of the bar at the corner, which would stay open until midnight, even on this, a weeknight. Alaric had gone ahead to get the Bronco, but Isabella, yawning, insisted upon waiting outside for him. Through the window, Simon waved to them cheerfully as Pat locked the door and dimmed the lights.

"That was a lot of people," Bella said, shaking her head.

"It was," Marty agreed. She felt exhilarated and exhausted, as though she should dance and sleep at the same time. "Too many." She turned to Caro, who, in the white light of the streetlight overhead, looked less pinched, but more ethereal. "Tell me, though. You bought the painting of Larry, didn't you?"

Caro turned wide eyes on her. "Oh, Marty, no! Someone bought it?"

"You didn't?"

Caro bit her lip and shook her head. "No. Oh, no, Marty. I don't think I can bear it."

"But you sold a painting," Isabella said, shifting on the brick sidewalk, to get a more comfortable position on her crutches. "Your first time in a gallery, and you sold a painting."

Marty shrugged, albeit ambivalently. "The show's up for another several weeks—I might even sell the other one. And if I do, Pat might hang some more."

She felt Caro stiffen beside her, and looked up.

Pete was approaching, up the hill from, apparently, the bar on the corner. The streetlights, above, shadowed his face, but his eyes were glittering.

"Well, well, well," he said. His glance raked the three of them. "Evening out, ladies? Though I expect one of you'll get picked up for underage drinking. Unless you're turning tricks on the High Street?" He laughed, an ugly sound.

"We've got nothing to say to each other, Pete," Caro said. Her voice shook a little.

"Oh, since I dropped the suit? Since the blood test proved you've been playing me for four years?" He took a step closer.

Marty edged in front of Isabella.

"I'm sorry. I don't want to do this in the street, okay?" Caro looked around desperately. During the day, when tourists thronged the town, the police were everywhere; there were none here now.

"Embarrassed to have the entire town know what kind of slut you are?" Pete held out both arms, turning from side to side. "Hey, everybody! Wanna know how much of a slut Caroline Pond is?"

Isabella drew in a sharp breath. Marty put a hand on her arm. "Now isn't the time, Pete," she said. "Not in front of Isabella."

Pete ignored her. His glittering eyes were focused on Caro. "Who's the father, then, Caroline? Or do you even know?"

Caro reeled back, as at a blow.

"Stop it, Pete," Marty ordered. "You've been drinking."

This time his gaze swung around to her. "I don't take orders from my ex-wife's lesbian lover," he laughed. Then the laugh slid away, as his eyes narrowed. "Oh. Oh, I get it now. It's your brother, isn't it? Your sainted brother."

Caro had her phone out. "I'm calling the police, Pete."

"The hell you are." With a swift movement, he smashed the phone out of her hands and into the street. He grabbed her arm and shook her. "Tell me, Caroline. It was Larry Ahearne, wasn't it? You were fucking Larry Ahearne."

The punch knocked Pete back a few steps, then he stumbled and went down on the bricks. Alaric stepped forward, his hands still fisted in front of him.

"Is everybody all right here?"

Matt Copeland had appeared just as Pete struggled to his feet and ran off downhill toward the harbor.

"Matt?" Caro turned.

"That was your ex-husband, wasn't it, Miss Pond?" Matt touched her arm, and looked past her toward the intersection, where the light had begun its overnight blinking yellow. She winced, and he dropped his hand quickly. "Did he hurt you?"

She laughed nervously. "I think I'm going to have a bruise tomorrow, but I'm okay." A car passed, and there was the crackling of glass as it ran over her phone. "My cell's bought it, though."

Matt slipped out and picked it up. He shook his head upon returning to her side. "Hope you've got insurance on this, because it's toast." He looked down the hill again. "Do you need the police?"

Beside her, Alaric was shaking his left hand, his right hand on Isabella's shoulder. Marty grabbed his knuckles and examined them.

"I don't know. He ran off when Alaric hit him. He's the type to call the police because he was just standing around when some guy punched him for no reason. Just to get Alaric in trouble." Caro put a hand to her head, which was beginning to pound.

"I'll call them. Best to file a report."

"My lawyer to the rescue."

He had moved under the streetlight and taken out his own phone; now he looked up, his wide face breaking into a grin.

"I'm not your lawyer now. I'm just a witness." He poked the screen. "In fact, I resign as your lawyer. I'm just your friend." He put the phone to his ear as the 911 operator squawked.

FORTY-EIGHT.

"You're back home late," Georgie said. She had been holding open the kitchen door as they pulled in. "Is everything all right?"

"You didn't have to stay up, Gram," Isabella protested. "I could have told you all about the fight and the police and everything in the morning." When she saw her grandmother's expression, she laughed gleefully. "There was swearing, too."

Georgie shook her head, looking over Isabella's shoulder at the three of them. "I should have known better. The bunch of you were too much trouble when you were teenagers, banging around in that Bronco. I see now that you haven't changed at all."

"Everything's fine, Georgie," Marty said. "There was a bit of excitement, but Alaric took good care of us."

Alaric pointed to Marty and Caro, then waved a hand in the direction of their house.

"I'm too tired to figure it out," Georgie said, yawning. "Isabella, what does Alaric mean?"

Bella shrugged. "He's going to take them home." She turned and wrapped an arm around her uncle, who bent to kiss her forehead. Then she, surprisingly, hugged Marty as well. Alaric looked pleased.

At the house, Alaric saw them to the door. Caro excused herself to head upstairs.

"Come inside and have a drink of something. I've got water, and seltzer, and I don't think the milk's gone bad yet." Marty flicked on the porch light. "You've never been in here, have you? Our humble hovel. Don't mind our mess."

Alaric grinned. He had long since abandoned his tie, and now he took off his jacket and folded it over the back of one of the wicker chairs on the porch. He turned away from the easel, though, making it obvious that he wasn't looking. In doing so, however, his eyes fell on the stones, now ranged on the windowsill. When Marty handed him a glass of something fizzy—she had one for herself—he pointed to the line of gaily painted stones.

Marty's cheeks reddened, and he resisted the urge to run a finger along her skin. "Just some rocks Sophie and I collected and painted over the winter and spring. When I wasn't painting pictures, because of Dad and everything." She picked up a deep blue stone, with a star and the word *shine* picked out in silver.

Alaric dug into his pocket and pulled out his own rock, the one he'd been carrying for weeks now, the one he'd found at the spring. He held it out to her, his talisman. *Hope.*

For the longest time she stared down at his palm, his stone, his hope.

"You found it at the spring," she whispered.

He shook his head. Then he pointed to her.

She shook her head.

He had to set aside his glass before he took his pad and pen out of his breast pocket. Then he wrote, still holding the stone.

I found it in you.

FORTY-NINE.

"NO SOPHIE TONIGHT?"

Isabella was working on the picture of the chickens in front of the barbed wire fence. This evening she had moved her chair further along the barnyard, where the chickens were milling about. The two calves had been moved out to the field with their mothers. Someone—probably Alaric—had set a little table next to her for her box of pastels. They were, Marty was pleased to see, wearing down with their frequent use.

"No." Marty set her chair alongside Isabella's and sat. She set two bottles of root beer on the table between them. "She came home from Joanne's this afternoon with a sniffle and a cough, so Caro's doing the early bedtime thing."

"I bet she's really pissed off that you didn't bring her."

"Don't let your grandmother hear you say that." Marty laughed. "But you're right, she is."

"I'm drawing this for her," Bella said. "She really likes the chickens. I don't know why. All they do is run around and peck stuff." She set the pastel aside and began smudging the lines of one of the chickens. It was mostly black, though with some white feather tips, and a red comb. Marty could easily identify which chicken, over at the fence, this was meant to be.

"I'm sorry," she caught herself. "I shouldn't be looking."

Bella shrugged. "I don't mind. Just as long as you don't say stupid things like Uncle Richard."

"No worries." Marty opened the bottles and put the caps in her pocket. She took a drink.

"And if you're looking for Alaric, he's out fixing a broken fence with Richard. Some of the cows got out, and I guess they were going to town or something."

Marty shook her head. "I wouldn't. Town's full of riff-raff."

"I'll say."

The root beer was gone, the drawing nearly finished, and the shadows long, by the time Alaric and Richard reappeared, riding the tractor and pulling a cart full of tools. They were putting the extra roll of fencing in one of the sheds when the first whistle blew.

Howard was out the kitchen door almost immediately, Red Sox game notwithstanding.

"What is it?" Bella demanded, shutting the pastel box.

Marty stood and looked around the yard, suddenly bustling with Morgans. The whistle blew again. "Fire call," she said.

Alaric paused for only a moment, on his way past to where Howard was backing out the farm truck. He pointed to the north.

"Wellman?" she asked.

He held up a hand nodding. Another whistle. He pointed to the southwest.

"That one's Danby, isn't it?"

Marty's father would have long since taken off in his pickup, in the days of her childhood when he'd served as assistant chief. Larry would have been close behind, as a junior firefighter.

Now Richard jogged past, shouting at Alaric to hurry up.

Howard braked, and both Alaric and Richard clambered into the truck. "Stay here," Howard ordered; Isabella had risen to her feet. His face looked anxious. Then, "Marty—can you stay here with Isabella?"

Marty didn't miss the quick glance Alaric shot at his father. Nor did she miss the subtle lift and drop of Howard's hand on the steering wheel. She hadn't been spending all this time with Alaric for nothing: *don't ask anything now.* As though Alaric *could* ask anything without taking the notebook out of his pocket.

"I can stay with her," Marty said, looking between them.

"Why can't I go?" Bella demanded, edging forward.

"Fire business." Howard reached through the window and tweaked his granddaughter's nose and grinned, but the smile did not reach his eyes. "Stand back now. We've got to get a move on."

Once she had moved out of the way, they tore off, leaving Marty and Bella staring down the driveway after them. The truck's taillights brightened at the road as they braked for a moment in the dusk, and then the pickup turned to the left and roared off toward the fire station.

"Fire business," Bella said, and it sounded like a curse.

"It's serious stuff, Bella," Marty said. "Something out there's on fire, and we're not trained."

"I suppose." She put her paper and pastels in their shopping bag and looped them over her wrist. "But now you're stuck being my babysitter."

"Or you're stuck being mine."

They could hear sirens now, several, heading down onto the cape. Marty tried to place them, from which direction they were coming along the highway. There seemed to be many. Mutual aid, and a lot of it. Must be a structure fire. With a twinge of anxiety, Marty wondered which of the buildings in Painter's Springs would be a mound of blackened timbers by morning, when she stopped by to deliver the mail. Because from the sound of it, *something* would be.

"It's not an accident?" Bella demanded, stopping in her tracks. Her voice quavered a little.

Marty shook her head, scanning the treetops for a hint of the smoke she knew had to be up there; despite the daylight fading fast, she could see nothing. "No. Too many sirens. It's a fire. Probably a big one."

Accident. She wondered about a world where telling Bella it was a fire would be reassuring.

"You don't need to stay with me," Bella said as they approached the house. "Grandad's just worried that I'll have one of *my spells*."

Marty rolled her eyes, but only spared a moment's glance at Bella before returning to scanning the treetops. "*I'm* worried you're going to have one of your spells."

Bella shrugged. "Now you're sounding like Sophie. 'You have spells. Something in your brain doesn't work right.' One would think you guys were related."

Marty cast another quick sideways glance. *We are.* Bella had probably gleaned as much from last night's brawl. That would be a topic for another day's conversation.

The screen door slammed. Georgie hurried down the two steps, pulling on a day-glo yellow safety vest. "There you two are," she called. She rushed across the yard to them. "Listen. I've got to go to the firehouse. Auxiliary and all that. It's probably going to be a long night, and they'll need water and coffee and food." She glanced from one to the other, clearly worried. "Can you stay, Marty? Keep Isabella company?"

"She doesn't need to," Isabella protested. "I'll be all right."

Georgie shook her head. "No, sweetheart. I'd just feel better if you had somebody here with you. In case anything happened. I might not be home until really late."

"It's fine," Marty said quickly. There was something odd about Georgie's demeanor, a kind of skittishness foreign to her. "Go on. We'll be fine."

"Thank you, Marty." Georgie kissed Bella, and then squeezed Marty's shoulder. Held on a little too long. Then Georgie, too, was off into the deepening twilight, leaving the two standing in the farmyard.

It was so quiet, save for the distant sirens.

"I guess we could get some cookies or something," Isabella suggested awkwardly, after a few moments. "Watch a movie, maybe."

They turned to the kitchen door, Marty staying back to let Isabella go first. She was holding the door when she smelled it: the first whiff of smoke. Slowly she turned again, searching the sky above the far trees.

There it was. Behind the barn, past the trees which edged the home field.

But that was the wrong direction. Marty had thought the fire to be somewhere in town, somewhere between here and the highway. That's why she hadn't seen it initially. She'd been looking in the wrong direction. To the southwest, and the mainland. Instead of further down the cape.

Then she heard the squawk of dispatch on the scanner in the kitchen.

"Listen, Bella," Marty said, trying not to sound frantic. "I've got to go. You said you'd be fine here. I know I told your grandparents I'd stay, but I really, really can't."

"What?" Bella demanded. She turned so quickly that she nearly fell, but Marty instinctively grabbed her to steady her. "What is it? What's happened?" She looked up at the scanner, on the shelf next to a trailing plant. "It's about that fire. What did it say?"

"I've got to go," Marty repeated.

"I'll go with you."

Marty was halfway down the steps. She spun hurriedly. "No. Bella. You stay here. Stay inside."

Panicking now, she ran across the yard. The Jeep was all the way back up behind the big barn, but the Bronco was over by the old stable office, and she had the extra key. She couldn't breathe. The smell of smoke was growing stronger, and now she knew the source. Scrabbling in her pocket for the keys, she managed to drop them, and then kick them partway under the truck. She threw herself to the ground, reaching blindly behind the tire until her fingertips looped into the carabiner. When she scrambled to her feet again, Bella stood next to the hood, her face reddened with exertion. How the hell had she moved so quickly?

"Take me with you."

"Bella, I can't," Marty gasped. She wrenched open the door and leaped up onto the seat.

Isabella did not move. Her jaw was set, her eyes hard.

"Get out of the way. Get out of the way, damn it!"

But Isabella, never dropping her eyes, came around to the passenger door and opened it.

"Bella—" The panic was in control now. Marty's eyes were burning.

Inexorably, Bella removed her crutches, tossed them into the cab, and then hoisted herself into the passenger seat. She slammed the door behind her. "Let's go," she ordered, reaching over her shoulder for the safety belt.

Time was wasting. Marty hit the ignition, and then slammed the Bronco into gear. At the end of the Morgans' driveway, she slowed only long enough to make sure the road was clear before spinning the wheel and heading right. The way Richard, Alaric, and their father would have gone, had they not had to get to the fire station first.

The road to the point was blocked off, someone in a Day-Glo vest with a flashlight standing next to the police car, all strobing blue lights, which was drawn across the tar. The sound was incredible, like the flowing of the springs into the trough magnified hundreds of times. Roaring. The flames were roaring, and for the first time ever, Marty knew what that meant. Even in the Bronco she could feel the heat.

"Oh, my God," Bella gasped, and started to cry.

The person in the vest was approaching—Marty couldn't tell who it was—but she jammed the Bronco into reverse and did a quick three-point turn in the road.

"Marty—where—?"

She couldn't answer Bella right now, couldn't think of anything but the house. *The house.* How about Caro and Sophie? A bit further along on the left was the old access road, to the far field, long overgrown now, that had been part of the small farm long before the property was hers. She had walked it often enough, known it was fairly doable for something with high clearance. She twisted the wheel, paused only long enough to throw the Bronco into four-wheel drive, and forced it into the tangle of low growth. Beside her, Isabella grabbed the chicken handle.

Marty forced the Bronco on as far as she could, following

the headlights. To her left the fire glowed like hell through the alder growth. She could hear shouting, but over the sound of the flames, it seemed muted and far away. The left side of her face felt hot, as though it were sunburned.

Just before the old farm pond, she felt the front wheels lose traction—even in the driest of weather, this part of the old road was always soft. She slammed the truck into park, and without even shutting off the engine, she kicked open the door and ran, her feet slipping in the mud.

"Marty!" she heard Bella shout. She did not stop. Her eyes were locked on the inferno that was her house. When she cleared the overgrown pond, she could make out dark helmeted figures against the red, dragging hoses, shouting instructions to one another. She could see the outline of the picnic table; the wading pool was tumbled away toward the side of the lawn. The smoke got in her eyes, which were streaming. Her nose burned with the acrid smell, and she began to cough.

"Caro!" she screamed. "Sophie! Where are you?"

She stumbled toward the firefighters.

Bella dragged herself out of the passenger door. When she turned to fumble for the crutches, she dropped one into the mud, her hands were shaking so hard. "Marty!" she called again, but Marty was long gone, and she hadn't expected an answer anyway. The dome light glinted on metal, off to the side near the bushes, but Bella couldn't reach for that crutch without falling. She grabbed the other one and shoved her right hand through the cuff, then, precariously balanced on the uneven ground, she struggled around the back of the Bronco.

It was so hot. She felt the sweat bead on her forehead, felt it run down the sides of her face, along her nose. Into her eyes. She squinted against the smoke.

"Marty!" she called again. "Wait!" And then, "Alaric!"

Ahead of her, figures danced like witches against a cauldron fire. She left the shelter of the Bronco and felt her way forward, leaning heavily on the crutch, pulling one heavy leg, and then the other.

Alaric hung back, feeling the heat on his exposed skin, feeling the sweat inside his gear. He could hear orders, he could obey orders, but he could not give them. He recognized his brother Richard's form, the way he walked, hefting hose over his shoulder. He heard his father's voice, shouting to someone else over the din. He fed hose. He dragged to the left or to the right according to command. He had knocked down the fence to set up the pump and the extension at the old farm pond, gauged the pump to pull as much as the low water would give up. Spring-fed. He thanked God for the springs. He knew the firefighters were emptying tank trucks to the front; mutual aid tanks would be emptying, driving to the nearest water, filling up again. Alaric was good in emergencies, though he used to be much better.

Through everything, he tried not to think about the blaze that engulfed Marty's house. *Marty's house.* He tried to block everything out of his mind except training: this was a structure fire. This was how you approached structure fires. This is how you fought them, and how you, when you could not speak, followed directions and helped as best you could.

Marty's house.

The thought kept intruding. Alaric shoved it back.

Because Marty was safe. She was back at the farm. She was safe.

"Caro!" Marty shouted again. Futilely. No one could hear her above the noise: flames, fire trucks, people shouting orders to one another.

The roof of the shed caved in with an enormous crash. Sparks flew upward into the dark sky. Marty cried out, a guttural sound torn from her throat. She stumbled, leaning back while throwing her arm across her eyes for protection.

"Oh, my God! Where's the baby? Where's Sophie?" She redoubled her speed, and reached the nearest firefighter. She grabbed his rubber-clad arm. When he spun, startled, she shouted out again, "Where's Sophie? Are they still in there? Has anyone seen them?"

"Get back!" the fireman shouted, his voice distorted. The firelight reflected redly off his protective goggles. "Get back behind the perimeter!"

Someone reached for her, grasped her shoulder.

"Sophie!" she cried out, and wrested her arm free of the grip. In the strength born of fear and fury, she knocked him aside and pushed past, toward the unbearable heat and the raging flames. "Sophie!"

His reaction was immediate. With a cry that was strangled, rusty, the sound of an animal in pain, he abandoned the hose and threw himself forward after her. Hard to run in the boots, the heavy gear. There was nothing for it. He tackled her low, at the knees, and they both tumbled into the blackened grass. Rolling. She fought him, shouting, with hands and knees, trying to wrestle free again, but he held on, sobbing. Sobbing.

He couldn't let this happen again. He held her down with all his weight. It took forever for her struggles to subside, for her to stop screaming and join him in the sobbing.

Bella saw Marty's flight toward the blazing house.

She saw the fireman—it could only be Alaric—abandon his post and start after her.

"No!" she screamed into the night, a sound no one heard, no one heeded. She took a step, fell. She lost the remaining crutch. Somehow she struggled to her feet, took a few more unsteady steps forward, fell again.

The third time she fell, it was atop her uncle, and she held onto him, crying hot, angry, terrified tears.

FIFTY.

MARTY HEARD THE voices, the shouting. She felt the rough hands.

"Get 'em outta here," someone ordered above the din. It might have been Richard. "Jesus, do they want to get us all killed?"

"Where's Caro and Sophie?" As she was pulled along, back toward the pond and the perimeter, Marty strained to look over her shoulder.

"At the ambulance," someone said.

Beside her, Alaric had lost his helmet, but held Isabella in his arms, sobbing against his chest. In the fiendish light, his face was streaked with soot and sweat. He jerked his head furiously: *follow me.*

She did not know how they made it out around the perimeter to the road, along which lights strobed: fire engines, blue police lights, the rescue truck, the ambulance from the hospital in Danby. Stiffly she broke away once again from Alaric, and stumbled along to where two medics were bent over figures wrapped in blankets, one on the other's lap.

"Caroline," she gasped. Caro made no move; the noise of the fire and engines, radios and shouting, was deafening. But Sophie looked up, perhaps at the motion, her eyes wide and reflecting the fire: eyes from the pits of hell.

"Aunt Marty!" she cried, and the impression was gone. She struggled to free herself of the blanket.

"No," Caro shouted, and held on all the more tightly. In the light from the flames, her face was carved, adamantine. "No, Sophie, don't you move. Don't you move—"

Marty hurled herself at the pair of them, dropping to her knees, wrapping her arms around them both. "Oh, God," she said, and could think of nothing else. "Oh, God, oh, God, oh God. I thought you were in there. I thought you were trapped." She pressed her face into Caro's blanketed lap, and found herself sobbing uncontrollably.

After a moment, she felt the hands on her shoulders, the small caress along her back.

"It's okay, Aunt Marty," Sophie said. "I was scared, but Mama saved us. It's okay." The little hands increased in pressure. "But we couldn't save the pictures."

A bustle, and then Alaric set Isabella down beside them. Bella's own sobs were interrupted by a fit of coughing. Someone pressed an oxygen mask over her mouth and nose.

"Hi, Isabella," Sophie said, her eyes wide above the blanket clutched around her shoulders. "Are you here, too?"

Marty had been wrapped in a blanket, and was seated beside Isabella, with a bottle of cold water in her hands, when Alaric appeared again, dark against the flickering lighting. His goggles were around his neck, and his eyes were white in his soot-blackened face. She felt her breathing falter, but this time not from coughing up smoke.

He slowly lowered himself to the ground, his gear creaking. He put his hands on her knees. His gaze was intense.

When he opened his mouth, a strangled noise came out.

Marty dropped the bottle and cupped his face in trembling hands.

"I know," she said.

Fire under control, they spent what was left of the night at the farm, at Isabella's insistence. Georgie opened the unused upstairs bedroom for Caro and Sophie, and Marty, after a prolonged scrub in Alaric's tiny shower cubicle, allowed him to wrap his comforter around her, allowed him to hold her while she tried to sleep.

"Are you sure?" Georgie had asked, frowning. "Wouldn't you rather go to your mother?" She had cast an uncomfortable glance toward the stable office. "Alaric's only got that futon in there—"

Marty had only shaken her head. From the back of the ambulance, as the fire was knocked down to manageability and the furor had abated, she had dialed her mother's number, which had gone quickly to voicemail. She'd left a message.

Now she lay in the dark, her face pressed to Alaric's shoulder, listening to him breathe deeply in his sleep. She hoped he wasn't dreaming. She thought now of the dreams he must have had, these past years, the ones he had at last tried to tell her about. The nightmares, which imprinted themselves in the dark shadows beneath his eyes. The nightmares in which he'd lost Larry, over and over again, the nightmares borne of an undeserved guilt.

Her right hip ached, where she had landed when he'd brought her down on her mad flight toward the house. She'd have a bruise, she knew. With a shaking hand she touched Alaric's forehead, creased prematurely. He'd tackled her and prevented her doing the ultimate in idiocy, running into a burning house. And she would have done it, she knew, for her best friend, and for Sophie, who was her niece: the only piece of Larry there was left in the world.

Alaric had saved her. Alaric had saved her life when he had not been able to save Larry.

She was his atonement.

Against her in the narrow bed, he shifted, and he made a sound. *A sound.*

"Hush," she whispered. "It's all right. Sleep, Alaric."

She pressed her lips to his, and closed her eyes.

FIFTY-ONE.

"You really shouldn't have, Mrs. Morgan," Caro said, looking at the spread on the picnic table in the grass outside the kitchen. She let the screen door swing shut, and turned to see the cake on the counter, iced and bristling with farm animals, with four candles evenly spaced along the circumference.

"Call me Georgie, sweetheart. We've known each other for a long time."

Bella had taken Sophie out back to look for the chickens.

"And besides—" Georgie handed her a covered tray of chicken for the grill. "We haven't had a good birthday party here in ages. It's about time we stopped being sad all the time and tried to celebrate some good things." She picked up a tray of watermelon slices and a pitcher of lemonade. "We've been stunted for a long time, that's what it is."

The thunk of metal on metal greeted them. Over at the horseshoe pits at the edge of the grass, Howard was clapping Matt on the shoulder. "Don't think those boys of mine will be having the last laugh now, do we?" He turned to Georgie. "Did you find that portable radio? It's one o'clock. Yankees today."

"It's on the windowsill, you foolish man," she called. "Pay attention."

Howard clapped Matt on the shoulder again, and came to adjust the radio. After a moment, the voice of Joe Castiglione rose up. He grunted and returned to the game.

"And it's nice you brought that young Matthew with you," George said, leaning in. She smelled of lavender, Caro realized, and felt a pang of nostalgia, though she didn't really know why. "Much nicer than that Pete Vargas, if you don't mind my saying." Her voice dropped lower, nearly to a whisper. "What did the police say yesterday?"

Caro shrugged uncomfortably. "Not much. They wanted to know if I'd noticed him at the house or around the neighborhood. But we were too busy trying to find that blasted giraffe before bedtime, so I didn't see or hear anything until the alarm went off."

This time when Georgie leaned in, she kissed Caro on the cheek, and patted her hair. "I'm just glad you had fire alarms. I'm just so glad."

Marty and the girls now appeared, coming down the long barnyard.

"Howard," Georgie called, "are you going to grill this chicken, or do you expect us to eat it raw?"

Alaric handed the horseshoes to Richard and pointed to his chest, then the grill. Immediately he laughed and said carefully, "I'll do it, Ma." His voice sounded hoarse, but he grinned.

Georgie handed him the tongs and nodded with satisfaction. "Good. Your father's liable to forget and burn it black, now the baseball's on." She paused then, for a moment, just looking at him—then she shook her head and kissed his cheek.

Marty watched Caro navigate the steps, carrying the birthday cake, four candles alight. Kneeling on the bench at the picnic table beside Bella, Sophie clapped. "Four!" she laughed. "I'm four now!" She held up four fingers and showed them to everyone. Alaric held up four fingers right back at her, and she collapsed into giggles. "You're not four, Uncle Alaric. You're big, like ten or twenty."

"Like that," he agreed in his unfamiliar voice. He still, Marty saw, looked on Sophie in wonder, as though someone had handed him a gift.

"Animals!" Sophie crowed, when Caro set the cake before her. "Look at them, Isabella!" She pointed to one after another. "A cow! A chicken! A duck! A horse—but you still don't have any horses here." She looked around at each Morgan in turn, hands on hips. They had obviously work to do.

"I chose them for you," Bella said.

Sophie opened her mouth wide in an exaggerated gasp, then threw her arms around Bella's neck.

After cake and ice cream, there were presents. At each, Sophie exclaimed in delight, and ran around the table to hurl herself at the giver. Even Richard got a sticky frosting hug.

One last large bag stood in the grass at the end of the table. "Is that for me?" Sophie demanded.

But this time Bella shook her head, her oak-colored hair falling around her cheeks and sparking reddish in the sun. "No, Soph. This is for your Aunt Marty."

"It's not her birthday, Isabella," Sophie protested, her lip jutting in that Larry way. "Her birthday's in the winter."

Bella shrugged. "We missed it. So our present is late."

Marty, standing at the end of the table, felt her face redden. She held up her hands. "I don't need anything."

Untrue, really: with everything in the house destroyed, she still felt like crying at night in Alaric's arms. The shorts and T-shirt she wore now were from the Goodwill store; she was husbanding her money until the insurance settlement came. But she looked around. Sophie and Caro were safe. Alaric was safe. They all had someplace safe to live until housing could be sorted out permanently. And all these people were here to celebrate Sophie's birthday, a birthday she might not have had. Only her paintings, burned in the fire, were irreplaceable; but Marty couldn't dwell on that. So maybe it was all right after all.

Bella swung her legs over the bench of the picnic table, and slipped her arm into the single crutch she was using now. She stood and picked up the bag with her free hand. "This is from Uncle Alaric and me."

"Got it, Bella?" Alaric asked, taking a single step forward.

She glared at him. "Of course I do."

He held up his hands and backed off.

When Bella, grinning, handed the bag to her, it was heavier than Marty had expected. Alaric was grinning, too, and the pair of them looked surprisingly alike. He cleared a space at the end of the table for her.

Slowly she reached into the bag and drew out a handful of brushes, the bristles all in protective wrap. Two flat, two filbert, a round, and a rigger. She fanned them out on the table and touched them reverently. She swallowed hard, and reached in again, this time, to pull out two palette knives, and then a glass palette in its packaging. There were canvases in several sizes, and at the bottom, tube after tube of oils. She spread them out next to the brushes: lamp black, ultramarine blue, cerulean blue, burnt umber, alizarin crimson, cadmium red, burnt sienna, raw umber, yellow ochre, cadmium yellow, titanium white. The tubes felt like old friends under her hands.

Marty opened her mouth, but could not find the words.

"We got you a new easel, too, but it's in the house." Now Bella shifted, embarrassed. "It wouldn't fit in the bag."

"Oh, Isabella," Marty whispered. She set the bag aside and wrapped her arms around the girl. "Oh, Bella." She pressed her eyes closed, and felt tears again, but grateful tears. "You understand, don't you?"

Against her chest, Bella nodded. "Yeah," she said. "But there's one more thing in there you need to look at."

Puzzled, Marty turned back to the bag. All that were left there were canvases—but wait, there was a small package, wrapped in paper and what felt like bubble wrap. Slowly she drew it from the bag and peeled back the tape, then the wrapping.

Larry's sardonic gaze stared back up at her.

"You bought it," she breathed, turning to Alaric. "You."

His smile was slow. "I thought you might need it back."

Her tears overflowed. She put her free arm about him, pressing her face into his shoulder. After a moment, though, she broke away. "There's someone who needs it more."

Marty held out the painting to Caro.

"No," Caro said. She took a step back.

"Yes," Marty replied, and thrust the painting into her hands. "This is yours."

For a long time Caro only stared down at Larry's face. She, too, was crying. Then they were in each other's arms, laughing and crying at the same time. Alaric sandwiched them in an embrace.

"Yuck," Bella said, stepping quickly back from them. "Gross."

"One last present," Alaric said, after the food had been cleared away. The Red Sox were ahead in the seventh, and no one seemed inclined to return to the horseshoe pits. Howard was dozing on a chaise longue.

"Not another present for your girlfriend," Richard joked. He took another swig from his beer bottle, and nearly everyone ignored him.

"For Bella," Alaric said.

"Is it your birthday, too, Isabella?" Sophie asked. She was seated in the grass, playing with the animals from the birthday cake, which, somewhat oddly, were nearly all the same size.

"August," Bella said. She maneuvered on the one crutch until she was facing Alaric. He reached out to place a key in her hand.

She stared at the key, turned it over in her palm, felt its coldness. Then she turned her eyes up to Alaric's face. He had his hands shoved into his pockets, and was leaning back on his heels. He met her gaze squarely. It was obvious. This was a challenge.

Bella didn't know if she could meet it, and found herself shrinking away. She felt suddenly unsteady on the single crutch, but she'd be damned if she was going back to two. "I don't— know what you want," she stammered. Even though she did.

He held her gaze unwaveringly, until she dropped her eyes. He always did that. Then, silently, he stepped to the door of the Bronco and opened it. Held it open. Waited.

"I don't know how to drive," she protested. Everyone was quiet. Joe Castiglione droned in the background. "I *can't* drive."

Alaric didn't move, didn't say a word. He only looked at her, his gray eyes calm, his expression firm and unchanging. Just his stillness was an insistence.

He waited.

Bella bit her upper lip, looking beyond him to the Bronco.

It was a long moment.

Then suddenly Bella took a long deep breath and lifted her chin. She pushed past him to the open door, seeing him bite his lip to keep that smile back, the one that infuriated her so.

"The seat's pretty high," she said. She slipped the crutch from her right arm and held it out. "Take this, will you? And help me get up there."

It was awkward, but then she was in. With Bella on the seat, Alaric pulled the lever to slide it forward. He tapped the brace locks at her knees, and she loosened them.

"Put your feet on the pedals," he instructed. Satisfied that she was close enough to depress the clutch, he shut the door and jogged around to the passenger side, to throw himself into the seat. Where he would have been sitting, she realized, if his friend Larry had been driving.

"I don't know how to drive," she protested again.

Alaric frowned, looking down at the braces, but then raised his eyebrows and shrugged. "Try," is all he said. "You've been working on bending in PT. Try." When she shook her head, staring at him, he pointed to the middle pedal. "Right foot." Then he pointed to the far pedal. "Left foot."

She depressed both.

"Rev 'er up." Alaric made a twisting motion with his wrist. She turned the key. The engine sputtered into life.

He grinned and rubbed his palms together.

Bella wasn't going to show him she was terrified.

"I tried to teach Marty how to drive this," he said. "In high school. After Larry gave up. Buck-and-stall. Buck-and-stall. He couldn't bear it." He reached across to do her seatbelt, then clicked his own into place.

"Scared?" Bella taunted him, but was embarrassed that her voice was shaking.

Alaric grinned again. "Move your right foot from the brake to the gas," he instructed.

She did, uncertainly. Were these the right pedals? The Bronco rolled forward a tiny bit, then stopped, the yard being flat.

Now Alaric held out his hands, palms vertical, left lower than right. Slowly he brought the one up while pressing down with the other. "Do this with your feet. More gas, less clutch."

The Bronco jerked and stalled. Bella pressed her eyes closed. "Not like that, I guess."

"Slowly."

From the corner of her eye, she saw Gram rush out of the kitchen door as though ejected. Her face was brilliant red, her arms flailing. She thought she heard Alaric's name, and then, more shrilly, her own.

The Bronco jerked into motion. Forward a few feet, then a couple of jolts and bucks, and it stalled. It rolled slowly to a stop.

"Shit," Bella said. Then, "Don't tell Gram I said that."

Gram was shouting again, and then she heard Gramp. She couldn't make out any words. She peered into the side mirror; her grandfather had his arm around her grandmother's shoulders.

"Again."

Bella glared at him. This was like taking those foul shots. She wasn't going to give in. Damn him. She wasn't. She moved her feet stiffly, then turned the key. Another moment, another series of jerks, and the stall. This time she said nothing, merely made her own readjustments, and turned the key again.

The engine roared this time, and when she lifted her foot on the clutch, they hurtled suddenly across the farmyard, toward the fence around the garden.

"Oh, my God—what do I do?"

"Steer!" Alaric pulled the wheel, and they nearly missed the fence. She heard a scratch along the passenger side and winced.

They stalled.

Marty watched them, passing the soft bristles of a number eight filbert brush back and forth over her palm. It was not an overly successful driving lesson—not unlike her own first attempts, at fourteen. She felt her empathy for Bella rise up; but she knew, at the same time, how patient Alaric would be. If not today, then Bella would drive the Bronco tomorrow. Or the next day.

She smiled. Then caught her breath, looking down at the brush in her hand. Because she knew, now, what had been missing all along from the painting of the spring.

ACKNOWLEDGMENTS

As always, I couldn't have done this alone. More thanks than I can say go to the following:

For the residency during which I wrote and walked and wrote and swam and wrote deliriously, the Hewnoaks Artist Colony, and the University of Maine Foundation. Special thanks to my cohort, Thalassa Raasch, Tessa O'Brien, and Ian P. Hundt, and to our caretaker, sculptor Pamela Moulton.

For information about psychological treatment of soldiers with PTSD, Mark Benjamin's *Salon* article, "Behind the Walls of Ward 54" paints a painful picture. (Benjamin, Mark. "Behind the Walls of Ward 54." *Salon*, Salon.com, 25 Sept. 2011, www.salon.com/2005/02/18/walter_reed_2/.)

For insights into the wars in Kuwait, Iraq, and Afghanistan, my friends and fellow teachers, Kevin St. Jarre and Jack McKay.

For the answers to my questions about speech pathology, Kristin Higgins and Jennifer Letarte Soares.

For the answers to my questions about occupational therapy, my determined daughter, Rosalie S. C. Bowman, M.S., O.T.R./L.

For the answers to my questions about oil painting and gallery contracts, the magnificent Jennifer Hallsey.

For putting up with the drafts of scenes, the members of the

CHS Writers' Workshop. Special thanks to Raolin Willis for allowing me to name a law firm after him.

For the theme song for *The Springs*, "Letting You Go," from the album *Hard Promises*, Tom Petty and the Heartbreakers.

For long, life-saving conversations about what it means to be a maker, Ian Blake.

For love and support always, Brenda Sparks Prescott and Rebecca Bearden Welsh of Simply Not Done.

ABOUT THE AUTHOR

ANNE BRITTING OLESON lives and writes in a small town in Central Maine. A frequent traveler to the U.K., she has published five previous novels, including *Aventurine and the Reckoning* (Encircle Publications, January 2022), and four poetry chapbooks. She has three children, five grandchildren, and two cats.

If you enjoyed reading this book,
please consider writing your honest review
and sharing it with other readers.

Many of our Authors are happy to participate in
Book Club and Reader Group discussions.
For more information, contact us at info@encirclepub.com.

Thank you,
Encircle Publications

For news about more exciting new fiction,
join us at:

Facebook: www.facebook.com/encirclepub

Instagram: www.instagram.com/encirclepublications

Sign up for Encircle Publications newsletter and specials:
eepurl.com/cs8taP

www.ingramcontent.com/pod-product-compliance
Lightning Source LLC
Chambersburg PA
CBHW030237120726
47903CB00005B/1516